The Earthrin Stones

Book 3 of 3

Muster of Heroes

(A novel set in the realm of Dhea Loral)

Douglas Van Dyke Jr.
(Cover artist: Joshua Scott)

The Earthrin Stones

Book 3 of 3

Muster of Heroes

©2021 by Douglas Van Dyke

Originally published 2008, 2016
This edition published through Ingram 2021

ISBN: 978-1-949060-10-2
BISAC FIC009020 Fiction: Fantasy – Epic

PUBLISHED BY Douglas Van Dyke Jr
Please Visit:
http://dhealoral.com
Retail Price: $15.00

PREVIEW

In the stillness of the room, with the sound of the hearth's fire crackling nearby, Petrow came to an agonizingly hard decision. He got to his feet, still tired and bleeding from his brush with death. The table had fallen in a way that blocked what he needed to get at. With a shove, he pushed it out of the way.

The floorboards in the center looked perfectly normal. There was no secret hatch, because Petrow never intended to recover what lie hidden below. Regardless, now he had a reason to dig up the past. He wedged the bloody blade of his axe in a narrow gap in the floor. Blood dripped and stained the floor as Petrow worked at the boards. The first one snapped in a puff of dust. The sound broke the reign of silence. Using the axe, he pried and chopped board after board out of the way. A hole opened up, through which he could see the bundle of blankets covering his hidden treasure.

Holding the axe aside, he reached down with one trembling hand and pulled the bundle out of its hiding spot. With a bit of reverence, Petrow drew aside the blankets to uncover the shiny leather-and-steel creation inside them.

At the end of their first adventure, Petrow had found this set of armor in a supply room of that keep on the sea. He had worn it when he had nearly suffocated Savannah back then. Magical in nature, it was light despite the steel breastplate and metal guards on the shoulders and upper thighs. The rest of the leather fit Petrow in a way only a magical item could. The magical enchantments laid upon the outfit would offer more protection than a potential foe would realize.

Footsteps at the door made Petrow turn. Inedra's face paled at the sight of the dead body inside their home, but a look towards Petrow holding up his suit of armor almost sent her into a swoon.

"No." Her denial was a bare whisper. "You can't leave me; you said you wouldn't."

Petrow's face was set and firm as he replied. "It's because I love you that I have to go."

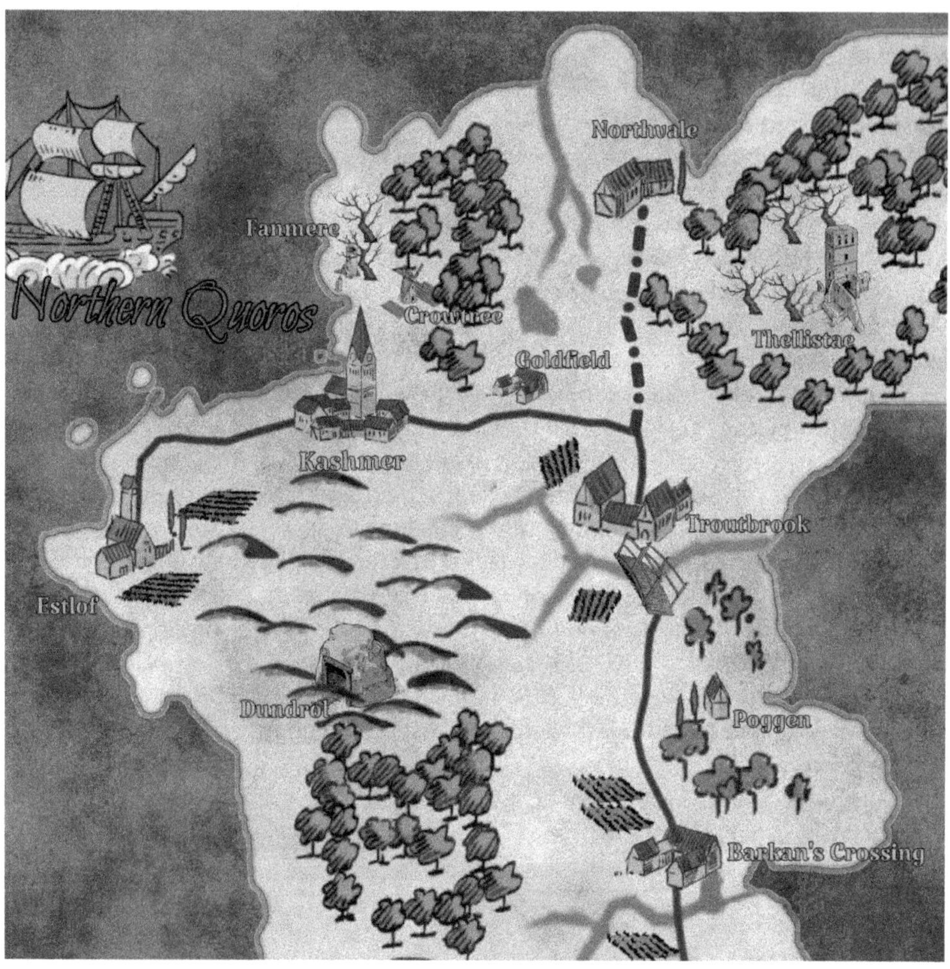

Map of Northern Quoros, including the lands of Kashmer's Protectorate.

Map of Southern Quoros, featuring Orlaun and the Kingdom of Gheras.

Map of Northern Shard, including the Stonelands and the great Tribal Expanse.

I dedicate this to my children. Who you will someday be, will be your choice…your adventure. May both of you be wise in choosing your destiny. I know that no matter how skilled I may write, my children will be my greatest work.

Prologue

The first day of Doyal, in the year 1254 After Covenant, surrendered to the evening sky. Six souls enduring a somber night camped in the wilderness of Eyldiian; a continent known to most humans as Wilder due to it's untamed, unexplored vastness. The group sat around a fire, recovering from injuries both physical and spiritual. They had fought with all their heart amidst the wreckage of the divine vessel which had carried them so far from human lands. For all their efforts, they considered the battle a defeat.

A shrouded, elf body slumbered in death beside them. Foyren had fought alongside their enemies, but not of his own free will. A mentalist had taken advantage of the honored warrior, twisting his anger so that he raised arms against his own kin. Regrettably, the fight ended in his death rather than his freedom. Beside the body, Cassyli brooded for his lost brother. The elf scout had performed his role in helping the others; now, he merely wished to return his brother's remains to his home and resume his life in the tree city of Serud'Thanil. Temptation drew him to follow them back to human lands and deliver vengeance upon those responsible for his brother's death. His conscience persuaded him against it. There was nothing to be achieved by journeying to strange lands to avenge his brother. His mother and people needed him at home.

For three of the travelers camped that night, the events which brought them here happened rather suddenly. The minstrel Lindon, the melee warrior Montanya, and the acolyte Sondra hadn't known any of the others until sabotage brought a god's flying vessel to its demise. The last several days brought an abrupt change to their lives, as they found themselves locked in a struggle for possession of ancient relics of power. They had very little idea of what was at stake, but for the moment, it seemed their efforts were a failure. The relics had been reclaimed by the elf wizard Revwar and a human cleric of DeLaris, named Savannah. The duo had fled back to Orlaun by magical means. This resulted in Lindon, Montanya, and Sondra patching their wounds beside a pair of adventurers whom had tangled with those enemies in the past.

Trestan, champion of Abriana, and his beloved Katressa, privateer from Kashmer, had fought to defend the relics four years earlier. Although victorious then, the current defeat erased those past efforts. They discovered the name of the three stone relics they had been chasing: Earthrin Stones. Much was still unknown about the origin of those relics, but it was accepted that the stones had somehow been used as weapons in the Godswars. The Godswars shattered the realm of Dhea Loral over a millennium ago.

Despite injuries and suffering from their latest clash, they would be offered one gain this night. Katressa succeeded in stealing a leather scroll that offered a glimpse into the history of the stones. With the help of a rune block once entrusted to her departed father, the half-elf had finally been able to decipher the encoded scroll. The others gathered around to hear the history and thus be enlightened as to the reasons they had struggled and bled.

Cat, as she was known to her friends, blushed as all the attention focused on her. She spread the scroll out, paper notes of her translation, and set the rune block beside it. She paused only to clear her throat.

"Know ye elves, this be one of three Earthrin Stones, entrusted to your care in the hopes they will never again be used in war. Yestreal chooses you to safeguard this terrible relic; a source of prosperity to some, and to others a means to destroy enemies. First, ye all should know about the history of these stones.

"They were fashioned from an unlikely alliance during the Godswars. Three gods commissioned their creation: Yestreal, DeLaris and Mothrok. These three greater powers shared inherent neutrality in the Godswars. Since Yestreal is a weather god, Mothrok an elemental goddess, and DeLaris carries out her disposition of the fallen...there was nay gain in committing their followers to the folly of the other gods. Yet, their combined influence could have major effects on any army, so an alliance was made for the mutual protection and survival of their mortal followers. Thus, the gods banded together in the creation of three relics. The power of all three deities would be pooled into each stone, and one returned to each god/goddess, where it would be granted to that patron's strongest followers for their protection. Against invaders they were a powerful tool, yet they were made to cancel out each other so that they could not be used against any of the gods who created them."

Upon reading those words, Cat paused for a moment as her gaze swept around the others. "By those statements, and others later, it seems we find the importance Savannah and Revwar held in controlling all three. If even one stone is in the hands of their enemies, that stone would cancel out the powers of the other two. I wanted to stress that message, for it may be important for us to remember later."

She resumed her translation from the aged document, *"From Yestreal, God of the Sun and Weather, the stones have the power to create sunlight at night or to eclipse the sun's rays. They can affect the weather to bring about favorable crops - his primary intent. Yet, they can also bring draught or spawn terrible storms.*

"From Mothrok, Goddess of Earth and Stone, the stones have an effect on crops due to her influence in the soil. Their greatest martial powers come in the ability to reshape stone. Stone walls can be raised or wiped to dust by this power. Castle fortifications are meaningless against the might of the relics. The stones can also summon warrior spirits composed of earth; automatons unafraid of mortals and highly resistant to weapons.

"From DeLaris, Goddess of Death and the Dead, the relics stood on the precipice between life and death. If an enemy lay near to dying, they could smite him over the edge. As a blessing, they could also be used to restore life to someone who had just died. Aside from these powers, they were most often used in the Godswars to summon undead spirits for combat or even menial tasks."

"In these ways, the stones became frightening for foes in the Godswars. The relics could bolster your rations while destroying those of the enemy. Favor one side with good weather while pounding an enemy with storms. Raise up stone walls while destroying any walls or ground cover that the enemy used. Summon spirits of stone or fallen corpses to fight, while impairing their enemies' ability to do the same. Deliver a widespread killing blow to badly injured foes, while bringing back the souls of one's own army."

Cat paused long enough for that information to be digested by her companions. Trestan stroked his mustache, a sign of deep thought. The rest hung onto every word, especially the storyteller, Lindon Taleweaver. Both paladin and minstrel shared the same thoughts regarding the dreadful Godswars. They came to understand even more of the calamity of that chaotic time. The war had split continents and leveled cities. These relics were but one weapon used in that war, and yet it was terrifying to imagine an army moving forward with that power at its disposal. Montanya, Sondra and Cassyli sat with mouths agape. Each envisioned nightmarish visions of that time in history.

"During the Godswars, an appalled Yestreal realized his two partners began to use their stones to attack instead of protect. Even the Death Goddess seemed to have a special appetite for keeping her death angels busy. The Earth Goddess sought to replace all mortals with a race of new creatures formed from the soil. Mothrok clashed with Krakus on many battlefields, shifting coastlines in their bid for control over the other element. DeLaris and Mothrok lashed out at any threat, real or imagined. Not only were the stones used to crush countless innocents, but it threatened Yestreal in an indirect way. It motivated enemies against his peaceful followers. Yestreal regretted that the alliance had ever been made.

"It wasn't until the end of the Godswars that Yestreal made a surprise move against his former allies. He foresaw the signing of the Covenant and the agreement that would bar the gods from mortal realms. Yestreal entered Dhea Loral one last time, before the Covenant was sealed, stealing the other two Earthrin Stones so that they might never be used for harm again. DeLaris and Mothrok were outraged, but with the Covenant in place they had no reprisal open to them.

"As with many artifacts and weapons from the Godswars, it was time for the Earthrin Stones to be destroyed or hidden away in obscurity. Yestreal chose the latter, preferring that these relics use their subtle nurturing effects to help the races recover in this dark time. This stone is the only one accompanied with a history, though even that history must be hidden from the majority of its guardians. Herein this document will also be a listing of the powers of the stone, in case it must be used to defend against the other two. This stone is hereby granted to the elves' protection, where its powers will help nurture the forest home in which they live. Mothrok's stone is destined for a fortress in the shattered city of Orlaun, where it will be treated as nothing more than an oddity and locked away by men. DeLaris' stone is also destined for obscurity. A holy disciple of Yestreal carries it to a wilderness location in northern Quoros, where a church will be built to house it in a region far from any bright points of civilization."

"Troutbrook." Trestan interrupted.

Cat glanced at him, "Aye, DeLaris' stone was in Troutbrook. It sat out in the open as nothing more than a small rock on a well. It stayed undisturbed for over a millennium of anonymity, even as Troutbrook grew around the church and the roads helped bring together the region under the Kashmer Protectorate. Mothrok's stone went to Orlaun, where over the years it would end up as an insignificant curiosity in a mage guild. Now, if I may continue?"

She threw a stern but not unkind look at Trestan, making it clear she wanted to finish without further interruption. Instead of reading directly out of the text, she summed up the rest.

"The document reveals its age to be only fifty years old; it is a copy of an original manuscript which had become brittle from time. This version ends with the signatures of several people who swear to protect the elves' Earthrin Stone, as well as the secrets behind all the relics, with their lives. Although using Elvish runes, it is encoded. The people who signed it could not read it unless they used this rune block. Two names stand out to my eyes: Reatheneus Bilil, who was my father and guardian of this rune block, and Revwar, who ultimately betrayed them and helped steal the relics."

Cat looked up again, her eyes going from Sondra to Trestan. "There is more here for both of you." At their upraised eyebrows, she continued, "There are priestly instructions on how to use the stones to command them as Revwar did. I don't know how he learned it…most likely DeLaris revealed their functions to Savannah and she in turn instructed him. Anyway, unfamiliar with the nuances of spells as I am, there are concepts here which you will understand better than me. I intend to go over them with both of you, so that you will be able to control the stones as ably as Revwar if we happen to get our hands on one. You both will have to learn this by the time we next face him."

Cat set down the scroll. Trestan interpreted it as a sign she was finished. The young warrior looked down at his right hand. He'd been idly twisting Faithful's Companion around his finger during the revelations. The ring reflected a polished, golden hue: a sign to return to Kashmer and be granted title as a full paladin of Abriana.

Trestan sat back and broke the silence. "We know when and where this battle will be fought. It will be sometime just before the coming of winter at Fortress Stone, on the continent of Shard. Savannah's mind hinted at an army of restless tribes coming out of the wilds to assault the castle. We will have to get help along the way in order to defend that place against an army. Yet, as Cat said, Sondra and I must be ready for our role. Their army could lay waste to any earth walls we try to hide behind, destroy the food supply of the land during the harvest season before the attack, pound us with storms, or send creatures without souls to battle us. If we don't get possession of an Earthrin Stone…if we are unable to use it to counteract the other stones…then nay matter what kind of army we bring, it will be our slaughter."

CHAPTER 1   **"Omens of Warning"**

The winds native to the plains gently tugged the woman's cloak. Pejena Cloud Whisperer raised a feather above her head and dropped it. By watching its dance upon the wind currents, the woman felt she could hear the voice of the air. The wind finished by dashing the feather against a rock.

The human mystic frowned, turning her gaze back to the valley ahead. The element of air whispered warnings to her. She hadn't received such dire warnings since they preceded her dead-born children. It wasn't that she misunderstood its message, but she could not predict the origin of the danger. Her green eyes tried to look past the things she expected, seeking that which lay hidden.

A massive tent-city spread out before her. She watched the multitude of horses, warriors, nomads, tents and pack animals, trying to anticipate the source of the bad omens from the clouds. They consisted the largest gathering of tribes that she had ever seen in her life. Orc tribes settled with unnatural closeness to elf and human tents. Banners of various other races displayed a crowded mix that seemed out of place, considering the natural competition between clans and races. It was odd to see so many, packed so closely, but that still didn't explain the anxiety of the elements.

She retrieved her feather. The mystic tucked it among numerous other trinkets in the pouches she carried. Pejena briefly considered the number of mystical tokens used for conversing with the elements. She had a beaded prayer necklace, a medicine bag hanging from a leather cord, and she leaned on a staff imbued with the power of the elements. To satisfy her curiosity, her fingers withdrew another token from her pouches.

She held a glassy rock in one hand, positioning that shoulder towards the sun. As always, whenever the clouds revealed the sun, the rock seemed to catch a message from above. A band of rainbow-colored light stretched across the lines of her opposite hand. She studied how they intersected the lines of life along her palm. Her face saddened at seeing the position of colors. The woman replaced the rock with a sigh.

The footfalls of a large man, one she knew intimately, approached from behind. Those heavy steps would have been frightful if one regarded him as an enemy. To Pejena, his presence offered a blanket of comfort in the face of these unknown anxieties.

His voice carried the power of his six-and-a-half-foot frame. "What message do the clouds bring to you? I can feel your unease."

She turned to regard the towering warrior, her husband. Kor Strongarm had earned his position as Com'der of the Spear Riders. His leadership guided the tribe through many seasons and endured several battles. Kor restrained the whitish-gray strands of his hair with a leather headband. The spear symbol proudly branded the surface. His eyes adopted a permanent squint after staring across the windy plains for all of his forty-eight winters.

The woman loved the reflections in those unmatched eyes: one brown, one blue. He cared for her greatly. Kor's muscular arms proved to be soft enough when Pejena needed someone to hold her close. He devoutly worshipped Dalios, the human's God of Strength and Courage. Only the strong and courageous could survive in the lands known to others as the Tribal Expanse.

He looked upon his soulmate through concerned eyes, awaiting an answer to his question.

Pejena Cloud Whisperer edged next to him. She leaned against his muscular frame as she shrugged her shoulders. "The clouds say nay more than the rumors we have heard. There is something amiss in the land. I have dark tidings about the gathered tribes before us. The numbers and races are unusual enough, but still…"

Her hands, lined from the endurance of forty-five winters, gestured ahead as if hoping to point out an answer, but none could be found. Her arms dropped to her side as she sighed, "The clouds offer only vague warning."

He offered comfort within his arm. Pejena snuggled close, tickling him slightly with her fur cloak. The cloak was mostly to keep the sun off her reddened skin. Hide coverings sheltered her from the cold winds. Many of the women of the Spear Riders rode with bare breasts, but too many men judged a woman by her breasts. For that reason, Pejena kept hers covered except to the eyes of her husband, Kor. Her gray strands outnumbered the brown, but she stayed lithe enough for life in the wild plains. Pejena's eyes never seemed to look directly into the face. Instead, they always focused somewhere beyond, exploring whatever lay hidden behind the reflections of one's eyes.

Kor turned his eyes from her, noting the position of the camps below. "I should go with you, for protection."

She started shaking her head, even as she leaned closer to him for support. "Nay. If there is something bad, it would not do for both of us to be caught in it. Nor should we take the whole tribe into the midst of the unknown. I am the one that is renowned for skills at negotetin, I have settled many disputes in the past. I should go."

The big man scoffed, "And that is supposed to comfort me if there is trouble? It is true that you are very skilled with words. Your skills and foresight have avoided many conflicts when Dalios would not have favored us. Still, I feel uneasy about sending you alone to negotetin."

The word, like a few words in the tribe's language, had been altered down the years from its true meaning. It began when the Spear Riders were a mounted regiment from some long-forgotten human kingdom. Men and women, side-by-side, fought during the Godswars across the open plains. In the midst of shattering continents and firestorms hurled by the gods, the troops were lost and abandoned by the time of the Covenant. Alone, without a country or any supplies in this strange land, they struggled for survival among former allies and enemies left in the same predicament. Over hundreds of years, the regiment became a nomadic tribe, dependent on the plains. The borders of the world shrunk to the distances a horse could cross during a phase of the largest moon.

Technologies and learned magic were lost. Metal weapons and tools could not be replaced due to the lack of miners and ore. They managed survival using the resources that were readily at hand. Food became scarce among warriors that knew not how to seed and farm. In those early years, most survived by plundering other stranded soldiers. In time, arcane studies were lost in favor of the old natura practiced by mystics, shamans, and druids. Clothing patterns shifted from tailored uniforms to the leather and hides taken from the wildlife. The Spear Riders used spears with stone tips crafted by their hands. Kor's maul consisted of a rock slab strapped securely onto a stout staff. The seasons forced them to migrate, searching for ripening wild fruits and the movements of animals. The tribes coveted the wild, mixed-blood horses of the plains due to their strong breed.

Like all the tribes in this land, the Spear Riders morphed from a professional army to a band of nomads living off the bounty of untamed land. In time, customs developed that originated from the shadows of imprecise memories. The members of the Spear Riders still had ranks. Instead of medals, stripes, or coloring on clothes, the self-inflicted scars on their arms increased in complexity the higher one ranked. Kor Strongarm displayed the most elaborate as Com'der of the tribe. Even "Com'der" had been distorted down the centuries, deriving from "commander". When not at war, tribes often had to meet and discuss barter or proposals. These sessions were referred to as negotetin. To other civilizations, the word "negotiations" might seem more appropriate.

As Kor and Pejena shared their concerns for the gathering of other tribes at the fresh well nearby, more advanced civilizations might have ridiculed the way their current traditions were based on a distorted past. Mighty cities and wonders of magic were being developed as other civilizations recovered from the old Godswars. Yet, in this seemingly rustic corner of Dhea Loral, people carried on their old way of life.

Even in this untamed land, modern craftsmanship could be found. Kor wore a steel dagger procured from the talented Stonelands artisans to the south. Pejena owned several glass bottles made in the Stonelands. The Tribal Expanse offered little luxury resources, yet the Spear Riders bred excellent horses.

Pejena turned her head upward to face her soulmate, "It is time for me to go."

Kor looked upon her, barely masking his concern. His hands remained on her shoulders. The close contact offered comfort before she would depart. He asked, "What if these people show devotion to this unnamed messiah? What if they also speak in crazed terms about this prophet? 'A silver-haired elf with golden eyes will herald the arrival of a new leader for all the tribes.' The image it provokes in my mind's eye makes me uneasy."

Pejena Cloud Whisperer, mystic of the Spear Riders, kissed her husband before stepping out of his strong arms. "Then I will move fast to get back to you. If you see me running like the wind, know that we should seek a safer water supply with tribes that have kept their sanity. We have nay patience for false prophets stirring the tribes to restlessness."

Pejena bid him farewell. She knew his eyes followed her all the way to the camp.

Like other civilizations, the neighboring people from the Stonelands mocked the cultures and primitive ways of the nomads of the Tribal Expanse. The immigrants that were forging their own kingdom around the Fortress Stone felt they had little to fear from the natives. No one from that small kingdom could predict how much they were outnumbered by the people of the plains. The citizens of Fortress Stone felt safe and sound behind their high walls. They could not know about the words of a messiah spreading among the tribes. No one would predict that the scattered tribes were about to come together in numbers unseen since the Godswars.

*   *   *   *   *

His image spoke to them from a mirror suspended in the assembly hall. A congregation of guild wizards and clerics of Ganden hung on every word as the figure in the glass relayed a tragedy. The person in the mirror stood a few hundred miles away, communicating through a long-distance spell. The elf speaker in the mirror wore the many-layered fashions of Orlaun. The decorated and jeweled outfit bore signs of damage from days spent in wild woods. The elf wizard looked as worn as his attire. The gathered audience could not tell whether it was mostly from lack of sleep or from the heavy burdens he relayed to them. As the figure spoke, he rubbed at the rough, golden stubble on his chin. Facial hair only appeared in elves once they reached middle age, though most chose to have it magically removed.

Korrelothar Balshav, "The Highwater Conjuror" and co-founder of the Brotherhood of the Circles mage guild, displayed it openly to embrace his age and demand respect.

The wizard's words continued to relay the tragedy. "…but I was on the last levitation boat to depart the ship. The *Doranil Star* continued onward with only a skeleton crew in the inner sanctum. Most of the pilots…pardon me…the Chosen, lie dead from some kind of explosive sabotage centered around the cauldron. The vessel sailed far into the untamed forests of this continent. We can only assume the worst: that the ship, piloting clerics, and magical treasures were all lost somewhere in that broad expanse. We can't even begin to search. Supplies are limited, or conjured on a daily basis, and we have guests to safeguard back to Orlaun."

Murmurings came from many; a few sad whispers between ears. The mages and clerics alike were still digesting the loss of the flying vessel. The clerics of Ganden had first sensed something amiss days ago. They suffered dreams of their vessel falling from Ganden's hands. In their night terrors, they witnessed the death of their brothers. Ever since the church alarmed the mages at the guild, wizards worked to establish some contact to their brothers on the flight. The apprehension in the room weighed on them like a heavy fog as the news they feared became reality.

One voice called out to the wizard in the mirror. "What about the noble families? What losses do we face?"

Korrelothar frowned at the question as he relayed some known casualties. "The Gandersen, Fedulacen, Vortess families are among those that have lost dear ones. They may demand compensation. Luckily, Duke MigRelke and his entourage were among the first to safely depart the vessel, though we have yet to find them in this land."

The elf gestured behind him, though the background remained blurry due to the limitations of the spell. "We sent a mage with each boat. Several of us have linked together and are making our way to the coast. Dangerous animals inhabit this land, but it is my hope that the worst is past. We will do our best to get the remaining nobles safely back to Orlaun, and then handle the emotional aftermath from their families."

One priest of Ganden, wearing a hat and robe signifying a high rank, queried the distant mage. "Can you give us more information as to what caused this disaster? *Doranil Star*, pride of our patron, was the last divine chariot known to fly. We must know more about why it was lost, along with several of our most talented clergy."

Korrelothar nodded, taking a moment to gather his thoughts before proceeding. The elf wizard could only imagine the pain this would bring upon the church. The *Doranil Star* had been the last flying vessel remaining from the volatile Godswars. A floating temple to the God of Duty, it had been one of the wonders of the world. Now, the spirit had fled and the body was lost to untamed lands.

Korrelothar answered, "I will try to sum up the important details as best I can, before this spell expires. On the vessel, featured in an exhibit, were numerous magical oddities and treasures. One particular display included two green stones that likely dated back to the Godswars. We thought them little more than trinkets, even though we knew something about their uses."

The esteemed elf took a long breath. "Four years ago, an elf wizard named Revwar and an abbess of DeLaris named Savannah made an effort to steal these stones for some unknown purpose. They failed. With the stones on board the vessel and outside of the guild walls, they found their chance to strike again. Jentan Mollamos became a traitor to our guild, aiding them somehow in getting access and sabotaging the ship."

Angry outcries erupted among the mages, cursing the absent mentalist.

Korrelothar did his best to continue despite the outburst. "Sadly, they seemed to have made an escape with the stones. We can't be sure if they are stranded out on this continent, or if they had a means to teleport back to Orlaun."

At some urging from those assembled, Korrelothar produced an illusionary likeness of their enemies. The audience studied the faces of those responsible.

"I have more to add," Korrelothar said. "Right now, we have a few allies who may know more about the situation regarding the relics than I. They are appointed guardians of those stones. It was their efforts that stopped the theft four years ago. I will show you two of their faces: Trestan Karok, paladin of Abriana, and Katressa Bilil, a privateer from Kashmer."

With that, Korrelothar allowed a mental image of the two companions to be sent to the mirror in the assembly. He continued, "If they are seen, they should be treated with all courtesy and comfort. I hope to get back to Orlaun before them and find out if they have any more news about Revwar and Savannah. Meanwhile, we should watch the harbor closely for the arrival of boats carrying any of these people from Wilder continent."

*   *   *   *   *

Days after Korrelothar's words reached his guild brothers in Orlaun, asking them to watch the harbor, their enemies attempted to slip away from the city. Two travelers stood among the hundreds of people going in and out of Orlaun's port.

Revwar hid his elven heritage under a large cowl. A plain, unassuming traveler's cloak hid most of his form from the summer sun. From the shadows of that large cowl, his intense golden eyes scrutinized the entire length of the harbor. Likewise, he expected there would be eyes looking for him. He could only assume the local wizards and clerics might be searching by magical means, wearing their own disguises so as not to draw undue attention. Revwar did his best to melt into the background of commerce. With all the flow of people from faraway lands moving through the docks, it would have been a hard feat to intentionally stand out.

His ship would not depart until later that day. Instead, Revwar accompanied his deadly partner to see that she caught her own chosen transport…or to talk her out of it.

Savannah was not as recognizable without her dark armor. The platemail armor she normally wore displayed designs honoring DeLaris, Goddess of Death. In conjunction with her skull-helm, it would have been impossible to walk the docks without attention. A number of other priestesses of Death walked the docks more openly, passing out words of warning about impending death and looking to convert followers. They did their duty for the church to pull at the guards' attention. Both Revwar and Savannah noted a lot of scrutiny attracted to those clerics. Too many guards and officials in Orlaun wanted Savannah, without knowing exactly where the abbess was hiding. Guards demanded that the clerics remove their helms, asked them their names, and tried to redirect them away from the docks.

The distraction served well enough that no one asked many questions of a certain blonde mercenary regarding her name and business in Orlaun. Savannah wore leather armaments. She did not even use dark coloring to shade her eyes to portray sunken skull sockets. A decorative, elvish, bastard sword hung in a baldric over her back. While the guards might search for her, or be on the lookout for Trestan, none would likely know anything about the stolen paladin's sword she carried. Instead, it helped her adopt a different persona. When port authorities casually asked her about her business, her story about being a paid guard for a chest of merchandise…(not worth stealing, simply some lord's crafted armor that she was entrusted to deliver, and nay, she wasn't allowed to carry the key to it for security reasons)…did not raise any suspicions. If anyone may have doubted her skills as a mercenary, her eyes still managed to express the cold promise of death. The leather outfit displayed the well-honed muscles that typically went unseen, normally hidden under the heavier layers of metal plates.

Revwar stationed himself casually far enough away to appear they were strangers. Yet, when no one was near, he was close enough to whisper to his partner. "It is nearly the hour of our most celebrated moment. We have months until it starts, yet there is much to be done. Must this task take precedence over your greater calling?"

Savannah frowned. She made a casual glance right and left to discern if anyone could eavesdrop. Since it appeared they were not under any undue attention, she whispered back. "This has become my one, true duty. This is my personal burden and only I can lift it. I must see it through."

The elf wizard noted the tense energy in Savannah's stance. The woman did not find it easy to stand around and wait for the future to come to her. His cowl seemed to point elsewhere as he watched her from his peripheral view. "He is not a threat, just a farmer. He does not seek us out…"

A hiss escaped the abbess' lips. "That matters not at all! And you do not need me to gather the tribes. Our powerful friends can do that easily enough. This trip won't take long."

Revwar loathed to be separated from his truest ally. Savannah shared a partnership with him for years. Whenever they stood together, they outlasted most foes; whenever apart, it seemed as if the God of Luck stacked the cards against them.

The elf knew she seemed set on this action, but he tried to talk her out of it anyway. "What will it matter in the end? War will come and he will be caught up in it like all the rest. He will die with his family. If you go, our efforts at raising our army may find unforeseen difficulty."

Savannah, concerned about ears listening, raised her voice and waved away the figure in the cloak. "Enough begging, old man! I have my own course in life and nay coins to spare for strangers."

When it seemed they were alone again, Savannah spoke in whispers. "I claimed Petrow's life four years ago. In my position…" (She did not have to say, 'as an abbess of

Death', out loud in the harbor. Revwar understood her position.) "I have to carry out that decree. Suffering the continuation of this unfulfilled deed is an insult to my matron. It gives hope to others that Death can be swayed. I learned in Wilder that he has fathered two children, and seeded a third in his wife. Those children were dead before they were born, as Petrow should have died before they were ever conceived."

Savannah risked one open look towards Revwar's concealing cowl. He saw the fear touching her visage, a rare emotion for one that worships Death.

The blonde woman continued, letting out her fears and anger whether Revwar cared to listen or not. "For four years now, the emissaries of my goddess visit me in my dreams. I am dead to her, until I carry out my oath to end Petrow's life and the lives of his children. By my oaths to my goddess, I declared him a dead man. He must die along with those who were spawned after my declaration, or I must die in their place pursuing that goal. This will only be settled with Petrow's death, or my death while carrying out my goddess' edict, or I will find no welcome in the next world."

Savannah turned to regard two burly men walking towards her from a nearby ship. They were coming to carry her burden: the chest that actually contained her black platemail, bearing the designs of her goddess. Her ship was ready to depart and head north towards Barkan's Crossing.

She finished voicing her feelings to her cloaked cohort. "It is time to end this. For all that I have suffered, it must end. I will butcher Petrow, I will murder his children, I will even kill his wife for the pain I have endured. On behalf of my goddess, I will claim any life that gets in my way. The only sad twist of this entire affair will be that this will seem merciful compared to what will happen when our secret allies join the war."

Savannah left on her ship, bound north for lands belonging to the Kashmer Protectorate. Later on, Revwar left on a ship that went south and west. He would land at the southern tip of the continent Shard at a rowdy place called Archer's Port. From there, he would sail up the western coast of that continent to the Stonelands.

CHAPTER 2   **"Kiss of a Demon/DeLaris' Assault"**

Long shadows stretched across the outside of the tent, signifying the lateness of the day. The sun retained only minutes of life before it would dip below the far plains. Kor sat on a cushion, contemplating his worries. He wasn't sure whether to have the tribe stake the rest of their tents, or be prepared to move despite the dwindling daylight. His mind tumbled through worries over his beloved. She should have been back by now. Kor had assumed that whether she carried good news or bad, his wife would have returned much earlier. The powerful warrior glanced at the heavy maul by his side. In a few more breaths he planned to take some warriors to get answers.

The rumors of a messiah coming to the tribes had many talking. Some spoke fearfully, some hopefully. Regardless of either stance, it added uncertainty when dealing with anyone. The nomadic clans began taking sides, though none claimed to have met the elf of which everyone spoke. Kor could not honestly know how he should react, though he viewed the situation with pessimism. He felt the tribes fretted over a small affair.

The tent flap parted, letting the evening rays spill over Kor. Although backlit by the sun, there was no mistaking Pejena's beautiful frame. The warrior rose to his feet as she stepped into the tent. She allowed the flap to fall closed behind her, shutting out the sunlight. The few lit candles were not enough for Kor to see any details about her face. He did not worry, however; she had returned safe and sound.

"What news my love?" Kor asked as he stepped closer. His arms parted just slightly, hoping for a comforting hug.

Pejena Cloud Whisperer accepted the gesture, practically throwing herself into his arms. He enjoyed her embrace. She whispered. "Much of this and much of that. Don't push me for details just yet. I have missed you."

As they hugged, Kor swung her partway around. He could finally make out her pretty face, her lovely skin. She seemed no worse off from her trip to the watering hole. He did perceive something out of sorts with the gaze from her green eyes. Kor couldn't place the emotions in her face.

"My love, is something amiss?" he asked.

Pejena pulled him closer to her height. She offered him a smile. "It's good to be in your arms. Pleasure me with a kiss. Give me that one offering before I go into details of what I have learned."

Kor eagerly obliged. He bent his sizeable frame towards her, eagerly seeking her kiss. Their lips danced slowly, coupled together. To his surprise, she opened the kiss a little further, tantalizingly teasing his lips apart with her tongue. He opened up for her as he held her close. His eyes had been closed, but he opened them now to glance at the face of his beloved.

She was crying. Something seemed very wrong at that moment.

With their lips still locked, Kor felt her body shake against some inner spasm. He tried holding her closer as her body underwent several convulsions. She responded the same way, pulling him tighter into the embrace. Her small, tender hands began to grip his arms like a strong titan.

Almost immediately as it started, he felt the foulest taste burst from her throat into his open mouth. Something rotted and cold ejected from her heaving body through her lips. It choked Kor as it started down his own throat.

He stiffened and pulled away, but Pejena's limbs became as strong as steel chains. He towered over her with his massive frame, yet strength from her own muscles kept her against him. There was no escape for his mouth as she forced herself on him. He choked and gagged as the wretched thing forced its way into his body. Whatever was trying to invade his mouth was alive!

He could still see her eyes, trapped a scant inch or two from his own. Pejena was in there, somewhere, but so was something else. Kor's muscles bulged as he tried to shrug off her strong grip. They both fell to the floor, rolling about.

A foul whispering noise welled up from *inside* his body. *A demon!*

He was helpless and losing strength. He tried to bite down, but could feel small claws holding his teeth at bay. The demon slithered down his throat, cutting off his air. He felt inadequate against this foe as he felt it turn his insides cold. The demon's voice began to hammer at his conscious thoughts. He heard a strange language in his head, yet somehow understood it. It was a sound that tore at his reasoning.

He became still enough to look into Pejena's eyes once again. Her body jerked slightly as the rest of the demon made its exit. Though this demon left her, she was still helpless to break free. Kor could see a faint trace of her spirit inside her eyes. She cried from her heart. He wanted to speak to her, urge her to resist, but he had no control over his own mouth. The demonic whisperings tore away at his will from inside his mind. It dawned on Kor that Pejena may be alive, but only as a prisoner inside her own body. She became a plaything of a demon babbling inside her own head.

The same fate loomed inevitable for Kor, as he felt control of his body slip away.

*   *   *   *   *

They learned of the danger too late to prepare for it. A strip of light blue coloring stretched across the eastern sky. The towering trees that dominated the continent blocked much of the morning's eastern glow. Torches from the trade outpost provided most of the available light. Sailors had been putting the last of the supplies into the boats on the beach. The rowboats were ready to cast off and board the mother ship. The crew chatted easily about their successful trip and how they might spend their trading profits once arriving back home. Amidst all the activity, a casual conversation between crew and the outpost revealed that the ship's arriving passenger was a woman dressed like death itself. She hadn't said more than a few words the whole trip, nor gave reason for her passage except that she insisted on fast transport to 'any Wilder port'.

It took only an instant to realize the significance of an abbess of DeLaris arriving in such a timely manner to this small trade post. Before anyone could be organized, the beach where the rowboats sat became a scene from a nightmare. Grisly forms crawled out of the ground. Long-dead humanoids rose from their eternal rest. Spirits animating the dead guided them towards their prey. They shambled forward on bony legs, reaching out with misshapen hands. The stench of decay permeated the air to the point where it gagged the sailors.

The nearby trading post, which owned the dock, hastily barred its shutters and doors. A few dozen people called this small settlement a home. They walled up their outer defenses rather than face the threat on the shoreline. This left the ship's sailors and a group of adventurers to deal with the threat.

Squire Trestan Karaok, the first of the would-be departing travelers planning to leave Wilder continent, threw aside his belongings in a hurry. Drawing forth a warhammer shaped like a bull's head, he stepped ahead to meet the foe. His armor reflected dents and holes from recent battles already faced in this land. An empty scabbard lie with his belongings in the rowboat. He held up his right hand, but not for the warhammer kept there. The undead spirits would never fear weapons. A golden light erupted from Faithful's Companion: the ring upon his right hand. That light illuminated the symbol of the coraross hanging from his necklace.

"By Abriana's will, begone foul spirits! Let the bodies of those dead find rest!"

The will of his goddess went forth. Channeling her miracle, the young warrior repulsed the spirits inhabiting the dead. The flow of energies banished undead spirits, ripping them away from the stolen cadavers. A wave of desecrated bodies began to fall apart before his eyes. The power of Abriana, Goddess of Love and Healing, restored the corpses to their restful state.

More forms came forward to replace the fallen on the shoreline. Some wavered, but trudged onward. Somewhere in the darkness, a follower of DeLaris exerted her will. Her priests had more direct control over the dead than a paladin-aspirant of Abriana could hope to overcome. As the zombies shambled along, Trestan met them head on.

"For Abriana and those that I love!" Trestan charged in, hammering away at the crowd of bodies.

His companions were likewise faced with threats. Katressa "Cat" Bilil strung her elven bow. The half-elf knew it would be useless against the walking dead, but she hoped to get a chance to send an arrow at the hidden cleric. As the undead closed, she slung her bow over her shoulder. She drew out her silver rapier to meet the attack. The pommel was made in the likeness of a hunting cat's head. She danced among the outstretched arms of her foes with all the agility gifted to her body. The closest corpse lost its hands to the enchanted weapon, yet still approached. It wasn't until it lost its head that the body went slack.

"Behead them or crush their spines. That's how you drive the undead spirits out!" Cat yelled to those companions around her.

Her voice was barely heard among the first screams of pain from the living. Numerous sailors from the boat cowered on the beach, though a few fought back with improvised weapons. Two sailors started clubbing the creatures with oars, even as a third companion stumbled backward while screaming for Krakus' forgiveness. Another threw a torch at the rags of one skeleton, doing little harm. The skeleton's soiled garments smoldered as it continued uninterrupted. One panicked seaman escaped the only way he could, going into the water hoping he could swim to the ship. A pair of officers drew cutlasses and attempted to hack limbs from the creatures. Some sailors fell victim to the encroaching multitude.

Sondra Oskires, an acolyte of Ganden, (God of Honor, Duty, Service), tried to gather her wits against this unexpected enemy. She was still new to adventure, having worked most of her twenty-three years in the poor sanctuaries of Orlaun. She wished her miracles allowed her to repel the undead, as Trestan had done, but Ganden had no influence over the dead. Instead, she could offer her companions a protective ward. Ganden's domain included support in battles, the majority of which granted boons to shield lives. She turned to face two of her friends. From a necklace, she pulled out a dog-shaped pendant she had reclaimed after once throwing it at an enemy. She prayed as she touched her pendant, touching both of them with her god's blessing.

"As Ganden's honor is your shield, I place a protection on your garments. May they guard you from danger."

Lindon Taleweaver and Montanya each felt a tingle. Neither felt a physical difference, yet a presence gave them confidence. Each felt that an angel of Ganden would be looking over their shoulders, at least for a short time.

Sondra readied her mace, yet did not rush to meet the corpses. As some sailors went down, she moved to help them. Her training in the church made her an accomplished healer. She would have to see to it that those still living remained so by the day's end.

Lindon Taleweaver had few weapons that would be useful against undead spirits. His throwing daggers and nonmagical smallsword felt feeble against walking corpses. The smallsword was a gentleman's fencing sword, light and thin, usually hidden in canes. For protection, he only had the metal buckler strapped to his left forearm and Sondra's prayer.

He relied on his musical talents instead. As a minstrel, he was skilled enough to tap into the harmonic web. This allowed him access to the magic of the world with his voice and tunes. Taking up his mandolin, he played to assist those around him. A good minstrel could stoke the feelings of those nearby, influencing their outlook. Since unable to attack the undead directly, he played music to bolster his companions and the nearby sailors. Bravery replaced fear. As Lindon sang, those nearby began to fight back with vigor. The minstrel incorporated Cat's words of advice into his song. The sailors began fighting with clearer minds, concentrating to hit the undead where it would count.

Montanya su Troyeal bara Westonhout, the orphaned child of a slain noble family, met the undead attack viciously. The young nineteen-year-old was lithe and muscular from training in the martial arts. Hardened leather protected her body, including a chest piece, armguards and leather greaves over her legs. A wooden elven clasp whipped around at the end of her braided red hair. She struck at the walking corpses with a beautiful elf-grown staff. The durable caleocht wood kept it strong and flexible as it whacked bones.

She listened to Lindon's music as she moved. The student of chiaso had learned that his melodies inspired her to find her inner balance. Wrapped in her own energy, her blows with staff and legs knocked the zombies off balance. The undead continued to shamble forward. Montanya heard Cat's continued warnings to strike at the nerve centers of the creatures: the heads and spines. Focusing her concentration, Montanya twirled her staff while jumping at one of the creatures. The staff came up, snapping the rotted skull backwards, followed by a jumping side kick to the vulnerable neck. Bones crunched. With its neck broken, the corpse fell to the ground as a lifeless husk once again.

Even skeletons with no shred of brain matter were destroyed when Trestan's warhammer crushed their skulls. The undead spirits summoned to guide such creatures housed themselves wherever the nerve pathways once existed. When those pathways were corrupted, the spirits fled the host. Blows to limbs and body, even broken bones, could be ignored; as could stabbing weapons through any soft flesh that remained. Without destroying the head or spine, a person would have to cause overwhelming damage to the rest of the body before the spirit would give up the host.

Trestan was well-versed in dealing with zombies. Even though he only had his nonmagical hammer, his training and muscles allowed him to topple several. Not far away, Cat's magical rapier performed gruesome work destroying corpses. Although her weapon was not ideal for dealing with the dead, it still had a magical edge. It simply took her a little longer to hamper a zombie's arms or legs before hitting the vital areas. Trestan and Cat had to fight slightly apart, trying to hinder as many creatures as they could, while forming a line with wild Montanya and a few of the sailors.

"We need to find the priest controlling them!" Trestan yelled amidst the fighting. Between breaths, he struggled to be heard above the shouts of others. "Her power over the dead is much stronger than my own; I can't use miracles to overcome her control."

Someone in the back yelled. "They are breaching this side."

Renewed screams and fighting filled the night as a number of the creatures pushed past a knot of sailors. Several undead created carnage behind the impromptu defense line. Lindon backed away while maintaining his song. Sondra abruptly ended her healing miracle on a wounded man in order to face one of the zombies.

Cat shouted orders. "Tighten the ring. Everyone step back four paces."

The fight became more chaotic as people moved in the face of the encroaching dead. One gap closed only to form another. Montanya danced in acrobatic destruction as she found herself becoming surrounded. Sailors on both sides of her were dragged into the chilling embraces of dead bodies. Teeth and skeletal hands tore apart those who fell before the foe. Montanya's staff sent one head spinning from a corpse, dropping it, but she was forced backward again. Some undead only slowed to feast on living flesh.

Lindon wouldn't be able to keep his song up for long if the zombies got any closer. He heard Trestan's call to find the enemy priest, so he attempted to work towards that goal. He tried something difficult for even the most accomplished minstrels. He managed to combine two songs into one. The notes from one song started to blend with another. The performer continued to inspire the combatants with song, yet now his command of the harmonic web also brought forth light. The beach area brightened, illuminating the nearby trees close to the shore.

Sondra Oskires had concerns of her own. A zombie came right at her, clawing at her robes, mouth stretched wide for a bite. She brought her mace down hard on its head. A solid smack echoed. Sondra hoped the thing was dead, but the blow only rocked it back for a moment. Some rotted flesh hung now from a strip, displaying the bare bones of the skull underneath.

The acolyte of Ganden stumbled backwards as the zombie chased her. It ripped part of her vestments as claws closed in. Its mouth opened to display its cracked, yellowish teeth as it prepared to feast on her. She panicked, frantically striking time and again without caring where it hit the creature. Her backward motion brought her into shallow water next to the boats. Sondra swung her mace again, but this time her wrist was caught by one of its misshapen claws. It held on tightly to her weapon arm as fangs came close to her face. She twisted furiously in her attempt to escape, unable to shake its grip. The undead seemed to have an unnatural strength. She was barely able to transfer her mace from her trapped hand to her left hand.

16

The two combatants stumbled and fell into the water. Sondra's right arm struggled for freedom as she felt those teeth coming at her throat. Under the murky waves, she couldn't see much aside from an outline against the glittering light from torches. Her left arm came up, thrusting the handle of her mace into that hungry maw. The rotted face stopped inches from her own, chewing on her mace handle. It was on top of her as she squirmed under shallow water. Its free claw reached up and sunk sharpened fingers into her left shoulder. She started to scream, but it only came out in the form of bubbles. Sondra stopped as soon as she realized she was losing her precious air.

"I'm going to die like this." She thought. The zombie's assault kept her body underwater even as it tried to devour her flesh.

"Trestan, I see her." Cat said, amidst their struggle. The bright light summoned by the minstrel allowed the half-elf to make out the form in dark armor. The priestess of DeLaris stood within some trees not far away. "I can shoot her once I get my bow."

Trestan shook his head, remembering the miracles DeLaris' clerics employed. "Savannah always has…a protective field around herself." He paused his thought, even as he hammered back another creature. "But, I bet clerics of Ganden could…enchant weapons with a miracle."

Cat glanced back, but didn't see the acolyte of Ganden anywhere. "Can you spare me?"

"Aye, go." Trestan immediately called on another banishing miracle like the one he had used just earlier. He bent his will towards trying to force the undead spirits to abandon the corpses. The cleric of DeLaris retaliated, reinforcing her commands.

It slowed the dead for a few precious moments, long enough for Trestan to slay another. Cat abandoned her spot, running back for Sondra. The half-elf saw the thrashing forms in the shallow water. She recognized the clerical robes around one kicking leg. The raven-haired adventuress ran as fast as she could. The zombie stopped moving when the silver rapier sliced through the back of its neck. Cat reached down and pulled the coughing woman out of the water.

Sondra was still trying to get her air back when Cat shoved an arrow before her eyes. "Can you put some blessing on this, *fast*…to pierce someone's magical defenses?"

The acolyte of Ganden knew such a miracle, but never used it before. She tried to gather her wits long enough to recite the prayer.

Any defensive line no longer existed. Everyone fought for themselves as the zombies and skeletons swarmed in. More corpses and sailors were lying on the ground than those actively fighting. Trestan and Montanya lost ground, but they concentrated on a few corpses threatening Lindon's songs. The minstrel barely held on to his concentration as two skeletons were smashed just before they could reach him.

Back in the trees, the cleric of DeLaris smiled at the destruction. She stood rigid as she channeled her concentration. The will of her goddess flowed through her with intoxicating power. She loved her goddess and the power of Death. She willed her mindless servants onward, crushing the lives of everyone in front of her.

She noted with only brief alarm when a female archer rose up between bodies and took aim her way. It seemed to matter little. The cleric had shielded herself from nonmagical weapons. Her armor and skull helm protected most of her body, leaving few spots vulnerable. The cleric paid little attention to the arrow's flight, preferring instead to focus more corpses on that attacker.

Cat's arrow found a gap in the armor, driving through the shields with Ganden's miracle. Just as an abbess of Death held more power over the dead than a paladin of Healing, so too did a cleric of Duty possess more power to enchant a weapon than a minion of Death could ward herself against harm. The cleric's eyes bulged in shock as the arrow tore through her. As she went down, so did her corpse puppets. The undead spirits abandoned their hosts, leaving the dead bodies to lay twisted on the beach.

*   *   *   *   *

As soon as the undead stopped moving, Cat and Montanya ran up the beach to check on the minion of DeLaris. Trestan took a step that direction, but changed his mind at hearing the agonizing moans from the wounded. A few sailors were in danger of succumbing to their injuries. Trestan looked for Sondra, the only one who could assist in healing the others. He saw the young acolyte of Ganden crawling out of the tide; red blood stained her tunic.

Trestan went to assist her first. He placed a hand upon her shoulder, causing her to wince, and spoke the prayer of healing. The grisly wound closed over, leaving only torn vestments as a reminder. He cupped her chin and gently brought her eyes up to meet his. Sondra obviously had a scare, but she didn't seem fearful at the moment.

Trestan prodded, "Are you well enough? We need to see to the others."

She nodded, blinking away tears. She didn't allow any residual pain from her shoulder to delay her as she went about healing the wounded. Trestan and Sondra moved from victim to victim, easing their pains. The miracles flowing from Abriana and Ganden allowed them to cure horrible wounds. The task wearied the healers, but it saved limbs and lives. Lindon stayed by them as they worked, bringing soothing words of comfort to those being healed. He foraged bandages and splints as needed. Trestan and Sondra couldn't heal all the wounds, but they were able to assist each man in some way.

The peasants and tradesmen of the trading post finally opened their doors. A few of them came out with bandages, willing to help.

At one point, Trestan looked up to see Montanya had returned. The red-haired youth, muscular and agile, was unhurt. Her martial training had served her exceptionally well against their foes, she wasn't even breathing hard.

Montanya waved to get his attention. "Cat wants to see you by the corpse of that cleric when you are nay longer needed here."

Trestan nodded as he looked over the scene of the fight. He and Sondra had exhausted all of their spiritual energy. They were unable to channel more miraculous healing without a rest. Trestan doubted any of the wounded were in mortal danger, though a few remained incapacitated. Trestan would have preferred to raise their health a bit more before taking the smaller boats out to rendezvous with the ship anchored offshore. His hand twitched as he reflexively went to reach for his sword.

A twitch of his hand was as far as he got before being reminded that his scabbard was resting empty in one of the boats. Wielding his blade, Trestan could transfer his health to a wounded person, taking on injuries to himself instead. One of their enemies, Savannah, had encountered him around a week earlier on a holy day of Abriana's. On the first day of every month, the faithful followers of Abriana may not attack their enemies, even in self-defense. It is a promise of faith that, if broken, expels them from her grace forever. Trestan had been tempted to throw away his faith to end a threat to a friend, but Savannah had taken the opportunity away from him. She stole his sword, a magical, elvish, bastard sword, from his scabbard.

It occurred to him that Savannah likely just died on the beach. Even now, his sword might be returned intact. Trestan asked Montanya to do a few things that would ease the injured sailors before hurrying to Cat's side.

The leather-clad privateer from Kashmer was kneeling over the body of their attacker. The half-elf had accepted his oathbond, the elf version of an engagement, just days ago. According to elf custom, Cat had a year to either marry Trestan, (known as 'spiritbond' to the elves), or refuse his hand in marriage. She wore a symbol of their engagement on one wrist. A bracelet of durable caleocht wood displayed designs of Laedelious in gold dust, and its emeralds matched the green in Cat's eyes.

The half-elf was an experienced adventurer when she met Trestan, a mere blacksmith's son. After all, she had been only a teenager when her parents died during a demon invasion of her home. In her youth she had scouted orcs before becoming a privateer in the service of Kashmer. The privateers were adventurers-for-hire that protected Kashmer's trade. Now at the age of forty-one she was older than Trestan by eighteen years, despite looking like she was slightly younger than him. Age had always been a touchy issue between them. Cat had accepted Trestan's proposal knowing that she would likely outlive him by over a hundred years if nothing killed her first.

Cat picked through bags and pockets as he approached. Trestan ventured, "Does she have my sword with her?"

She leaned back, answering, "This isn't Savannah."

The skull-helm had been removed, revealing long locks of dark hair tumbled about a stranger's face. Though dressed similar to the blonde abbess, this was someone they had never met before. Trestan looked over this stranger, averting his eyes from lingering on the bloody arrow. Although he had chosen the path of a warrior, the sight of a dead body still bothered him. He wondered how long it would be before he could casually, coldly, examine the remains of a once-warm person. In his heart, he hoped he would never view a body in a way bereft of any passion for the spirit that had once lived there. He didn't expect that this person, if alive, would ask any forgiveness for the deaths they had just caused. As he looked over her face, he simply thought of how this woman could have grown up to be a performer, a mother, an artisan or anything other than a bringer of death.

Cat spoke, echoing thoughts that were just creeping into Trestan's head. "This woman was here for us…specifically looking for us at this port. Her goddess has to have known that we'd be at one of these small trading posts, looking for passage off this continent. How many more clerics of DeLaris are between here and Fortress Stone?"

Trestan frowned. "DeLaris is using her other followers? This isn't just us against Revwar and Savannah anymore. Apparently, the Goddess of Death sees us as enough of a threat to send murderers after us."

Cat nodded grimly. "We won't be getting much rest until this is over. Mothrok may feel the same way, so we shall use caution around her followers as well."

Trestan shook his head. The quest became far more dangerous with every minute. It felt like the first time they had left Troutbrook to rescue Lady Shauntay. Their enemies had multiplied with each step down the road. This time, two goddesses were sending minions against them.

Trestan felt unarmed without his magical sword, despite his heavy warhammer. His gaze drew to the tiara on Cat's head. It shared the identical healing properties of his sword. Trestan crafted the golden tiara with the help of the elf mage, Korrelothar, and molded the weave of golden strands from designs on his magical sword. Unbeknownst to even Trestan during its creation, Korrelothar had put a bit of magic into the *Taef' Adorina*. The headpiece deflected blows better than a steel helmet, and it could also be used to heal if the healer sacrificed some of their own health.

The champion of Abriana put a hand on Cat's shoulder, *"Faunlessa,"* (He often called her by the elvish term for "cherished lover"), "I would like to borrow the *Taef' Adorina* for a few minutes. There are some who could use another touch of healing before being moved."

"Nay, you may not." Cat faced him. She could see the surprise her rejection brought to his expression. The half-elf spoke quickly to assert her reasons. "I'll make one thing perfectly clear. You are the holy champion who needs to be healthy to wield the Earthrin Stones if they fall into our hands. Also, this is my tiara, and my means of healing. So, from now on, whenever you need to use this for healing, you will only do so after I have used it first."

Trestan started to object, but Cat motioned with her hand that she wouldn't abide disagreement. She continued. "Don't try arguing this with me. This is mine to use for the good of others before you need to make a sacrifice on your part. I won't back down. Now, tell me which of those men you need me to heal first."

Trestan had known Cat long enough to realize she wouldn't be budged from her stance. He nodded his head in agreement. As Cat stood, Trestan once more considered the unknown face of the dark-haired abbess. He realized that their journey would be that much more dangerous. DeLaris was mobilizing her other clergy to take part in her bid for power, possibly Mothrok too. Abriana would have to do the same.

CHAPTER 3   **"Orlaun Inquiry"**

After the attack on Wilder continent, Trestan, Katressa, and their companions returned to Orlaun with news for the Brotherhood of the Circles mage guild. Word of their presence in Orlaun reached the ears of the guild well before they made the walk up to the gates. Their timing proved convenient for those inside the guild. A number of people with vested interest in the affairs surrounding the downing of the divine chariot, *Doranil Star*, were staying as guests at the mages' estate. As word spread, several influential people readied for a meeting behind closed doors. A host of unfamiliar faces, plus a few recognizable ones, confronted the companions.

Foremost among the people conducting the session were members of the Brotherhood of the Circles mage guild. They had been entrusted to help preserve and protect the last divine chariot that retained the ability to fly. One of their members assisted in sabotaging the ship and bringing about its destruction. The guild demanded to hear all that had transpired from those who witnessed the sabotage. Their questions were led by the elf wizard Korrelothar, who had just returned from Wilder continent over a week earlier. One of the other mages present was recognizable to one of the returning companions. Wendall, the gnome illusionist, had met one of them before under a brief circumstance.

The second group of representatives hailed from the church of Ganden: God of Honor, Duty and Service. The *Doranil Star* had been a sacred vessel of their deity, blessed during the Godswars. It required several clerics chanting in prayer to give the ship its ability of flight. The sabotage within their vessel murdered several of their clergy, and most of the other high-profile priests perished trying to keep the ship aloft while others escaped. Of the two acolytes that had been on board, one received the task of informing them of fate of their Chosen. The other one, thought lost, had just arrived with the last group of survivors known. A veteran paladin of Ganden lead the church's delegation: Sir Penvos "The Steady", renowned for his unwavering loyalty in severe situations. He needed to hear what the other remaining acolyte could share.

The last interested party consisted of a mix of nobles and appointed officials representing either the king of Gheras or the city of Orlaun. Their interest focused around the lives of many nobles that had been lost during the incident. It had been established that the cause of the accident was a theft unrelated to the presence of such personages as the duke who ruled Orlaun's province; however, they stayed to investigate further due to the rumors, falsehoods, and conflicting reports that always accommodated such a calamity. They also attended on behalf of the many influential noble families suffering from the loss of their loved ones.

Across from all of these influential people, the companions who had a unique perspective on what had happened sat in chairs lined up before witnesses. They sat together with some discomfort over the scrutiny by which their stories were received.

Lindon Taleweaver did most of the talking on behalf of the companions. Despite Trestan's quest, and the background that Cat provided, Lindon was the most at ease talking in such intimidating company. The minstrel was no stranger to this chamber. This large, almost coliseum-like chamber was the same acoustically perfect room in which entertainers competed to determine who would entertain on the *Doranil* Star's flight. Upper rows of seats were packed with numerous guests of the interested parties. The native of Orlaun also retained an advantage in his familiarity with some of the attending representatives. The minstrel had learned much of Cat and Trestan's history from their time together. He managed to sum up events well, in a way that painted them very favorably. He spoke in an educated manner between well-cleaned teeth. The emotions that Lindon revealed seemed either really genuine, or the best acting that Trestan had ever seen. The red hair that framed his face with a beard, the multi-layered style of Orlaun clothing, his light blue eyes, the broad, red-feathered hat, and his graceful dance of movement...all drew attention as he helped unfold the story.

Much of his rendition of events centered on Squire Trestan Karok. It felt right to associate the details of their struggles with the story of the young champion of Abriana embarking on his final quest to become a paladin. Trestan was asked for his input often, and the young, twenty-three-year-old former blacksmith answered as best and yet as little as he could. He preferred to let Lindon showcase a minstrel's skill with the human tongue. Trestan held his composure well, knowing those on the other side of the room observed and judged his every action. He certainly looked the part of an adventurer. He had grown a manly mustache that he often smoothed over when in deep thought. His muscles were well-honed under the metal armor he wore. His visible skin was tanned from spending days traveling under the sun. Trestan felt some scrutiny coming from Korrelothar. The attention wasn't unfriendly. It appeared Korrelothar was eyeing the empty scabbard on his back. The elf wizard knew the importance of the Sword of the Spirit to the young man. It had been passed on to Trestan from the mentor who introduced him to Abriana's teachings.

Trestan hid any discomfort he felt under the inspection of all these important people. His silent support came from the half-elf sitting by his side. His fiancée, Cat, always seemed to have a reservoir of strength behind her emerald eyes. Cat fully invested her heart in Trestan. She promised to marry him and enjoy the years they were offered. On one wrist, she proudly wore the bracelet of caleocht wood adorned with emeralds that signified their oathbond.

For this meeting, she dressed in her black adventuress leathers. The silver rapier hung by her side. There was no way to know how many hidden daggers she had tucked away. When Lindon made introductions, he made known to them that she was a privateer in the employ of Kashmer's Protectorate. As such, she was an adventurer paid by Kashmer to hunt down thieves, pirates, bandits, monsters and anything that could adversely affect Kashmer's commerce. Though she looked as tough as the leather she wore, she crowned her head with the magical *Taef' Adorina* that Trestan had given her as a gift. The thin, golden wires that composed it gave no hint that they were magically reinforced to deflect strong blows. Her other hidden tricks included a shroud covering one bracer. When unbuttoned, and a command word was spoken, the tiny gnomish disc within could launch an unfolding grapple hook several floors up.

The next companion in line often had her eyes downcast, shying away from the attention of those across from her. Her wheat-blonde locks dangled low enough to obscure her face. The few times she did raise her blue eyes, they were met by her superior in the church of Ganden, Sir Penvos. The paladin was eager to hear the words of Ganden's long-absent acolyte. The church had begun to suspect she had died during the voyage. Sondra Oskires wasn't sure what she would say when it came her turn. The young woman lacked self-confidence. She hoped she had handled herself relatively well, considering all the strange situations in which she had found herself since the voyage began. Sondra tried to sit up straighter as she felt Sir Penvos' eyes linger on her. She wore her finest ceremonial robes. Her belt buckle displayed a symbol of her service to Ganden: a shield with two open palms on it. Sondra wore another symbol hidden around her neck: a dog-shaped pendant representing selfless service to man. Her rust-colored, leather, healer's satchel rested by her chair. Her mace hung at her side. The weapon had seen no use until she bludgeoned to death the man everyone held responsible for the crash of the great vessel.

A red-haired youth whose face seemed to scowl, even when she didn't realize it, sat last in line for the companions. Only recently had Montanya begun to show a smile from time to time. Her loose clothes allowed freedom of movement, while hardened leather padded the vital areas. The nineteen-year-old had long legs capable of delivering powerful kicks. Her long hair was braided through an elvish clasp. Montanya spent her life training in the martial arts of the chiaso. Her goal had been revenge for the death of her parents at the hands of thieves. Montanya allowed her bottled rage to fuel her attitudes towards life. It also had the unintentional effect of holding back the inner balance required for a chiaso.

At some point, that attitude had changed. It might have started with guidance from the minstrel Lindon. Minstrels and chiaso tap into similar flows of magic in the world. Both methods are born from blending one's heart, mind and soul. Lindon felt the disharmony in Montanya's soul, helping to guide her meditations with his musical gift. For once, the young chiaso felt the true strength within her body. Aside from the minstrel, other changes forced perspective on Montanya. The youth had aimed a lot of anger towards Sondra until Trestan intervened. Through a miracle, Montanya and Sondra were forced to share their memories…each reliving the other's past. Much of what had been shared was slowly fading from memory, yet it made a change. Montanya and Sondra formed a friendship with their renewed understanding of each other. Yet, even those changes may have only seemed minor until Montanya came face to face with her life's goal. Her training had been focused on dealing justice to thieves. She finally caught a thief she had chased for many miles. She fought until victorious, but her efforts nearly killed her in the process. Victory seemed meaningless as she realized how much her quest for vengeance had robbed her of all enjoyment of life. Even now, she faced the future with no more possessions than the clothes on her back, an elvish quarterstaff, and an empty family locket around her neck. Montanya had no clear direction in which to continue her life beyond one last obligation. A mask, currently hanging from her belt, had been recovered from the thief. Its magic allowed short races to appear human. Montanya still had to return it to its rightful owner, whom she spotted at this very meeting.

For now, it was Lindon Taleweaver's time to give his rendition of events to the gathered assembly. He spoke about the three Earthrin Stones. He mentioned the theft of the one up north, transitioning to Trestan's and Cat's efforts to protect the two on *Doranil Star*. When Lindon mentioned the member of the Brotherhood of the Circles who had turned traitor, he provided more details and motives than were offered by any previous survivors' renditions. The mage guild members muttered a few insulting comments directed towards that dead mentalist. Lindon recounted how Revwar, Savannah, and their two accomplices had escaped the vessel despite the efforts of others. He went on to mention the companions' own abandonment of the Divine Chariot.

Korrelothar interrupted during this phase of the story. "I thought you may have found a way to chase after Revwar and Savannah. You have been gone for so much longer than everyone else, I was worried for you."

Trestan offered an answer. "It wasn't specifically the other band we were chasing." Trestan continued as Korrelothar's eyes showed interest. "Only after our departure, we found out that the stones were actually still on board the divine chariot."

Korrelothar almost fell out of his chair. "How did that come about?"

Trestan shrugged, "After Montanya was knocked into the hold with the bag, Revwar must have grabbed the wrong bag. Montanya didn't realize what was supposed to be inside it. Only later did she recall seeing the stones still inside the hold after Revwar had escaped. Thus, our course led us to track down the resting place of *Doranil Star* and recover the relics before the other band could get there."

The mage expected a lengthier response, but at Trestan's hesitation he prompted for more, "As you have not produced the stones as of yet, I must assume the worst?"

Trestan, his shoulders barely slumping at his own failure to protect the stones on the holy day of Abriana, nodded at Korrelothar's observation. "They got away with the stones. We found what we believed was a teleport circle nearby. That may have allowed them to escape to Orlaun very quickly."

"If I may pose an inquiry?" Sir Penvos asked Korrelothar. The elf wizard motioned for the representative of Ganden's church to proceed. The veteran paladin addressed the pupil who served under him. "Acolyte Sondra, the decision to search for our lord's chariot in that wilderness instead of returning to Orlaun must have been a hard one for you to make. I would hear of your account."

Sondra couldn't respond before swallowing a lump in her throat. "It was hard to even abandon our vessel. I would not have left had not Mother Evine commanded me to do so. My wish after being sent from her side was to make it back to Orlaun, even if it was just to report our loss."

She was unsure what else to say, but Sir Penvos and a roomful or delegates hung their attention on her words. Sondra managed a dry swallow. She responded even though she felt like she needed to apologize for some unknown wrong. "I was…outvoted. And so, unable to do anything else, I followed these others hoping to find out what I could. They headed for the remains of our holy temple, therefore, as the only representative of Ganden, I was bound to accompany them. I hoped to recover what remained of our relics, and in that respect I was successful."

The young woman awkwardly reached down to a large bag by her chair, dragging it forward several inches and allowing the top flaps to fall back slightly. She simply stated, "They are here. The artifacts from the cauldron were recovered amidst the remnants of our holy vessel."

Sir Penvos and the other clergy beside him all made motions to their deity, giving thanks to his blessings by returning what was lost. The paladin asked, "What of the Chosen?"

The question immediately brought tears to the corners of Sondra's eyes. "They were there to the end. We buried them as best we could, offering proper respects to Ganden as we worked. We couldn't carry the bodies. I don't think they would have minded a burial on grounds sanctified as the final resting place of the Divine Chariot. When I found the cauldron, I felt as if I stood on holy ground. I recognized all the bodies of the Chosen. There was one missing. Mother Evine's clothes were there, but her body and holy symbol had been consumed." Sondra showed them a wooden piece from the ship. "Her symbol branded itself on this piece of wood before being taken from this world by Ganden."

"Mother Evine was not a Chosen." Sir Penvos stated.

Sondra almost broke down in tears as she remembered her mentor's sacrifice. "She was one at the end. The surviving Chosen were very weak. She couldn't be sure they would stay aloft long enough for the rest of the passengers to escape. Mother Evine knelt by the cauldron before asking me to leave. She gave her voice over to the mantra to keep the ship floating…until the end."

Sir Penvos stood and walked over to comfort the acolyte. He held her head against him as he spoke softly to her. "Do not cry; you did well. Mother Evine shall be entered into the books as a Chosen, as it should be. We will talk more about this later. Compose yourself, daughter of Ganden."

Korrelothar urged the meeting to go on and cover all the other pertinent facts of the voyage. One of the next issues that came to light revolved around Montanya.

"There are those here who remember this young woman," Korrelothar was saying, "as a stowaway. She was apparently a guest in our brig, though I hadn't known that when I saw her on the deck. Montanya, is it? I would like to hear what brought you to our vessel."

Montanya had once dreamed of carrying out justice to thieves and being hailed as a hero from their victims. After chasing and beating to death the thief from the other band, she found that she took no pride in her actions. She answered with straight facts.

"I came aboard chasing a thief whom I felt was up to nay good. She wore a disguise when she boarded. I suspected something foul would happen. I didn't feel anyone would believe my story, and they didn't, until it was too late. By the time I caught her and dealt with her, the damage to the ship had been done."

Korrelothar turned to regard all the companions in turn. "So not all of them escaped."

Lindon interceded, "Revwar and Savannah escaped. Jentan Mollamos and the halfling rogue died."

There were excited murmurs at the news of Jentan's death. Korrelothar tried to bring some order back to the assembly. "Very well, I believe I should move on to ask…"

Montanya interrupted the wizard, "If I may, I wasn't done talking."

The elf wizard looked at the fire in her eyes and actually offered a hint of a smile at her feistiness. "Please say what you have to say."

Montanya looked across at the gathering of mages. "As I mentioned, the halfling snuck aboard with the help of a disguise, a stolen mask. She took it from one of your own, and that is how I came to follow her trail."

The youth stood up, reaching to her side and producing the mask Kemora had worn. The gnome, Wendall the illusionist, hopped out of his chair with a gasp as soon as he recognized it. The two met each other halfway as Montanya continued, "I chased her down to reclaim the stolen property. I offer it back to the owner."

Wendall gratefully took back the mask. He studied it briefly in wonder before squinting up at the woman. His eyebrows went up in recognition. "It was you I saw right after she attacked me!"

At her nod, the gnome was flabbergasted. Wendall exclaimed, "You spent the last few weeks chasing her onto a flying vessel and all the way through the untamed lands of Wilder?"

Montanya blushed a bit, "Aye. It became rather personal for me. I'm glad I was able to return your rightful property."

Wendall laughed. He found humor in the woman's simple words for such a long adventure. "Well done, my champion! You don't mind if I nickname you 'Bloodhound'? Hee hee. I don't suppose you can help me relocate a recipe book I lost two months ago?" He chuckled some more. "I will be happy to offer you a reward when this meeting is done."

At the mention of a reward, Montanya's first impulse was to refuse. She hadn't been motivated with any thought of reward except for how she had hoped to view herself afterward. The red-haired youth began to wave away the offer. Wendall began to insist, until Sondra interrupted.

"Take the reward, you could use it."

Montanya started to scowl at the young cleric. At seeing Sondra's concerned expression, Montanya softened a bit. Maybe it was the result of a new connection between the two since Trestan's miracle brought them to an understanding. Montanya felt Sondra's reasons without the cleric having to voice them. The wheat-blonde woman had once noted that Montanya's life of vengeance didn't account for any way to earn wages while doing it. Montanya had no means of supporting herself.

Turning back to the gnome, she accepted his offer. They resumed their seats, while Wendall enjoyed a smile. The illusionist happily fidgeted with the mask in his hands, which brought a grin and some satisfaction to Montanya's soul.

The meeting then revolved around Katressa and the translated scroll. The half-elf wasn't sure how much news she should share regarding the power of the relics. If she felt she had a choice, Cat wouldn't reveal too much at all to this gathering of various strangers. However, Trestan had plans in mind, so a full accounting needed to be brought forth. She shared most of what she knew. The Brotherhood of the Circles, especially Korrelothar, had the right to know what was at stake. She described the powers of the stones and their creation. The mages reacted with shocked expressions, even audible gasps, that such an item had lay hidden in their protection as nothing more than an oddity. The implications of such weapons began to weigh heavily on those present.

"They could cause destruction on a grand scale," Sir Penvos lamented. "All the struggles we have endured, over an era of rebuilding, seem insignificant in the face of Godswars-era weapons being unleashed. The mere fact that there are gods once again pitting their champions against others bodes very badly."

Korrelothar sighed, "They could easily carve out a small kingdom with those relics to back them. We can't even know if that is the limit of their intentions. If they have an army available, they could wreak havoc without anyone being able to easily stop them."

Trestan interrupted, "If I may have the floor, Korrelothar, I know of their plans."

The elf gestured an open palm toward him. "Speak, Squire Trestan of Abriana."

Trestan drew himself up straight. For all appearances, it was as if a noble of high birth stood to address them. The young paladin did well to hide any unease. For this role, he needed to speak with all confidence. "Savannah is a high-ranking abbess DeLaris chose to initiate her plans. The abbess and I linked in a duel of minds. She invaded some of my thoughts while I ventured into hers. They intend to take a large castle that will serve as their launching point. Their target is called Fortress Stone. It resides in the Stonelands, so named after the castle which is their capital, on the continent of Shard. I saw their planned timeline. It will be close to the approach of winter. Restless tribes from the open plains will descend like an angry horde. If they can take the castle, something even more malicious and evil will spew forth to attack the rest of the lands. If their plans are not stopped there, they will work their destruction back towards Orlaun."

When Trestan paused, Korrelothar filled the silence. "So, we at least know where the chaos will be sown first."

Trestan nodded, then looked sternly at the rest of the delegation. The most influential members of Orlaun society, whose anger had already been stoked by prior events, gave the young paladin-aspirant their complete attention. "They attacked your loved ones for this purpose. They took the relics from us so they could use them against us. They did it to make Orlaun defenseless against a future onslaught. They sabotaged your Divine Chariot to get it out of their way. We do know where the first battle will be fought. And…we have time to send the Stonelands enough help to quench the assault before the realm may be engulfed in another Godswar."

Korrelothar raised an eyebrow at Trestan's boldness. The meeting had been called to ascertain the full details of the events of the *Doranil Star's* crash. In a wink, Trestan was turning the emotions of that meeting into a demand for action. The elf did well to hide an approving smile behind an impassive face.

*   *   *   *   *

After the meeting ended, Korrelothar was chatting with one of his colleagues when he noticed Trestan and Cat lingering nearby. The couple lurked on the fringes of his conversations as if seeking his attention. As soon as politeness allowed, he concluded his chat. Once the other mage departed the two companions stepped closer.

"I think I've been played by a master," Korrelothar declared with a knowing gaze. "You had the minstrel subtly stoking our emotions with his account of events. Then, when the time was right, you switched the subject to plan for retribution."

Trestan shied away from his look, "Well, we needed to rally them into action to stop Revwar and Savannah's plans. I wasn't sure when I'd have the next opportunity to address so many influential people. We're going to need all the help we can get to prevent this invasion."

Korrelothar waved a hand to dismiss any further comments. "I quite understand, and I'm in agreement with you. It won't be hard to convince my brothers to act. They are still stung by Jentan's betrayal as well as flustered by our inability to protect the relics and the ship. I'm sure you'll be able to count on several angry mages for support."

Trestan nodded towards several well-dressed attendees. "And the Orlaun nobles?"

The elf shrugged, "Always hard to tell, but don't set your expectations too highly. They are…" Korrelothar glanced around to make sure no one overheard his words, "somewhat spoiled. The loss they suffered was hard, but the battle you mentioned is far away. Don't count on them to provide much help beyond what might be sufficient for diplomacy's sake."

Trestan stroked his mustache as he thought on the wizard's words. He had expected that winning over support from some might be difficult. Katressa stepped in during Trestan's pause, "There was something else we wanted to ask you about."

"Oh? Do ask."

"Revwar found another one of the items that had been on display when he was at the crash site. A golden necklace, with several jewels. They mentioned its name, 'Gitouro', saying that it had been worn by an immortal during the Godswars."

Korrelothar's worry increased noticeably at Cat's words. "Gods, that is even worse than I expected. I knew we shouldn't have brought that item for display."

The elf paused to light the pipe he carried and sample a puff. "It is another relic from that time. The necklace has as much power as the Earthrin Stones, I'm afraid. Rather limited, yet able to tip the scales unbelievably in their favor."

Cat beseeched him, "Please, tell us what it can do. Even better, how might we counter it?"

The elf responded, "There is nay method to counter it except to get it out of their possession. The only bright side of the Gitouro necklace is that, unlike the Earthrin Stones, the imbued necklace has only a small, limited number of times it can be used."

Korrelothar paused a moment, gathering his thoughts. "During the Godswars, there were two other gods forced into a position of neutrality. One was the God of Luck, Kelor; the other was the God of Balance, Foyul. These two differed in how they faced the wars, yet their goals were the same. Foyul, by his nature, was forced to balance out the opposing gods so that nay god got too strong. Therefore, Foyul's armies flipped loyalties often. Kelor was frequently called to intervene due to the luck needed by combatants in war. Kelor is a powerful enough god in his own right, having much influence over the fates of mortals. He could have easily picked a side and helped it win. But, like Foyul, he knew that he also had to achieve a certain balance. Between those two gods, the Godswars raged on longer than they normally would have, due to the shifting of loyalties. Foyul and Kelor kept any one side from completely dominating another.

"The necklace came into play as one of a few that were bestowed to Kelor's champions. Usually this was an immortal, but not always. It changed hands a few times. Its owner could change luck, over a large influence. Since it was possible that such an artifact might fall into the wrong hands, Kelor imbued those necklaces with only a few charges each. The Gitouro necklace was so named after the original hero who wielded it. The necklaces are not as uncommon as the Earthrin Stones, but few are found that still possess those active powers of luck. Unfortunately, they have an almost unmatched ability to change the fate of those around them."

The wizard sighed. "This makes it every bit as deadly as those stones. It basically has the power to obtain whatever the owner wishes. However, as I said, it can only be used a limited number of times. Yet, even such wishes have limits. The necklace can certainly affect a battlefield, or one person, but it can't reshape a continent. It can change fate, affect luck, or save the person wearing it, but it can't hand them the world in one blow."

Trestan, still stroking his mustache, interceded. "There is one hope that we can turn this to our advantage."

Korrelothar and Cat looked to him, astonished. He continued, "We were worried that we had to capture an Earthrin Stone to counter the other stones. Yet, if Revwar isn't guarding that necklace as well as he guards the stones, the necklace might also be a means to stop the powers of the stones."

CHAPTER 4   **"Plans made in Bedchambers"**

Although the castle belonging to the Brotherhood of the Circles was not often a place to acquire a room while passing through Orlaun, the companions were granted a few rooms under Korrelothar's generosity. The furnishings of their chambers proved fancy enough, even if dinner was an affair by which one had to walk down to the dining hall during certain times of the day, dressed in better clothes than any of them actually owned. Thankfully, the guest rooms also came with a wardrobe. An efficient seamstress visited each, sized them up, and had an array of garments ready for them.

The companions were grateful for Korrelothar's charity in letting them stay under that roof. It proved to be an interesting stay in more ways than one. For example, they found that wizards tended to display all sorts of odd trophies on the walls to impress guests. There was a touch of magic in many of the amenities provided. A marble slab in the tubs heated the water once touched. An abundance of magic illuminations in the rooms responded to verbal commands, such as voice-activated lights. A horn on a nightstand sent out a silent summons for cleaning maids to service the room.

This last oddity was discovered by Lindon Taleweaver by accident. He had picked up the horn to sample its musical qualities. After blowing on it for several minutes, puzzling at its inability to produce sound, a swarm of harried maids arrived and lectured Lindon on its proper use.

Once the castle servants had departed, the companions were left to sit and chat. They carried on their conversation in the room belonging to Trestan and Katressa. Lindon, their only guest for the moment, blushed and apologized over the horn incident. Montanya was supposedly just down the hall. Sondra had been absent ever since the meeting earlier that day. The young acolyte, along with the holy items of Ganden she recovered from the crash site on Wilder, had been ushered away to the church. Trestan wondered how Sondra was reacting to the questions from her superiors. Her actions on Wilder, guided in part by Trestan, had been brave and honorable. The young champion of Abriana only wondered if Sondra's low self-esteem would stand up in the face of the questions from her teachers.

His worries for Sondra lingered in the background as he listened to Lindon and Cat share an interesting conversation. The two travelers had seen much more of the world than Trestan. Both were comparing notes on their different experiences in famous cities. They discussed people's attitudes, style of dress, strange customs, and famous castles. It was all new to Trestan, so he tried to soak up every word. For all their time with the minstrel, they knew more about his songs and stories than anything about his past.

Trestan had that thought on his mind when he managed to find a break in the conversation. "Lindon, you certainly have done a lot of traveling. You call Orlaun your home, but when did you leave to explore all these places?"

Lindon relaxed back into his seat. "I left Orlaun as soon as was feasible after my tenure at the Artistic Enlightenment College. Within a week of concluding my studies, I set sail to see the world. I wanted to see everything if I could…and I mean everything! I wanted a tour that would even go beyond the boundaries of the known kingdoms."

Trestan felt he could identify with Lindon's feelings. "Like your home was too small, and there were all those tales of faraway wonders?"

"Aye," Lindon nodded, "Aye, indeed. At least, that is how it started out. When learning about music and folklore one learns about a lot of fantastic things out there in the world. It opened my eyes to places I wanted to visit and experience firsthand. You must understand, my youth was spent in one of the poorest districts of an otherwise rich city. Even when I walked through the cultured areas of the city, they treated me poorly. I was a cretin in dirty rags. People thought of me as crazed, a beggar or even a thief."

"And your parents?" Trestan ventured.

Lindon sighed, "There was only my mother. Very supportive of me throughout my youth. She showed me how to cook dirt in an alley and make it seem tasty. Elles. A simple name that couldn't begin to touch the depths of her character. We spent a lot of time begging for food. She taught me how to run and hide from trouble. I even found out she'd…" His voice caught. Lindon paused a moment before shaking his head. "Nevermind that. Some things aren't meant to be shared. I will say, mother made it clear to me that she had one goal she could hope to attain: giving me a happy life. She even showed me a spot where we could peek over a wall and observe high-society plays, and we'd laugh at the outrageous dress styles of both actors and patrons. Illness took her from me. I watched her die over the course of a few days, unable to save her."

The minstrel glanced upward. His light blue eyes were usually lit with an inner happiness, yet the ghosts of the past could be seen lurking there. "It's not a subject I usually discuss. I am quite happy to forget about that existence. If Korrelothar had never given me this…"

He reached into his vest. His nimble fingers plucked out the bamboo flute that seemed longer than his vest pocket could accommodate. Trestan and Cat had been witnesses to how well the minstrel could play the instrument.

"…I may never have escaped that prison of society. I am eternally grateful to that elf. Aside from hunting for food, I had nothing to do but practice. The more I practiced, the more the flute paid for my meals. When my fortunes changed, I had the bardic college to house me while I learned from the masters. Once I was free, I flew like a bird that just found his wings."

When it was apparent that Lindon reached the end to his discourse, Trestan voiced his feelings. "I'm still stretching my wings. I've seen more wonders in the world than a younger me could have imagined. I just wish my course in life didn't seem to be focused on matters of such worldly importance."

Lindon offered a look to Trestan that silently voiced his encouragement even before he spoke his feelings. "The good in this world is a beautiful thing. I have seen many reasons for the heroes of the world to have convictions to back up their sacrifices. Your quest draws me by the magnetism of its importance. As a minstrel, I would go along simply to record the deeds. As Lindon, the world traveler, I feel a need to take part in the struggle. The realm is a flower, pretty enough to look at but doomed if plucked by a thoughtless conqueror who feels the need to own it."

A forceful knock on the door interrupted them. A muffled voice outside revealed her to be Sondra. As soon as they told her to enter, she burst into the room practically dragging Montanya along. The chiaso wore an expression of bewilderment. Apparently, whatever had gotten Sondra all excited hadn't been shared with the red-haired youth as of yet. The others stood amazed as Sondra urged Montanya to take a seat while she made an announcement. This change in demeanor really surprised the others. The shy acolyte of Ganden often stayed quiet and reserved...never one to seek attention. Now the woman seemed all giddy with excitement.

Montanya commented to her friend, "You look as excited as if you'd just found a leprechaun's gold."

"Oh, it isn't any news that exciting," Sondra grinned, "But important enough all the same. I wanted to share the news with you all at once."

With no further interruptions, Sondra continued. "None of you will see me tonight. I will be spending the evening in solitary meditation inside the church sanctuary..."

Only Trestan quickly grasped her meaning. She noticed his grin, and even flashed him a bright, knowing smile. Of course, the squire of Abriana allowed her to finish her grand announcement to the others without giving it away.

"...and in the morning...I emerge as a full-fledged cleric of Ganden!"

A hearty round of congratulations emerged as the companions applauded her ascension. Trestan praised her, "It seems they must have approved of your retrieval of Ganden's relics from the crash site."

Sondra was beaming with energy. "They said it went above and beyond expectations for any acolyte."

"Well, wait a second," Montanya interposed. "I should go down and mention to those clerics that you voted for going home."

Sondra wasn't bothered by Montanya's jest. "Oh, I let them know that. Regardless, they seemed to be impressed at my tale, and Lindon's recollections of the adventure earlier today. I still can't believe they bestowed me this honor."

"We all saw how well you handled yourself in the wild." Cat gave the woman a congratulatory hug. "You helped us get back on our feet and your miracles made a difference. You have certainly earned the honor."

Sondra blushed, as she so often did in the face of compliments. Although Montanya had teased her a moment ago, the red-haired youth now spoke in a serious tone. "You saved me, maybe three times at least. I can't thank you enough for that."

The statement connected with Sondra full of meaning. Once Montanya wouldn't have thanked anyone, especially the acolyte with whom she had taken a dislike. The youth had come a long way from her original feelings. The two women now acted as best friends...indeed, neither had many other friends at all to boast.

"Are you able to celebrate the occasion with a drink?" Lindon asked. "We should see if we can call for some wine."

Trestan maintained a serious face. "Maybe you should use that horn again. Didn't the maids say it could be used to order wine as well?"

Lindon laughed, "Anyone else may feel free to try that; however, if you are going to blow the horn, I will be making a swift departure before more angry servants arrive."

*   *   *   *   *

The companions spent some time in their room in counsel. The conversation switched to plans for the near future. Trestan resolved to go north. His reasons revealed a mix of practical and personal issues. One reason for venturing to Kashmer would be an attempt to mobilize Abriana's faithful. Trestan intended to enlist help from the church, much as he had attempted to do here during the recent meeting with Orlaun representatives. In that regards, Sondra also brought a ray of hope. It seemed that the church of Ganden committed sending help to the Stonelands. The young woman had overheard many conversations at her church, which lead her to believe that the details were being discussed.

"…but they may take some time to decide exactly how they will move. They understand the timeline you discovered, Trestan, and that they likely have at least a month to plan and prepare." Sondra looked to the champion of Abriana. "I hope the vision you saw in Savannah's head doesn't alter. If our foes move quickly, then any delay could bring ruin."

Cat proved nervous about the postponement Trestan's journey north would cause, yet she supported his decision. "That has been my biggest fear. All our delays are based on the plots in Savannah's head back on Eyldiian. If things are altered, then gods need to help us. We may require the effort to gather more allies wherever we may find them."

Trestan shrugged, "Somehow, Revwar and Savannah plan to raise an army in the wild lands near the Stonelands. I don't know how they will do it, but I'm sure it will take time. We must be ready to meet them with our own army. I have heard that the fortress out there is huge, but stone walls can be made into vapor with the relics."

Sondra frowned. "I must stay with my church and be ready to leave with them. I will be sorry to see you depart." The disciple of Ganden threw the briefest of glances towards Montanya as she spoke.

Trestan's next reason for heading north came in the form of a ring upon his finger. The ring, Faithful's Companion, sparkled a golden hue. Where once it displayed symbols of tasks Trestan's goddess had set before him, now its luster shined unblemished. It called upon him to return to the seminary in Kashmer and become a full paladin. Sondra wasn't the only one of their group receiving accolades from a patron deity.

The third reason Trestan wanted to head north wasn't directly related to the conflict. He had to warn his friend Petrow about a direct threat to his family. Savannah, following the edicts of her goddess, had once tried to prove her goddess' control over life and death by claiming Petrow's life. She failed to kill him. What followed was years of divine punishment heaped upon the abbess of DeLaris. An individual evading the death claim left a message of hope to others that DeLaris would not suffer to endure. It was vital that Savannah carry out her edict. Through her mind-link with Trestan on Wilder, the abbess gained two important pieces of information. First, she learned exactly where Petrow lived; second, she discovered that Petrow had fathered children in the time since his life was supposed to have been terminated. The affront to Savannah could not be ignored. The goddess would not allow Savannah to rest until Petrow and his children were dead. The former hero of Troutbrook, now farmer, was oblivious to this threat. Trestan had to warn his friend that their family was in danger.

Trestan and Cat laid out their course. They would take a ship to Barkan's Crossing, and go by horse from there to Troutbrook and Kashmer. Sondra had already mentioned her plans to stay with the church in Orlaun until it sailed. Lindon and Montanya had said relatively little about their plans. Even as Trestan considered the two, he realized he may be assuming too much from them. After all, he already endured disappointment on the road he and Cat tread after the Embarking. His best friend Petrow refused to ride forth, citing his responsibilities to his family. Mel Bellringer had also stayed behind with a new love interest. It occurred to Trestan that Lindon and Montanya owed no special loyalty that was worth their lives.

He faced them. "I would ask, Montanya and Lindon, of your plans. I have been going on and on about my reasons for this quest, yet I have not asked your feelings on the matter. The danger is to the whole realms, yet there is certainly risk in going out to meet the threat. Will you ride with us?"

Montanya was caught unawares by the question. "Well…I feel that…how do I put this? It's not like I have any greater calling to my spirit. I guess I devoted so much of my life to one thing, and I haven't been sure where I can go from here." The others knew that Montanya's life had been spent in pursuit of thieves. The woman adopted the life of a vigilante. Her one encounter with a thief had shown her how hollow her pursuit had been. "I don't know how I can best help…but I plan to go."

Trestan nodded his understanding and turned to hear Lindon's response. Cat didn't show it on the outside, but she watched Montanya with interest. Something was out of place from the woman's message. It wasn't that Montanya seemed lying…more like she kept some truth hidden. There was more to her answer than what had been voiced.

Lindon Taleweaver made a flourish as he spoke. "My road lies northward with you. I have only wanderlust flowing through me, as I mentioned earlier. There is more of the world to see! On top of it all, there is a tale to be sung about these events. I wish to remain near both of you to learn the story that will unfold."

"Then our course is set. All we need do is follow the stars to our journey's end," said Cat. The raven-haired half-elf looked to each of them. "Does anything need to be taken care of in Orlaun before we leave?"

Lindon and Trestan shrugged. Montanya bit her lip at some indecision. The youth's reaction was not lost on Cat as she heard Trestan say, "I could pick up Belgard and depart at any moment." Trestan referred to his warhorse. The steed had been kept in safekeeping at the guild during the doomed voyage of *Doranil Star*. He continued, "Though there probably are a few things, maybe people I should talk to, before going. I want to make sure we have as much support as possible."

Cat spoke, "I, too, have business that might be best concluded while in the city. Maybe we should set forth after a couple days of rest and preparations?"

"You have some plans in mind?" asked Trestan.

Cat had one hand absently stroking the hunting-cat figure that was on the pommel of her rapier. "I like the big, hunting cats as you know. I also have a responsibility as a Kashmer privateer to seek out enemies that would disrupt Kashmer's trade."

The half-elf pulled her blade partway from the scabbard, examined the pommel figure, and allowed the blade to slide back home.

"I need to prepare for a hunt."

*   *   *   *   *

After some time, Montanya happened to catch Katressa alone. The chiaso intercepted the half-elf and steered her aside for a private conversation. "I needed to talk to you."

Cat motioned for Montanya to speak. "My ears are yours."

The red-haired warrior looked nervous as she spoke. "I'm worried that you will do something like what I did. I'm worried your life will be consumed by your hatred for that elf wizard."

The half-elf tipped her head to one side as she considered the youth's words. Like the others, Cat noted the change for the better which had come over the haughty young woman. It surprised her to receive the same scrutiny. "What makes you think that?"

Montanya reminded Cat of the way she had yelled at Revwar back in the elven city of Serud'Thanil. "You swore an oath that if it was the last thing you would do, you would hunt him down and kill him."

"Ah," Katressa understood. "You think my hate may drive me beyond consideration of anything else? Let me assure you, if that goal is never accomplished…if Revwar lives…my main goal in life is to love every moment Trestan and I have together."

Montanya felt relieved, and responded, "That is good to hear. Of course, I don't want to sound like a hypocrite. I still hate thieves. There are things about them that make my blood boil when I think about them. Yet, I can say that I now seek a more positive purpose in my life."

"As I hate Revwar." Cat put a comforting hand on Montanya's shoulder. "My parents were killed when I was young, as yours was. My home and other children I knew were ravaged in a terrible fashion. Now, I find out years later that Revwar stood behind all that. He still plots to finish what he started back then."

In her mind, Cat could still see the past as it was. She remembered her father touching the gold unicorn earring she had given him as a present, just before he stepped through a portal to the demons' home dimension. The portal closed before he could ever escape from that hellish world. In Serud'Thanil, Revwar informed her of her father's death, saying it had been merciful compared to most. He told her she might recognize the coldast demon who killed him someday, for it wore the ears of its foes openly. She would know the demon by the sight of Reatheneus' earring-adorned ear on its body. The news inflamed Katressa; she swore to hunt Revwar until he died by her blade.

Cat looked into Montanya's greenish-blue eyes. "I can't deny my hate for him. I do have a plan for my future, and it involves bearing children for Trestan…not for some time, of course! But for now, I have to be prepared to fight the nemesis that has scarred my childhood memories and threatens my lover."

"I was just worried that you might do something foolish." Montanya admitted.

The half-elf shrugged, "Quite the opposite. The last time we fought, Revwar had a few new tricks. He wore a robe that easily deflects even my magic blade. I plan to be a little more prepared with tricks of my own when next we meet."

      *   *   *   *   *

Trestan stood to one side of the open door as Korrelothar swept into the room. The aging elf wizard noted packs of equipment and various objects lying strewn across the bed.

"Well, I have come not a moment too soon. Looks like someone is preparing to leave on a journey."

Cat stood next to the pile of supplies, smiling mischievously. "No, we decided the bed was too comfy for our adventuring tastes. We made it more to our liking by using our packs as pillows."

Korrelothar offered a small chuckle. "Ah, there are days I still long for sleeping under a canopy of stars next to a warm campfire. Sadly, my body offers more complaints than it once did. The spirit is there, but the bones seek better rest."

The companions thought he had finished but he added an afterthought. "Of course, it was more comfortable going out in the wilds with *Dovewing*. At night, I threw a shield over the vessel while I napped quite comfortably on the couch at the stern. To be safe from predators, I hovered ten meters above the ground. I miss that comfortable couch."

Cat rolled her eyes to the heavens, "He is never going to let us live that down! We will have to buy him a new one."

Trestan closed the door and interjected. "I should point out that it was Cat's idea to steal it and I objected."

"Oh, thanks for the reminder my love," Cat's voice dripped with sarcasm and feigned hurt.

Korrelothar privately enjoyed mirth despite laying the guilt at their feet. "In fact, I find it odd that I invite you two on board another rare flying vessel, and that one crashed also. You sure you didn't have anything to do with that?"

Cat hid her emotions. After all, the *Doranil Star* started dropping out of the sky when she shoved Revwar's staff into a magical trap. She changed the subject. "You must have heard I was asking for you."

The wizard nodded, chuckling at the companions' discomfort over the previous conversation topic. "I heard you needed some favors from me. I thought that was good since I had trouble finding something for *you*." He specifically indicated Katressa.

Continuing, he moved closer to Trestan and handed him a vial from beneath his robes. "I found something for Trestan to take on your journey. I heard you were heading to Kashmer, and I must stay behind to ready my guild for their part at Stonelands. It is my hope to find you both well, yet if nothing else, I have this gift to offer."

Trestan took the vial. It's style and symbols gave credence to ancient origins. Carvings and symbols on the vial paid homage to the god Dalios. To humans, he was the God of Strength and Courage, though other races called him the God of War.

Trestan handled it carefully as he examined the fine workmanship on the sides. "What is this?"

"It is called 'Blood of Dalios'. It was one of the treasured items here at the guild. We owned two such rarities, but this one was mine from younger days. I offer it to you."

Trestan looked up. "This is something from the Godswars as well, isn't it?"

The wizard nodded. "When Cat mentioned the Gitouro necklace in the hands of the enemies, after they already have claimed the three Earthrin Stones, I thought it important to put a powerful weapon in your hands. This container was among several given to Dalios' followers. It is indeed a potion made of his blood, from when he walked mortal lands."

Trestan's mouth gaped open, "I can't take such a prize!"

36

He tried to push it back into Korrelothar's hands. The elf refused to take it. "Would you prefer it to sit on a dusty shelf for another millennium of uselessness? This was created to win the Godswars. If Revwar and Savannah have their way, we will be embroiled in another bitter war. I'm hoping this will give you the strength when you need it to stop them."

Unable to get the elf to back down, Trestan asked. "Fine then, what does it do?"

"Drinking this potion will boost your strength and your vitality beyond most mortal means. Its effect lasts a relatively short time, so use it wisely. You will be able to throw boulders like a giant, take weapon blows that would drop a raging boar in its tracks, and it will also regenerate your wounds even as you fight. For a brief period, you will be an unstoppable fighter. It will be as if you are Dalios' earthly avatar."

The champion of Abriana offered his sincere thanks as he took the potion. Korrelothar turned to Katressa. "I could not find an item that I would consider so suitable a gift for you. If there is anything I can do…"

As he trailed off, Cat answered, "There is, which is why I left word that I sought you. I have a few things I need, magical in nature, and I have the gold to acquire them."

Cat started to pull out a scroll on which she had listed several things. Korrelothar looked over it, "Don't be too hasty throwing around your gold. I'm sure with your deeds I can go about pulling a few favors from my fellow guildmates." He continued to read down the items on the scroll. His brow furrowed as he read the unusual list. "Dare I ask what you plan to do with all of these things?"

Cat smiled, "Just a little hunting."

*   *   *   *   *

Sondra wore her new vestments, adorned with the fresh trim signifying her recent change of status to a full cleric of Ganden. Her blue eyes perused a scroll inside her new room at the church. Her small room barely housed a bed, a desk, and a chest of garments. No one knew, but tucked into that chest of clothes hid Sondra's lone vice: scrolls of love stories and romantic poetry. It was a humble living space, yet more than she needed.

A knock sounded at her door. One of the younger acolytes announced from outside. "Sister Sondra, I have Montanya from the house of Westonhout here to see you."

Sondra couldn't help but crack a smile at the introduction. Montanya generally did not use her family name. The cleric set aside her scroll and stood up. "Show her inside, thank you."

The door opened and the long-legged chiaso sheepishly stepped into the unfamiliar room. Montanya definitely seemed out of her element. Sondra knew the youth felt uncomfortable in church structures. The woman had refused the services of the Sanctuary for Those in Need where Sondra had worked, storming out after showing an ungrateful attitude towards the clerics who had saved her life. The young chiaso slandered those houses as being "copper pens", since the clergy asked for a copper coin a day to house and feed the poor. For these reasons, it surprised Sondra that Montanya chose to come for a visit. The truth hit Sondra's thoughts a moment later. Montanya was likely here to say goodbye before leaving to go up north with the others.

Sondra decided to put Montanya at ease. She wasn't sure if what she had in mind would actually work or have the opposite effect. Inside, Sondra was still a shy person who found it hard to express herself well around others. The healer had resolved to be more open to those around her.

She greeted Montanya with a big smile and a warm hug. Montanya hesitated before returning the hug, yet return it she did. Sondra spoke as she pulled away, trying to set a positive note.

"I'm glad to see you here. I wish I'd known you were coming; I would have made things more presentable. It's a pleasure having you visit."

Montanya gave a small smile, "Your room looks comfortable enough, nay need to make any special preparations for me. I'm sure you may be wondering about my use of my family name with that acolyte. I thought it might help me get in the door if I sounded more important."

Sondra chuckled at that. The wheat-blonde woman stepped backward until she could sit on the edge of her bed. "I figured as much."

Montanya didn't take a seat. She still seemed nervous as her weight went from one foot to the other, wringing her fingers. The red-haired chiaso lowered her eyes, studying Sondra's garments. "Your new robes look nice. Your old ones were beginning to look worn. I'm glad you achieved your dream."

"Thank you," Sondra held her arms apart to show off the new look. There was very little difference between an acolyte's robe and an ordained cleric's, but the new look and feel did much to improve Sondra's outlook. Of course, her previous clothes had become horribly stained and discolored from their weeks-long romp in deep forests. "Well, my dream was to be a Chosen. That wish crashed in Wilder. Trestan got me thinking I could pursue some other dreams. I'm still figuring what I want to do. I haven't really explored too many interests outside my studies."

Montanya nodded, "Same for me. I trained all my life as a warrior. It turns out that I want more from my life than just that. I don't even have a home or a trade. My future is clouded."

A bit of silence passed. Sondra decided to get things out in the open. "So, did you come to say goodbye before you take the ship north?"

"Aye…err, nay…well…" Montanya seemed to get a lump in her throat.

Sondra could see the nervousness radiating from the younger woman. Was that how Sondra had often looked before Mother Evine? In fact, Sondra had never seen Montanya look so uncomfortable. The cleric sat forward on her bed, waiting for the chiaso to sort her thoughts.

Montanya didn't know how to phrase her words. Instead, she took a seat next to Sondra on the edge of the bed. Sitting side-by-side allowed her to speak her thoughts to the walls instead of facing the woman directly.

"This probably sounds foolish…" She began, staring at the small cracks in the surface, "but I'd rather not head north with Trestan. Don't get me wrong, I intend to be at Fortress Stone and fight, but I don't want to take that route."

Montanya absently twiddled some fingers as Sondra queried. "You have something to ask that I can help you with?"

Montanya swiveled her face to look into the cleric's eyes. "Can I stay with you?" She turned her head back to the wall, adding as an afterthought, "Please?"

Sondra's soft, blue eyes widened at this unexpected request. It was the last thing she thought she'd ever hear from Montanya. "This doesn't sound like you."

"It doesn't sound like the *old* me," the youth clarified.

"Hmm," Sondra mulled it over. Secretly, she was excited that her friend would seek to stay until the journey to Stonelands. Sondra tried to keep her true feelings from showing. "I'll have to see about having a guest over. I can remove the desk…writing space is plentiful enough around here…and add a second bed. That's the only way they might let you stay. They don't just give rooms out to people. You'll probably have to work in the church somewhere. Would you be willing to handle some chores?"

Montanya took a deep breath before dropping her next unusual request. "I thought about that. I was thinking…well, I could help feed people at the shelters."

Sondra's dark-red lips fell open in shock. She quickly recovered so that she didn't make things harder on the youth than the discomfort she must be feeling to make these requests. Luckily, Montanya still stared at the wall, and missed Sondra's gawking.

The priestess revealed, "You realize…when I work at the Sanctuaries for Those in Need, I also sleep there overnight. I thought you hated those places?"

The nineteen-year-old's mouth twisted something awful as she swallowed that news. "I would have to sleep in a copper pen?"

Sondra's voice took on a tough tone, "Sanctuary for Those in Need! I won't sponsor you volunteering there if you go in and call it a copper pen."

Montanya's head sagged. The youth remembered the rat's nests and bug-infested places she had slept in since being kicked out of her monastery. She compared that to the notion of sleeping in a poor house. Her voice croaked out, "I've slept in worse places. I'll learn to like it, or at least I'll try."

"Montanya, my friend," Sondra reached out and gently pushed back Montanya's closest shoulder in a clear sign that she wanted the younger woman to look her in the eye. It was not something Sondra did often, as the cleric also had preferred talking to the walls or floor on many occasions when with people. "You have asked these things, and I will see them done for you. I would be honored to have you stay with me and help the church. Yet, I must ask a question, for you seem rather…reluctant. Why do you want to do this?"

Montanya's greenish-blue eyes beseeched Sondra, "I tried to do a noble thing but I went about it the wrong way. I lived only to be a fighter, and yet I have done nothing for the people whom I thought I was saving from harm. Even though I know, in your heart, you haven't felt much satisfaction from those you tried to help…" She stopped and swallowed. "Well, you have dealt with some very bad parts of the city, and you carry hidden wounds from it. Maybe you haven't paid enough attention to the worth of your actions, but you have helped many and put smiles on those with little hope. I want to try on your shoes for a while. I want to help people in a way that doesn't depend on me looking for someone to hit. I want to do something for suffering folk that I think I will be personally very proud of, before war calls me to Stonelands."

*   *   *   *   *

Within a couple days, Trestan, Katressa and Lindon set sail northward. They bid goodbye to Sondra and Montanya, who would rejoin them again once in the Stonelands. Korrelothar also appeared to say his farewells, before returning to his guild for several preparations. He had to ready the mages for war, as well as craft several magical items at the request of Katressa.

As Trestan looked northward on this sea journey, he could not know that Savannah already had half a month's head start, 20 full days, on her way north to kill Petrow.

CHAPTER 5   **"I *am* Death!"**

"I do admit, I couldn't have asked for a finer place to build."

The speaker looked up to the distant castle: a structure sitting on a raised plateau overlooking the coastline and the town. "You have a mighty work o' stone walls nearby for defense…human crafted as they may be, yet proudly constructed. A lot o' care and planning went into that toil. A fine place to be named Fortress Stone."

Men nodded as the speaker praised their castle. They politely waited as the dwarf downed a swig of potent brew before continuing his speech. "Now, I have seen some impressive stone fortresses…dwarven to be sure! Their strength lay hidden in extensive tunnels under the earth. Many a goblin o' minotaur army would break their weapons trying to hammer through impregnable defenses. Sadly, you only get to glimpse a small piece o' the dwarven maze at a time. There is always a lot more hidden behind the next turn. But humans, like the ones who built that castle, lay their masterpiece out in full view. To a dwarf, it might even be considered arrogant! You are saying, 'Here we are, this is our walls! Come and try smashing through them!' Yet, where many castles fail to invoke my interest, this structure gives me pause out o' respect. No wonder many feel the calling to dwell here in its shadow, far from what others consider to be the 'civilized' lands."

A few hearty cheers of agreement rose, launched from those laborers sharing drinks with the dwarf who honored their nearby fortress. The drinkers were able to share the view of the castle in question since they were sitting in the shade of an outdoor pavilion tent. Next to the tent, workers continued construction on a building. A mix of stone and wood began forming shape in a construction larger than most simple businesses around their town.

"Hey Salgor, how much longer before we can enjoy having a drink indoors?" One shouted enthusiastically.

Salgor Bandago…adventurer, past bouncer, and currently brewer…wiped a hand across the ale drops on his beard as he answered. "Hard to say, depends how much drinking instead o' building I get done." His future patrons shared a laugh. He raised his mug in salute to the construction going on. "I reckon we'll be sheltered within walls and roof, gathered around a hearth fire, before the winter onslaught strikes with its cold breath."

The muscular dwarf walked among the crowd as he spoke with them. Hired helpers of his dispensed what drinks were available. Though the tavern itself barely consisted of a cellar and framework, Salgor made sure he had space to brew some drinks. He wanted to attract some patrons even before the walls went up.

Like all self-respecting dwarves, a proud, full beard hung low from his chin. Thick, brown, braided tails of hair on the sides of his head swung to the level of his beard, ending in a hammer-shaped charm on one side and an axe on the other. Indeed, Salgor always had his large battleaxe nearby. It had been blessed by a cleric relative before he had set out to find his fortunes. When an axe wasn't enough, he also had a solid mace as his favorite back-up weapon. Though he usually just used one at a time, he had been known to swing one in each hand as needed. Usually, his left arm carried the metal shield currently propped next to the makeshift 'bar'. It displayed his personal crest: a large ale cask, supported by what appeared to be a dwarven temple, with a hammer standing ready to tap the cask. A tattoo on one arm represented the only other symbol sacred to this dwarf: Daerkfyre, dwarven God of Strength and Courage. It was represented by a fist holding up a fiery hammer, surrounded by a field of flames. Standing at four feet, every bit as wide as he was tall, Salgor radiated strength to those around him. Few would have dared do anything to anger such a figure.

"One thing I will miss when the walls are finally up," he lamented, "is that they will obstruct this fine view."

The geography around them grew from a cove, which had been transformed to fit the needs of a growing town. It sat on a strip of coastline which ran between the ocean and the edge of the plateau. Beyond Fortress Stone, standing sentry on the raised ground, the plateau stretched into a seemingly endless expanse of flat grasslands. The town of Pilgrim's Bay connected the castle to the ocean by a road and harbor. In terms of size, it was not as large as Barkan's Crossing. Pilgrim's Bay could not boast any plentiful bounty of artisans or scholars. It did not have many outstanding merits that would make it stand out from many other coastal towns. What it did have, however, was that it stood away from many other points of civilization, perched on fertile plains that were, for the most part, unclaimed. The nobility residing in the castle were relatively quick to assign or rent land in order to grow their relatively young kingdom. Many pilgrims, settlers, missionaries, and occasional shady characters trying to escape their past identities, migrated here to settle this untamed land. Most settled within sight of the shoreline and castle. Only a few delved deeper into the grasslands bordering the Tribal Expanse. South of the plains, a large jungle creeped farther southward to the foothills of a visible mountain range. The Stonelands were mostly comprised of Pilgrim's Bay, Fortress Stone, and a number of small hamlets and scattered farms which seemed to form no definitive border.

Refugees from other lands viewed Stonelands as a new land ready to be settled. The Godswars had wiped the old cities from this land, allowing for a new country. Few inhabitants paid mind to the nomadic tribes who claimed this land as their own. The understandings of land ownership differed between the native nomadic tribes and the new settlers. Clashes and hostilities erupted from time to time, but also open bartering of goods and exchanges of ideas. Though the fortress had already been inhabited for several generations of humans, the area had seen little growth until recent years.

The Stonelands were not the only portion of the continent of Shard inhabited by civilized races. The disreputable swashbuckling town of Archer's Port lay on the southern tip. Miles of jungle and mountains segregated north from south, stunting the growth of the notorious pirate haven and allowing a natural barrier between both lands.

The drinkers raised a toast in response to Salgor's assessment of the view. After downing their drinks, Salgor contentedly whispered under his breath as mugs were filled. "Aye, a pleasant sight, a lack o' needed taverns in a growing place, and the occasional weak orc tribes to drive off. The Stonelands are a perfect place for me to build." The dwarf sighed, "I only hope it isn't too quiet out here. I need a little excitement now and then."

Little did he know, Kor's Spear Riders and several other restless tribes were marshalling their strength on the plains, rallying in support of the messiah who would lead them. Meanwhile, the silver-haired, golden-eyed, elf "prophet" that would precede that messiah was on a boat headed for Pilgrim's Bay.

Douglas Van Dyke Jr.

*　　　*　　　*　　　*　　　*

Petrow walked the fields of his home, noting the wetness of the soil. Although he owned a good pair of boots, he liked to walk his land with just his open sandals. Petrow felt it might be a bountiful year for crops, despite the theft of the relic, at least in such fields with enough hands to work them. The villagers knew their crops and livestock were at increased risk of disease and weeds, so they stayed vigilant against both. He had been busy helping neighbors who had lost fathers and sons in the attack on Troutbrook earlier in the season. The blue-eyed man had seen the carnage firsthand as raiders killed lifetime friends, before he turned and ran to see to his family's safety.

Despite being a hero of Troutbrook from his actions four years ago, the scene on the street that year had scared him to the bone.

Petrow still lived with the nightmares of his previous adventure. He had suffered a night of torture, at the hands of the priestess Savannah and her minotaur accomplice, which lived on in terrifying dreams. He had become more prone to jumping at loud sounds or imagining scary figures at the edge of his vision. An uneasy feeling gnawed at his heart; he may forever carry hidden scars from that adventure.

Forcing his mind to the present, he made his way to a pile of wood which needed to be cut down into more manageable firewood size. Petrow readjusted the straw hat which his wife, Inedra, crafted for him. He set about his work with vigor. Taking his old woodcutter's axe in both hands, he brought it down time and again. He swung every blow with all the effort he could muster. His muscles strained as he worked to cleave every piece in his way. Wood broke with sharp sounds, sometimes reminding him of *Dovewing* as it snapped apart, or maybe the crunch of his own bones when the minotaur hit him.

Sometimes, in the darkness between logs, he could see those eyes staring back. Cold, blue eyes representing DeLaris…representing Death. Eyes ringed with black make-up, imitating the hollow orbs of a skull. Eyes staring dispassionately into his soul as she slowly wrapped her hands around his neck and squeezed his throat shut.

He had fought her with all of his strength. Petrow paused to consider the black mark on his axe handle, a persistent reminder from when her enchanted flail had struck it. That blackness linked memories of her dark armor. Despite his strong body, he had been powerless before her prayers. With a few words, she paralyzed him and proceeded to slowly suffocate him.

"On this day Petrow, your life is claimed, and shall be extinguished by the will of my patron deity. May the Karet-Atriul speed you swiftly to your judgment."

If not for Cat's timely intervention, he would have died there. Yet those words still echoed in his ears even though it had been four years. His traveling days were long over. After returning from that adventure, he married Inedra and started making babies. Lil' Willy and Leane were the most important things in his life. Inedra carried their third child.

For all that his land mattered to him, he found his gaze drawn southward often. Trestan and Cat had passed that way, asking him to come with them on a new adventure. Petrow convinced himself that he couldn't go. He had to stay and watch his crops and children grow. At least, that is what he kept saying in his mind. The handyman-turned-hero-turned-farmer did not dwell on the question: even if he had no ties holding him to Troutbrook, could he have gone south?

In the blackness of the scorched mark on his axe handle, Petrow saw Savannah's eyes staring back.

Aware of unimagined eyes upon him, he looked up and saw Inedra staring across the field. She frowned, for she had often caught him staring into his axe handle, motionless like a statue, lost in his thoughts. Petrow tried to shrug it off with a wave at her. He kept the smile on his face as he resumed chopping wood…acting as if he had only stopped for a slight break.

As he worked, he tried to convince himself that Savannah was just a memory.

*   *   *   *   *

To Savannah, Petrow was a painful memory. Her soul ached to find and kill him in order to free her from DeLaris' nightmares. Her fingers flexed as she imagined choking the life from him while staring into his eyes. She had claimed his life once and failed to execute him. That circumstance affronted her goddess. Savannah had to carry out her decree for DeLaris to forgive her. Even worse, she learned he had fathered children in the years since he was supposed to have died. As her responsibility, they would have to die as well. She had no qualms about murdering children. When one worships the tenets of Death, and carries out the end of life, they are merely doing the will of their goddess. DeLaris' faithful stood on different moral ground than others. Savannah could kill whoever she wanted, whenever and however she wanted, and be justified by her church in doing it. The laws of nations might condemn it, but her church made their rules apart from the morals of men.

Savannah looked northward, intent upon reaching the farm where Petrow lived. She could not see it as yet. It wasn't just distance that impaired her sight; a rolling blackness and mist surrounded the merchant ship. The wind barely rippled the sails. Feeble gusts changed direction randomly. Despite the crew's efforts, no wind meant no motion. Lanterns on the masts and railings sought to chase away the dark. It was the noon hour, but no light nor warmth got through the black clouds at all. A cold dread drifted about the deck along with the lingering mist. The ship did not sail so much as it drifted through this perilous haze.

"What dangerous game do you play, Yestreal?" Savannah's lips uttered the words in a whisper. Her eyes searched the unseen horizon, seeking her future. "To plague me with such darkness and lack of wind; it is recklessness. My goddess plays by the Covenant: mortals moving against mortals. This unnatural darkness for so long makes me think you seek to break the Covenant by targeting me. You are barred from interfering."

"A week of nay sun over our heads, and barely a breath of wind to stroke our sails," shouted one crewmember within easy hearing distance of the woman at the bow. The ship's crew had managed to put a finger on the cause of their cursed voyage. "This woman be not only a handmaiden of Death, but the shadow of Kelor!"

Kelor was the God of Luck. The act of referring to something or someone as the shadow of Kelor indicated them as a cursed figure, emanating bad luck.

Savannah rounded angrily on the voice. Raindrops swirled off the curves in her custom black armor as she turned. The woman had donned her DeLaris-inscribed plate suit days out of Orlaun's port. When the journey started, unrelenting dark skies and a lack of wind power had them drifting anyway…and spreading rumors. They could not return to Orlaun, indeed, they had no reliable way to direct the vessel at all. As the rumors spread, she dropped the facade. Sailors turned aghast when she shed her mercenary disguise and proclaimed her true nature by the designs in her dark armor. The specter of Death spooked many to silent whispers, yet whisper they did. They knew about the Orlaun officials looking for a certain cleric of DeLaris. Stories passed around, growing in scope as they went. The crew threw angry looks at their deceitful passenger, yet did no more than that. They were afraid, even more so that their voyage seemed forsaken. As the days set adrift ticked onward, the sailors became more desperate to rid themselves of their curse. They began voicing their concerns loudly.

Another crew member gave an imploring shout to the captain. "She is an anchor that will drag us to Krakus' embrace. The gods have forsaken this woman as well as doomed us for giving her passage!"

The captain shouted to them all, "Silence! Have a care what words you utter on my deck, lest I heave you from it! Man your stations and manage what little wind we have as best you can. I will have words with our guest while you do your duties."

The men grumbled. Savannah noted that few complied with the captain's orders. He approached her, yet his own fears halted him a very safe distance away. The captain put on a brave front which did not fool the abbess. Savannah sensed his unease. "What manner of crimes have you caused, woman? All of Orlaun was looking for you, and it seems the gods themselves have been angered. You have brought trouble to my ship and I would know why."

Savannah's eyes flared angrily behind her skull helm. "I do not answer to you, nor any of the laws of men! I am an abbess of the Death Goddess. I carry out the will of DeLaris. Do not curse me, for it is other gods who betray both of us by letting this foul weather linger." The wind roared once in response, in a direction useless to the sails.

"You have not answered my question," the captain spoke, though he seemed unwilling to take action against the dark, armored figure at the bow. After a moment's hesitation, he suggested an answer that he judged fair without causing undue trouble. "You got your passage out of Orlaun, but we will carry you nay further…"

Before he could complete the thought, Savannah came to her own conclusions of his intent. Her right hand drew forth her flail. She spoke the prayer that empowered it with dark shadows. Her left hand moved also, holding aloft Sword of the Spirit. She glared back at them, jutting her chin forward defiantly. She raised both weapons high on each side. Dispassionate eyes offered no mercy.

"If you move against me, many of you will die."

The captain shrank back. Despite his fears, he found the strength to draw his own cutlass. "I didn't mean we'd kill you, only set you on the first land we spot. If you resist or threaten us, you can't stop all of us from killing you."

Savannah laughed. A cold, mirthless laugh sent shivers down the sailors' spines. Men who heard it might have guessed the woman was half crazy. Even Savannah wasn't sure how much of her mind remained sane after four years of continuous nightmares. Under her skull helm, she wore a wild look. Since failing in her claim over Petrow's life, one of two things had to happen to redeem her soul to DeLaris. Petrow and his offspring must die. Failing that, Savannah herself was to die in his place, as long as she was attempting to carry out her claim on his life. If her death occurred on this ship, traveling north to kill Petrow, the act would satisfy the second option and rid herself of the nightly terror.

Her blue eyes glared out from the helm, staring through the captain. The benefits of death outweighed the allure of life. "Look at me. I do not fear Death, I *am* Death!"

The crew and captain stepped back, unsure and afraid of how to react to this crazed woman. Savannah noted they were too cowardly to carry out any threats against her. Instead, she turned to face her true enemy. The cleric vaulted over the bow. She took a stance in the dangerous area above the base of the forward spar. Her legs couldn't keep her steady enough with weapons in each hand, so she leaned against the ropes stretching up to the masts. Below her plate-armored legs, the sea swirled against the bow. She looked to the heavens from her precarious stance. The abbess showed no concern for her life.

She challenged the heavens. "How long will you play your game, Yestreal?"

The crew cowered as Savannah chastised a god.

"I am here! The mere mortal who killed your precious High Priest Gerlach! You stole from my mistress; therefore, I brand you a thief! I took what was rightly hers from you! So here I am, standing in full admittance of my 'crime' if you wish to strike me down yourself!"

If anything, the air around the ship darkened even further. The wind picked up, swirling randomly, and rain fell again. Through the gathering storm, Savannah stayed perched atop thin beams of wood. She stood inches from a slip in which her armor would carry her to the depths.

Savannah laughed in the face of the toothless threat. "Aye, you coward! Call upon Krakus to capsize this ship! Ask your sister, Westrealei, to blow her winds until I find myself falling over the edge of the world. Unleash Juliustan's storms on me! Part the sky and smite me with pure light from the sun! I am without defense, with nay means to go anywhere 'til you finish me!"

The wind tried to pull at Savannah's short, blonde hair. With two fingers from the hand that held Trestan's sword, she ripped her helm free and allowed it to fall upon the deck behind her. Her hair was tossed about her face as she stared skywards again. Savannah seemed half lost from her sanity. Her eyes, surrounded by black circles of make-up, looked upon the heavens with contempt.

"Can you hear me, or have you blotted your own ears as you have the sky? Have you turned such a deaf ear on your followers as well? You did not stand neutral in the past, and your people suffered!"

Behind her, sailors took cover from whatever death the gods might hurl upon them. A few pulled out holy symbols and uttered prayers. The captain considered pushing her overboard right then, but his fear overtook his reasoning. He stepped back as he contemplated the impending loss of his ship and life. Rain pummeled downward, running off the deck in streams. The boat rocked as the wind kicked up large waves. Lightning flared in the distance, steadily coming closer. Savannah teetered on the edge of the bow. The ropes she leaned on for support pulled and swayed as roaring wind assaulted the masts. Rough water broke upon the bow and sprayed her with mist.

"I AM RIGHT HERE YOU OATH-BREAKER!" Her voice screamed at the wind, almost drowned by it. "Yestreal, come kill me yourself! Break the Covenant right now and let us have another Godswars! Set one foot upon this mortal realm, cast me from my human shell, and let the gods flay each other with war again, while DeLaris simply collects the cascade of the dead."

For breathless long moments, the storm swirled about the ship. The cowering sailors feared a god's voice would boom from the skies at any moment, striking them dead.

Suddenly, the storm stopped. The darkness remained, the mist remained, but the rain shut off in an instant. The waves eased their thrashing. The boat ceased rocking as calm prevailed. Those on the deck could only guess at what was going on between the wills of the gods. Savannah, confused, tried to see through the darkness. She had to really wonder if she wanted the weather to end, or if she preferred that Yestreal sent down a bolt of fire from the sun to take her life, igniting a new Godswars. A few tense breaths passed in relative calm.

Krakus, God of the Sea, intervened in the way he thought best.

A large wave suddenly slammed into the boat. The helmsman yelled in fright as the wheel spun out of control. Crewmembers scrambled to hold on as the ship swerved. Savannah lost her footing at last. She plunged towards the sea. Her left arm released the Sword of the Spirit, allowing it to clatter on board the deck. Her body was falling in front of the hull. The abbess did something she didn't think she would do. She grabbed hold of a rope and held on to save her life.

"Land, ho!" Someone shouted.

A large, rocky formation jutted from the sea. The ship barely missed a scrape with it. As the gloom began to fade, they sighted more rocks ahead. The captain managed to bark a few words before the hull heaved against dry land. Wood snapped and buckled at the impact. It jarred sailors from their posts as the vessel came to an abrupt stop. The impact jerked Savannah free of her tenuous handhold. The abbess fell without a scream towards whatever fate waited below. The momentum of the ship caused her skull helm to roll off the deck, as well as Sword of the Spirit to slide overboard. A moment later, an impact rattled Savannah as her body landed on a hard surface. Her helm clattered past, while the magical sword fell point first into rock and stuck upright.

She felt the solid surface beneath her. The mist and clouds parted to allow the sun's rays to fall for the first time in a week. A rocky beach stretched into the distance.

The ship had run aground. Portions of the front and one side suffered gashes and would need repairs. As Savannah called forth a minor healing miracle to soothe the bruises of her fall, the captain and his crew checked over their vessel. The captain noticed her standing on the rocky beach and called out to her.

"This is goodbye between us. I said I'd set you off at the first land I saw, and so it happened." Crew members tossed Savannah's packs overboard. Her items joined her on the beach. The captain continued, "My ship isn't going anywhere soon anyway. Go find whatever ill fate you have in store for you. Don't drag us down with you."

Savannah glared at the man but said nothing. The abbess did not care to enforce any threats. She meant to continue on her trail to kill Petrow. A part of her was surprised at what she did: standing there begging for death from Yestreal. She moved to collect her personal things. Her skull helm went back on her head; she strapped her pack on her back. She allowed the shadow of her flail to disperse as she put it away. She found concern with the magical sword; it had buried itself a few inches into rock. Its ability to easily cut through such stone began to intrigue her. A quick tug pulled it free, much to her surprise. She re-sheathed it in the scabbard acquired in Orlaun.

With the sun burning the mist away, she observed in her surroundings. She cursed as she saw that she was on a relatively narrow stretch of level land, before foothills to the west went steeply upwards into mountains.

The abbess muttered, "A week spent on that ship and we never even got far enough north to get past the mountains. How far will I have to walk until I see civilization?"

Savannah commenced to walking north along the shoreline. She knew it would be a dangerously long walk through hostile wilderness before she found her way to Dunker Keep. Built at the northern edge of the mountains, it was the southernmost town of Kashmer's Protectorate.

CHAPTER 6 **"Eyfan/The Gnome who Dreamed of Flying"**

The month of Doyal waned, bringing a close to the calendar days of summer despite many warm weeks yet to come. In Kashmer, the naval fleet had already enjoyed the High Summer's Tide festival. The occasion marked the longest days of summer, when the three moons aligned just right and the tides rose to their highest peak. The fleet put on naval exercises and staged mock battles in Kashmer's bay. The event honed the ships' youngest recruits, yet also drew crowds and gained a few coins for many businesses.

Throughout Kashmer's Protectorate, the people who worked the land were judging the growth of their crops. The harvest season would start all too soon for many types of produce. Landowners were already trying to tally their expected gains for the year.

In one part of Kashmer's Protectorate, Trestan glanced over a field that was familiar from a previous visit. This field produced horses and cattle instead of crops. Out in the pasture, several horses enjoyed a leisurely time chewing grass under noon sunlight. The squire of Abriana stood next to his stallion, Belgard. He patted his horse while engaged in conversation with Lindon. The red-bearded man's wide-brimmed hat shaded him from the sun. The minstrel made small talk as they passed the time waiting for Cat to do what she needed. As much as Trestan and Cat wanted to ride north with all speed, they decided that a few stops were in order. This farm stood beside the road between Barkan's Crossing and Troutbrook. Even though they had warnings to deliver and a battle to plan, there were some small things that needed to be done.

As they waited, Lindon inspected a rip in his coat. "They tried to catch us unprepared, and that would have gone very badly if they had done so."

Trestan nodded, "I'm thankful that Cat's senses are as attuned as they are. It could have been us lying dead on the road back there, instead of those clerics."

Lindon counted out loud, his eyes considering the dried bloodstain near the tear. "Two clerics of Mothrok and paladin of DeLaris. What an odd group to attempt ambushing someone on the trail."

"Aye."

The minstrel prompted the paladin, "Just like the cleric of DeLaris that attacked us on Wilder. Think we can expect more attempts on our lives?"

Trestan only responded similar to the words Cat offered after the first attack. "How many more clerics of DeLaris and Mothrok are between here and Fortress Stone?"

The half-elf put one foot ahead of the other as she walked up to the fence. Cat fought the tears as she looked into the big, dark eyes that watched her approach. She stopped just short of the fence, as a long nose sniffed the air about her.

"There you are, standing as if I just walked away only moment ago. It's been a long, few weeks." Cat commented.

The equine ears perked forward, listening intently as its familiar rider talked. Its nose picked up the familiar scent of dried fruit treats.

Cat looked her former horse in the eyes. "I'm back."

She stepped forward. The horse nuzzled her eagerly, taking in the scent of its former rider and showing interest in the fruit smell. One nimble hand, then the next, rose up and petted the horse's neck. The horse didn't mind. It continued to sniff around Cat.

"I missed you terribly. I thought about you often, even though a part of me didn't want it. When we rode south, I couldn't stand the thought of watching a friend grow old and die. Now, I can't stand the thought of being separated from a friend who needs me. You helped me many times; I'll be there to help you face the advance of time."

As the long, equine nose brushed against her chest, Cat laughed through tears, "Is that all I am good for? Treats?"

She took some dried fruit pieces out of her pocket. The horse eagerly devoured them. Its ears stayed attentive on Cat. Although its tail swished back and forth to chase off flies, it almost seemed like a dog wagging its tail for its returned master.

"I'm sure you've enjoyed this pasture. Maybe you don't like the adventuring life I lead. If you'll be by my side again, I could use a reliable friend in the next few months. You are more a part of me than I realized."

The horse's nuzzling seemed to convey a message to Cat. She freely shed tears as she hugged close her old friend. "I'll never leave you behind again…never. I once was afraid to watch a dear loved one grow old," she glanced to Trestan, though he was keeping himself distracted from her emotions, "but it's a crime to put walls in a relationship when you think things will end badly for a companion. You're my friend, and I know you have more miles to travel. I'm buying you back. Wait here for me."

Trestan was atop Belgard again, Lindon mounted beside him, as Katressa rode away from the farm on her old horse. The minstrel had the good sense to not inquire as to why Cat wanted to get a horse here, half a continent away from Orlaun and already a far hike from the edge of Barkan's Crossing.

Cat had come to an understanding with her relationship to Trestan. She knew she may outlive him by long decades, yet she was willing to endure that pain for the closeness they had found. During their plans to go north, she rethought her situation about needing a horse for the ride and the coming battle. Taking a strange horse into combat wasn't a good idea. In the end, she applied some of the same feelings she had discovered for Trestan and decided that he had been right. Cat let her old horse go too soon. Reunited with her friend, she was ready to continue onward.

Cat rode up to Trestan. He could see she had been crying, though she did her best to hide the evidence. The squire nodded to her horse. "I'm glad to see the two of you reunited…for the second time outside Barkan's Crossing!"

Cat chuckled at that, for indeed she had rescued her horse from the area of Barkan's Crossing during their first adventure.

"You have ridden that horse before?" Lindon stated the obvious, plying for more, "What is her name?"

Trestan knew Cat wouldn't have an answer. She never named her horses, for they came and passed all too soon in her eyes. This horse had been no different.

Cat surprised him by turning to Lindon and answering, "She is named Eyfan, the Elvish word for traveler." Cat slid her grinning face towards Trestan. Her eyes were full of meaning.

50

Lindon admired the horse, "She looks strong. Maybe she has traveled a few roads already? Eyfan is a good name; I bet she will serve you well."

Although Cat responded to Lindon, her words were for Trestan. "Aye. I know she will. I was there when she was born; I taught her the reins and saddle. If she is ever parted from me in death, I'll be there to pray as her soul leaves."

Trestan felt good to hear those words from Cat. She had been afraid of watching a friend grow old and die. Now, she was willing to forget the pains of the future in trade for enjoying the time she had with her faithful mount. Trestan decided to give a distraction to get them on their way.

"Belgard has a question for Eyfan."

Emerald green eyes swiveled to meet his. "Aye?"

Trestan gave a slight twitch to the reins, turning Belgard towards the road. "Belgard was wondering…when was the last time Eyfan galloped down a long road, seeking adventure? He wonders if she can keep up with him."

Trestan and Cat playfully urged their horses on with all speed. Lindon tried to catch up behind their dust as they rode hard. Belgard and Eyfan, side-by-side again, tore up the road on their way north.

*　　　　*　　　　*　　　　*　　　　*

The two gnomes rode carefree through the wood. Atop the big wardog that served as a mount, the two conversed about many things. At least, one gnome talked about many things. The male went on and on about a large variety of subjects, from the beauty of the woods to their future as a couple. The female, ever loving of her mate yet not one to talk much, merely smiled and listened to his ideas as she guided her mount.

The male gnome rode taller, boasting almost three full feet in height. Since he was a full head taller than his companion, he could see the path ahead without obstruction. He had a mustache and a small goatee, looking very handsome. His fashion sense prompted him to wear colorful clothes that stuck out amongst the backdrop of the forest. A pipe stuck in his belt. A tiny mace hung from his hip. An overlapping and confusing array of straps and pouches crisscrossed the gnome's tunic.

One had to wonder how Mel Bellringer, (of the Bellringer family: makers of fine bells, chimes, gongs and other acoustical instruments), kept track of all his spell reagents.

Sitting in front of him, guiding her dog, was the love of his life. Aijak, slightly older than Mel, proved to be a quiet person. That worked great with Mel since he loved to talk so much. Dark, slightly curly hair fell to her shoulders. At times she half-turned to listen to him, and Mel could make out the tree tattoo on her cheek. The dark ink of the tattoo on that tanned face represented her druid link to nature. Aijak often called herself a daughter of the forest. She wore leather of mixed colors to blend in with the forest, much like the way that Faer'Seelie elves disguised themselves in the woods. Her only weapon showed her druid heritage. The wooden thacca was a "T"-shaped weapon, held with the top bar of the "T" clutched in the fist, while a long, wooden stake jutted out to stab an enemy. Some druids carried a version more akin to a claw, having three wooden stakes that jutted between the clenched fingers, but Aijak's weapon had only the solitary stake. It was a weapon of last resort, since the gnome druid had other talents at her disposal.

The two gnomes rode through the woods on Aijak's mount and friend, Cathag. The druid had an affinity with animals that led her to this special dog. Cathag was a big, dark-gray mastiff. His gnomish name meant the alpha of a pack.

One would think that just the sight of the big dog would prevent them from being disturbed, yet on this day a group of goblins would test their luck. A sizeable band of them lie in ambush in the woods. They had been waiting for travelers, gnomes or others, to walk down this often-used trail. It wasn't out of necessity that they needed victims, for they had food in plenty. The lust for gold and adventure made them try their luck as highwaymen. They did not appreciate the ferocious appearance of the dog. Some whispered fearfully, yet they outnumbered their prey. The leader of their band suggested they would simply use threats, and see what that earned them.

Mel, unaware of the danger, carried on his conversation in Gnomish. "It was as huge as a human-sized carriage…and a luxurious one at that! *Dovewing* carried seven of us during one trip from the nearby wilderness and up to Troutbrook. And, well, it flew so fast! We covered miles of ground that would normally take days of tiresome walking. I'd love to recreate such a device. I had a chance at the controls for most of a day. So pleasurable to fly that piece of artwork over tall hills!"

Mel paused only long enough to put a hand on the pipe in his belt. He briefly considered lighting it, but changed his mind when he recalled how agitated Cathag could get if any burning embers drifted onto his fur.

Returning to his other desires, Mel continued. "Of course, such a creation is far beyond my means. I'm rather saddened that I never took the time to study a spell of flight. I am beginning to think I don't need to, though, as long as you can help me."

Aijak uttered a brief noise, encouraging him to explain more.

"Well, I was hoping…since you have a way with animals…if you could help me find and train a flying mount."

The gnome druid rolled her eyes at such a suggestion. Mel couldn't fathom the degree of her relationship with animals. To her, they were all potential friends with wants and needs like any two-legged humanoid. Cathag was as much a friend as any other gnome she'd known, and certainly not considered a pet. Druids felt comfortable whether they were talking with people or having an empathic communication with the animals of nature. Curious about his plans as she was, she didn't deflate his suggestion. She merely listened as he kept talking.

"I was thinking maybe something fierce, a beast known for being trainable to fly riders. A gryphon sounds about right. I've heard of people riding them, well, not that I ever actually met anyone who has laid claim to it. Imagine the prestige of flying such an awe-inspiring creature!"

Aijak chuckled as she offered a brief comment. The female gnome never talked near as much as Mel did. Mel amended his reasoning. "Well, I suppose you have a point. I might not want to try training something that could eat me so easily. There aren't many flying animals that would work well. I suppose I could try an eagle, but I think I'm too much of a burden. Even though, if the stories be true, eagles can easily carry off gnome babies…"

A scratchy voice interrupted the sorcerer. The voice spoke brokenly in the human tongue, yet well enough to convey the meaning. The goblin leader demanded that they stop and leave their gold on the trail, even as a number of his fellow thieves came out of hiding to appear menacing. Cathag growled and tensed, looking ready to bite heads off. The big dog scared the goblins. Mel could see them nearly shaking in fear even as they tried to look brave. The goblins held aloft a few meager, simple weapons. They did well to hide their own fear even as they made threats.

Mel replied to them quickly. He intentionally replied in Gnomish at first. The goblins looked at each other in confusion before the leader tried to repeat their demands in the goblin tongue. Mel then responded in the human language. "My companion doesn't speak the human tongue," (which was true…Aijak didn't have a good grasp on the human language), "allow me a moment to translate for her."

The goblins did indeed pause. Mel had bought some time while he whispered to his love. "They want us to leave our gold and weapons on the trail and ride on. They are too scared to push a fight. The goblins don't understand Gnomish. They all looked confused when I spoke it to them. I think we should give them a surprise."

Aijak noted that Mel spoke true. The goblins seemed clueless to Mel's words. They tried to look like they were tough, even though the ones in front stood ready to bolt if the war dog leaped at them. The druid wasn't sure what Mel planned, but she readied a surprise of her own. Even as Mel seemed to comply, reaching for one of his many pouches, Aijak silently sent her will among the plants nearby.

The woods suddenly came alive. Urged by the natura magic of the druid, the trees, bushes, and plants began to thrash about wildly. The goblins were quite surprised as the flora around them began to beat or whip at any goblins in their midst. Branches snapped across as surely as if someone had pulled them and let go. Long blades of grass whipped hard against any exposed skin. Some plants expelled seeds at the goblins, while others dropped acorns. The green assault knocked down several goblins, though seriously injured none of them. Leaves rustled and fell. It happened as if a tornado had descended to twist the trees every which way, yet no wind accounted for what was being done. More than one poor goblin howled as thorny branches scratched them.

Just as suddenly as she started it, Aijak allowed the plants to relax. Stunned goblins tried to regain their feet…or for those still on their feet they moved randomly away from the trees.

In the middle of that confusion, Mel caught the eye of the goblin leader and yelled. "You may seriously want to rethink our vulnerabilities. We are not defenseless, yet we are sympathetic to our fellow forest dwellers. Here, have this bag of gold nuggets as some compensation, and let there be nay hostilities against us again."

Aijak frowned as she saw Mel willingly surrender one of his pouches. The gnome sorcerer threw the bag over to the leader. The goblin caught it despite the surprise on his face. Its greedy eyes looked between the bag and the large dog, which was still growling at the closest goblins. As leaves still fell past his face, he decided not risk his own blood for anything more than the reward in his hand. He turned and ran into the woods without examining his prize. The remaining goblins, faithful to each other as thieves could be, ran well around the dog to catch up with their leader before he hid any of the spoils. None were brave enough to challenge the two gnomes after that impressive spell.

With the goblins out of sight, Aijak urged Cathag to simply continue down the trail. She threw a disapproving look back at Mel. When he asked what was wrong, she criticized his choice to willingly give some of his cash to goblins. The big dog plodded onward as if nothing had happened.

"Oh, that wasn't really gold nuggets," he offered. She kept half-turned to him, waiting for more even as she tried to keep watch for additional dangers. Mel explained. "All it had were some pieces of enchanted clay, just the little ones. You remember my 'Timed BOOMY' spell? Well, I'm quite good with it. I can set the time as I cast it, so that it delays as much as I want before exploding. Anyway, I gave them a pouch containing several small pieces that should go off with small bangs. Not anything impressive, just enough to give them a scare and maybe some blackened fingers…"

They both heard the sounds of several popping noises from deeper in the woods. The sound was immediately followed by more goblin screams as would-be thieves ran scared in every direction. Some actually fled into low branches, then wailed that the trees were attacking again.

Amidst the background of terrified goblin screams, Mel said, "I forgot where we were at. Did we already rule out gryphons as a possible mount?"

*　　　　*　　　　*　　　　*　　　　*

They had said their goodnights, yet he lie awake in the dark, staring up at the ceiling. Inedra slept next to him and had been slumbering for some time now. She had fallen asleep as Petrow stroked her back. He had ceased his massage in order to keep her from lingering awake like him. Three-year-old Lil' Willy curled in the bed with them, huddled content under a blanket. Leane rested in her crib, within arm's reach of her mother. It was dark around the shutters of their bedroom. The entire household had gone off into their dreams, leaving Petrow alone in the waking world.

Petrow would have liked to sleep, as long as it went peacefully. The nightmares of Savannah often found him there, and that scared him. The woman still haunted his dream world as an enigmatic phantom that he couldn't hide from, couldn't stop. He tried to convince himself there was nothing more to fear. Petrow had grown up smug during his youth, putting up a wall of bluster and false confidence. Sometimes he drew on his old self to dismiss his feelings. There could be any number of reasons why he found it hard to sleep. It was possibly too warm to sleep comfortably, or the bugs intruding, or the lump in the mattress, or Inedra's occasional snores…anything but fear of a harmless nightmare…

…a nightmare that often woke him like a slap of cold water, chilling the warmth from his bones, and drawing him awake just as his lungs desperately gasped for air.

It was bad enough that it affected him, but it wore on Inedra as well. Verbally, she offered him support, which Petrow appreciated. Yet, he knew the truth. Under her surface emotions, it disturbed her that he suffered from such irrational fear. He could not describe to her the panic he felt when waking. Both of them wished that the nightmares would go away. Petrow hated when his outbursts woke the kids, which happened often.

When he tried to close his eyes again, he heard a noise. It sounded like the jingle of a horse's harness. Petrow opened his eyes, looking around at the shutters. They were closed. There were a few gaps he hadn't gotten around to fixing, yet through them he saw nothing. His heart began to beat anxiously. Another noise from outside. Was a horse next to their home? Petrow did own a horse, but it resided in a stall a short walking distance from the house. Even if his horse got loose, it didn't have anything on it. The horse he could hear, if it was a horse, had jingling reins and a leather-creaking saddle on it.

54

Petrow slowly sat up. He pondered the implications of this surprise visitor, not liking what it could mean. Images in his mind conjured up Savannah, coming to claim him like she had promised. He tried arguing with himself, after all, just because he heard a horse didn't mean there was a rider. It could have strayed.

He doubted it even as he considered it. Something odd felt afoot. His skin prickled with goose bumps from some formless threat. His eyes darted from shutter to shutter when he saw it. The window facing towards the front had a dark, human-like shadow pass between it and the moonlight.

A deep fear began to grip his bones. A nightmare seemed to be turning into a reality. Petrow slid off the bed and quickly crossed into the main room. He wore barely anything to cover himself in the middle of that warm night. Even if fully clothed, he would have felt almost naked before the fear of whomever lurked outside his home. Petrow glanced at the door, noting that someone had carelessly left it unlatched.

A soft knock rapped upon the wood, done very quietly. It forced a surprised gasp from him. Petrow stood unsure. He hadn't expected a knock, yet it had been a quiet one. Inedra and the kids hadn't noticed; they continued to sleep unaware. It could be a friendly visitor being polite. On the other hand, it could be someone who didn't want to reveal their intentions before some unwitting person opened the door. Ever so quietly, Petrow reached up to the wall and grabbed his axe. The wooden handle bore the blackened mark where it had deflected Savannah's flail years ago. He felt better with his axe in his hand.

He heard the outside figure shift their weight, and Petrow heard the unmistakable noise of armor. Petrow certainly didn't expect any armored visitors. He took a cautious step closer to his door, axe balancing in hand.

Another knock, louder, made Petrow jump. Inedra stirred. The woman turned in bed, her hand sliding across her pregnant belly. The one-time hero of Troutbrook became afraid for his family. They slept unaware…vulnerable. He had little doubts as to the person standing on the other side of the door. He could still hear the plates of the armor rubbing slightly as they moved. With the door unlatched, they could walk in at any time.

Petrow decide to act first. He grabbed the door handle and flung it open. Moving swiftly, he got both hands on his axe and hoisted it for the swing. The armored figure filled the doorway…and it was someone that Petrow indeed knew well.

CHAPTER 7   **"Forsaken Fruit"**

Montanya wasn't sure she had made a good decision when she asked Sondra about staying, only to be told she would have to help in a Sanctuary for Those in Need. The daily ritual never varied. Evening fell and a number of poor and homeless dregs lined up for their allotment of food. A number of folk looked like they hadn't had a good meal in some time. Many were dirty, their clothes worn or stained, and a few reeked of cheap ale. Too many arrived towing children with them. The children filled Montanya with the most pity. A few children who seemed to have no parents begged for food; none were ever turned away. The sanctuary workers treated and fed them, though they rarely had a coin to offer. Montanya felt a special connection to them, having grown up as an orphan. She wondered if their lives would be any better than hers, or if theirs would end tragically on the streets. All who came in needed help; some probably did not deserve it. In every group there seemed to be those who probably made part of their living outside the law. Montanya reminded herself that it wasn't her place to be their judge. They came for assistance, and the church unquestionably offered it.

More often than not, Montanya and Sondra worked and slept at the church, and the chiaso performed chores as rent. Montanya had already worked on several occasions at the homeless sanctuary, helping with several different jobs. She cooked, served food, cleaned up messes, assisted the clerics who were healing the injured, restocked the meager supply of burning candles in the dining room, and washed whatever needed it. The experience had left her with a mix of emotions.

She understood how Sondra viewed it as a thankless job. They worked so hard to care for others, yet it never seemed enough. They couldn't get everything folks needed, and sometimes people who weren't so needy would take advantage of the church's generosity. The few thanks that came their way were appreciated, but always in short supply.

The youth remembered one night when a visitor laid his head down to sleep at a table. No one knew how long he sat there dead before someone realized it. They carried him out to a backroom to be prepared for a burial. People had turned away from the procession that carried him, perhaps distracting themselves from their own fears that it could be them someday.

For all Montanya regarded some of the bad things she felt and saw, the faithful were helping people who needed it. Some families had nowhere else to go and no dependable source of food other than the sanctuary. A few smiles surfaced, shared between the common folk. Some people were so accustomed to their surroundings that they managed to share jokes and stories. People didn't come here because they wanted to, yet this place existed to fill their needs. There was more warmth than could be found in the shadows of great towers. People came hungry and they left...less hungry. The faithful of Ganden that ran these sanctuaries gave them a meal and a sleeping place when they normally wouldn't find either. Montanya recalled how it was just such a sanctuary where Sondra had saved her life. From time to time wounded or sick people came in the doors and were escorted to the back for miracles to be performed.

Sondra worked with Montanya this night, along with a handful of others from the church. The wheat-blonde cleric oversaw lot of responsibilities arising from her recently bestowed rank. She moved constantly, tending to many needs. Sondra found herself directing the actions of others who had once been her fellow acolytes.

It was also Sondra who had just exiled Montanya from serving in the soup line. The conversation remained fresh in Montanya's mind.

"Montanya, you can't keep filling some people's bowls past the fill-line. You're going to make things worse." The cleric had told her after pulling her away from the serving area.

"I rarely do it! Besides, she is pregnant and already breast-feeding one other babe…"

Sondra was already shaking her head. "Was she really pregnant or hiding a bundle of clothes under her dress?"

The notion surprised Montanya. Sondra continued before the red-haired chiaso could say more. "There are many here who deserve more than we can provide, but we are limited. Others notice when you fill some bowls with extra helpings, then they try to play on your gullibility. Before long, more and more will try to get extra helpings from you. A few extra spoonfuls won't really make a difference to them, but by the end of the night it means that others won't get any food in their bowl at all."

Montanya, normally the more outspoken of the two, hung her head. "I'm sorry. It's just…when I see the orphans, they remind me of myself at that age. I'll try not to give in, but it's hard for me to ignore them."

Montanya's best friend shrugged, "I know, I can't help but feel the same way. We can't give in to our personal desires. We have to think of the greater good, and not try to spoil some by cheating others. Take a break from the serving table, collect some bowls to be washed."

Thus exiled, Montanya stood to one side, looking over the crowd of people she had chosen to serve. She could see things about the sanctuary that must lay that depressing effect on Sondra. People came in feeling bad about themselves or their lot in life. Many looked bereft of hope. Montanya enjoyed providing them food, but sometimes she wondered if she was doing the best job she could. She remembered Trestan asking Sondra once if she ever played music or knitted for people in the sanctuary. Given the apathy of some of the people they served, it was easy to see how the clerics who served them might feel mentally drained.

The youth wished she had the means to liven the mood of the place. It would be nice to spread smiles, but she had no special talents. Montanya was a fighter. Her life focused on the pursuit and punishment of thieves. She hadn't allowed herself any room to take up leisure hobbies. Montanya couldn't play an instrument as masterfully as Lindon. Sondra recently took up knitting, but it didn't appeal to Montanya. The chiaso doubted she harbored a good singing voice, yet she knew few enough songs anyway. The one thing she excelled in life was training her muscles and reflexes. Strength. Flexibility. Agility. Those traits by themselves didn't seem to have much worth in this place.

Alone in a dark corner Montanya stood, looking over the room for any bowls she could take back to be cleaned. As one middle-aged man slowly pushed away his wooden bowl and got ready to leave, an inspiration struck. Montanya hurried over before the man could walk away from the table. She wasn't sure if she could perform what her mind had planned, but she knew if she failed it would still send some laughter through the building.

She got in front of the man as he was about to go. "Excuse me, sir, I'll be happy to take that bowl if you're done, though I could use your hand with something first."

The confused man's eyebrows rose. "How do you need help?"

"Just a moment and I'll show you."

Montanya glanced around at the arrangements of tables and aisles leading to the wash area. She hurriedly tucked her tunic into her pantaloons, not wanting the shirt to fall up and cause a scene. Wasting little time, she sought the balance of mind and body required of chiaso. To the astonishment of those near, she stepped back and went into a handstand. Her braided ponytail dragged on the floor as she balanced on her arms. The middle-aged man was now looking more at her soft, leather slippers rather than her face.

Montanya said, "Balance the bowl on my right foot please, if you would be so kind."

Onlookers gasped and pointed their acquaintances towards the upside-down youth. The middle-aged man looked unsure as he grabbed the wooden bowl, empty except for a few stains, and gingerly balanced it atop the offered foot.

Others began to watch in amazement as the youth stood there, her weight balanced on her arms, supporting the bowl atop that one foot. All the attention in the room swiveled in her direction. Montanya called to the kitchen, "Sondra, get ready! A bowl headed your way!"

Followers of Ganden, volunteers, and poor folk watched in awe as the woman started turning in her handstand. Montanya went deep into her concentration. All her trained muscles and agile limbs worked in harmony to walk on her hands. She took only tentative steps at first, testing her balance and the stability of the bowl. As everyone noted the feat that the youth was attempting, a hush settled over the room.

Montanya went hand after hand, slowly advancing up one of the aisles. She paused often, regaining her balance and keeping the bowl from dropping. Her braided hair proved a nuisance, but there was nothing she could do about it now. She slowly advanced past several amazed onlookers. Everyone politely gave her extra room. Sondra watched from the kitchen area; her head cocked to one side as she tried to figure out her puzzling friend. People in the far corners of the room stood on chairs to get a better look at the legs that bobbed between tables.

Montanya endured her stunt through gritted teeth. She was comforted by the fact that even if she fell, she would likely cause a lot of laughter among those who wore grim faces minutes earlier. The wooden bowl would not be harmed by a small drop. Hand after hand, inch after inch, she carried that bowl past one aisle and into the next.

Her voice called out as she saw feet nearby. "Excuse me please, bowl coming through!"

People chuckled and moved out of the way. Montanya continued to walk on her hands up to the windowsill counter where kitchen helpers were awaiting the dirty bowls. Montanya stopped before the wall, hoping she wasn't too far to the left or the right.

Montanya spoke blindly to the person at the windowsill. "Here you go! Another bowl to wash!"

As the helper inside reached out and claimed the bowl, people started chatting in amazement. Montanya rolled to her feet, then bowed for the crowd. Pleasant laughter, cheers, and applause erupted. Sondra smiled as she also applauded her friend. The room wasn't so gloomy a place as it had been before. People smiled, and as they smiled they talked, and as they talked they shared stories and jokes. Though their bellies weren't any fuller than they might have wished, they were in a good mood.

As Montanya was still accepting her applause, a voice called out from the other side of the room. "There is another empty bowl sitting here!"

With a sigh, Montanya flexed her arm muscles a bit. She shook out any weariness from her first trip, and readied herself for another stunt. Her face enjoyed a rare smile as she once again went out on her hands.

*   *   *   *   *

The leaders of the united tribes gathered under the night sky. Bonfires lit the assembly, casting light on the faces of humanoids from many different races. There were no tents large enough to house the entire get-together of chieftains. They did have a line of hides and tent skins stretched vertically around them. This wall helped shield them from the rest of their people. They could not allow themselves to be heard by the unpossessed.

Nor could they allow themselves to be seen, as various demons walked about freely under the cloak of night. Chortling and cackling, they relished their dark plans.

Kor Strongarm silently witnessed to it all, a prisoner within his body. He couldn't stop seeing through his eyes, hearing with his ears. Kor couldn't control his body at all. The giant of a man remained captive from the demon whispering inside his brain. It was torture. The demon could read his mind and his memories. It often played games with his emotions by using his past.

The Com'der of the Spear Riders did not suffer alone. All of the tribal leaders within that gathering had been enslaved by mind-controlling demons. All were subject to the will of their possessors. More joined them week by week, as others were subjugated. There were not enough demons for all the tribesmen, but they had numbers to capture and direct the leaders. It seemed enough. The demon issued orders through Kor to his tribesmen, and they followed the man who was their leader. Some questioned the new events, but they obeyed. Every now and then, due to supplies and food, the gathered hordes would split up, scavenge, seek out more tribes that hadn't been assimilated, and reunite briefly again to keep in touch. The numbers had grown vast, devouring many of the resources from any one place they stayed at for too long.

Pejena "Cloud Whisperer" shared Kor's fate, which injured him most of all. It hurt to know that she suffered the same torture as he felt. He longed to look into her eyes and try to offer some comfort, but he could not control his eyes any better than she could. He treasured every glance of her. Sadly, the demons inhabiting their bodies knew of their affections and played games with them because of it. When alone, the demons often spent time terrorizing their captives. Kor would hear Pejena's voice talk to him as the demon controlling her told him twisted things about her thoughts. In turn, Kor's demon would tell Pejena things Kor would never say to her.

Kor heard the demon lie, but it also mentioned the occasional half-truths. It spoke of things that made the couple suffer and sabotage the most solid foundation both clung to: each other. Pejena's womb had been left barren after her second failed birth of a child. Kor heard his voice tell Pejena that he had always hoped for a stronger woman to bear his child, and that he planned to find one despite the love he professed for her. His unstoppable voice told her that he desired rekindling passions with another member of the Spear Riders tribe who had been a love interest of his when younger. Kor didn't have such feelings, yet that exemplified the kind of things his demon would tell Pejena. Kor was sad that they had never, and would never, be blessed with children, yet he loved Pejena more than he could possibly express. His world would have no light without her. The demons even tortured both souls at once, insinuating that they might try to sample what human sex was like. They hinted that they might be able to give the couple a child…a demon child.

Pejena's voice told him all sorts of nasty things, and he tried to ignore the words. He viewed them as twisted lies designed to hurt him, and nothing more. Pejena's demon also made her walk around immodestly. Pejena was one of few women of the Spear Riders that only bared breasts for her husband, but the demon controlling her made her act differently to extend her pain. Now she walked around topless all the time. Kor could only imagine her shame at this treatment. Even as Kor winced at the lies his demon told to her, he had to endure things her demon said that latched onto his own fears.

Of all the Spear Riders, only Kor and Pejena were possessed. That proved sufficient for the demons' use. The couple ruled the tribe, and the demons inside them used their influence to bring the tribe under their banner. It was the same with other tribes. All the nomad tribes of the plains, and even a few permanent settlers, were forcefully recruited into service. Among them were orcs, elves, goblins, raulgans, domids, and the lizard-like ithyska. A few trolls from one of the shorter subspecies were found. There were many tribes of humans as well. All of these nomadic people had once fought in the Godswars allied or as enemies, though that was almost a forgotten memory now. Past rivalries and alliances had meant nothing for centuries. They had never gathered in such large numbers since that war, until now. As the new union of tribes gathered at a watering hole, the farthest tribes faced an effort carrying back water and fruits. Despite subduing the will of the nomads' leaders, opposition arose among the masses. The demons would insist that a prophet would arrive, and that he would precede the arrival of a messiah that would lead them all too greater glory than any before. Some dissented, and those people were made known. Sometimes the demons would possess the doubter, other times they would have them killed. There had been some deaths among the Spear Riders, and the demon inhabiting Kor did his best to deceive his followers. The possessors had magical charms at their disposal, which they used.

Although the demons enjoyed access to Kor's thoughts and memories, the Com'der in turn learned much about them. He could see their past, and in that past lay a foreboding prediction of Dhea Loral's future.

The demons came from another world once named Illutheus. The word meant "garden", and the description matched their world long ago. It was beautiful and bright with life, much like Dhea Loral had been before the Godswars. There existed a multitude of humanoid races, and they worshipped the same gods. There were some disputes and wars as in any world, but it had been a world worth fighting to defend.

The strife of the Godswars came to Illutheus before arriving in Dhea Loral. The gods committed acts there that they hesitated to unleash in Dhea Loral after seeing the effects.

They forced living things to mutate into creatures of war. Magic, of the gods and their followers, worked to reform the nature of its inhabitants. A once diverse population of

60

people with hopes and dreams were stripped of anything that wouldn't assist in warfare. Some became more animal than intelligent, bred for savagery. Many willingly succumbed to this change, attempting to serve their gods and further the divine needs in the expanding wars. Every succeeding generation carried the choices of their parents.

The land and plants turned poisonous against some, which in turn caused others to change and adapt. One god would create a fearsome type of creature, and then another god would counter it with a design of his own. The original races lost their individuality as new races were defined. The inhabitants of Illutheus, forever altered, clashed in endless battles for the sake of gods who had betrayed their trust as caretakers of the world.

Thus, even as the Godswars raged, the pantheon of deities observed and came to an unvoiced agreement. They saw that whoever might actually win the battle for Illutheus would win only a shattered shell of a world. At that time, the Godswars were erupting in Dhea Loral on a grand scale. The gods refused to begin the same game of altering people, worried that they would be salting the fertile ground for all time.

When the Covenant urged an age of peace for both worlds, Dhea Loral recovered…Illutheus didn't. Already bred for war, the inhabitants could only do what they were made to do. In the centuries that passed, they formed a society based on competence in warfare. As individuals, they differed in how they viewed the gods due to the changes made to them. Many still hold to one god or another, even though the majority shuns the heavens for what was done. From what Kor could learn of his captors, they harbored a mix of followers. A majority had belonged to Mothrok or DeLaris, but several others came to play a part in conquering the new world. Though they would normally fight each other, the lands of Dhea Loral offered them a paradise the likes of which they had been deprived.

Illutheus lost its name. The garden had been despoiled. They now called it Ibleu Taraz: "Forsaken Fruit". The demons who inhabited its remains called themselves taraz, which labels them as forsaken. Now, the taraz have turned aside some of their disputes to set their eyes on this world of prosperity. Here was a chance to win something more appealing than simply survival in their native, bleak landscape.

Kor took one hope from this revelation, albeit a slim one. One he could not communicate with Pejena. The native vegetation of Dhea Loral seemed to cause illness and irritation within the taraz. The warrior had a hunch that whatever god planned to release taraz upon this world, they did so knowing that the taraz were too corrupted to thrive on the fruits of this world. Thus, Dhea Loral would somehow be safe from converting fully into a new Ibleu Taraz. It seemed to be the only thought that spurned his possessor into anger, but it did not believe his observations. In any case, Kor would likely be dead or used up if an end ever came about.

The taraz, veiled by the encircling tent skins and darkness, gathered together and discussed their plans of conquest. Kor was disgusted to hear the sound of his own voice adding to the discussions as the demon within him spoke. Numbers were discussed, information was shared, and preparations were made. The demons used the knowledge gathered from the captured tribes to find and subdue other nomads. They wanted to have as large an army as possible in order to stage an attack on the Stonelands. To Kor's horror, he learned that the taraz didn't even care what the tribal losses would be in the assault. To them, any unpossessed residents of Dhea Loral, whether they were Stonelands soldiers or humanoid tribesmen, were all potential threats against their conquest of this world. They just wanted the Fortress Stone secured, and if the nomads trampled themselves in their rush to conquer it…all the better they would benefit in the end.

To ensure the eager participation of all their unpossessed tribe members, the demons possessing the leaders continued to instill a vision. They continued to speak of a prophet, an elf wizard, who would appear when the time was right. The demon inhabiting Kor didn't know where this elf was; only that he would bear relics that would help their cause. This prophet would precede the messiah. From what Kor could guess, the messiah was actually a demon, though one he had not yet seen. The messiah would form the tribes into a force unmatched since those Godswars of their campfire tales.

Kor and Pejena knew the truth. The demons were not out to lead any of the tribes to victory. Their goal was to subjugate all of the realms. The invaders were abandoning Ibleu Taraz so that they might have Dhea Loral as their own. All of the humans, dwarves, orcs, gnomes, and other intelligent races of this world were to be replaced by demons bred during centuries of war. Even if the people of the world resisted in time, Dhea Loral might only become a mirror of what Ibleu Taraz had become: a world locked in endless wars.

CHAPTER 8   **"Sharing the News of the Journey"**

"Petrow?" Trestan asked, surprised that his friend stood at the door with the woodcutter's axe poised to swing.

Petrow's heart and lungs had been racing. Some inner voice had convinced him that the armored person could be none other than Savannah, returning to torture him. Recognizing his friend Trestan in the doorway, wearing metal armor which had creaked with his movements, Petrow lowered his axe and worked to steady his nerves. He reminded himself that his fears of Savannah were unwarranted. There was nothing special about her except a bad dream.

He saw other faces beyond his friend. Katressa stood slightly behind Trestan, one hand rested on her sheathed rapier. She seemed prepared for trouble. A man with a wide-brimmed hat and reddish beard, a stranger to Petrow's eyes, stood nearby. Petrow quickly studied him, noting the mandolin he carried, the sword at his side, and the crossbow hanging from a strap over his back.

"We didn't mean to scare you," Trestan offered as they stood frozen in the light of the three moons.

Petrow sheepishly allowed his axe to dangle from one hand, down by his side. His voice answered in a whisper, since his family still slept in the next room. "I hope I didn't scare you. My mind plays tricks on me some nights. You picked an odd hour to return. I thought you might be Savannah come to harm me."

Katressa raised an eyebrow, "Why? Have you heard any new news about Savannah?"

The farmer, only a year older than Trestan, tried to shrug off his fears. "Nay. Troutbrook has been quiet since you two rode through. It's just my mind," he paused, embarrassed to say anything about his nightmares. "My dreams sometimes play tricks on me. I've had nightmares involving her ever since our adventure. More of them than usual ever since she passed through and attacked the church. I'm glad she's just a memory."

Trestan looked him in the eye. "Petrow, we need to talk. Inedra needs to hear what we have to say."

    *   *   *   *   *

Inedra, dressed in a simple gown, sat down at the table with their unexpected visitors. Voices were hushed as they tried to keep from waking the children in the next room. A few candles provided scant illumination.

Katressa whispered, "Proper introductions first. Petrow and Inedra, meet Lindon Taleweaver, minstrel of Orlaun. We met him there on our journey and he has been a supportive friend. Lindon, meet our good friends Petrow and Inedra. You will recall Petrow from our stories."

"A pleasure to finally meet you, good sir, and your lovely bride." Lindon offered his handshake to both, which they returned.

"So, you've been telling stories about me? I hope you put the proper exaggerations in where needed." Petrow chuckled as he spoke. Inedra tried to smile at his humor, despite her fears regarding this visit.

Petrow reclined in his chair as he looked between Cat and Trestan. Neither seemed quick to delve into the serious matter behind their nighttime visit. He decided to prod them further without being too obvious, "So tell me, what have you been up to since we last saw you? It has been weeks."

Trestan and Cat shared a look. The two companions could share conversations using only their eyes. The more time spent together, the more they could anticipate what the other was thinking. Trestan came to a decision, "There is a lot to tell, but perhaps we should start with the happier moments."

Katressa smiled as she looked to Petrow and Inedra. "In elven terms, we have taken an oathbond; in human terms, we are engaged."

Katressa showed them the bracelet of caleocht wood, laden with gold dust and emerald gems. Petrow and Inedra smiled and congratulated the couple.

During the compliments, Lindon added, "I witnessed when it happened. It was in a place of unmatched beauty. Trestan proposed in the elevated gardens above the elven forest-city of Serud'Thanil."

Inedra asked, "Where is that?"

Lindon responded, "On Wilder continent. The elves call that land Eyldiian."

A pair of jaws went slack as their hosts reacted with shock at that news. Few ventured to Wilder. The denizens of the legendary wilderness continent fervently guarded its interior. Petrow murmured loud enough for them to hear, "Sounds like I missed one grand adventure. How did you get to Wilder?"

"We flew." Trestan answered simply, enjoying their surprised reactions a little more before he would venture into the full explanation.

The half-elf wouldn't keep them in suspense. She answered before he could say more. "You recall Korrelothar talking about the last divine chariot known to fly being housed at their guild in Orlaun?"

Petrow's face twisted up as he tried to remember the details from long ago. "I have a vague recollection flitting around my thoughts like a fairy. Tell me more about it."

Lindon was only too happy to embellish the details when Cat and Trestan glanced to him to describe it. "The *Doranil Star* was larger than most sea-going vessels you've ever seen. Part warship and part angel. Decorated to be a flying church, for it was the faith of Ganden's priests that allowed her to slip free the bonds of our world. The Brotherhood of the Circles hosted an event on board that flying wonder. We soared over the clouds looking down on Wilder, treated to the best wizard illusions as well as the best minstrel entertainment." Lindon made a flourish with his arms to clearly indicate he was among those who entertained. "The cream of Orlaun's nobility attended, a few hundred strong."

Petrow, blue eyes lit with astonishment, spoke out of the corner of his mouth to his wife. "By the gods, you see what kind of wondrous adventure I missed by not going south?"

Auburn-haired Inedra rolled her eyes even as she playfully elbowed his side.

Chuckling, Petrow continued, "Think of it! Maybe we can go there someday and Korrelothar will set us up for a flying journey."

The faces of their three visitors changed tune. Trestan spoke, "Uh, Petrow. You know our luck with magical flying vessels?"

"It didn't!" Petrow gaped.

Lindon's hand motions indicated a fall and a fingers-splayed splat on the dining table. Trestan summarized. "You missed your last chance. But count yourself lucky."

A thought came to Petrow. He turned back to his longtime friends with a smile upon his face. "Did you find Salgor and Mel? Were they there?"

Trestan shook his head sadly, "We don't know where Salgor is hiding. We did run into Mel. He still lives with his people just south of here. He has a new love interest now, a druid named Aijak. We tried to get him to go south, but he ended up staying behind with her. We rode past his home again on the way here, hoping to talk with him. He wasn't home, so we left him a note and continued on our way."

Petrow smirked. "I don't think Salgor would 'hide' from anyone, Tres."

Abriana's champion chuckled as he considered how Salgor would react to his choice of words. "I would agree. Well, wherever he is…killing minotaurs or such…it is far enough away we couldn't hear the sound of his axe."

Petrow sat back from the candlelight, smiling, as he commented, "It sounds like you went on a grand quest. How did things go?"

Neither Petrow nor Inedra missed the momentary frown that flitted over Trestan's features. Whatever caused it, Trestan switched to a positive subject. He raised one hand, indicating the ring on his finger. "You recall me mentioning Faithful's Companion?"

"Aye, you mentioned it was part of a task given to young paladins to complete your training. Am I right?"

Trestan nodded. "Aye. This ring is our last guide before we reach the end of our training. It is marked with symbols representing challenges we must conquer in order to be recognized as a champion of Abriana."

Trestan turned his hand, displaying it for his friends' eyes. Petrow stared at the shiny, metal band. "I don't see any symbols."

Trestan grinned, "I have finished all my tasks. I journey to Kashmer to be knighted as a full paladin."

"Congratulations!" The word came from both Petrow and Inedra, yet Inedra added, "Now, before you dance around anymore, tell us the bad news."

The words did put a stunning stop to the conversation and removed all smiles. There was no mistaking the serious tone in the voice of the farmer's wife. Inedra spoke again, "You didn't come back and wake us late in the evening just to tell us the news about your ring, or your travels. Something is amiss. I can feel it behind your words. The dread I sense is tying my guts into knots."

Lindon and Cat looked to Trestan. The champion of Abriana had seen the visions in Savannah's head, and his lifelong friend would be affected. It was his news to share.

Trestan took a deep breath. "In short, the relic stones, which we now know are called Earthrin Stones, were on that flying vessel. Savannah, Revwar, and two new friends of theirs attempted to steal them. They sabotaged the ship, dropping us into an adventure deep in the forests of Wilder. We fought them more than once to take back the stones. We lost."

Trestan paused, approaching the worst part. "Savannah and I met face-to-face, at a time when I couldn't really fight her off. She somehow used an empathic ability, similar to one I can employ, to search for information inside my head. At first, I tried to block her, but then I realized I had more to gain by letting her inside while I explored her mind. It was a chance to examine and reveal her plans. We both found what we wanted. For me, I found out where they intend to put the stones to use. They will start a war, and I know where and roughly when it will happen. For her…"

"For her?" Petrow whispered, his throat gone dry.

Trestan leaned forward, an intense gaze locked on Petrow. "I'm sure you remember that fight years ago. You said Savannah said something about claiming your life, and went about trying to choke you to death."

Petrow's hand reached over and clasped Inedra's. "Aye. That moment still haunts me in my dreams."

"It haunts Savannah's dreams too." Trestan remarked, much to Petrow's surprise.

Petrow felt old fears bearing down on his mind as he asked, "Why?"

Trestan met Petrow's gaze squarely. "She failed to take your life after she claimed you for DeLaris. You probably don't understand the gravity of that importance. She is an abbess of the Death Goddess. Once she claims a life, she has to take it or die trying. Savannah can't ignore the will of her goddess; she must finish what she started."

Petrow felt the weight of all his nightmares upon him. His breathing quickened, as if he could imagine those feminine hands coming at his throat. Inedra tightened her grip on Petrow's hand, even as she began to go white in the face.

The farmer mumbled, "That seems so long ago…"

Trestan shook his head sadly. There was compassion in his eyes for his longtime friend. He wished he could bring some comfort, but all he could express was the bitter truth that Petrow would have to face. "Time doesn't matter. Savannah has been busy with bigger plans, but she can't shake this need. It is burned into her soul. To ascend into DeLaris' graces after death, she has to either kill you or die in the attempt."

It brought Trestan pain to admit more. "She went into my memories to find exactly where you live. She knows you are here."

Petrow's thoughts were a jumble. He feared for his life, and felt scared for the vulnerability of his home.

The squire continued, "There is more, it hurts to say this but you have to know."

Trestan awaited some response from Petrow before continuing. He knew this was painful to hear. When Petrow at least seemed to mouth the words, "Go ahead", Trestan continued.

"In Savannah's eyes, you died back when she claimed you. Your children were all fathered after she claimed your life. Savannah knows about them too, as well as the one Inedra carries within her. She will need to kill them for DeLaris as well."

Petrow lost all color from his face, though it was Inedra who let out an unintelligible squawk before fainting.

*   *   *   *   *

It took some time before they could resume their talk about the threat to Petrow and his family. They helped Inedra recover from her fainting spell. As soon as she returned to her feet, she refused to let them fuss over it. Inedra tried to be strong for her husband, even though the ghosts of his past were now coming for her. The woman feared for the fate of her love, her two children and the baby growing within her womb. Her husband's nightmares would now be her own.

Inside, Petrow felt more dread than he would reveal. He had hoped the memories of the past would stay in the past. A cold fear shook his arms, giving him goose bumps, when he remembered lying helpless under Savannah as she tried to strangle him to death. He almost killed her in return, now he wished that he had finished the job.

When Petrow returned to the subject, he expressed feelings of helplessness. "I don't know how to respond to such news, Tres. Our home has now become a trap? Savannah will be looking for us someday and for that one fear we must leave our home? Is that what we must do?"

Trestan wished they had returned with better news. "It may be that you should leave, if only 'til we catch Savannah. Is there anyone nearby you can ask for refuge?"

"But, for how long?" Inedra cried. She kept quiet so as not to wake the children in the next room. "Must we forever live in fear that some evil woman will lay in wait for us at our home, or even in the village? How long will the presence of this phantom haunt our doorway and stalk us from the dark corners of our vision?"

Cat offered, "Savannah has been distracted of late. The last four years she has focused on DeLaris' greater plans. All of her efforts have been invested toward an invasion that Trestan has foreseen in her mind. The tribes in the wilderness around the Stonelands will rise up to conquer that area. It is her current focus. There is hope that she will remain on that one goal until she sees it through. Trestan and I go to meet her in the Stonelands. Gods willing, we will return to report her death."

Trestan nodded. "Savannah's need is great to complete what she started, but she has been called by DeLaris to carry out a more important mission. I hope to battle her hundreds of miles from here. Stay with Inedra's family if you can. We passed by Hebden at the smithy earlier and told him everything. He promised to be here in the morning to help, in case you planned such a move."

"And yourselves?" Petrow asked. His grim expression spoke more than his words. He knew the only protection offered by his friends was a fragile shield made only of optimism. "What are your plans? Are you not staying?"

Lindon remained more or less a silent witness as Cat and Trestan responded. These moments a minstrel needed to see and hear, rather than be heard.

Cat said, "We ride to Kashmer even this night. When the need to rest overtakes us, we will sleep wherever we stop. We have pressed hard to get there as fast as possible and warn the church of the threat we face. The battle Trestan has seen in Savannah's mind won't occur until close to the winter winds, yet we may have much to do to prepare. The relics Savannah and Revwar wield, as well as a necklace Revwar obtained, will make such a battle very difficult for us."

"An army of wild tribes…to take a castle? It almost sounds, well, too simple. A massacre for their army." Petrow commented.

Trestan shrugged, "There is probably more we don't know. I don't think we have found all the pieces to the puzzle. However, with the powers of the relics they could take a castle easier than you might think."

"I would not underestimate them." Cat said. "I have done so before and it cost us. They may have thousands under their banner, but the odds would shift greatly if we can control at least one of the relics. I wish I knew what surprises lie in wait for us."

Muster of Heroes

She could see uneasiness growing on Petrow and Inedra. She caught herself, saying, "Don't confuse my words. I only mean that we plan to be very careful, and get all the help we can muster."

"I hope to return with good news," Trestan said, "Though it will be months before you hear from us again. It would be a good idea to stay with someone...Inedra's family, or anywhere that isn't within sight of the village. Try to limit your trips to Troutbrook if strangers are about. She can't do anything to you if she can't find you."

Petrow found himself trying to comfort Inedra in a hug. "We will be out of this house in the morning. I'll have to figure out what I can take and what to leave. Thanks for your warning. As unpleasant as this news is, at least I can prepare for this threat."

"Take some food for the road. If you intend to spend so much time galloping instead of sleeping, at least be well-fed." Inedra, being a proper hostess despite the terror she felt, moved to gather some meals for the travelers.

While Inedra occupied herself, Petrow looked between Lindon, Cat and Trestan. He whispered, "Is there anything else I should know?"

Trestan frowned, "Savannah has my sword."

Blue eyes widened with alarm, "Sir Wilhelm's blade? I still remember its power. So, Savannah might be coming after me with a sword that can hack wood as if it was air?"

"I'm so sorry, Petrow."

The farmer waved off the apology. "I'm sure you tried your best, Tres. You're the hero, not me. I regret only your own loss, that you might not have that weapon when you go to war."

When a silent moment passed, Lindon spoke up. He leaned closer to the table. "Trust in yourselves and your gods. In my studies I have heard many tales where heroes and good folk alike felt overburdened by some worrisome foe. Many of those stories ended in triumph. While some are only just stories, there are many others based on truth. Never let despair defeat you before your enemy is even in sight."

Petrow nodded, "Good advice, that last message." He seemed to direct his words to Inedra, who was trying to keep her tears silent as she bundled some food.

While Inedra worked, Lindon suggested such a tune. Petrow felt in no mood for music, and he objected using the sleeping children as an excuse; however, Lindon persisted. Using a wooden bamboo flute, given to him in younger years by Korrelothar, the minstrel played softly. The flute's music had been described as a soft breeze in a sylvan wood. There was little worry of it waking the children. Lindon's notes drifted so smooth and mellow, they helped relax some of the tension arisen from the bad news. By the time his song ended, Petrow and Inedra felt much better.

Trestan, Cat and Lindon thanked Inedra for the supplies as they mounted their horses. The three rode into the deepening night, hoping to travel many miles before the need for rest overtook them. The light from all three moons proved enough to keep the line of the road in sight.

Petrow and Inedra did not sleep. They talked, made their plans, and began to pack their things.

*   *   *   *   *

68

False dawn lit the eastern sky. A few farmers moved about their barns getting the early chores done. One distant rooster called its greeting to the morning, though the man jogging along the back roads felt it was giving its song prematurely. Petrow ran with axe in hand, just in case he would need it. He had only traveled a short distance across a few fields to get to Inedra's father's house. The blue-eyed man hated waking them so early. He told her father of the threat against Inedra and his children. Of course, the man welcomed them into his home to stay for however long was needed. He and his wife proclaimed their support. Petrow stayed around the house long enough to clear out a room for use by his family.

The once-hero of Troutbrook considered that he might be giving in to paranoia by rushing their move…yet every movement, shadow and unknown noise made him think Savannah might be upon him. As he went down familiar roads to his house, he couldn't get the woman's deadly eyes out of his mind. It made him shiver to think that even if Cat and Trestan were right, even if they defeated her in some far away battle, he would have to live with this paranoia for months before finding out the truth. Troutbrook would be one of the quietest corners of the world to live in, if it weren't for the occasional bloody visits from that cleric. Every time her and that wizard Revwar came through, they left good people buried in the ground.

Petrow admitted the dread in his heart. The years of nightmares since the night he suffered the nonexistent mercy of Savannah and the minotaur, Bortun, had left him fearful of even her name. He was brave at the time he faced her. The fight between the two of them in that castle out at sea had ended with her unconscious and tied up on the floor. Yet, it had been a very near thing that Petrow had almost died instead. If Cat hadn't happened along when she did, Savannah would have choked the life from him. Clerics of DeLaris preferred to take lives that way: paralyzing their victim with a miracle, then choking the life from the individual while staring into their eyes. As their prey died, they shared the power of Death with their goddess. Petrow had felt firsthand that awful experience. Savannah had claimed his life for her goddess as part of some ritual she observed. Instead, he had survived. For that crime alone, he had earned the eternal hatred of one of DeLaris' minions.

Petrow had almost strangled her to death in return those years ago. He often felt sorrowful that he had never finished killing her. On the other hand, if he killed her, he'd have likely felt guilt over it ever since. Hindsight always made one yearn for the feel of the road not traveled, wondering how things could have been different.

He felt like a hunted man who could not run far from the phantom that sought him. For all his heroic efforts, he had earned a powerful nemesis. Petrow didn't even view himself so much the hero as he once did, but he never let known that opinion since all his old friends in Troutbrook beheld him with awe in their eyes. People looked up to him, more than they ever had before. That felt good.

Petrow jogged down the last turn towards his farm. Worries tugged at his mind, but he kept reminding himself that once he got his family into hiding, they would be safe. He could not empty Savannah from his mind, yet he tried to convince himself that he was blowing his fears out of proportion.

South of his house, on the edge of some trees on an adjacent property, Petrow saw a horse tied to a branch. It struck him as odd, since the property belonged to a man who owned no horses. The horse wore a saddle on its back, either to be ready for a ride or concluding one. He paid it no mind, returning his focus on his home. A modest amount of smoke arose from the chimney. This also struck him as odd. The morning felt warm. Inedra was going to have the children ready to leave the house, so why should she be cooking anything?

He looked once more to the horse, and back to his house. Trestan had said Hebden would come in the morning to help if they moved. Maybe the fire was for Hebden's sake, but Petrow wondered about the new horse that wasn't far from his field.

A horse tied far enough away to seem inconspicuous, yet close enough for sneaking up on Petrow's home.

His imagination likely sparked his worries; nevertheless, Petrow picked up his pace. He ran without much morning light, past his crops, as he shifted the axe in his hand. His bad memories of Savannah were likely making him paranoid. All the worries in the back of his head set his heart beating faster. It should be nothing; that's what he tried to tell himself. The phantom woman who stalked him in nightmares seemed to always find a way into his waking world. Petrow's fears assaulted his mind.

Coming closer to his home, he forced himself into a stealthier walk. His ears trained on every noise, so that even his own breathing became a loud interruption. No sounds from the house. Petrow was almost around to the door when he heard a slight crying sound from Leane. That actually put him more at ease, just hearing her voice.

Petrow held his axe less threateningly when he opened the door. His first look at the scene inside his home took the breath from him. His worst nightmare had materialized in the flesh.

A cozy fire flickered in the hearth. The flames illuminated Inedra's body lying on the floor at a crooked angle. The woman's chest moved as she breathed…her eyes open and moving…but her body motionless in a pose that indicated she had fallen rather than lay down. Not far from her, Lil' Willy also lay immobile. He still wore his bedtime clothes. The only noise from the small boy was the slight whisper of breath still passing his lips.

Sitting in the center of the room, cradling baby Leane in one armored arm, while her right hand clutched her deadly flail, Savannah watched the door with a rare smile on her face.

CHAPTER 9   **"Savannah Returns for Her Claim"**

"You have nay idea how long I have been waiting to meet you and your family, Petrow." Savannah purred quietly, pleasantly, barely letting her voice rise above the crackling logs in the hearth.

Petrow looked directly into those haunting eyes; her blue orbs surrounded by black make-up to symbolize the hollow sockets of a skeleton. Her skull helmet sat at Petrow's end of the dining table, turned so that its empty sockets faced him in the flickering light from the fire. Savannah looked more akin to a skeleton even without the black make-up. Her eyes reflected the lack of sleep she had endured for the past few years. Those fine cheeks of hers sunk from more recent weeks of hunger in wilderness areas. Dirt smeared parts of her face and her blonde hair hung greasy and unwashed. After returning from Eyldiian, her stay in Orlaun had been much too short before being stranded in a drifting boat for days. Once left ashore, the abbess marched through the dangerous foothills between Quoros' mountains and Krakus' watery province. She had been forced to survive alone amidst lands dominated by giant-kin races. Savannah proved dangerous and powerful enough to send a few predators to DeLaris' domain. Tired, lean, and starving, she eventually exited the wilderness at Dunker Keep, the southernmost outpost of Kashmer's Protectorate. Since then, she had ridden a horse hard up the road without any pause.

Now, she sat comfortably in Petrow's home, holding his baby daughter in one arm as she swung her flail in lazy circles with the other.

She grinned at him as much as any spider expressed glee at a visitor to its web. "Set down that poor excuse for a weapon, and let's talk a bit."

The abbess masked her insincerity well. She had no real intention of getting into any discussion with Petrow. She simply hoped he would put down his axe so that it would make it easier to deliver the full measure of her revenge.

If anything, Petrow secured a firm, two-handed grip on his woodcutter's axe. "I won't give it up so easily. If you harm my daughter, nothing will save you from my wrath. Let her go; you don't really want them."

"Don't force me into an impasse," her eyes narrowed dangerously. "I could simply do things the easy way."

Savannah set Leane on the table. The abbess made her threat clear. Still sitting, she dangled the head of her flail just above Leane's chest. The baby playfully reached up towards the object dangling over her. Small fingers batted at the instrument that could be her death. Petrow's mind raced for ideas, yet he could think of nothing. He had no advantages, and there was too much space between him and the abbess to risk beating her speed.

He spoke while hoping to delay her in any way. "I know I can't give up my axe. You want all of us, Trestan told me so!"

"Trestan?" Savannah was surprised. "How could this be?"

Petrow tried to think on his feet. "He was here, he still is in town!" (A lie that Petrow hoped would give him some leverage.) "He looked into your mind and saw you want all of us dead. How can I lay down my axe, when you have already pledged to kill my baby?"

Savannah chuckled, "If he is in town, then you have just handed me a valuable warning. What else did he say?"

Petrow didn't reply fast enough for her liking. The young man tried to think up some story, but nothing came to mind. He stepped slightly closer to the table.

The abbess hopped to her feet. In a fast motion, she drew out the Sword of the Spirit with her left hand and pointed it down the length of the table at Petrow. He was almost ready to charge her then, but the point of the sword held him back.

Savannah sneered, "Don't try to sneak closer. You want to talk, let's talk. What else did he say?"

Petrow's silence wasn't a good enough answer for the abbess. She started spinning the flail with her right hand. The deadly head of the weapon whistled inches above Leane's form. Off to the side, a pained moan escaped Inedra's lips. Unable to move, she remained aware of everything happening around her. Savannah had used her paralyzing miracle on Petrow's helpless wife.

Exasperated Petrow cried, "If I talk, you still plan to kill her!"

"If you talk, maybe she'll live a little longer. If you don't talk, she dies now."

Petrow's axe head wavered inches from the point of the sword…a sword that could cut through the handle as if it wasn't there.

"He knows about your invasion!" Petrow hated to give away that information, but he didn't have anything else. He hoped Savannah felt confident enough in her plans that she wouldn't be concerned.

Savannah allowed the flail to stop swinging. "And?"

"He will stop you. He knows you are raising the tribes against the Stonelands!"

Petrow felt guilty, yet his baby daughter lie in immediate danger. She cooed as her tiny fingers touched the spiked ball. He had to say anything he could to find an opening. His mind raced to come up with some misleading stories that might buy him time without revealing precious information. Nothing good inspired him.

The dark cleric hesitated at this unexpected turn. She wondered if all her secrets were out. Petrow nervously looked from Leane, to motionless Willy, and groaning Inedra. If there was any moment he felt a failure at being a hero, it was now. He needed a miracle to save his family.

The abbess stared at Petrow's eyes with an intensity he found hard to match. "He only mentioned the tribes? He didn't say anything more?"

Petrow had a feeling he had lost an advantage instead of gaining one. He asked, "What more is there?"

"So, you don't know everything," she purred. Whatever secret Savannah hid brought a grin to her face.

For a moment they stood poised on the edge of a confrontation. Savannah still held her deadly flail over Leane's helpless form. The Sword of the Spirit stayed rigidly pointed at the farmer. Petrow stood with his legs separated for balance and his simple woodcutter's axe in hand. He stared into her grinning face, wondering how he could possibly save all of

72

his family. She stood slightly triumphant, as if she had already won and was savoring the moment.

Without warning, the abbess relaxed her posture. "Have it your way, Petrow. Since you will not drop your axe, your force my hand. Such a lovely creature a baby is. So sweet and innocent, far from Death's embrace…yet so vulnerable if Death should visit."

Savannah turned the sword away from Petrow. She set the point on the floor and leaned it against the table. As she talked, she moved her empty hand to Leane. The hand holding her flail drooped to one side, as she half-turned away from Petrow. The one-time adventurer knew she was probably trying to force him to act, or simply had no respect for his fighting skills. Either way, it seemed the best opportunity to strike even as her fingers reached out to harm his daughter. He had no choice but to step into her trap and hope he could thwart her.

As fast as he could, Petrow closed the distance with the abbess. Inedra feebly tried to voice protest, but garbled incoherently. Petrow had both hands firmly gripping the handle, which bore the black mark left by Savannah's enchanted flail four years ago. Savannah turned her head back at him as she registered the motion. She would not be able to deflect the axe blade in time. Petrow cleaved.

Petrow's axe stopped short of Savannah's head as it bounced harmlessly off the protective, invisible shield woven around her form. The impact shocked his fingers numb.

Savannah grabbed hold of one of his arms with her empty hand. It was a dangerous position for Petrow: while touching him she could speak a prayer that would paralyze him as she had done to Inedra. The once-hero of Troutbrook, father of children, couldn't allow that to happen. He tried to fight.

Without Savannah speaking a word of prayer, Petrow lost all feeling in his limbs. He watched himself pitch helplessly forward. She hadn't even said a word! Now he felt as paralyzed and helpless as his family. He heard his axe clatter to the ground as his body dropped next to the table. Inedra seemed to be wailing, though her jaw and muscles continued to disobey her will. Petrow sprawled supine, staring up at Savannah's triumphant smile.

"My abilities have improved since you last met me in battle, Petrow," Savannah gloated. "If I know who I intend to paralyze, I can pray beforehand and intone their name. It doesn't stay active indefinitely, but it lasts long enough. You were lost the moment I touched you."

She knelt on the floor, staring into his eyes with her cold, blue orbs. "You can't cheat your death, Petrow. You were claimed, and so your soul must go."

Petrow fought with all his heart and mind to move, to speak, to even lift a finger. His body wouldn't respond. His mouth, so recently paralyzed compared to Inedra, could form no sound. Inside, his mind screamed louder than his voice could ever achieve.

"Try to scream all you want," Savannah whispered amidst the crackling flames nearby. One leg crossed over his torso as she straddled his form. Her slender hands loosened his shirt buttons, exposing his neck. "Your farmer friends might actually hear you. Maybe one of them owns a magic pitchfork to pierce my protective miracles."

The abbess examined Petrow's vulnerable neck, watching his carotid arteries pulse under the skin. "Once, I nearly strangled you to death. Then, you nearly strangled me to death. We both lived." She leaned in closer to his ear, enjoying his helplessness as she spoke softly. "Let's make it the best two out of three wins."

Inside, Petrow's heart felt crushed, and not by the abbess' weight. Despair gripped his soul. His only reprieve would be to hope there were no nightmares in the next world. He could hardly feel the abbess' fingers gliding across his vulnerable neck.

Her hands started to clamp down hard on his throat, as he stared into the madness revealed in her eyes. His lungs demanded air. His diaphragm reflexively convulsed, but the air passage was closed. He heard Inedra's sharp breaths, but could not see her. Those deadly eyes of Savannah's hovered right above his face. Helpless, he couldn't avert his eyes from her cold stare. Darkness crept into the edges. Suddenly, she released her grip.

"You thought I would make it that easy, did you?" She asked, malice driving her expression. "I endured four years of torture, and you shall suffer before I finish you!"

The abbess sat back on her heels, hands moving away from his neck. "So, first of all, know this: Trestan didn't see everything I had planned. If he is going to fight at Stonelands, I say give him a fast horse and make sure he takes a wooden box. More than simple tribes will attack Fortress Stone.

"The Covenant didn't stop the Godswars; it just changed the rules. It's an old game being played with a new twist. The gods still crave power over this world, as men do. Since the gods won't allow themselves to interfere directly, the burden has shifted to mortals."

Savannah lifted a finger to accentuate her point. "Ah, now there is the rub. The war is to be fought by mortals only. DeLaris and Mothrok have plenty enough supporters to accomplish a good amount of conquest with their mortal followers…if they do one thing. You see, the people of the world Illutheus also fought their own Godswars, but it turned their home into a nightmare. My goddess still has plenty of followers there who seek a new home. Do you know who those mortals are, Petrow?"

Of course, Petrow could not respond, helpless as he was. She obliged, "They call themselves taraz, but we refer to them as demons."

Petrow's eyes couldn't have widened if he had tried.

"Mortals versus mortals, as the gods have decreed." Savannah grinned, "But we're borrowing our mortals from another world; a world that shaped them into monsters of destruction. Let people come to defend Fortress Stone; they will find demons waiting for them. With legions of demons on our side, the world will fall swiftly." She paused a moment in thought. "Taraz can not survive on Dhea Loral over a long term. Our world is too soft for their needs. By the time it matters, DeLaris' and Mothrok's native followers will preside over an empire larger than the glory of old Diara."

A brief period of silence resumed, as Savannah stood and stretched to her full height, backlit by the flickering radiance from the hearth. Her victims fell under the dark shadow of her decorated armor.

She leaned over once more, bringing one hand down to Petrow's face. "And now, the rest of your punishment for eluding me for four years, and fathering three children after you were claimed for death. The youngest of which is still in her womb."

Savannah turned Petrow's head to one side without resistance; his gaze directed towards Inedra's helpless form. Streaks of tears ran down her cheeks. Savannah walked over to the woman; heels thumped across the wood floor.

The abbess kneeled over Petrow's lovely wife, whispering into her ear. "That's the last look you get at him in this life; however, he will be watching you until you are nay longer here."

The gaunt, travel-weary abbess cast one more look at Petrow. "Death is a matter of business with clerics of DeLaris. Generally, we don't take pleasure in it; we just recognize it as something that simply exists. Today, though, I take great pleasure in ending my nightmares."

The abbess turned Inedra face-up into her cold eyes. Petrow could not move no matter how hard he tried. Somewhere behind him, Lil' Willy gasped as the paralyzed boy heard everything that was going on. On the table above him, Leane cried for her mom. Petrow could only stare helplessly at his wife as Savannah's hands wrapped around her small throat. The abbess' legs straddled the woman's pregnant belly.

Savannah recited the words that Petrow had heard only once.

"I act in accordance of the tradition of my goddess; who brings death or spares it, escorts lost souls to their judgment, and ultimately decides the fate of many by her power. You must respect and acknowledge the control she has over your fate. On this day, Inedra, your life is claimed and shall be extinguished by the will of my matron deity. She also takes the unborn child in your womb, which was claimed years ago. May the *Karet-Atriul* speed you both swiftly to your judgment."

The abbess proceeded to take the life that was claimed. She commenced in the way clerics of DeLaris prefer: by choking their victim to death with their bare hands as they stare eye-to-eye. Savannah's grip on Inedra's throat tightened. The farmer's wife ceased making any noise as her air ended. Her fingers twitched feebly, desperately; the only movement her body could achieve. Petrow could only stare as Inedra's life was fleeing before his eyes.

In that moment, Petrow became aware of movement at the corner of his vision. Someone else stood in the doorway of his home.

*   *   *   *   *

"What the…"

Those startled words from behind warned Savannah of the unexpected intruder. She released her hold on Inedra's throat only to reach for her flail. She jumped to her feet. The figure in the doorway looked with surprise at the fallen bodies of Petrow and his family. The newcomer realized with a shock who Savannah was by her dark armor. Fearful of his own life, he reached for the solid iron spit by the hearth.

He entered Petrow's vision as he tried to attack with the spit before Savannah could set her stance. It was Hebden Karok, arriving as Trestan said he would, to help Petrow move his family. The muscular smith, a veteran of swinging heavy hammers, slammed the bar across the top of the abbess' unarmored head.

Any temporary relief Petrow gained suddenly wilted by the knowledge that Savannah was a more dangerous threat than anyone in the village could handle. He feared that Hebden was only adding himself to the woman's death list. Petrow wished he could put all his strength together just enough to yell at Hebden to run.

His fears seemed justified as the heavy blow glanced off Savannah's head without causing much distraction. She cocked her flail, suffering a backhand swing as Hebden gave her another shot. Any unprotected human would be reeling from such blows, yet the abbess stood strong, covered by her shielding miracle.

Just save yourself Hebden! Just run! Petrow shouted inside his mind. Only a groan escaped his lips.

The smith wouldn't even consider the open-door escape behind his back. Although Petrow lost sight of some of the action as Savannah backed Hebden up with a swing of her flail, he did catch the noises their feet made.

The smith of Troutbrook retreated around the other side of the table. He must realize that his attacks were futile, yet something kept him from fleeing. Petrow realized it was Leane, crying on the table, which forced the smith to hold firm. Hebden and the abbess traded swings as the man tried circling the table. Petrow heard metal hit metal as the weapons twirled in close proximity to the baby.

Petrow and Inedra remained unable to act. All they could do was pray that Hebden could at least grab their daughter and run with her. At least some small victory would give them relief before the end came for them. If Yestreal was willing, Savannah could endure a lifetime of more nightmares if she could never find Petrow's surviving child.

Hebden tried with all the effort his heart could muster. Savannah proved more battle savvy than the aging smith. She saw his goal and masterfully guarded her small victim. Hebden suffered a stinging hit from the flail which foiled a temporary grip he gained on the child. He tried swinging the spit one-handed and made another grab with his free hand. The abbess blocked the blow easily with her arm. Even had her arm not been covered with plate, the miracle of her dark goddess was formidable. The flail whipped around again and painfully knocked aside the smith's arm. As much as he tried to save Leane, he could not win past Savannah's skill and determination.

Savannah leaned over the table, grappling with the larger man. Leane's perch wobbled as Petrow listened to the scuffle. Hebden tried to wrestle with the woman. He had mixed luck. Savannah did not have any augmented strength such as Revwar frequently cast upon himself, yet the miracle protecting her made it hard to do any physical damage or even get a proper hold on her. Whether Hebden launched at Savannah or Savannah pulled at him, both came back over the table to Petrow's side. The table holding Leane rocked as the flailing arms and legs came over it. The two resumed their struggle on the floor, at the feet of the paralyzed couple. Hebden and Savannah still had their weapons and resorted to using them in close quarters.

A new nightmare fell into Petrow's vision. The Sword of the Spirit, which had been leaning casually against the table, was shaken loose by the movement. The extended handle and elvish runes crossed his vision as the blade toppled towards him. The elvish magic had given the blade an amazing quality to slice through most anything easily. It now sliced a path at Petrow's chest. He could do nothing to avoid its cut. One small consolation: the sword would present a quicker end to the nightmare than Savannah offered. Petrow winced as it arced closer.

The blade glanced against a stool as it fell, putting a spin to it as it came down. The flat of the blade bounced on Petrow before coming to rest.

Like someone had opened a door, Petrow's nerves sprung to life. He could feel everything about his body. His fingers jerked alive to his commands, even as Petrow opened his mouth wide for a gasp of air. The paralysis was gone! Petrow looked down at the sword lying across his chest. He remembered Trestan talking about its properties long ago. It could disperse magical fields at a touch. The weapon had dispelled the miracle holding Petrow hostage in his own skin. Even as he glanced downward, he saw Hebden on the losing side of his battle with the abbess. She was getting to her feet, lashing out repeatedly while Hebden tried to parry with the spit. The smith had no chance to strike back any powerful blows. Even if he could, it would be useless against her miracle. Petrow, with the sword lying across his body, now had the only weapon in Troutbrook which could sunder her miraculous protection.

The one-time hero scrambled to get off his back. He wrapped his fingers around the hilt, testing how lightweight the sword felt. Even as he rose to a crouch, he turned towards his immobile soulmate. He carefully allowed the flat side to touch her shoulder, freeing her from the abbess' miracle. Inedra pulled in a deep gasp of air as her limbs worked to get her off the floor. Petrow was already turning his attention back to Savannah. DeLaris' minion flailed at Hebden. Her weapon knocked the iron bar from his grip. He tripped as she advanced.

With one last flex of his fingers on the handle, Petrow made sure of his grip before lunging forward. Savannah had her back to him, unaware of the danger. Petrow aimed for her spine, between the shoulder blades. The magical, elvish blade jabbed true.

It hit her barrier and stopped.

Petrow saw the energies from the protective miracle scatter away from Savannah's form. The field had protected her for that one blow, even though now the sword's magic had stripped her of her invulnerability.

Behind Petrow, Inedra sobbed even as she ran to grab her two children. She hoped she could carry both out of harm's way. The woman picked up Leane even as Savannah turned to the noises behind her.

Hebden was down on the floor, not badly hurt, but not much of an immediate threat compared to the attack that Savannah felt behind her. Although surprised, she responded as a skilled veteran. Greasy, blonde hair twirled around her face as she spun with her flail. The spiked head of the weapon missed Petrow, yet the chain tangled with the sword. They were locked, weapon against weapon.

Savannah's eyes widened with worry as she realized how the situation turned against her. She began to fight wildly, recklessly, as her revenge was slipping away. Hebden got up as she fought and twisted with Petrow. Both struggling combatants turned and danced about as they sought to loosen the entangled arms. The magical blade was tugged between both sets of blue eyes, reflecting firelight off its keen edge as it waited for blood. The chain was made of the finest enchanted craft, holding the blade without being cut. Despite Petrow's superior strength, he was at a disadvantage. Savannah possessed armor and more skill at fighting, while Petrow had just his clothes.

Petrow was trying to keep the blade away from his face when he felt Savannah knee him near the groin. Her efforts would leave a bruise on his inner thigh. She attempted a second time when Petrow pulled some dirty tricks as well. He spit in her dark-ringed eyes. They both twirled around as Hebden rushed into Savannah with a flying tackle. Weapons went flying outward to the corners of the room.

Inedra somehow stumbled past the deadly projectiles. The mother carried Willy's limp body against her, holding Leane in her other arm, as she ran out the door of the home. Her voice yelled out in the dawn hours to any who might hear, screaming for help.

Savannah found herself trapped against the back wall by the two men. Petrow paused to look for the missing weapons, while Hebden tried to corner the abbess. The hero-farmer found a weapon at his feet. He reached down for the handle as he heard the abbess begin a prayer.

"Don't let her pray!" Petrow yelled.

His warning was too late, as it went off simultaneously with the abbess' miracle. "DeLaris, move him away from me!"

The force of the miracle shoved Hebden backward, dashing him against the table with enough force to topple it. The impact dazed the smith.

Petrow stood with his old woodcutter's axe raised. The blackened mark on the handle matched the darkness of Savannah's etched armor. He made a move towards her when she spat out a few more words. The abbess stepped to the side and was gone.

It was also a trick Petrow had seen once before. As surprising as it was, Petrow felt the cold dread of knowing where she reappeared. Savannah had used that trick in the past to get behind her opponents for an opportunistic blow. The young father spun around, letting his axe arc outward. The axe collided with the dark armor even as a dagger slid across Petrow's shoulder. Savannah's dagger might have done worse had not his axe softened her blow by moving her body. The axe blade dented the armor, but did not draw blood.

The attack backed Savannah up, but she came forward again. The abbess was mad with rage and intent on killing the source of her nightmares. She knew she had to get at him before Hebden got up to interfere again. Petrow relived his worst nightmare, stranded with the woman who had haunted him for years. He swept his axe towards her attack.

A sickening crunch echoed in the room, followed by a terrible scream.

"Aaaiiiieeeee!"

Savannah's dagger dropped from her broken arm. The armored joint at the elbow caved in from Petrow's heavy hit. Petrow came at her again, without pause. She turned to flee. Her only goal now was to live to kill him another time.

Before she had stumbled far, Petrow laid another hard hit into her side. The axe blade once again put a dent in the armor designed to honor DeLaris. It didn't draw blood, but the blow pushed Savannah away from her course. Petrow felt like he was trying to hit a turtle with a twig. It didn't feel like he was doing enough. A mixture of fear, anger, and desperation spurred him to keep attacking. Hebden slowly regained his feet, but he refused to come close to that swinging axe.

Savannah tried recovering her bearings but the heavy axe head slammed across her back again. Her broken arm bobbed in pain. Every breath she took was blasted out of her body by repeated blows to her platemail. The door seemed ever far away, and yet the distance to it paled compared to the distance to her horse.

The axe came at her again like a battering ram. Her legs went unsteady as she tried to right herself on the move. Her feet tripped over some object rolling on the ground. The abbess didn't even register that it was her skull helm, rolling beside the fallen table. It sent her sprawling next to the entryway of the home.

Petrow tried a heavy, two-handed, overhead chop. His axe stopped as it chipped a ceiling beam. Below him, he heard the abbess crying out words.

"DeLaris, please heal…"

This woman had seen many battles with the companions in the past where she had healed an opponent that should have been beaten near death. As long as she could pray, she was a threat. All of the damage suffered by her body was only a few words away from being totally healed.

Petrow stooped lower and gave an overhead chop into her prone form. The axe head glanced along the side of her lovely blonde hair before smacking into the top of a shoulder. With a pained grunt, her prayer spoiled. Blood ran through her hair and down her face.

Feebly, she crawled towards the light of the open door. Petrow's axe came down on her back, then her hip, hammering her again and again. The durable platemail suit, adorned with dark images honoring DeLaris, became bent and pounded out of shape. The crafted steel worked to keep the sharp blade of the axe from cutting through, yet that only prolonged Savannah's agony without saving her.

"DeLaris…" she croaked out once again, as Petrow's rage caved in a section over her good shoulder. "Oh goddess…"

Dents in her armor became gouges as repeated axe blows rained down. Anger and fear fueled Petrow's blows. He could not make her die, and yet he could not allow her to live. The repeated force of the axe began to rend sections of the armor. The axe blade opened one hole in the tortured steel, only to be drawn back with red blood dripping onto the black metal. Her blonde hair still oozed blood when a second hit glanced down the back of her head. More blows blasted through her metal barrier. The designs of Death were spoiled by dents and torn sections. Her blood seeped through the gaps in the armor to coat the threshold of Petrow's home. Savannah stopped moving or making noise, yet Petrow made sure she would never rise again.

The young man wheezed from the effort of the repeated axe swings. Exhausted, Petrow dropped onto a footstool that still stood, laying his bloody woodcutter's axe across his knees, as he stared at the corpse at his front door.

*   *   *   *   *

The former handyman, and current farmer, flinched when he felt Hebden's hand gingerly touch his shoulder. "Are you alright?"

Petrow didn't truly know. He was glad that he and his family were alive, yet appalled at how he had to end it. He looked over the bloody form of the woman who had given him so much pain over the years. Nothing seemed real.

In the background, he heard Inedra shouting and screaming out in their field. His mind turned to her. "Hebden, find Trestan's sword." The farmer motioned blindly at the room behind him. "Lil' Willy is probably still paralyzed. A touch of the flat of the blade will cure it."

"Petrow?..."

"Just do this quickly, please, for me. Let her know everything is alright and I'm ok. Don't let the children come back and see this."

Hebden nodded. The aging smith found the sword lying on the floor. He shook it to untangle it from the flail's chain. Taking it in his hands, Hebden warily stepped over the body on his way out. He glanced back at Petrow, but didn't say anything to him before he went to console Inedra.

Petrow thought about what the abbess had unveiled about the attack on Fortress Stone. His first thought, with Savannah dead, should have been that he and his children were safe from harm. Instead, he found himself worrying about her confident revelations. Demons from another world? His mind envisioned an even darker morning than this one. He imagined nightmarish forms darkening the sky and fields as his children cried out in fear. Trestan and Cat were blind to the demon threat.

In the stillness of the room, with the sound of the hearth's fire crackling nearby, Petrow came to an agonizingly hard decision. He got to his feet, still tired and bleeding from his brush with death. The table had fallen in a way that blocked what he needed to get at. With a shove, he pushed it out of the way.

The floorboards in the center looked perfectly normal. There was no secret hatch, because Petrow never intended to recover what lie hidden below. Regardless, now he had a reason to dig up the past. He wedged the bloody blade of his axe in a narrow gap in the floor. Blood dripped and stained the floor as Petrow worked at the boards. The first one snapped in a puff of dust. The sound broke the reign of silence. Using the axe, he pried and chopped board after board out of the way. A hole opened up, through which he could see the bundle of blankets covering his hidden treasure.

Holding the axe aside, he reached down with one trembling hand and pulled the bundle out of its hiding spot. With a bit of reverence, Petrow drew aside the blankets to uncover the shiny leather-and-steel creation inside them.

At the end of their first adventure, Petrow had found this set of armor in a supply room of that keep on the sea. He had worn it when he had nearly suffocated Savannah back then. Magical in nature, it was light despite the steel breastplate and metal guards on the shoulders and upper thighs. The rest of the leather fit Petrow in a way only a magical item could. The magical enchantments laid upon the outfit would offer more protection than a potential foe would realize.

Footsteps at the door made Petrow turn. Inedra's face paled at the sight of the dead body inside their home, but a look towards Petrow holding up his suit of armor almost sent her into a swoon.

"No." Her denial was a bare whisper. "You can't leave me; you said you wouldn't."

Petrow's face was set and firm as he replied. "It's because I love you that I have to go."

Hebden also appeared in the doorway. Petrow could hear others, neighbors, outside comforting the children. Hebden also looked to Petrow inquisitively. The smith judged the man's posture and expression, comparing it to Trestan's when Trestan first came to Hebden intending to go out on an adventure. Inedra's face was already streaked from tears as she looked to Petrow with reddened eyes.

"But why?"

Petrow looked between Inedra and Hebden. "Trestan doesn't know about the demons." Hebden's eyes widened, since this was news to him. "He is going to need more help than he realizes. If he doesn't, then today's victory is meaningless if tomorrow there are demons in the fields where our children would play. He also will need his sword. Someone has to take it to him."

Petrow set armor and axe aside as he walked to Inedra. "I'm not trying to be the hero; I'm just doing what I need to do. Give me your blessing, and know that I'm doing this for my family."

Inedra sought his arms and held him close. They had almost lost each other, and now she would lose him again, hopefully for just a short while. She whispered her love for him, as she asked him to stay safe.

Hebden still held the Sword of the Spirit in his hands. He looked down at his son's sword, appraising its designs with an experienced eye. The smith thought about what Petrow said, and he contemplated words he had shared with Trestan once. Back then, he had admitted how, as a younger man, he had sought adventure and yearned to protect his fellow man. Of course, Hebden had stayed in the humble role of a blacksmith. Despite the current danger, despite Hebden's years, he felt a need stirring within him.

"Petrow, let me make some quick arrangements with Mikhael before we go," the smith looked up from the blade, "Because if you don't mind, I'd like to go with you."

CHAPTER 10 "The Prophet in Pilgrim's Bay"

A figure moved furtively through the darkness of the early morning, originating from the gloomy light of the harbor, when few would note his passing. He was worried that his public stroll was timed later than he'd prefer. That did not deter the golden-eyed elf wizard from making his path through the streets. Revwar's long, silvery hair trailed him as he slipped through the smaller byways. He glanced up the high ridge on the far end of town, where the Fortress Stone sat as sentinel on the plateau above.

As he made his way through the port town of Pilgrim's Bay, a sudden chill entered his spirit. The odd feeling made him pause. He felt as if he was momentarily connected to his fellow conspirator Savannah. Her presence called out, in pain, from far away. Distressed emotions accompanied her phantom. Revwar closed his eyes and could see her face. He couldn't see or know what she was doing, but the connection took a worrisome turn. He felt Savannah's spirit go cold. The feelings of anguish accompanying the vision died into a perception of bleak emptiness. Revwar tried to digest the unfamiliar experience. He got the impression that a link between him and the abbess severed by some catastrophe on her end. Revwar felt a barren sensation as if she had really become death.

Revwar could no longer see or feel her as he reopened his senses to the sleepy town around him. Her presence had been there, then it had abruptly suffered something which separated them again. The wizard hadn't imagined it. Some spell must have linked them for a brief moment.

An answer dawned on him. Savannah kept a link on all her companions to let her know if one of them met their death. The link must work both ways. Savannah's spirit gave the impression that something had taken her. It was discomforting, but not at all unexpected. Revwar had worried that Savannah's dogged pursuit of an inconsequential man would end in some disaster. He had done his best to coax her from that course, and now his most trusted ally was gone.

Revwar felt angered over her foolish decision and the disastrous result. At the same time, he regretted the loss of a truly supportive partner. She had been the only real friend he had. He had known Savannah longer than any of his cohorts. If there was any one person he would trust with all his schemes and plans, it had been her. Savannah channeled death itself, delivering many opponents to their fate in the years they had traveled together. The woman had lived life from a different perspective, preferring allegiance to the world of the dead. Her faith encouraged fearlessness. Revwar wondered how she faced her own fate. He was curious on whether she delivered vengeance upon her obsession before she died. The wizard couldn't pause to contemplate it for long. Her death felt far away, and yet he had a job to do here. She deserved to be mourned, but not until he had accomplished his task and moved from this town.

As his attention returned to his surroundings, he noted a figure exiting an unfinished structure. The building taking shape down the street looked large. Revwar noted an ale tent pitched out front that served as a temporary tavern. The apparent resident of this construction caught Revwar's attention. A dwarf with muscular arms, brown hair with braids ending in charms, an axe dangling from a belt and a frame that was four feet tall and seemed just as wide, stepped out into the early morning air and stretched. Despite the early hour, the dwarf began sipping a mug of ale as he looked towards the dark harbor.

Revwar recognized Salgor Bandago despite the years that had passed. He had once restrained the dwarf and used him to set an example for an angry mob at a pub. A short time later, the same dwarf came after him despite a number of magical tricks at his disposal. Revwar was brought close to death from the incident. Although the wizard had survived, the unfortunate situation had set back all their plans.

The elf wizard was dismayed to find the dwarf had settled here, directly in the course of their latest goal. Seeing such a fierce opponent, coupled only seconds after the revelation of Savannah's death, did not bode as beneficial omens. Revwar did not expect one person to be of any real threat to their plans, yet Kelor's luck had been favoring those who stood against him.

Of course, Revwar realized that now he had some of Kelor's luck running in his favor. Even as he ducked out of sight of the dwarf, his hands rose up to touch the Gitouro necklace. It was Kelor's own gift for his faithful. The magic empowered within the relic could change things miraculously on a whim. The wizard resisted the urge to use it against the dwarf here and now. There were more pressing matters awaiting his attention. Revwar could not afford to react with some short-sighted plan.

Despite the loss of Savannah, Revwar would have many more allies soon. His secret acquaintances were even more powerful than most mortals that walked Dhea Loral.

His sharp mind committed the locale to memory, saving it until he could enact a proper retribution. He ventured onward towards the plateau where the fortress overlooked the cove. There were few people moving about at this hour, yet too many for Revwar's comfort. He strode with purpose to put as much ground behind him before the full rays of the sun struck the towers of the castle. His steps carried him up a long, twisting incline. When he ascended the top of the plateau, a few hundred meters to one side of the fortress, he had his first glimpse of the land he planned to assault.

A number of farms cultivated the relatively flat ground around the fortress. Houses which could shelter a few generations under one roof dotted the horizon. Irrigated waterways from small streams brought moisture to the fields. The smaller streams eventually fed a larger river which split around the fortress. The natural moat cascaded down rapids before falling into wetlands. From there, several smaller waterways branched off until they flowed into the ocean.

The fortress stood as a titan of stone made formidable by skilled masons. It had an impressive overlook of Pilgrim's Bay. Even on the plateau, it dominated the landscape in all directions. A traveler from miles away could set his bearings by the distant spires. The first post-Godswars craftsman carved the base directly from the stone. Within the past few centuries, skilled workers had built up the remainder. Some of the stone had been dragged from a nearby dwarven community; many of those dwarves assisted with the development of this bastion.

The simple name, Fortress Stone, seemed fitting. It conveyed all the strength that characterized the structure. It even went with the rather spartan design: no elegant carvings or décor. Only the resident king and queen shared a lavish lifestyle, constrained within one of a few separate castles that were part of the greater structure. It was built layered and strong…and impressively large.

Revwar felt a twinge of temptation. For all the might offered by this titan, it was helpless against the Goddess of Earth and Stone. With a wave of his hand, Revwar could send out Mothrok's power of the Earthrin Stones to topple the mighty walls. Stone would be reduced to dust, centuries of work would be eradicated in minutes, and the entire garrison force would be crushed in their sleep. Wizards were intimately familiar with the intoxication of power. Revwar felt the inhabitants should rightfully crown him king, just to spare them his wrath.

The elf wizard reached a hand into a bag at his side. He withdrew one of the three egg-shaped stones. Even though his eyes were accustomed to the dark, the relic seemed black in the pre-dawn light. He claimed sole possession of all three, though he only needed one to perform feats worthy of the gods.

He held up the stone before the backdrop of the stone castle. Destruction seemed tempting, yet he had other plans. The inhabitants would live another day, though their fate would likely still be sealed. Revwar's cohorts had designs centered on this castle, so he could not simply destroy it. He may have to demolish portions of it later on, yet it was best to preserve as much of it as possible. Though most of his accomplices were dead, one close ally still remained. His last partner was even much more powerful than he, and that one represented Mothrok. DeLaris' faithful had met an untimely end, but Mothrok's servant still remained. His deal with that companion would make him a far more powerful mage than he might otherwise attain.

His eyes barely made out the markings on this Earthrin Stone. It was fitting that the one in-hand was the relic originally entrusted to DeLaris' faithful. Although the powers of all three gods were needed for his next actions, the final result would foster death.

Delaying his actions no longer, Revwar began to use the stone for the purpose which brought him up on the plateau in the early hours. First, he used Yestreal's powers over the weather and sun to slowly bring in a fog. The morning light had flourished too much for the wizard's liking, so it was time to conceal his magic. The mist rolled in, not too thick or heavy, but enough to make it hard to see for much distance…at least, for anyone but Revwar.

Satisfied, he began to channel other powers of the stone. A green light seeped forth, spreading across the nearby land. It turned the fog an eerie color, but observers thought it a trick of the morning light. Without the fog, they would have seen a green glow cast across the land. Hidden inside the mist, Revwar sent the light among every farm field, cattle pasture and store of food. The miasma blew aside the morning scents of the dew flowers. The combined powers of Yestreal, Mothrok, and DeLaris clutched the land in a subtle yet dominating grip. Animals grew restless as they felt the change. The farmers noted nothing odd, save for the heavy mist itself.

Revwar, standing still, concentrated for many minutes. The stone drew from the influences of all three gods. A blight seeded the land, as Mothrok's will took root in the earth. The ground fortified itself to reject the life-giving warmth of Yestreal's sun. Energy seeped out of the plants and their fruits. Mothrok poisoned the soil in her own way, as rocks formed and fertile earth was displaced. The touch of Death from DeLaris brushed against the plants, the cattle, and the stores of food secured in their cellars. Revwar's magic was very slight in its course, invisible to all. Days or weeks would likely pass before the failure of crops and the sickness of the cattle would be felt. The stored food might seem unaffected for some time. Eventually, even those stores would begin to spoil at an alarming rate. The relic cast its powers out across the whole community. Pilgrim's Bay and Fortress Stone would be in for a rude shock when they found out that all their food was spoiling. Such was one of the intended powers of the Earthrin Stones during the Godswars. They were given the ability to sabotage an opponent's food supply or enrich one's own. After all, no army can fight effectively when it is starving.

Revwar closed off the flow of magic once he felt the effects would be sufficient. He looked indifferent at the landscape, undisturbed by the suffering these people would face. The wizard was vacant of any sorrow for what he sowed into the farm lands. He had chosen his own future, and his own clout would only improve. As long as he stood to gain power, there was no sympathy for what others had to lose. The wizard placed the relic back in the bag with its two companion stones. Looking through the mist at what little he could see of the Stonelands, he couldn't resist making a comment.

"You've already been given a crippling blow, in a war you don't even realize is coming." He whispered to the dark mist. "So many people are scared of wizards lobbing balls of fire or channeling the lightning from the air. The most dangerous things we do in war are those which are hidden…sometimes not even felt until they are too late. If you prefer fire and lightning instead, well, that time will come soon enough."

Revwar's golden eyes turned away from the fortress. Ahead, beyond the morning mist, stretched a flat expanse of untamed lands belonging to nomad tribes. The elf wizard set foot in that direction, walking calmly from the chaos he had just implemented.

*   *   *   *   *

The couple arrived at their humble abode. Aijak and Mel dismounted from Cathag at the base of a large tree. The full tree grew on the side of a hill, with many roots trailing down the open face. Although they were deep in the forest, the air hummed with the sounds of their gnomish kin going about their daily lives. Gnome villages had remarkably little evidence above ground that a community thrived there. Though anyone could see the footprints, trails, markings on trees and rocks and any items that might be left carelessly in the open, the gnomes liked to hide their dwellings as much as possible. A human traveler could walk through the town square and think they were only on the fringes of a village. There were no threats in the woods to be seen, so a number of the little forest folk were out harvesting, playing and socializing. The delightful laughter of children added to the comforts of home. The flowers around the entrance, nurtured by the druid, added to the familiarity and solace. Aijak removed the leather saddle from Cathag as she thanked him for carrying them. Not many riders thanked their mounts, but Aijak saw Cathag as a willing friend. Mel went to the door of their house. The house belonged to Mel, but Aijak had her own space set aside. He turned a rock set in the network of roots, opening a hidden door which led inside. The sorcerer returned outside a few moments later, contentedly puffing smoke out of his pipe.

This earned him a slight rebuke from Aijak. The female gnome brought his attention to some dry grass and plants nearby, requesting that he watch where any embers fell. Mel sighed. He loved the druid dearly, but she disapproved of his habit of smoking. Her comments heeded, he tried to look concerned and moved to a different spot in which to enjoy the weed.

Mel spoke between puffs. "So, as I was saying…it's a pub that sits on the road between Barkan's Crossing and Dunker Keep. The owner built it at a place often used as a good resting spot for travelers. Of course, the road sees many soldiers going back and forth to the keep, so he had lots of business! He was a smart man, but he kept a tight leash on all his copper coins. Turns out it cost him some money to get regular supplies from Barkan's, and he owned the only pub on a good section of road, so he started watering his drinks."

Aijak listened as she continued giving attention to the big mastiff. She brushed out the tangles from his fur. She stopped to pluck any burrs she found. Mel went on with his umpteenth story that day. "Of course, he denied doing it, but everyone kind of knew about it. It was a rumor that everyone accepted, since one could so easily taste how weak his drinks were. Of course, the owner blamed the taste on a number of other things, but everyone knew it was watered. The soldiers and merchants started calling the pub 'the watering hole'.

"Just a couple years ago, I guess, the owner passed away. That's why I was asking the new owner about the changes. Knowing the reputation of the place, he decided, with a little humor, to name it as he did. That's why I chuckled with surprise when I found out they renamed it 'The Watering Hole'."

Mel paused to listen for Aijak's laugh, but the woman only nodded and smiled as she continued primping Cathag. The son of the Bellringer family paused to take a puff on his pipe before launching into his next subject.

He never got to start it. Another gnome, whom he had never met, walked their way and greeted them. "Are you Mel Bellringer?"

Mel's face lit up, assuming he was becoming more of a local celebrity since faces he didn't know were asking for him. "Aye, I use that name around human settlements. They know me as Mel Bellringer, from the Bellringer family: makers of fine bells, chimes, gongs, and other…"

The other gnome interrupted his introduction, "Aye then, I found the right person."

He fished a note out of one pocket. It was written on good quality paper, and looked large enough to be either sized for humans or useable as a large sign for gnomes. "Three travelers came by here two days ago; two humans, the other had the looks of an elf. You weren't here so they left a note. They said it was important."

Mel took the note from the gnome's hands. He opened it and saw letters in the human language. Glancing at the signatures, he smiled as he saw the names. He half-turned to Aijak, "It's a note from Trestan and Katressa!"

Looking back at the gnome who delivered the message, he remarked, "You said you saw three people?"

The gnome described Lindon Taleweaver's appearance, but Mel had never met the man and didn't recognize him. Mel offered the other gnome a tip for his service, which was gladly accepted. After the other gnome left, Mel announced to Aijak his intention to have a seat inside and read the letter.

Aijak smiled and entered their home. Distracted by the note, Mel stumbled into Cathag's furry posterior. The big dog liked to be as close to Aijak as possible, leaving the door temporarily blocked for Mel. After he brushed some dog hair from his coat, he followed the tail into their sitting room.

Mel took a comfortable seat in a slouched-back chair as Aijak kindly made them a snack. The sorcerer could read the human language easily. His eyes eagerly scanned the page for news from his old companions. By the time Aijak brought him some bread and jams, she noted that his expression had turned grim. Few things could trouble Mel Bellringer. She asked him about it, but he motioned for her to give him a moment. He wanted to read everything to make sure he knew all the facts.

Mel mumbled, "Two days ago, they must be in Troutbrook or even beyond by now."

While Aijak quietly sat in her chair, Mel thought about old friendships. He would love the chance to adventure with them again. He was offered the chance when Trestan and Katressa last rode through to the south, but Aijak hadn't been pleased, so he had stayed. By the words included in this letter, it seemed that Trestan and Cat's adventures were turning more serious.

Mel knew Aijak would not want to go, yet his own philosophies would be at odds with hers. Mel was an unusual gnome in that he worshipped a god outside of those revered in gnomish society. Having felt shunned by his own gnomish deity, Mel had once been in a situation where he passed a rite from a dwarf god. Following that experience, he turned his worship to Daerkfyre the Valorous, the dwarven God of Strength and Courage. Of course, the gnome sorcerer wasn't at all a typical representative of such a god. His muscles didn't bulge from the constant exercise of swinging a hammer or axe, such as those of the dwarf worshippers. Mel felt that, if anything, the concept of Courage was weighed towards those who didn't have the strength of arms of their foes. Mel's strength and courage hid on the inside. In battle, he carried his wits, his wands, and bore no heavy metal armor. Dwarves mocked him or acted insulted when he informed them of his loyalties. He wasn't sure why they would feel that way, but at least Salgor had tolerated it. Mel was perfectly happy with his chosen deity. The drawback for worshipping such a patron was that the gnome felt he shouldn't shun a fight when he believed in the cause.

He slid his fingers down that dry paper, readjusting his grip as he reread some parts. Trestan and Cat were going off to a fight, and it sounded like the stakes were high. The sorcerer didn't overlook Aijak's patience. She silently waited to hear about the letter's contents. Mel's spiritual calling told him to catch up with Trestan and Cat and join them. Now, if only he could convince Aijak of that.

CHAPTER 11   **"A Message to be Heeded"**

Belgard, Eyfan, and the mount Lindon had bought in Barkan's Crossing were left at the seminary stables. The horses enjoyed a nice midday rest after the hard run north. Belgard felt at home within the seminary grounds of Abriana; he had been born and trained as a warhorse on the grounds here. The three horses contently nibbled a meal and enjoyed the freedom without saddles.

Meanwhile, Trestan Karok, Katressa Bilil, and Lindon Taleweaver were escorted into the inner workings of the seminary hierarchy. The first followers of Abriana to meet them asked Trestan if he had succeeded in the quest of his Embarking, to which Trestan showed them the golden glow of his ring. Faithful's Companion rings were carried by all the squires as they went into the world to fulfill a quest. Its smooth and shiny appearance proved that Trestan had fulfilled all the requirements Abriana set forth in order to become a full-fledged paladin.

Even before the companions had left the courtyard, a familiar woman recognized Trestan and sought him out. The woman's tabard represented her position as a senior acolyte of Abriana. Her short, curly, brown hair bounced as she ran within easy shouting range. She wore her hardened leather armor and a mace dangled from one arm. It appeared they had interrupted her from a training session. Cat remembered this young cleric of Abriana as Rhijin. She had been a classmate of Trestan, taking the tests of the Embarking when he did. Unfortunately, Rhijin failed too many of the challenges, including a frightening one called the challenge of the beast. The price of failure was to stay behind and endure more training before she would be ready to venture as one of Abriana's champions.

"Trestan!" She called from a distance, "This is amazing, two of my friends returning from their quests on the same day!"

Trestan was being escorted, so he continued onward as he called back, "Who was the other?"

"Leander arrived only an hour ago. He is still in audience up there."

Trestan smiled; Leander had been one of his closest friends at the seminary. He turned back to Rhijin before they entered the doors. "I hope you are studying hard. I want to see you succeed your next Embarking."

"If Abriana is with me, I will!" She answered.

Rhijin performed a motion: hugging herself while bowing to Trestan. Trestan paused just long enough to return the gesture to her. Among followers of Abriana it conveyed a silent message: "May the goddess keep you in her arms and watch over you." There was no time for more words before the companions were indoors.

Trestan and Cat had their minds inward on what they should say when they met Trestan's superiors. Lindon simply soaked in the grandeur of the holy keep. His mandolin hung over his back; nevertheless, his right hand moved like he was trying some notes on the instrument. For the minstrel, every moment and place had its own music. He always sought to find the proper tune for any situation.

88

The companions had to wait outside a door while some proceedings concluded. While they waited, Trestan stroked his brown mustache. The squire turned to Lindon, "I think we should go about this like in Orlaun. You should do most of the talking."

The red-bearded minstrel shook his head in disagreement, "Why? This is your church. We stand within sight of your goddess."

Trestan shrugged, "Your gift of words is much better than mine."

Lindon waved off the notion, "Oh, don't fool yourself. You are quite talented with words. You will make a good orator, even if you are a bit untrained now."

The squire returned an empty look, "What's an orator?"

Cat giggled over Trestan's facial expression during his response. Before anyone could say more, they were ushered inside.

Beyond, they stood enraptured in the shelter of the grand hall. Trestan shared awe with the others, for this was a place he had never witnessed before. This was where the elders oversaw the seminary and administrated all the church's affairs in the northern half of Quoros. Cardinal Alunetar Gracegiver sat in high, throne-like chair, looking across at the new arrivals. The lines across his face reflected the many matters that had weighed upon his thoughts during his journey under Abriana. Although his robes of office hid his form, one could tell he was neither frail nor portly, and he seemed to walk and talk with strength of spirit. The high chair he occupied was topped with the coraross symbol of Abriana. A half-circle of chairs and desks extended to each side, with ink and quills for writing. The majority of the seminary's elders seemed to be present. Most were at least middle-aged, though their differing dress reflected their history in Abriana's service. Some still wore swords at their sides, while the garb of others suggested their role as clerics. They were in equal numbers men and women. One quality shared by each elder was the ability to hide their true emotions while sitting in a perfectly erect posture.

A grand mosaic tiled the floor, depicting a river of love flowing from the high chair to the door. Rows of chairs, reserved for high-standing visitors, faced the half-circle of elders. Leander stood to one side of those chairs; respectfully leaving them empty in case some king should happen to walk in the door. Many stained-glass windows occupied the exterior wall. Each had a picture story to tell from the holy scriptures. They were quite elaborate, and Cat couldn't begin to appraise their worth. The ceiling had a grand painting which showed Abriana giving half her heart to the world.

A towering statue of Abriana stood near the entry, facing it. With one hand she held a large decanter which spilled water into a pool. The fluid in the decanter represented the flow of her healing power into the world of mortals. In her other hand, she carried a shield with the coraross symbol.

As custom dictated, Trestan knew to face this statue in prayer before approaching the elders. He did so, bowing his head and offering silent words for the plea he was about to make of the elders. Trestan reflected on how Abriana had guided him through incredible adventures to wondrous places. He could only hope that she would continue to illuminate his path. For now, he also needed the church to recognize the importance of his quest. This would be a long waste of a detour if no help was acquired. It would also hurt his faith if his concerns were turned away by the church.

Trestan turned back to face the assembly of elders. One offered him a greeting to summon him closer. "Come forth, Squire Trestan, we have been awaiting your presence."

Trestan stepped closer; his companions trailed a step behind him. He wished he could offer a brief smile to his old friend Leander. The thoughts in his head kept him focused on the importance of the moment. Since Leander was no longer the center of attention, the fellow paladin-aspirant allowed himself to smile for both their sakes.

The young squire from Troutbrook felt a little uncomfortable that he had disrupted Leander's return. Trestan offered, "I hope I am not interrupting. I had an important message regarding my Embarking."

One of the elders answered. He did not make any comments in reference to Trestan's message. The words he spoke were from tradition, asking Trestan if he returned with Faithful's Companion aglow with his worth. Trestan answered that it was, and offered his ring for them to view its shiny, smooth qualities.

Cardinal Alunetar allowed the traditional questions and responses to continue as long as might seem proper, before he leaned forward and intervened. "We may want to dispense with further customary responses for now. It is indeed a blessed day that two of our promising champions, Squire Leander and Squire Trestan, have returned bearing the favor of our lady Abriana."

The cardinal representing all the clergy from northern Quoros stared at Trestan. The former smith felt pinned by that intense gaze. It seemed the cardinal knew he should be looking for something, but didn't know what. The holy patrarch continued talking.

"A dream came to me and others here, delivered by Abriana herself. We were given to know that today a squire would return to us with most dire news that we needed to heed. When Squire Leander arrived, we assumed it was him." The cardinal swiveled his gaze over to the other young champion. "I apologize if it seemed we were being extremely inquisitive of your adventures."

Leander's curiosity peaked. He hoped the elders would allow him to stay present for Trestan's announcement. In reply, he offered, "That is quite alright, considering what you just said. I just did my best these past few weeks to help a privateer boat rid Kashmer of some pirates. While it was a grand adventure, I was surprised that you took so much interest in it. Nay need to apologize, your Grace."

The cardinal made no further comment to Leander, instead turning his hard gaze upon Trestan. "Do you come to us bearing important tidings?"

"I do, your Grace."

Trestan stood nearly within the half-circle of elder chairs. Following Leander's example, he did not take a seat in any of the renowned visitor chairs. When Trestan seemed hesitant on his answer, whether due to nervousness or unsure if the cardinal would ask more questions, Alunetar tried to set him at ease.

"Blessed of Abriana, feel free to indulge us with the story. Just stab right to the meat of the matter, including only what smaller details you feel are pertinent."

Trestan started to reach up to stroke his mustache, as he often did when in deep thought. He caught himself and settled for a deep breath instead. Cat and Lindon could only offer silent support behind him as he faced his most influential superiors.

Trestan began. "Some of you have already heard, either from my words or the rumors that came from others, the adventure I was involved in before I came to the seminary for formal training. Three old stones of unknown magical potential were stolen. I, my friend Katressa here, and others returned them to their rightful owners."

There was a slight pause as Trestan considered how he could condense this newest grand tale. "When I left on my Embarking, the first thing I discovered was that the one in my village had been retaken by force. Two villains we had fought on our last adventure had returned with friends to regain all the stones. When I found out, I raced to Orlaun, where the other two stones were guarded. They were normally kept on display at the mage guildhall of the Brotherhood of the Circles."

One of the elders interrupted, "I heard that a band of raiders attacked Troutbrook. Even the people in Kashmer were exposed to the details. From what we knew afterwards, a company of swords and mages from Kashmer hunted them down and destroyed the raiders."

"Well, I can't comment on what happened to the raiding force," Trestan spoke. "But I know that the leaders who orchestrated the attack got away with their prize and went after the stones held in Orlaun."

There were some murmurs among the elders, but the cardinal waved them silent. "My brothers, if we let our young champion speak, we will be educated beyond what rumors have passed along."

Trestan continued, "The stone relics in Orlaun were moved from the guild as part of a magical exhibition on *Doranil Star*. You may or may not know that it was the last known divine chariot that still retained the power of flight. Through some treachery, the enemy band managed two fell deeds at once. They brought down *Doranil Star*, bringing her and Ganden's guiding clerics to their deaths." Despite the elders' restraint, there were a number of gasps at this news. "They also managed to steal the relics, as well as one other important necklace. This is a much-abbreviated tale, of course. We fought them in air and on land…but I should not dwell on those details right now."

Cardinal Alunetar allowed himself the freedom to comment as Trestan wrestled with where to take the story next. "It feels as if the end of an age has come, to hear that the last divine chariot is lost. I feel sorrow for Ganden's church. Such a tragedy that must have been." The older man looked across to Trestan. "I will want to learn more of the details later, but for now, go on."

Trestan re-straightened his posture as he continued. "The two who led that band managed to escape out of our immediate reach. So, we ended that adventure with my ring whole, yet the true objects of my quest were now in enemy hands."

Cat and Lindon sensed that Trestan was stumbling. The young man struggled to say everything perfectly, yet his hesitation at finding the words might take away the momentum he needed to carry out his overall goals.

Trestan was still speaking. "I guess that leaves two things that need to be explained. One is the significance of the stones themselves, the other is how their recovery demands Abriana's involvement."

Cat felt that Trestan was hesitating at a crucial moment. Here, standing in the center of his superiors, dwarfed by the immense holy chamber, Trestan seemed to be asking his elders for guidance. The young man had developed many qualities of leadership in the time of his training. Trestan had shown how much initiative he could take even when confronted with adverse situations. In this place, Trestan became a student looking to his teachers for acceptance of his decisions. Cat felt that he needed a push away from surrendering his self-reliance to his teachers' opinions. His last statement seemed as if he was asking his superiors for an answer…Cat decided to answer the perceived question first and put him on the right track.

She stepped closer to him, yet spoke loud enough for all to hear. "I believe it is important that you enlighten your brothers as to the importance of the relics. They should know the terrible powers commanded by the stones. After that, it would be proper to warn them of what lies ahead…and where."

Trestan nodded. She had chosen her words carefully. It was Trestan's job to enlighten, playing the role of teacher. By referring to the elders as his brothers of the faith, instead of his elders, she helped him elevate his importance.

Before the squire could speak, Cardinal Alunetar Gracegiver fixed Cat with an amused expression. His words were aimed at Trestan. "Pardon my rush to get to the heart of matters. I rudely ignored your companions. I would appreciate if introductions could be made."

"Of course! I am honored to introduce Katressa Bilil of the Kashmer privateers." Trestan swept his arm out to indicate his beloved.

Even as Cat gave a respectful bow to the elders, the cardinal responded. "Oh, I recall the lady who dared shout out to you during your interrogations at the Embarking." His eyes betrayed an amused twinkle as he spoke. It seemed he had not been angered in the least by her actions back then.

Trestan, beginning to blush, added, "She is also my betrothed."

Cardinal Alunetar made a comment to help loosen the feeling of suspense that hung in the air. "Engaged!? Why, Squire Trestan, it seems you have entered a riskier Embarking than most young men undertake!"

A few terse chuckles answered the cardinal's comment, though with the topics that had already been discussed, it seemed there was little true mirth in the room. Cat responded by simply saying. "It is an honor to have audience with you, voices of Abriana."

"And it is an honor to finally be introduced properly. Abriana watches over your safety within these walls."

As attention shifted to the red-bearded human, Trestan turned to introduce his other companion. "This is Lindon Taleweaver, minstrel of Orlaun and world traveler."

The cardinal addressed him, "And what part do you play in this?"

With a smile, Lindon responded in a way to broaden what little amusement had been kindled by the cardinal. One hand patted the instrument over his shoulder. "Why…I play the mandolin, of course!"

Indeed, this brought some more chuckles from the cardinal. The mood helped put Trestan at ease. Alunetar looked at him and said, "Now that things have been put proper, continue your tale. Don't allow worries to weaken your confidence. Just speak, and Abriana will guide your words."

Trestan puffed up his chest slightly amidst regained self-assurance. Even the nearly-forgotten Leander, standing to one side, looked up to Trestan. Having gone through the training at the seminary together, Leander knew Trestan possessed a gift with words.

Trestan declared, with more confidence, "I should tell you the specifics of the relics. They are of the utmost importance here, and their value reflects the importance of Abriana's will in this struggle.

"Much of our understanding of the stones comes from either firsthand experience or a translation from a leather scroll." Cat displayed the scroll in question as Trestan spoke. "These relics are called Earthrin Stones. Three were made during the Godswars. Crafted on behalf of an alliance between Yestreal, DeLaris and Mothrok, the stones lent the powers of all three deities to the individuals entrusted to carry them. A person who wields a stone has the influences of all three gods at their command."

Trestan paused only slightly as the elders digested the implications. "The wielder of the stones has access to powers greater than many priests of those gods. The stones call on Yestreal's powers to shift weather patterns, either subtle changes over time that can induce or restrict crop growth, or massive changes that can bring about storms or even hide the sun for days. When this stone sat hidden in plain sight in my village of Troutbrook, it quietly nurtured the land over the long years. If one so desired, any of those stones could actively control night and day."

Elders made notes with the quills and paper at their chairs. Many seemed almost aghast that such power was loose in the world again.

Trestan continued. "They also have mastery over stone and earth. They can lay low castles with a thought, or rebuild new walls from the rocks in the ground. They can summon elemental monsters of earth to fight their enemies. The stones have all the power Mothrok invested in them for such tasks. Between the Goddess of Earth and the God of the Weather, I believe the stones could destroy an army's food source while even bolstering your own.

"From DeLaris, they have mastery over death. A wave of the stones over a battlefield can whither the strength of those enemies whose grip on life is tenuous, forcing them into the next world. At the same time, it would restore those recently dead from your side back to life. It can also summon forth a small army of undead warriors. Such creatures lack fear and withstand blows that would drop a living man. DeLaris could also affect the food stores of an enemy, killing the plant life or affecting the rotting of meat.

"This is the power now stolen by those who wish to wage war again."

Trestan finished, allowing a reaction from the clergy. There were scattered responses of disbelief and concern. The rest quieted once Cardinal Alunetar's words echoed across the great chamber.

"I had hoped that all the terrible weapons of the Godswars had been hidden away or destroyed. Such a tragic era. Can any of us truly imagine what it would have been like to live during a time of the wrath of gods? Even the immortals swaggered about the land dispensing terrible power upon those who didn't share their faith." Gracegiver returned his gaze to Trestan. "Was there any means built into the stones to limit their powers?"

Trestan replied, "As part of their alliance, any one stone could cancel the other two. They prepared so that if the alliance ever went sour, the stones couldn't be used against themselves. Indeed, once DeLaris and Mothrok started using their stones for more than just defense, Yestreal tried to end their arrangement. Yestreal stole and scattered the stones before the Covenant barred gods from the lands of men. As long as any stone was safe from the influence of enemies, it could be used to counter the other stones. The Covenant went into effect with Yestreal in possession of all three stones. Thankfully, Yestreal sought only to hide the stones and use only their passive beneficial effects."

At long last, Trestan sighed, "Which is why the band I have been chasing needed to possess all three stones. As long as they hold all of them, they can move the skies, the land and the undead to do their bidding, without a rogue stone countering the effects."

"This is indeed a serious matter you have brought before us." Cardinal Alunetar had also written notes on the table next to his chair. His quill stopped above the paper, held back in indecision even as it was poised to make more notes. "They would be formidable foes against any army or bastion, especially with surprise. How much more do we know about those who know hold the stones?"

Trestan responded, "I know when and where their attack will land."

The elders raised their eyes in interest. Trestan proceeded to describe Revwar and Savannah first, letting the clergy know their main foes. After that, he went into the details he had seen in Savannah's head.

"…while we stood there locked in mental combat, I went into her thoughts to find their plans. Her thoughts pointed at the Fortress Stone, on the continent of Shard, as their next goal. When the winter snows are almost felt, they will ride out from the untamed lands with an army of tribes at their side. There are a host of humans and humanoids on the plains near that fort, and somehow Revwar and Savannah have a plan to get them under their control."

When Trestan paused, the cardinal asked, "Is there any more we should know about their attack?"

"I only know that we have until late in the waning season. Other than that, I foresaw that if they succeed in taking the fortress, some greater evil will rise up from that land to engulf the world in shadows. I also know that it isn't just Revwar and Savannah that we need to fear. We were attacked by a cleric of DeLaris on Wilder continent who tried to stop us from getting word out. A second ambush awaited us just outside Barkan's Crossing, composed of faithful of Mothrok and DeLaris, but they failed to surprise us. DeLaris and Mothrok have mobilized their clerics to cover up their intents for Shard. The quest has led me to see that it is not just individuals who seek power…it is the goal of the goddesses themselves."

"These goddesses are acting more aggressive than I can believe. Is it their intent to start another Godswars?" Cardinal Alunetar paused as the door to the assembly reopened behind Trestan and his friends. He didn't pay it much attention, thinking about what was said. Trestan heard voices at the door behind him. It sounded like an argument, yet he kept his focus on his message. Gracegiver continued speaking despite the distraction at the door, "And yet, terrible as this news implies, DeLaris' actions seem so small by comparison. If she is daring conquest, why summon an army of under-equipped tribes at the edge of civilization? What possible goals can DeLaris or Mothrok hope to accomplish before there is a backlash from the other gods and their followers?"

Trestan was about to offer some comment, but Cat had looked behind them to see the cause of the interruption. She reached out and tugged Trestan on the arm. "Look behind you," she urged.

The majority of the elders focused on the ruckus at the entry. Squire Trestan turned to face the door, and his mind emptied of whatever he had planned to say.

Petrow jogged inside the door, after shouldering his way past the door guards. Behind him, trying to block a guard from entering the room, was…his father! Trestan could only stare with mouth wide as he witnessed this unexpected arrival. Petrow approached the assembly, having heard those last words and having an answer for them all. Trestan saw that his friend carried Sword of the Spirit in his hand. The presence of his old sword implied a lot. Petrow wore armor that Trestan had only seen on him at the end of their first adventure together. Enchanted leather and steel covered his body. Petrow looked so different without his straw hat and open sandals. Both Petrow and Hebden looked sweaty, trail dust coated their clothing. Trestan's mind began to worry over what may have happened in Troutbrook to cause them to race to the seminary.

Petrow spoke in a low tone. His voice sufficiently resounded throughout the large chamber. "I have an answer to that one from a cleric of DeLaris. They are not just attacking with tribesmen. DeLaris plans to use demons in the assault."

Stunned silence overtook the assembly. Cardinal Alunetar reassumed his composure and poise, addressing the man inside the door. "Introduce yourself speaker, and tell us how you know this…after you put away your sword."

Petrow responded, "I came to return this sword to its rightful owner."

Petrow came close enough to Trestan to hand him the sword. Trestan, the surprise still registered on his face, took the sword and cradled it close. The squire whispered the question foremost on his mind, "Family?"

Trestan was still staring into Petrow's blue eyes when he responded. "Safe, thanks to your father showing up not a moment too late."

"He gives me too much credit," Hebden said, even as the guards forced their way into the room. The guards paused, unsure how to treat their unannounced guests now that they had already gotten the attention of the elders. Neither Petrow nor Hebden seemed intent on harming anyone. The guards took up posts near the two men, awaiting orders from their superiors.

"You said demons." Cardinal Alunetar stated from the other end of the room.

"Aye, sir. My name is Petrow. I am a friend of Trestan's." Petrow glanced between Trestan and the cardinal, unsure who he was really addressing yet afraid to look into the eyes of the powerful presence in the high seat.

The hero-turned-farmer continued. "A cleric of DeLaris had me helpless and wanted to torture me by telling me what my friend didn't know. They plan to have the aid of demons from Illutheus in their attack. DeLaris plans to use mortals from that other world to spearhead her conquest here."

The elders were aghast at this news. Cardinal Alunetar frowned as he considered all the consequences of this revelation. The leader of Abriana's followers in northern Quoros digested all the implications as a multitude of elder voices spoke out.

"Abriana did foresee bad tidings would be brought to us this day…"

"…this will be chaos, panic will spread…"

"Help should be sent there at once. We must marshal every paladin and priest who is not otherwise occupied…"

"…nay time to overreact…"

"Their food stores will be in danger; we should acquire some to be sent as well…"

"…can contact a friend there by magical means, we can confirm if they see any threats from the tribes."

"…should summon him, he is an expert on studying demons…"

"Would the Kashmer authorities be counted on to help us?"

"…as long as trade may be disrupted, they may be convinced to assist…"

The voices went on for a while in separate, confusing conversations. Eventually, they died out as Cardinal Alunetar stood. The man paced a few steps, which by itself brought silence to the other elders. He stopped and glanced up at the great painting on the ceiling, staring at Abriana's form.

Finally, he spoke, "There are two dangers here, and we are only looking at the smaller of the two. After the long peace created by the Covenant, it seems that the gods grow restless again. DeLaris is testing the boundaries of this Covenant along with her ally, Mothrok. Now that so many people are beginning to prosper, she seeks to make a first move towards advancing her plans in the world. War will come again. Just because the gods can't enter the realm, doesn't mean their followers can't wage battles here for them. I fear that even if we win, there will nay longer be a lasting peace such as there was."

The cardinal looked at every person in the room in turn. His words were for all to hear. "We, of course, are obliged to take a stand. Abriana said there would be a message today to heed, and one was presented. We must look to ready ourselves for this fight by any means possible. If it is to be us or demons that will control the fate of the Stonelands, then let it be us."

The cardinal swept his gaze across the assembly, "However, let us not forget that there may be even more at stake. DeLaris is playing by the Covenant, sending mortals forth even though she is testing the rules. So, Abriana sends us in order that she may wage war on the same scale, with mortals only. We are her mind and body in this world. We are her only tools.

"Yet, the greater danger may be if we fail. In the effort to preserve what peace we can, will the other gods be unprepared against DeLaris and Mothrok's plans? If we lose, the best we might hope for is to settle for the demons controlling a continent. The worst, would be that some god may decide to break the Covenant in order to react directly to any threat against their followers. Would even our wise Abriana break the Covenant to stop the hatred of the demons?"

Everyone in the room, from elders to squires, silently envisioned such a catastrophe. The cardinal continued, "We may stand on the brink of another Godswars. If pushed hard enough the Covenant may break, and then none of us will know peace in our time ever again. A second Godswars will sweep away our world worse than demons could ever scour it."

CHAPTER 12 "Surname"

"Let's see what's stocked in the larder." Salgor Bandago bellowed in his usual dwarven tone, as he led a human helper into the only finished portion of his inn.

The cellar was carved out over the whole foundation of the large structure. Casks and boxes were stacked against the walls and in aisles down the center. It would be less cluttered after the inn was more complete, at which point some of the stored items would be in the upper rooms. The Temple of Ale was coming along nicely. Salgor benefitted from drawing interested drinkers to the outside tent on a regular basis. Some patrons even joined the construction team.

His helper asked, "Why are we taking inventory of the food? Are you worried over a farmer's tale?"

Salgor shrugged his shoulders at the question. "That farmer is one o' my chief suppliers. He told me he's worried about his yields this year. Said it looked good until just recently, when it seems like some disease o' maybe insects have turned some o' the crop sour."

The inn helper nodded, "I can see why you'd be nervous. Still, we should have plenty to last us."

Salgor lit a lantern to enlighten the subterranean chamber. He did it more for the sake of his human friend than for the needs of his own dwarven eyes. He paused to look around the inventory. His inn planned to be the largest in Pilgrim's Bay. Such a status required a lot of supplies and miscellaneous items.

The dwarf's nose, gifted to help sample the aromas of good drinks and meats, sniffed the air as he detected something out of place. "Smell that?"

The human shook his head. Salgor followed his nose to the smell. In disgust, the dwarf came to the source of the slight odor.

"Looks like we've got some rotten food too." His beard twitched as he frowned.

"But…I just bought these yesterday, they looked fresh!"

Salgor poked around the food bin. "Odd. I'd blame wizards. Trust magic to foul up things when you aren't looking."

*   *   *   *   *

The stained-glass windows, dominating the side walls of the church sanctuary, made lovely mosaics of history when the outside sun cast its light through the colors and shapes. At this nighttime hour, they appeared dark and mysterious. The moons outside did little more than offer a pale glow; creating an ashen and blanched network within each portal that suggested altogether different personas to those images.

Warmth came from lights closer to the main altar. A number of candles burned in front of the steps leading to the center of worship. Anyone kneeling upon the steps would be humbling themselves before the statue representing Abriana's presence. A tapestry depicting many annals of her history hung beyond the golden figure. The few candles that burned created a multitude of shadows behind that lone statue. Their glow illuminated little else. The hall of the sanctuary could seat a few hundred people easily, even offering second floor balconies from which to observe religious rites. The church served as a bastion of Abriana's strength, despite how dark and cold the corners appeared for the two figures kneeling in that small pool of light.

Both had already spent one night of sleepless meditation in this very sanctuary. All of Abriana's senior acolytes observed a night of prayer in this hall before undergoing the tests of their Embarking. Except for students who have to repeat the Embarking after failing their first try, the only other time her disciples had to spend a second night here was after satisfying the symbols etched into Faithful's Companion. On the eve of their induction as a true paladin or ordained cleric, they spent the entire night without sleep as they reflected on her virtues. These two young men had just returned from the quests of their Embarking. They kneeled in quiet contemplation as custom dictated.

Squire Trestan went without armor, despite his calling as a paladin. He wore only a tunic and leggings designed with the coraross, covered with a cloak on his back which also displayed her symbols. It was custom for even the paladins to bare themselves before Abriana. No armor and no weapons were carried in. On the lonely night of their silent vigil, one had to feel that their armor lay in their faith. The scent of fine soaps clung to him, as it was proper to bathe one's body from all impurities just prior to entering the sanctuary for this event. Cleaned and clad in such simple yet elegant garb, he stared into the statue and tapestry images. As often as he looked at the designs, his mind actually wandered inward into the decisions of his own past. He reflected on all he had learned on the road and in the adjacent halls of study.

On Trestan's right kneeled his friend, Squire Leander. The other paladin-aspirant bore similar dress. His long, blond hair once again was tied back in one long tail. They had already been in silence for hours when Leander's whisper seemed to carry to the far corners of the divine house.

"Pardon my interruption of your meditations, but I hoped to share a few thoughts with you before the dawn."

Trestan turned to his friend, allowing a grin to let the man know that Trestan wasn't offended. The former smith whispered back in return. Any words louder than a baby's breath seemed to disturb the peace of the hall. "I assume your words will add to my spiritual reflections. You may proceed."

Leander nodded his thanks. "I recalled our training with the sword here. I think everyone, myself included, criticized your style of swordplay. You favored speed of motion and agility, over large swords and heavy swings that would dent armor. Your choice affected the armor you wore…we all thought you were exposing too much of your skin without the protection of steel.

"The amusing twist was when I found myself having to adopt a similar style. I fought pirates while serving on privateer ships out of Kashmer. In the midst of rocking ships, toppled masts, foul weather, and trying to leap across a watery gap to board an enemy vessel…one does not want to burden themselves with steel plates. I wore as little armor as possible. I had to strike quickly and return my sword to a defensive position. My sword was as much my protection as any shield, so I had to strike and guard." Leander blushed as he admitted. "I borrowed some of your moves."

"If my style kept you alive so that we might share our friendship for more years, then you may borrow as much of it as you want." Trestan smiled. "I never took offense to those words back then. I even dwelled on a few in order to expand my swordplay."

"I guess I'm trying to make an apology of sorts. I'm sorry we bothered you, especially since you taught me a few lessons in return." Leander shifted slightly on his bent knees. "That was only part of what I wanted to say. I plan to journey with you to the Stonelands. I know the elders will be asking many to go, possibly they may even *tell* me to go, but I wanted to personally offer you my sword."

Trestan glanced back at the statue of Abriana, then returned his gaze to his friend. "I am very grateful. I could use all my friends and every friend they can bring."

Trestan's smile lowered as he looked to the giant tapestry. His eyes fixed upon an image of a humble man who later ascended to immortal status during the Godswars. Looking upon that hero, he mused. "When did I outgrow the small concerns of my youth? I used to only worry about our stock of iron...the size of the fish I could catch and brag about...whether I could get the local lord's daughter to look at me or if I'd settle for a farmer girl. When did I let myself become so involved in something so much bigger?"

Leander commented, "I suppose the same way I left my future as a fisherman and joined Abriana's side. Things happened in my life to change my outlook of the world, and I was young and energetic enough to turn towards making a difference. Of course, once I undertook my Embarking, I was all too obliged to give some payback to the pirates that were found."

Leander decided to change topics slightly, "Rhijin would love to join us. I saw her and told her about your vision. She is still discontent that she failed her Embarking, yet she has been hard at her lessons to make sure she doesn't fail the next one. I don't suppose it makes a difference; the next Embarking was scheduled for the end of Tiquierum."

Trestan nearly interrupted. "The elders were talking outside the meeting hall. They may move it up to late Novak. That may still be too late in the season, but those who graduate by then may be able to make it."

Leander turned towards the altar. "She may yet be able to go. Do you think that will be enough time?"

Trestan shrugged, "Hard to say. I hope to be sailing for Stonelands even before then. I can't be certain when the battle will happen, but I must make sure I don't miss it."

Silence followed. When Leander seemed to speak no more, Trestan offered a question of his own. During his time in prayer, a thought nagged him. The young favored of Abriana was unsure about something he would be asked in the morning.

"Leander? Will you be taking a surname?"

"Aye," the warrior with the fair hair nodded. "I have one picked. It reflects an event during my campaign against the pirates. Will you take a name?"

Trestan's eyes were downcast as he answered. "I'm not sure."

Leander thought he might drop it at that, but Trestan needed someone to confide in. Trestan spoke several breaths later. "I have a name I am considering; however, I have always felt that I am Hebden Karok's son. If I choose a name other than my own, what am I saying about the Karok family name?"

"Well, the difficulty of your choice is understood. I, on the other hand, will be happy to do away with my old name. Only gods know what some fishing ancestor of mine did to earn the name Carphunter and pass it down the family line."

Trestan, despite himself, gave a snort of laughter at that. "You never told us your real last name!"

Leander raised a stern finger towards Trestan. "And as far as anyone knows I didn't reveal it here either. We're not supposed to be talking, after all."

When Trestan seemed to be holding back his lingering amusement over Leander's name, the other man prompted him with another question. "You said you learned the tenets of Abriana from a mentor in your village. What was his choice?"

Trestan thought back to Sir Wilhelm Jareth. "He kept his family name; at least, he never mentioned a given name other than the family name we knew."

"Well, I think I have an idea for you." Leander explained, "You can go ahead and pick a surname for the eyes of the church and your brothers of faith. Assuming that you do, nothing says you have to go by that name outside the church. You can use your father's name whenever you like, and still have a name for your path under Abriana."

Trestan nodded, "That is one good way of looking at it, I suppose."

Leander added, "Your bride-to-be, will she be taking your father's name according to human custom?"

The notion stunned Trestan. It threw thoughts into his mind that he hadn't dwelled on much.

Leander recalled her name from earlier. "Katressa…Katressa Karok. Has a nice ring to it. You would also then be honoring your father even as you have a name set aside from Abriana."

Trestan was digesting that name in his head when Leander offered another question. "What name are you considering, if I may ask?"

"Oh," Trestan was obviously thrown into distraction at the mention of Cat's name with his last name attached. "I'd…like to keep it secret…just in case I change my mind."

Leander respected Trestan's decision. Both young warriors returned to their contemplations, once again leaving silence to reign in the large sanctuary. Both resumed a motionless bow toward their matron as they continued their quiet vigil. Candles flickered lower as the night lingered.

Trestan's thoughts were interrupted often by a repetition that would not be silenced in his head.

…Katressa Karok…Katressa Karok…

It had a nice ring indeed.

*   *   *   *   *

The morning sun's glory shining upon them, Trestan and Leander kneeled on rugs laid out on a grass-covered hill outside the sanctuary. Neither were yet allowed to bear armor or weapons. Oil anointed their heads. The cardinal traced the coraross symbol on their foreheads. A small gathering of elders surrounded them. Both men were allowed to have close friends and family near as they ascended Abriana's favor. Petrow, Hebden, and Cat gathered for Trestan. Petrow bore his sword for him…just as he had for his trip north on Trestan's behalf. Leander had no family nearby, and few friends outside the seminary walls, therefore he had asked Rhijin to carry his sword for him. This left Rhijin as the only student that could even come close to the time-honored proceedings. Other students and seminary hands watched from afar.

The elders encircled the kneeling squires, as if shielding them from impurities or evil. A few of them held censers which gave off the powerful smell of burning incense. All those of Abriana's worship wore tabards displaying her symbols and colors.

Cardinal Alunetar Gracegiver continued addressing Abriana, looking up to the sky with eyes closed as the rest bowed their heads to his words.

"…your newest champions kneel before you, ready to give their pledges and affirm their hearts. As they were once born as mortals, then reborn as your students, they have cleansed their bodies and minds to fully accept the devotion required of them."

Cardinal Alunetar came before Leander. "As you were first to arrive yesterday, so shall we commence with your paladin's oath. Do you, Leander, swear your fealty and devotion to Abriana; pledging yourself to take her virtues to heart, to spread her love and healing, and to defend those worthy of that love; and furthermore, will you always obey her teachings 'til life flees you? Speak now if you can affirm such with all your honor, courage, honesty and compassion."

Leander replied from the kneeling position, with arms wide and his closed eyes humbly turned downward. "I do so swear with all my heart."

The cardinal held a hand forth. "May your bearer present your sword to me, please."

Rhijin stepped forward and reverently extended the hilt of the sword for the cardinal to take. She kept hold on the scabbard as he drew forth the blade. Once he held it before him, she quietly stepped back to her place, slightly behind Leander's side.

The cardinal addressed Leander again, with the man's sword in his hands. "You have the option to take a surname, which will be your name within the church. If you want to take a name, please state it now…feel free to share your reasons if you so desire."

Leander raised his head to answer. "Swordbreaker. I choose the name Swordbreaker due to one of my own ideas during my Embarking. We had found an island where a group of pirates held their booty. The ruffians there were killed or arrested, and we confiscated the stolen loot. Sadly, we failed to capture the ringleader of that band. I decided to send them a warning message. I suggested to my captain that we take the weapons of those pirates and break them all, leaving them in a pile where the gold was once stored. We visited that island once more before returning to Kashmer. No one has used that island since, and the pile of broken weapons still resides there."

The cardinal smiled briefly, yet returned to a solid expression as he finished his solemn duties. He tapped the flat of Leander's blade ever so softly on both shoulders. "On behalf of Abriana, I name you Sir Leander Swordbreaker. Rise, knight of Abriana, paladin of Love and Healing, and be her champion."

Leander stood, accepting his weapon from the cardinal, bowing respectfully as he stepped back. As the cardinal moved to face Trestan, Rhijin handed Leander the scabbard so he could put away his blade.

Trestan tried to appear patient while awaiting his turn. His insides churned with the excitement of the end of this long road. He wished Sir Wilhelm could witness this moment. After his youthful trepidations about what service to Abriana might entail, he was ready to embrace the responsibilities and the gifts of such service.

"Now for you who brought such important tidings to our attention. Do you, Trestan, swear your fealty and devotion to Abriana; pledging yourself to take her virtues to heart, to spread her love and healing, and to defend those worthy of that love; and furthermore, will you always obey her teachings 'til life flees you? Speak now if you can affirm such with all your honor, courage, honesty and compassion."

Trestan responded in the same traditional fashion as Leander. "I do so swear with all my heart."

The cardinal once again extended his hand. "May your bearer present your sword to me, please."

Petrow tried to mimic Rhijin's poise as he duplicated the way she handed the cardinal the sword. He had the urge to warn the cardinal to be especially careful with Trestan's keen blade, but he forced such thoughts silent. It would likely embarrass Trestan if Petrow questioned the cardinal's ability in handling a weapon.

In actuality, the cardinal was very respectful of the power he felt in the blade. The man had once carried weapons into battle, and he admired the craftsmanship that had gone into this piece. He looked down to Trestan, "You have the option to take a surname, which will be your name within the church. If you want to take a name, please state it now…feel free to share your reasons if you so desire."

Trestan gave a brief moment of hesitation, mindful of his father. The young man had considered Leander's words, concluding that he wanted to use the surname he had picked. To his father and the villagers of Troutbrook, he would always be Karok.

"I do have a name I want, in reference to that sword you have in your hand. That sword is an inheritance from a dear friend who helped me find faith in Abriana before his untimely death. He died fighting the enemies who still test me to this day. The Elvish runes on the blade say, '*Fa Iblearol re fa Dolingomo re fa sen-Salustrel*'. Literally translated: 'the sword, of the spirit of the soul'. I call it Sword of the Spirit. Before I wore Faithful's Companion, this sword had been my spiritual guide, reminding me of why I took this road. With this sword in mind, I choose the surname Spiritblade."

The cardinal tapped the flat of the sword on both of Trestan's shoulders, pronouncing, "On behalf of Abriana, I name you Sir Trestan Spiritblade. Rise, knight of Abriana, paladin of Love and Healing, and be her champion."

Trestan Spiritblade stood as a full paladin of Abriana. His friends and his father stood by him for support as the cardinal prayed for his and Leander's future. In the back of Trestan's mind, he remembered the long road that brought him from the smithy to this point in time. Silently, he spoke to himself as if Sir Wilhelm could overhear his thoughts.

I did it…I'm finally here.

CHAPTER 13   **"The Chiaso Healer/Aide-de-Camp"**

Line after line of elegant ink swirls danced across the paper scroll, yet at the moment the writer was frozen in pause. Sondra's quill hovered over the inkwell, so that any drops that escaped might be recovered for some future words of wisdom. Flickering candlelight illuminated the text already scribed on the yellowish surface. Perplexed that the words she sought weren't coming to her, she began to let her eyes wander about her small room. The first thing that caught her eyes was the yarn work that lay abandoned near her bed. As much as she had tried, she wasn't as gifted at weaving patterns as Mother Evine had been. Sondra had attempted it with thoughts of clothing some of the poor people as her mentor had done. Every pattern and project never seemed to come out right. Sondra had given up that pursuit and taken a new hobby.

As a priestess studying holy scriptures, she was well-educated in letters and words. She admired the artful, neat calligraphy of the church scribes. Likewise, Sondra could articulate her handwriting in a style that brought emotions in the appearance of the words, even before their meaning was read. In Dhea Loral, distant lands utilized the common human letters differently. Sondra's writing explored the possibilities of playing with those different forms, seemingly creating new words by combining different known styles.

Sondra opined that she wrote very well. She had already filled more scrolls than she could easily fit into her shared living quarters. Of course, she was always very self-conscious of her writing. Many times, she looked over something she had written and realized she could have done better. With ink and paper, there were no means by which to clear a mistake. Even scratching out the sentence and starting anew, left the obvious mistake glaring in the middle of her otherwise fanciful creations. She continued to explore new things to write. The more she wrote, the more she surprised herself with her expressions of emotion. Mistakes came less often, replaced by imaginative words even as meandering thoughts coalesced into well-structured points of view.

Sondra often penned reflections based on her opinions of Ganden's scriptures. On most occasions, she simply wrote in self-exploration of her deeper feelings. Sometimes she went on a different line entirely, writing something akin to the romances she had tucked away and secretly read during her teenage years. Perhaps, in those written passages, she found something else she dreamed about but never thought attainable…a loving partner. She locked away all such writings soon afterward. Someday, she might get up the courage to share her religious writings with her brothers and sisters, but the scrolls containing her personal feelings and romantic ideas were too private.

A telltale knock at the door interrupted her thoughts. Her roommate had a peculiar knock that she always used. The door didn't even have a lock. Montanya respected Sondra's privacy enough so as not to barge in unexpected. Sondra began to put away her writing tools as she told Montanya to come in. The arrival of the red-haired teen meant that it was even later in the evening than the young priestess had realized. Montanya had been working at a sanctuary that night, although neither woman had been required to work this day.

Montanya's labor was done, and she bounced into the room possessing more vigor than Sondra ever remembered having after her nights in those places.

Montanya's greenish-blue eyes glanced over Sondra's writing tools as she began to settle in for the night. The chiaso undid the clasp holding her braided hair. "You're up late. Scribing anything interesting?"

"Only for myself," Sondra offered a grin as she banished her papers to a chest.

Noting that Sondra was acting shy again, Montanya pushed the issue as her hair came free. "I thought you were taking up knitting or an instrument? You've been so busy working over scrolls that you hardly leave any time for other pursuits."

The blonde cleric sighed, "Well, this is a pursuit. I've…I guess it has helped me to be a better person."

When Sondra looked back to her roommate, she noticed the youth had one eyebrow raised. "A better person?" Montanya asked, "How do you mean?"

"For one, I have been thinking hard about my choice of words and looking up the meanings of some. I feel I am better able to articulate my vocabulary."

The chiaso offered a blank stare in return. Sondra wasn't sure she liked the way Montanya was looking at her. The blonde cleric asked, "What did I say?"

"That's what I was wondering. You lost me around artic-late and voca-brewery."

Despite herself, Sondra burst out laughing. Montanya reverted back to her old scowl as she turned her back and retrieved her nightshift. The youth threw it onto her bed with a huff.

Sondra fought against the urge to laugh as she tried to answer her friend. "I'm sorry. I just meant that I can use a larger variety of words to properly state my points of view."

"Is that all?"

"There is more." Sondra paused in thought for a moment. "You know I have a hard time speaking up or conveying my feelings. In writing, I can state whatever I want. I can express emotions and messages I couldn't bring myself to say out loud. I've surprised myself with the number of things I'm willing to write about that I would never talk about."

Montanya nodded, "That's good to hear. If it makes you a better person and makes you happy, then by all means you should pursue it."

Montanya dressed for bed. She pulled down the covers as Sondra added, "Did you ever read that scroll I left out two days ago? I wanted your opinion."

The chiaso kept her back to her friend. "Uh, what was it about again?"

"Some improvements the Sanctuaries for Those in Need could use that we might be able to get city taxes to help support. What did you think? I'd love to go through with getting those plans presented to the elders. Of course, I don't think I could stand there and propose the idea without my knees shaking."

Montanya slid into bed as Sondra spoke. With her face still hidden, the younger woman responded, "Well, your writing is pretty. I think you wrote it rather well."

Sondra hoped for more of an answer. Suddenly, a thought dawned on the cleric. Weeks of being with Montanya, as well as the memories from Montanya that were still fading from Sondra's mind, left clues that Sondra finally pieced together.

"You can't read!"

Montanya turned over with a huff, casting an angry eye at her friend. "Speak a little louder; I don't think the cleric in the confessional heard you."

Her hand slapped her forehead as Sondra realized the truth of Montanya's lack of education. "I'm sorry, I just didn't realize…"

"I can read many Tariykan symbols, especially anything dealing with the martial arts. The monastery gave me that much. I can read some of the common language, but I was too little when my parents died. I barely remember any schooling other than how to punch and kick." The chiaso rolled over again, facing the wall. Any shame remaining on her features was known only to the stone.

Sondra recalled how easy it was to bruise Montanya's fragile pride. The wheat-blonde cleric thought carefully before speaking. "There is nay shame in that. Even many merchants' sons know how to count coins but not how to read words. I'm sorry if I embarrassed you. I'd be happy to help you read if you ever wish it."

A muffled thanks was her only reply, although that word in itself was one Montanya rarely used.

Sondra Oskires decided to change the topic. "I didn't mean to put you in a bad mood the moment you arrived. Actually, I've been wanting to compliment you."

The youth stirred in the bed. Her face half-turned back, though Sondra could only make out a portion of her profile. "Hmm?"

The young priestess of Ganden walked a few steps closer to Montanya, taking a seat on her own bed but facing the younger woman. "I worked so long to help the poor and sick people in those sanctuaries. All the chores I did, and the intense training I put into my healing, it all wore on me. I guess I felt dulled by some of my work. Maybe it was thoughts on how I'd given my life over to be an endless witness to suffering…but whatever it was, my soul was burdened. Mother Evine commented that she rarely saw me smile."

Montanya turned back towards Sondra, a perplexed expression across her features. "You smile all the time."

And at those words, Sondra did smile for Montanya's eyes. "Because of you, my friend! You brought a light and warmth into the sanctuary that rarely existed before. Your balancing antics with the bowls, the way you juggled rocks for the kids yesterday…you've made the people around you smile. It reminded me of when my mentor put her knitted clothes on those who were cold. I remember how their world brightened for that moment. You've been doing that ever since you came to the sanctuaries."

The younger woman seemed to go a shade of red at all the praise. "I just like being able to help out. I didn't realize my performances pleased you so."

Sondra nodded. She began to change for bedtime even as she attempted to say more. Montanya could tell she wanted to make clear a message, but it took Sondra a few moments to find the right words. "You heal injuries that I've never touched."

Montanya understood. The youth smiled towards the wall as Sondra went on. "I can feed them and give them a place to rest, but you've given them the next thing they need. You've brought joy to their hearts."

Sondra blew the candles out and climbed into her bed. In the darkness, Montanya viewed her own worth in taking care of those who had little else. The chiaso could not even claim to own more than a few coins or a home other than that which was provided for her work there. Despite that, and considering her years of isolating her thoughts around revenge, she finally felt as if she was in a place that she was happy.

"I'm glad you let me stay with you here, Sondra," she spoke to the darkness. "I've felt more alive than I ever have before."

"Goodnight, Montanya."

"Goodnight, my friend."

           *   *   *   *   *

The day found Trestan, Petrow, and Katressa sharing a moment together. The trio chatted on a balcony overlooking a portion of the seminary grounds. They had finally finished settling into the seminary, discovering that the hosting clergy offered rooms for all of them. From a nearby workshop, they heard Hebden putting his smith skills to work. Hebden decided to volunteer his part to ready tools and weapons the seminary would need when marching to the aid of Stonelands. Trestan planned to pitch in and work alongside him soon enough. For now, the three friends talked about the days ahead.

Trestan kept glancing down to the seminary training grounds. Lindon Taleweaver was down there, trying a few notes on his mandolin. Every so often, the minstrel would look up towards the three companions. It wasn't difficult for Trestan to comprehend that Lindon's observations were being translated into the notes on the instrument.

"Tres, you seem nervous." Petrow observed.

Trestan stroked his mustache, attempting a subtle nod towards the red-bearded man below. "He's making me nervous. It is discomforting trying to have a decent conversation with friends when a minstrel is watching your every move."

Petrow snorted in amusement, "I think we once wondered if rescuing Lady Shauntay Tessald would get us into song. I don't know that it ever did, though from what you said, I guess the tale did spread even to Kashmer."

Cat snickered, "If you consider a story about, 'armed farmers from Troutbrook ambushing a fleet of pirates and returning the noble to her home using a divine chariot', an accurate portrayal of events."

The companions could not help but smile at the way stories were exaggerated. Petrow scratched at his collar, unused to the feel of the leather. "Well, feel honored. You two are heroes, and you deserve some praise for your adventures."

Trestan glanced at his childhood friend. "I'm sure he's putting in some verses about you too!"

Petrow seemed unconcerned. "For what? If I'm lucky he may mention my name once. I haven't done anything."

"I better go down and enlighten him," Cat mused. "After all, didn't Petrow capture the abbess of DeLaris by himself those years ago? Also, how she hunted him for four years before he slipped out of her ambush and killed her with his simple axe."

Petrow perked in alarm at that. "Nay, please, nay. The last thing I want is to be immortalized in song for killing a member of the church of Death."

"Well, now you know how I feel." Trestan turned away from the minstrel, not wanting to have his every expression and thought shared to strangers in song.

They shared silence between them as they soaked in the sun on that balcony. The harvest season was fast approaching, and it would be accompanied by colder days.

At length, Katressa brought up a different subject. "I saw some representatives from the church riding down to Kashmer this morning. I found out they were going to ask the king for help with the fight. Hopefully Kashmer will assist with its navy, or at the least muster some privateers to help."

Trestan looked out to the western skyline, where waves swept into Kashmer's harbor. The continent of Shard sat somewhere past that horizon. "I talked with a former mentor. He has connections with a friend in Stonelands. Sometimes they speak to each other using a miracle to bridge the distance. Anyways, he inquired about any troubles. There were nay ominous signs regarding the tribes of the region, but they had disturbing news regarding their crops. Crops are dying in the fields; even stored food is spoiling at a fast rate. This friend of his expressed concern for the health of the livestock. There is a sickness spreading, and even the grasses the cattle feed on seem to be withering."

There was brief silence until Cat spoke. "Revwar must be in the Stonelands already. The power of the relics has been used to starve the area before the battle."

Petrow, lost in his own private worries, felt Trestan's hand on his shoulder. The blue-eyed man looked to his friend as Trestan asked, "Petrow, are you sure you want to go? We will have wizards from Orlaun, clerics from both Ganden and Abriana, and the Stonelands' own army. It will be dangerous, but we'll have a lot of help. We wouldn't ask you to go and leave your family behind."

Petrow looked out over the seminary grounds and thought about it. He shook his head. "I have gone this far; I can't go back. I know I can't offer much. I'm not a warrior like you are, Tres, but I wouldn't be able to go back to Troutbrook without looking over my shoulder and wondering what is going on. I guess I have one more adventure in me. I want to make sure my children can play in fields free of demons."

The paladin of Abriana nodded at his friend's choice. "I wonder what other help will come to our aid. Will Kashmer assist? Will their help be useful against demons and magic? I hope we can muster enough numbers."

"Well, you know how that one saying goes," Cat started to say. Trestan and Petrow looked to her, and saw a broad smile. As she talked, her attention locked on the road leading to the seminary. "Short help is better than nay help at all."

At Trestan and Petrow's puzzlement, Cat pointed to the road. The men turned to regard a distant sight. Lindon noticed the gesture and paused in his composing to look in that direction. The humans had trouble seeing details from this distance. They were momentarily confused as to the shape of the approaching subject. Cat, with her superior elf vision, was able to make out better details.

Cat jubilantly announced, "We have a 'little' bit of magic on our side now."

The four-legged creature speeding towards the seminary moved like no horse they had ever seen. It took a moment to realize that its smaller size deceived them as to how far away it truly was. The sight puzzled Petrow longer than the others, for he had never seen a dog used as a mount before. Yet it was a dog, of good size, loping up the road. The reins bounced along as did the small feet in the stirrups to each side. The small person guiding the dog wore her camouflage-cut leathers, making it hard to spot her exact shape among the moving patterns. It also disguised the fact that there were two riders, although that fact soon became apparent as a second gnomish head peeked from behind the first. From a distance, they recognized the thin mustache and beard on the second gnome's smiling face.

Mel Bellringer of the Bellringer family, (makers of fine bells, chimes, gongs and other acoustical instruments), had persuaded Aijak to join him as he rode forth to please his dwarven battle god.

The two gnomes didn't realize they had been spotted by friendly observers, until their ears caught the whooping and hollering from the men on the balcony. Mel met their eyes and waved. In the field, Lindon allowed his mandolin to dangle by its strap as he rose to gaze at the newcomers. Trestan and Petrow ran inside the building to get downstairs.

Cat chuckled to herself at an inner realization. "Now there won't be any breaks in the conversation."

Unlike the men, Cat took an easier route to the ground. She vaulted the balcony, caught the bottom ledge with her hands, bounced lightly off of an overhang and landed like an acrobat. It was another half-minute before Trestan and Petrow burst out the door and wondered how she had gotten there ahead of them.

"My friends! We came as soon as we heard you needed us!" Mel shouted as Cathag came to a stop. Aijak said a few comforting words to the mastiff as her lover jumped from his perch. Pouches strapped to Mel's bandoliers bounced as the gnome trotted to join his former companions. "Petrow, a pleasant surprise to see you here. Trestan and Cat, I hope you had a fun adventure despite the worries you relayed to me."

The companions hardly got a word in as Mel went on and on greeting them. Mel asked a few questions but never waited for an answer before going on to the next subject. Lindon was likewise introduced but soon partly ignored as long-standing friends caught up on old times. Despite the seriousness that brought them here, Mel's uplifting chats never dwelled on dark worries. He drifted among semi-related topics until interrupted by Aijak. The woman cleared her throat to get his attention and then gave him a stern look.

"Uh, oh." Mel turned back to his friends with a look that, for him, seemed slightly nervous. "It took considerable convincing to get Aijak out here. I had to convince her that I had an important position, or would at least be put in an important position, fitting my skilled status. I think she wants to make sure I have a high rank that pays a lot."

Trestan looked over the druid woman. He remembered, from their brief meeting over a month ago, she couldn't understand hardly anything of the human language. "Well, I don't know that we'll have anything to pay. We'll be coming to the rescue of a castle under assault by demons."

"Demons?! You didn't mention that!" Mel acted more animated, but as always, he quickly filtered away the information and went back to the positive aspects. "The fact that we'll be fighting demons will help. Druids hate demons, they consider them abominations. But as I was saying, don't worry about payment, I'm here for friends. Just tell me I'll have an important title of some kind. She wants to know I'm someone important out here."

The gnome was looking at Trestan, but the paladin drew a blank. "Uhh, um…let me think." Trestan turned to Cat. "Help me out here. What is a good title?"

Katressa, who was more knowledgeable of the world from her travels, thought on it. He hoped she had heard of something in her journeys that would fill in the gap Mel needed. She tried to think of some rather obscure titles, ones that would *mean* something important without necessarily *being* important since they all didn't know their parts yet. Since Mel seemed educated in a number of various random subjects, she hoped she could find one that would be useable even if his experiences made him familiar with its meaning.

"You can be Trestan's…aide-de-camp." She smiled, hoping that would be sufficient.

Trestan quietly awaited Mel's response. The gnome smiled, "Oh, like over in the Counties of Diara! That's an important position! Perfect!"

It wasn't a total surprise to Cat that Mel knew what the position entailed. The gnome nodded eagerly while Trestan held a smile and wondered what an aide-de-camp was. Mel was telling the good news to Aijak as Trestan threw a questioning look at Cat.

"That is great, which is…?"

The half-elf made it appear as if she was just reminding Trestan of the position instead of educating him on something new. "You know, an officer assigned to an officer."

Trestan naively nodded, expecting more. When Cat said nothing else, and Trestan realized how nicely vague the answer was, he began to smile and think that was a perfect rank.

CHAPTER 14   "The Prophet and the Messiah"

After months of circulating rumors regarding a prophet who would lead the tribes to a messiah, the appointed messenger arrived and his passing marked by all. Hair of silver, eyes of gold, the elf radiated power and confidence as he appeared before his people. They watched him walk, alone, out of the endless sea of grass. They couldn't believe this figure dared walk the open plains unguarded. His regal stride carried him through the multitudes of awed nomads.

Revwar noted the many varied peoples and banners that had been brought under the sway of the demons. The nomads of the Tribal Expanse remained different in many ways. Their one commonality: their ancestors had once fought the Godswars until the hardships of the war's aftermath scoured away their pre-war history. Since that downfall, they remained primitive wanderers. Lives were spent fighting over the plains, wandering from well to well, scrounging wild fruits, bearing children on the move, and trying to recover what was lost to memory. They avoided crowding any given area. Today, under the sway of demon puppet masters, they massed together in numbers that spread to the horizon.

The elf arrived at a water basin that had dried up from the multitudes of thirsty warriors. The hardy grass which thrived throughout the plains lie trampled many times over by feet and hooves. Almost every tree in sight had been cut down to feed large cookfires. Solid ground had become churned and muddy in many places. The air about camp filled with animal noises, singing, arguments, drinking toasts, storytellers…hundreds of voices mingling as a continuous, rumbling expression. Some druids likely lamented the blow suffered by nature. Some had been turned away from such concerns by demonic lies that hinted at the greater danger Stonelands' people supposedly poised to their way of living.

In the outer boundaries of the gathering, Revwar first passed gliel scouts patrolling the windswept stalks. They would have been harder to spot if so much tall grass had not been trampled. The diminutive, elf-like race, had been pushed to the edges of the encampment. Few enough members of their race survived the Godswars in all the realm. Their descendants were growing up in a world better suited for the larger humanoids. The gliel peered out of hiding to view the one that would lead them to their rumored savior.

The golden-eyed wizard passed a disorganized layout of tents belonging to an orc tribe. A number of torn banners identified the tribe as the Moon Slayers. The orcs displayed a pale, blue moon painted on their foreheads. Revwar had heard of their savagery. They possessed large numbers and a reputation of driving off any neighboring nomads wherever they traveled. It was a testament to the powers of demonic persuasion that such a group willingly shared camp space with so many others. Even as he reflected on it, he saw one orc wiping fresh blood from a jagged axe blade. Apparently, scuffles still broke out between tribes living in such close quarters.

He passed between two tribes where posted sentries stared across at the opposite group. On one side was a band of humans with painted faces. They freely shouted insults at their neighbors while drinking some thick beverage. Across from them, sentries from a tribe of raulgans answered insult for insult. Raulgans were about the size of humans, sharing many traits in appearance, though their upbringing and warrior values bred well-muscled survivors. The thick ridge that formed in the middle of their scalp was often used to deliver a devastating head-butt. The humans would likely stir up more than words before long. Raulgans were eager to fight yet held to their own codes about honor. If any of the humans got foolish enough to insult that code, a large melee might ensue. Revwar's passage between the two camps made both sides pause their slandering. Human and raulgan alike beheld him with curious eyes. Revwar ignored the faces as he went. The elf wizard wondered if the verbal sparring between those two tribes would lead to bloodshed before the day was out.

Other races and tribes watched the prophet pass. Some even bowed and prayed to their gods. Revwar wondered how many prayed favorably versus how many prayed to deliver them from the madness that seemed to envelop so many. A crowd began following him as he made his way deeper into the gathering. Whispers exchanged among the nearby nomads. It was as if an aura of hushed voices led the way for Revwar, flanked him on his sides, and even followed in his wake. In a number of languages, the word 'prophet' rode the waves of murmurs in the vicinity of the elf. Revwar walked between tents of stretched animal hides, tether lines of horses, stacks of weapons, and curious nomad children. The eyes of hundreds scrutinized him as he approached the center of the water basin.

The leaders of many tribes gathered together at the edge of the nearly-empty reservoir. Revwar marched directly to them uncontested. Some chieftains and elders motioned for guards to encircle the meeting. Kor Strongarm, easily recognized and seen by many due to his six-and-a-half-foot frame, stood next to his love Pejena Cloud Whisperer as he pointed out guard positions for his Spear Riders. Although the Spear Riders had questioned their leader for the past several weeks, much of their dissent had been quieted or even crushed. They no longer asked questions as they formed a wall of spears against those attempting to follow in Revwar's steps. The elf wizard stood face-to-face with the demon-controlled elders. Other nomads were stopped some distance away.

The meeting between Revwar and the demons inhabiting the elders' bodies had been planned and rehearsed months in advance. Unknown to the hundreds who observed the meeting, the elders and Revwar had already opened communications through magical means to fine tune their rehearsed play.

An elder known by many spoke to the lone elf. "Who are you to attend our gathering? The tribes of this land stand united!"

The elf responded; his voice magically amplified so that all could hear. "United in what? You are gathered together here, but I, Revwar, will guide you where you need to go."

Kor's voice spoke out next. The trapped soul behind those eyes watched helplessly as his body participated in the charade. "What do we need that isn't here? These sacred plains provide for us!"

The elf mage gestured to the muddy, drained spring. "Do the plains truly provide for all your needs? Look upon this watering hole and think of the lands you roam. There are many tribes, growing larger each day. This expanse of grassland is bordered on three sides by impassible bodies of water. To the south, you allow yourselves to be hemmed in by those who build stone walls to keep you back. As your tribes grow larger, your resources shrink, and you wage war amongst yourselves."

Revwar paused for a breath to let his words sink in. "Your sacred lands are slowly absorbed by invaders. More arrive in the Stonelands every turn of Nirahha. They build their walls farther out, taking your land to feed themselves. You have met these new people, and you have seen many that do not respect you!"

Even reluctant heads nodded at that statement. Numerous tribespeople could recall incidents with immigrants who settled the wilds around the Stonelands and clashed with the nomad natives. Even voyages to the Stonelands to barter for trade could result in insults or injustices. Some natives died facing Stonelands' justice system or lack thereof.

Revwar turned to face the people as he spoke. Although he was supposedly talking to the elders, the demons controlling the elders wanted his words to persuade the masses. "Some gods turned from you during the Godswars, but others never left you. I bring message of a messiah who will come, bearing the words of gods who would see you a strong people once again!"

The crowd showed mixed reactions, but all shared curiosity towards Revwar's words. Revwar and the demons knew that some tribes had turned completely from the gods. Some preferred worship of the land itself, which led to the presence of many druids, shamans and mystics. For those who mistrusted the gods, it was important to appeal to those who also revered the land.

One elder, a respected mystic, stepped towards the elf wizard and addressed him. "There are those of us who listen to the land and the gods. We have heard a message of one who will come with their blessings. How can we know this foretelling to be real? How do we know you do not fool our minds?"

"To prove that my words come from your gods and the land you serve, I will make an example for all to see." Revwar once again turned to the nearly empty oasis. He spoke to all nearby, pulling their attention to his words. Using magic to amplify his voice, he conversed with those at the edges of vision just as easily as if his calm voice was in their ears. "The land is harmed when too many drink from it. This dwindling pool is an example. The gods are shamed that so many must fight when hunger gnaws at young bellies. Those who come and take your lands must be thrown back to the sea from where they came. They rob you of your fair share of the land. The gods will give you strength, and the land will give you nourishment in plenty."

Revwar tucked one hand inside of his robes. His hidden hand gripped one of the Earthrin Stones. The other motioned towards the muddy water. "Nay simple magician or trickster can duplicate what the messiah has given me power to do. The messiah is blessed by land and gods, and he shares that blessing with those for whom it is intended!"

A low rumble echoed from the heavens. Tribesmen looked to the sky and saw dark clouds blotting out the sun. Many cowered in fear. In the heavens, Yestreal felt the misuse of his powers through the Earthrin Stone, but was forbidden by the Covenant to directly interfere. In her plane of existence, the goddess Mothrok felt her powers used and she smiled. As Goddess of Earth and Stone, she felt the land under the plains undergo changes. She knew one of her accomplices in Dhea Loral was putting her schemes into motion.

Dark clouds blocked sunlight directly over the gathering. In the distant horizon, the edges of the clouds could be seen. The nomads realized that a storm formed directly over them and nowhere else. The land buckled and shifted. The tremors were light, but enough to topple items and cause some panic. Under the surface, rock displaced mud. The clouds let loose a downpour in the basin, even as the stone underfoot pushed water up to the surface.

Minutes slipped past as the sudden rainfall soaked the nomads. Revwar concentrated on the Earthrin Stone hidden in his robes, while pretending to call the rain down with his free hand. People who had been standing close to the muddy water retreated as the edges expanded. The water basin filled and then overflowed as amazed tribes stood in awe. Revwar used the powers of Mothrok to force the mud to settle to the bottom, turning the water supply clear. Just as quickly, Revwar allowed the clouds to disperse, bringing back Yestreal's sunlight.

The tribes stared openly at the filled pool, gleaming with purity under the sun's rays. Their minds wrestled with the fact that no one man could work the magic Revwar had just done. Conjuring a small amount of water would be one thing; the ability to form large storms and cause so much water to erupt was another. Most conceded that they had witnessed a miracle of epic proportions.

Revwar removed his hidden hand, throwing his arms out wide. "Thus, will your desires be fulfilled under the messiah. Drink and be fulfilled! Make yourself ready to be led by one who shares the favors of gods and the land!"

*   *   *   *   *

Revwar used more "miracles" and magical deceptions to appeal to the masses of nomads. The demon-dominated elders did their part, feigning awe and validating Revwar as the prophet who would show the tribes to their messiah. For those hundreds of massed nomads who still questioned their leaders, they were slowly convinced that there was something special about this elf. Some even adopted a passionate fervor. The ones who knew the truth and wanted to complain most vehemently could not…they were trapped inside their own bodies by the demons from Ibleu Taraz.

Support of this new prophet grew from a curiosity to fanatic fealty. Despite scattered events of violence between some rival nomads, the tribes banded together. The tribes still retained some sense of illusionary sovereignty under their demon-controlled leaders, but in the end, all were directed as one.

The tribes took their own pilgrimage. The procession gathered up more numbers as they went. They enslaved more wandering nomads, whether by subtle words or open force. The crowds would have been a strain on the natural resources of the land, but Revwar used the relics to bring forth what was required to sate the masses.

More time was needed before the Stonelands would be accessible. They spent those weeks training the skills of the tribes' warriors. Revwar and the demons sorted out the best natural leaders among the tribes, the best archers, the best horsemen…they planned the roles in which all would participate once battle started. They spent time solidifying the nomads' support and allowing them to believe Revwar was indeed a divine-sent blessing. Revwar did have a messiah that required summoning from Ibleu Taraz, but to do things too quickly would risk unnecessary exposure of the demon that would play the part.

While Revwar led the tribes through fertile lands, the Stonelands suffered from famine.

*   *   *   *   *

Late in the harvest season, during the last couple weeks of Novak, the amassed nomads came to a place considered holy to them. In the expanse of plains resided one large, rocky hill standing tall amidst the grasslands. They called it Lethnurial. Tribal lore revealed that a great battle had taken place here, between the jaws of three separate armies. The battle had been one of the last of the Godswars before the Covenant caused the tribes' ancestors to be stranded on this land. They no longer knew the reasons or importance of the battle, except that during a few days of fighting each side struggled to capture this hill in order to obtain the higher ground. Remnants of that battle were still discovered from time to time. Metal arrowheads, rusted blades and blackened rocks could be found.

Revwar led them to this hill because it was known as a place of great loss of life among the nomads. A few tribes claimed their ancestors fought here, though the haze of time did much to reshape memories. All of the tribal shamans and mystics considered this place hallowed ground. The people remained standing on the plains as Revwar ascended the hill. In the shadow of some rocks, he turned to address them. The elf wizard, and his demon conspirators, had done a masterful job convincing the nomads that he was nothing short of the right hand of all their gods and even the land itself. They listened as he proclaimed to be ready to call upon their messiah. From their vantage, they couldn't see the runes drawn on the ground at Revwar's feet. Only if the Companions of the Relics were here, would anyone recognize the pattern as the same one drawn in a keep out at sea. As it was, the nomads saw nothing other than their hero standing upon the ledges of their holy ground.

The air cracked with energy as the mage brought forth his spell. He expressed the words written on a tome from long ago. The effort would have been less taxing if Savannah had been here to help him. As things were, the demons controlling the tribal leaders hummed mantras which lent him their strength, and made the nearby tribesmen feel as if they assisted in the summoning.

All of that combined effort produced a small gateway to Ibleu Taraz, beckoning the coldast demon to come forth. The large figure, Norzal by name, willingly embraced the expected portal. His essence left his home world, the realm appropriately named as "forsaken fruit". The taraz swept through the curtain separating the two worlds, arriving in Dhea Loral an instant later. His appearance on the summoning circle seemed as if he stepped from the face of the rock itself. The nomad people of the Tribal Expanse got their first view at the savior they had begun to worship…a cruel being that harbored no love for them at all.

Norzal's large, bulky frame stood higher than Kor Strongarm's tall frame. His width compared to his height made him seem blocky enough to compare to a dwarf's proportions. Covered as he was in his cloak and robes, no one could see details of his features. They accepted him as humanoid, even if he was taller-than-life. For some reason, it seemed appropriate that a man heroic in stature should appear to lead them.

His robes hid his foreign nature. The nomads could see wisps of some strange, ethereal mist that swirled around his body. They had been told that even the air and water stood by to serve him. The essences were only a whisper away and would do his bidding. Those who saw him up close thought he had a hard, stony shell of a mask. His gloves looked like rock. They simply assumed it was part of his miraculous heritage, since he had been born of the earth to lead them.

The nomads bowed at his appearance. Their heads and shoulders dipped as if a wave of wind bent a field of tall grass. Some went so far as to prostrate themselves with bellies

114

pressing the ground, crying their praises. They prayed for thanks and for forgiveness. They prayed for victory over those who had built homes on their land.

His words came to them as a deep rumbling. It sounded as if his voice emanated from vibrations in stone. "My people, my family, it is *you* who have given *me* life, yet it is *I* who will lead *you* to a better way of living. Your hearts have called out to me, and I am bound by your wishes."

Inside, the taraz found amusement in the whole spectacle. He cared nothing for these soft, indigenous slaves. The people of the tribes were as much a threat to his conquest of Dhea Loral as the people of Stonelands. It brought him some mirth that his fellow demons had inspired the nomads to a fanatical following. With the powers of the Earthrin Stones, he could level Fortress Stone, yet it was far better to shred apart the nomads and the defenders against each other. Let them destroy themselves, before the demon army would be summoned to conquer all.

He kept such feelings guarded deep within while he placated the masses. He spoke words to their hearts. Norzal moved among them, keeping his face in the shadows. They received his passing like a god among men. Many continued to kneel; they lacked the right to stand and face this titan who towered over all. Those who looked saw a dark-brown face, though one that looked out of the ordinary. It looked hard as stone and rough in places. Any inner warnings set off by that glimpse of his visage were soon discounted and ignored.

Norzal and Revwar soon retreated into the largest tent which had been found among the nomads. Some of the tribal elders joined them for a time. Whatever was said in the presence of the demon-controlled leaders was brief. Norzal and Revwar wanted a private meeting. The elders came out and continued to play their part for the crowd, praising the messiah that now walked among them.

*   *   *   *   *

Norzal had been Revwar's first ally. Before the wizard had even met Savannah, he had plotted with Norzal decades before. Since they had known each other for so long, the demon had no need to wear his disguising cloak once they were free from the sight of others. The coldast let the cloak fall open and uncovered his head.

Revwar knew the truth behind the mist shrouding the taraz's rough, brown appearance. The nature of the coldast demon meant he was part undead and part elemental. Once upon a time, he was a hero for Mothrok in the Godswars that ravaged his world. So great was his devotion and resourcefulness, that after his death she resurrected him as earth and spirit. The Goddess of Earth and Stone did not restore true life to him; therefore, he had no need for food or even air. Instead, he resided in a stone body, with the essence of his undead intellect wreathing him like mist. One could see his dark-gray, stone skeleton peeking through parts of his rocky exterior. His fingers ended in such bony claws as could rake a numbing cold through any creature they touched. The bones were so smooth as to seem polished. A shifting mass of brownish-gray rocks covered much of his body. They were bound together by Mothrok's power within him. He could shift and move around the rocks to match his tastes. He could cover his skeletal face with those rocks, maintaining a brownish, rough appearance partially enclosed by his hood. If one only had a passing glance, he might appear humanoid when covered in shadows. More often, Norzal would simply allow the stone to migrate elsewhere to display his skeletal face.

This creature of rocks had little need for clothing or coverings under the cloak. The holy symbol of Mothrok had been branded upon the large slabs composing his chest. In those long ago Godswars, he must have been a paladin or cleric that was highly devoted to her. After his death, her reward was undead immortality inside a resilient elemental covering. Even as he shed away the front of his robes, Revwar could see the wide straps across his torso. It was a gruesome sight to behold. The straps had numerous dried and twisted pieces of leather attached. The uncounted ears of his defeated enemies hung as trophies.

The elf mage reserved a lot of respect for this demon. The Godswars may have ended a millennium and a half ago, but this coldast survived all that time fighting in a world that endured endless wars since the Covenant.

Norzal's face assumed his skull appearance as he looked upon the mage. The taraz could see clearly, yet he allowed the ghostly mist to form the pair of glowing blue orbs which represented his eyes. It had an unsettling effect on anyone who witnessed it.

The transformation finished as the creature rumbled in its deep voice. "Your work here appears good…with exceptions. I worry for whom I do not see. Once, you had a powerful minotaur at your side. You also had a mentalist who would have helped with our situation in these tribal lands. Let us not forget our most important missing ally, Savannah."

Revwar did his best not to shrink from the demon's stare. "Never underestimate the power of young, adventurous fools. I tell you truly, I only mourn the loss of Savannah. Her goddess forced her down a conflicting path; one I could not follow if I was to carry out our goals here."

The evil coldast released a sound that could have been a snort of amusement. His ghostly mist danced around his solid bulk. "I could refer to you as a young, adventurous fool."

Revwar's eyes narrowed at the reminder that his long elf years were short compared to the centuries of this undead demon. Norzal continued, "Before you glower, I must grant you an acknowledgment. I owe you more than any others. Only you have brought us to this point. Many seasons passed in both worlds as the relics languished in hiding. Our own harvest is at hand. You have been instrumental in bringing us to this horizon."

The golden eyes of the elf mage received his praise gladly, while hiding the anxiousness of his promised reward. He could not restrain himself from reminding the demon of their past agreements.

Revwar's words attempted to do so in a subtle way. "Mothrok was indeed deserving of my devotion. I knew she could offer the power I sought, and her request was an honor to carry out. I look forward to what havoc her minions will bring forth upon this world."

The taraz seemed to chuckle at this. "Fickle mortals. They always dream of power, yet each bit achieved only makes them insatiable for more."

Without warning, the cold arm of the demon clasped Revwar near the collar. The elf belatedly tried to jerk back, but he was caught by the necklace clutched in the demon's stone claws. "The Gitouro necklace. An impressive bonus in your adventures. I require it."

"To the conqueror go the spoils!" Revwar protested in his quiet, yet commanding, voice.

"So," the demon reasoned, "I must conquer you to own it?"

At the dangerous glimmer in the coldast's ghostly blue eyes, Revwar relented. The elf wordlessly ducked his head, allowing the necklace to slide freely into the demon's grip. Only this powerful ally, one who would repay him with arcane power, could humble the wizard.

Norzal placed the necklace around his neck. He sighed in content, making a low rumble within his stones, pleased with the power represented in that item.

Revwar would not be ignored. "As long as I have your word that my reward will be all as was promised. I believe I have served you well."

"Have I not taught you enough in these past years? You must realize my lessons granted you more control of the elements than many Dhea Loral wizards understand. I assure you, there is much more I can offer to enlighten your mind. Practice the patience inherent in your chosen field of study. You would do well to remember, that it was *you* who first approached *me…*"

…and with those words Revwar finished his spell of summoning. Rather than pulling a demon into the realm of Dhea Loral, he opened a communication link to speak to one whose name he had discovered in old scrolls. If the elves of his community discovered such magic in practice, Revwar would be immediately exiled or killed. He didn't care.

The mirror made of flowing water misted over, before a skull made of stone gazed back at the elf mage.

"Who dares speak my name and attempt to compel me to obey the call of a lesser world?" The voice of the coldast rumbled.

Revwar did not reveal much at first. The elf mage explained his needs to the demon, yet was rudely interrupted.

"Power and immortality!" Norzal roared, his blue eyes nearly aflame. "You and every mortal of Dhea Loral seek to learn our secrets for your own private ends! What makes you think I am able or willing to grant either? How will it help me in my world?"

"It will serve you through your devotion. I'm told you champion Mothrok's cause…is this correct?"

The demon stared back, "It is; I am bound to her will. I doubt you share similar allegiances."

"For the mysteries of the elements and the powers of magic she can share, I would gladly pledge myself to her. The elves who dabble in magic here place too many limitations due to their beliefs in nature. I would place myself in a position to control nature, not be controlled by it."

"Words…only words. What can you give to prove your worth?"

Revwar thought carefully before responding. He weighed how much he should admit. "I was recently assigned to protect the location of a relic from the Godswars. It is something that may be of great value to Mothrok."

The elf hoped that would be enough to glean some more information from the coldast. The skull in the mirror displayed no emotions. The low voice uttered forth, "Tell me more. What is the item in question? Speak and it may be worth something."

"It is an Earthrin Stone."

Revwar paused to let that sink in. Norzal leaned back and considered the information. It almost seemed a test of patience, as the seconds passed by.

The taraz hid any emotion as it asked, "Only one?"

"Aye." The elf wizard decided to add more, feeling that Norzal was not totally satisfied with that answer. "There is a document that describes more. It was copied from an older scroll years ago. While I don't know the entirety of the document, I am aware that it describes where the other stones were sent after the Covenant."

Norzal nodded to the wizard, "You have indeed accomplished a small favor for She Who Is The Foundation. One of those stones is not much by itself. The relics were made to counter each other. Can you obtain this…document…of which you speak?"

"Nay, not by myself. It would be very unlikely. The guarded text is kept with the stone, yet it is encoded. I know part of it from helping to translate the earlier scroll. However, those of us who performed the task were only allowed to do small portions each. There is a key to decoding the scroll. I believe an acquaintance, Reatheneus Bilil, holds it."

The demon made a rumbling noise which Revwar interpreted as the 'hmm' sound some humans make. At this, Revwar volunteered more. "Even if we don't get this scroll, I do recall the general locations of where the others were sent. One was sent to a fortress in Orlaun; the other was carried by a priest of Yestreal into the wilds of northern Quoros. We may be able to find them if we look."

Norzal's blue eyes flared a moment. "This will be good. Yestreal cheated Mothrok's followers out of their joint venture. DeLaris would find this interesting as well, but only if my mistress wills it. Say naught of this to any priests of DeLaris. They may be of use to us, but my goddess will make such a decision. I will pray to Mothrok and share this with her. I'm sure she will find a suitable reward for you. I must ask, is this all you plan to offer? Will you be willing to search for the other stones for her?"

Revwar nodded. "I would gladly serve her to become a wizard unmatched in power in this realm. Immortality is worth the price."

With that, the coldast seemed to utter a cold, rumbling laugh. It looked down upon its own elemental body. "Mortals often think so…the truth may surprise you…"

CHAPTER 15   **"Preparing to Sail"**

Visitors crowded Kashmer's seminary of Abriana. It had become the focus for the city's efforts to handle the impending problem in the Stonelands. The government took the threat to Fortress Stone seriously, though they were partly guided by the value of gold. Kashmer profited well from trade with the Stonelands. Ongoing magical communications stressed the starvation problems that had taken hold in that frontier country. The land would not support crops and the livestock were all dying.

Ships in the harbor were being loaded with provisions to aid those people, though not all of it was donated in the spirit of goodwill. Stonelands sent money in return, promising more once the threat passed. More ships were being readied with nearly empty holds. These would carry the people who crowded the seminary.

Abriana's faithful had heard the call for arms and journeyed to take part. The goddess manifested in their dreams and sent a summons over much of the continent. Paladins and clerics filled the halls around the church.

Outside the seminary, a motley crew of the most unusual variety appeared and set up camp. There was little order to the layout or types of tents. There was even less order observed among those who camped there. Kashmer had put forth a lot of effort from their navy to support the coming battle, but they had fewer to spare in the way of a standing army. Instead, they sent privateers.

Adventurers and mercenaries pitched camp around the seminary grounds. Some generally only worked as individuals, though most were part of small, chartered parties. There were guilds present such as the Sword & Sail that catered to adventurers. Even such notorious guilds were loosely structured in the field. A wide variety of races, appearances, and attitudes could be found. While Trestan and his companions had been pleased to see help forthcoming, they were soon dismayed at the troubles these groups created. It seemed that although Kashmer invited the privateers and offered them pay for their service, the city did not want to take full responsibility for them. No one directed the small army. Kashmer simply sent them up the hill to the seminary since it was Abriana's worshippers that seemed to be organizing everything else.

To complicate matters, a number of merchants who dealt goods from their carts or donkeys decided they might be better off setting up shop next to all these people rather than attempt to do business next to the city. Many hoped to cater to the deep pockets rumored to belong to adventurers; instead, some adventurers thieved and swindled from the locals.

The only one of the companions who really enjoyed walking into the sordid tent city was Mel, who explained to Trestan: "So many people to meet down there! I normally haven't seen so many non-humans around a city like Kashmer unless I walk into the slums. It's good to meet so many gnomes and dwarves. Well, there was one group of dwarves who didn't seem to want to talk. I mentioned my fervent devotion to Daerkfyre. Despite the beards, I could see their veins sticking out of their skin. I thought they were honored since their faces went red, likely blushing that a lowly gnome would call on their god like he was my own father. They may have been embarrassed, because they all turned their back to me.

I'm guessing they were all red and ashamed, and since dwarves don't do well showing emotions, it was more honorable to turn their backs. Anyway, I even asked if they had a spare holy symbol of Daerkfyre, (since I'm slowly trying to convert Aijak over), and one offered to brand the symbol into my hide…which of course wasn't what I meant at all, so I excused myself.

"Oh, and I saw someone that seemed half-raulgan and half-human. Since I'd never really met a raulgan before, I asked her about her race. After asking her a few questions, it seems she didn't want to tell all of her story. She didn't share what happened with her raulgan father, only admitting that she was raised by her human mother. Well, I was so excited to learn about the race, I asked her all kinds of things. She couldn't answer most of my questions. She didn't know anything of the raulgans' language, she didn't know where to find any of them, and when I asked her how much raulgan anatomy differs from human anatomy she just kind of stared and pretended she didn't hear the question. About the only thing she did voice was a generalization, indeed a correct one, that gnomes are too nosy for their own good. Well, I happen to agree with her! Hence the old saying, 'curiosity killed the gnome'.

"After that, I had a fun discussion with some other sorcerer who was trying a magical experiment. During the entire time we talked he seemed distracted, so I tried to offer a few pointers. He got clumsy after that, set his tent on fire, so I moved on…"

Apparently, Mel was the only one who enjoyed the distraction of the tent city. The camp persisted as an eyesore to the seminary's owners until a message from Kashmer arrived addressed to Katressa Bilil. She took it back to the room she shared with Trestan. When she opened it and read the beginning of the message, she mentioned, "It has to do with the camp of privateers."

Trestan asked, "Are they finally going to do something about it? Have they taken our complaints seriously?"

Cat's face went pale as she continued reading, until she sat down heavily on their bed. Her jaw hung open as she reread the words on the paper.

Trestan saw her expression, and simply said, "Uh oh."

"Damn right it isn't good!" Cat yelled, her face beset with worry, "After considering my vast experience and successes assisting Kashmer in disposing of many bandits, and due to my personal history dealing with this matter…*they put me in charge of that mob!*"

Kashmer's officials decided it was less stress on them if they simply appointed a privateer in charge of the privateers.

*   *   *   *   *

Weeks went by as final preparations were carried out to the fleet in Kashmer. The companions kept busy in their own separate ways.

Lindon stocked up on paper and ink. He found ways to insert himself into every part of the seminary grounds and worked on composing songs or stories on whatever happened to catch his fancy. Shortly after watching him entertain some privateers, Cat cornered him and drafted him into her service. The half-elf faced the seemingly impossible task of maintaining peace in the tent city. With Lindon's assistance, the job slowly became easier. The minstrel helped influence people. Soon, Lindon helped Cat find a number of respected adventurers that worked to help put some order and function into the tent city. The job wasn't as simple as words might imply. A few bones got broken, by Cat or by someone defending her, causing a few privateers to realize that they hadn't signed up for easy money. She ran her rapier through a couple of them. Some were chased out of service altogether, tents aflame in their wake. For Cat, disposing of such degenerates helped send a signal to the rest while getting rid of blades that might turn tail and run when battle was imminent. Once she restored some semblance of order, the seminary could actually sleep at night without stray spells exploding outside their windows. Cat and her core of entrusted aides began to shape the privateers for organization in a large battle. There was much the half-elf wasn't knowledgeable about, yet she delegated to those who seemed capable.

Petrow often felt like the odd man on the outside of anything except where his friends were involved. He wasn't a follower of the seminary, though he shared a room with Hebden and some other servants. His roof and meals were earned through carrying out odd jobs like when he had lived in Troutbrook. If it wasn't for the occasional presence of one of the companions, or the distraction of the jobs that came up around the grounds, Petrow would have felt a depressing sense of loneliness. He didn't care to visit the tent city much. The adventurers who sang and drank there did not appeal to him at all. When he wasn't doing chores, he went into the training fields where the students of Abriana studied weaponry. Petrow practiced with his axe. Wearing the enchanted leather and steel breastplate he had discovered years earlier, he mimicked what other students did as they went through their routines.

As Petrow practiced, a paladin of Abriana joined him inside a corral fence. "Petrow, do you remember my name? I am Leander, a friend of Trestan."

Petrow paused in swinging his axe to consider the warrior. "I remember you. A pleasure to meet you again. What brings you here?"

"Trestan was busy with something, yet he saw you out here alone," Leander explained. "I know the seminary won't train you, since you aren't an acolyte. Luckily for you, I don't mind keeping my skills up. Trestan suggested that maybe you wouldn't mind someone with whom to practice."

Petrow accepted the help graciously and learned a few things from the paladin. The two men sparred almost daily. Petrow enjoyed being able to prepare for the upcoming showdown, as well as have someone distract him from some of the loneliness he felt being separated from his family.

Hebden Karok worked tirelessly. Never before had he put so much effort into something. Racks of weapons, metal shields, and pieces of armor stacked up for the seminary to use. The weapons weren't fancy at all. Hebden had made many more plows than swords in his days. The armaments were practical and would simply perform well. The privateers from the tent city even approached him and gave him some of their business. They set higher expectations, and Hebden gave what effort he could without taking time away from his main focus.

Trestan stayed busy with many projects. He tried to give Cat a hand with putting things in order with the privateers, but she gently rebuked him. Apparently, he was 'too soft' on people for what she needed to do. It was better for him to let her do things her way. When evenings came, and she found her way to their bed, he massaged the worries of the day out of her muscles.

Trestan's focus switched to the seminary instead of the privateers. The paladin who would lead the seminary's forces to Stonelands would be Sir Theros Lightshield. He was a warrior with much experience. The veteran was not too old in years that he was unable to swing a sword powerfully. He reminded Trestan of Sir Wilhelm Jareth. The man seemed to have a fatherly appeal as well as a bold sword arm. One of Trestan's duties was to pass along knowledge, from the scroll Cat had translated, on how to control the Earthrin Stones if they ever came into possession of one.

For those acolytes that knew Trestan from his time studying at the seminary, he lived true to his kindness and helpfulness. Trestan worked with the students who were fast approaching the time of their Embarking. He helped them in their lessons. They asked of his adventures, and he didn't mind sharing some details and how it affected his faith. He spent much of this time with one particular student. His friend, Rhijin, hoped to join them in the Stonelands after her Embarking. Rhijin should have graduated with Leander and Trestan, but she failed her Embarking. One particular challenge, in which she faced an angry animal, had worried her. Trestan did his best to ready Rhijin for her next test. He told her about how the test wasn't about facing a fearsome creature; it was the conviction to help someone who needed it, despite them not understanding your good intentions. The curly-haired woman applied herself hard to her lessons. She did not want to fail again.

Trestan also found time to work side-by-side with his father. He enjoyed sharing time around the anvil again. His arm muscles kept warm as he pounded metal into shape.

Mel and Aijak set up their own tent somewhat distant from the tent city of the privateers. Mel wouldn't have minded the people, but Aijak preferred to camp closer to nature, away from all the ruffians. Needless to say, the spot suited Cathag better as well. Much as the dog sniffed at the cooking smells riding the wind, it distrusted the strange humanoids. Sometimes, the sorcerer could be seen studying scrolls of arcane text, while nearby, Aijak would be tending to a garden. This late in the year the garden was not obvious, and even Mel made remarks that Aijak's efforts would not be seen until next year…long after they had moved camp. The gnome druid, maintaining her tranquil demeanor, simply responded that the garden would still be there even if she didn't see it. In this way, she kept busy even as Mel pondered arcane magic. He focused on the subject of demonology. The sorcerer hoped he could find some arcane formulas that would help against the taraz.

*　　　　*　　　　*　　　　*　　　　*

Sondra's mind swam with thoughts as she made her way through Ganden's church in Orlaun. The cleric took little note of the path to her room. Her thoughts focused inward, sorting through the words spoken at the meeting of clergy.

She almost ran into her roommate. By comparison, Montanya wore a broad smile and practically bounced with energy. "There you are!"

Sondra was shaken from her thoughts as Montanya blocked her path. The red-haired youth couldn't contain her exuberance. "I was looking for you and someone said they had the priests cooped up in a meeting. What was that all about?"

The wheat-blonde woman was going to respond, but found herself at a loss for words. She didn't know how to share the news with Montanya while the younger woman was obviously in such a good mood. Sondra gently reached for Montanya's arm and guided her to a side alcove.

Her words gently deflected the chiaso's query. "I'll tell you in a moment. First, tell me: what has gotten you so excited?"

"Oh aye," Montanya was glad to impart her good news before listening to the reason for Sondra's glum looks. "I'm sure you remember that stray alley cat that keeps wandering around the docks' sanctuary?"

Images of the cat in question did lighten Sondra's expression. "The one you and a few others kept feeding and encouraging? Of course."

"Well…guess what?"

As those greenish-blue eyes stared at her, Sondra realized that Montanya was trying to drag out the story as long as possible. The cleric didn't feel in the mood for games, but she spoke without being harsh.

"Don't keep me hanging on here. We're both going to be busy shortly. Crack the treasure chest open already!" She said, a popular saying in Dhea Loral.

Montanya giggled and conceded, "All right, I'll get to the point. The reason we haven't seen the cat around the last few days is that she gave birth to a litter of babies!"

"Wow, I thought it was just fat off the portions people kept feeding it."

Montanya cupped her hands like a ball. "Nay, it had a few little ones smuggled under its fur. She gave birth to them, now she's created a nest for herself and her babies in Thorson's alley. Some of the people have brought milk and food scraps to the family."

Sondra chuckled as Montanya continued. There was a happy gleam in her eyes as the chiaso stated. "I bet that must be a cute sight! I'm going there tomorrow evening too and see for myself."

The happy expression on the cleric's face fell as her roommate said more, "I plan to bring a few food scraps also. Oh, can you imagine how cute those little kittens must be?" Montanya couldn't miss how suddenly the smile vanished from Sondra. "Why are you frowning all the sudden?"

Sondra sighed and looked to the side. She took a little too long to voice her thoughts, so Montanya maneuvered herself back into the older woman's line of sight. There was no ignoring those questioning eyes.

The shy cleric got past the lump in her throat. "We won't be here tomorrow night. The ship is ready and stocked. My superiors have decided not to wait any longer. In the morning, we sail for the Stonelands."

Montanya stepped back, as if Sondra's words had physically pushed her. This time, it was the red-haired youth who averted her eyes. One nimble finger went to the side and traced a mosaic on the wall before she could speak again. For the first time, Montanya's mind seemed to pay attention to the hubbub in the church. Clerics and acolytes rushed around in a fuss, asking questions and talking about what to bring and what not to bring.

The red-haired youth asked. "So, it's time for war already?"

Sondra nodded. Realizing Montanya wasn't really looking at her, she offered, "Unless you have decided to stay here? Some clergy have to stay behind to run the church."

"Stay here?" Montanya's gaze snapped back up. There was a flash of emotion in her visage as if she had been insulted. It smoothed over immediately as the chiaso spoke. "Nay, I planned to go and help see this quest finished, and that is what I will do. As long as you are headed to a fight in the Stonelands, then that is where I need to be."

Sondra nodded with a grin. "But you'll miss working at…a copper pen."

Montanya, realizing the cleric was making one of her few attempts at humor, adopted the same stern disposition Sondra had shown at times. She shook her finger at Sondra like she was giving a lecture.

"The proper term is Sanctuaries for Those in Need. I won't have you disrespectfully calling them copper pens." As Sondra gave a little laugh, Montanya relaxed. The youth's expression turned sincere when next she spoke. Her eyes glanced over the decorated halls of the church. "I will miss this. In some ways it doesn't feel like, 'me', but then again, I'm still trying to find what 'me' is. Regardless, it has been something that has made me feel truly proud. I've felt like a part of something. My actions here have contributed something, and lifted my spirits."

Sondra grinned. "The poor admire your antics and ask for you when we aren't there. They will mis you while we're gone. You'll be happy to come back here when our task in the Stonelands is done?"

Montanya smiled, "Aye. I think I'd like to come back here and see if this lifestyle grows on me." The chiaso offered her friend a big hug, "Now, I guess we better get packed for the journey."

*   *   *   *   *

The ships carrying the companions, the followers of Abriana, and the Kashmer privateers were already a few days out at sea when a letter arrived in Troutbrook. It was carried to the small village by Kashmer Protectorate soldiers marching to replace some of the garrison at Dunker Keep. The letter found its way to a small farm where a woman and her children had taken refuge with her parents.

Inedra's heart caught in her chest as she recognized Petrow's poor handwriting addressed to her. Although her family was interested in what the note had to say, Inedra left them with her children as she excused herself. Taking a handkerchief, she sought out a secluded corner of a barn. She sat on a stool inside an empty stall. She glanced around her surroundings, judging as if she were truly alone except for the baby she felt kicking inside her abdomen. She took a deep breath, pulling some of her auburn strands aside so she could see the paper easier. With shaking fingers, she broke the wax seal Petrow had found and she set her eyes on his words.

"Dearest Inedra, my one and true love,

"The ship will be leaving soon, and it has not been easy coming up with the words that express my feelings. It would be wonderful if the gods could grant me the tongue of a minstrel just this once, that I might best say what I want to say. Although I would like to assume the confidence I display for everyone else, and thus assure you that I will be alright…I also know that there is a chance this may be my last letter. It pains me enough that my words come to you by this indirect route when I long to feel your kiss.

"We both want to grow old together, watching the tall harvests of our field as our children mature and bring us many grandchildren. These many weeks I've been living in the bustle of the city. It is hard to believe I once thought I would chase my dreams in a big place

124

such as this. I've learned that the quiet life we live is the best life for me. I want our children to grow strong and free in this open land. I gave you my reasons for leaving. Though the danger seems far away, it will find us soon enough and destroy the future we plan if it isn't stopped. Fate calls me to go forth.

"I'm sure you remember why you fell in love with me, but allow me to remind you in my own words. You said you saw something special in me when I returned from my adventure those years ago. You felt that I had something in me which put me above the others in our small community. You always called me, 'my hero', and ever since that title I've tried my best to be the greatest husband and father I could be, because of your belief in me. It is that same special something in me that tells me I have to do what I'm doing now.

"You know I don't like it when anyone else but you calls me a hero. I may have once dreamed of being a hero, but the events from that adventure never made me feel like one. Our society has made the mistake of labeling someone a hero because we place them on pedestals that none can truly touch. We say our heroes have the strength to move mountains, are blessed with the gods' own luck, never make mistakes, have the wisdom of a seer, and can stand against armies by themselves. I have always rejected such a vision of heroes. I guess my definition of a hero is a person willing to do what he feels he has to do for those he loves, even though it scares him terribly. To that end, a hero is entirely mortal and ultimately may end up offering his life…but it is a risk that he must take. If you agree with this definition of a hero, then maybe I can be your hero one more time.

"I'm told that even if we win, we are not likely to return until after the winter. It will be a long wait for both of us. I will do my best to find my way back to your arms. If I should fall, yet succeed in keeping the demons from ever coming close to our home, then you must live to see our dreams come true. Tend the land and raise the children until their children are playing in our fields. If you do this, my soul will always be by your side, because that future is my vision of heaven.

Loving you forever, Petrow"

CHAPTER 16 "Reunion in Pilgrim's Bay"

Scouts from Fortress Stone were reporting a large mass of tribes gathered out on the plains, just as the first ships arrived on the horizon. Kashmer's and Abriana's pennants waved proudly in greeting to the harbor of Pilgrim's Bay. The vessels bore more food than they did troops…and the food was welcomed first. The Stonelands had been hit hard by famine. Eager dockhands helped unload the precious cargo and distribute it to guarded warehouses. The nobles of the Stonelands set about managing how much to hand out to the populace, and how much would be moved up to the castle in anticipation of the fight. They argued regarding the large amount of food that was reserved on the ships. Sir Theros Lightshield, overall commander of the forces of Abriana and Kashmer, proved uncompromising about the extra food stores. He knew that if all the food was placed inside the castle at once, it could once again be rotted away easily by the Earthrin Stones. Instead, a large store would stay safely offshore and to the south. If the battle was won, they had more food to distribute, but if the battle was lost, less food would fall into the hands of their enemies.

As the companions disembarked from the boats with the army, they got their first glance at the place they would defend.

Pilgrim's Bay sprawled under the plateau which supported the old castle. The castle itself stood impressive in scope and length. Many generations had added more and more to its defenses and size until it could claim to be one of the largest castles ever built…even as large as some built during the prosperity preceding the Godswars. The walls stretched long and tall, with no less than a score of towers reaching for the clouds. The castle enjoyed protection on all sides by a set of rivers and the edge of the plateau. The Hossan River brought water out from the Tribal Expanse and then split around the rocks at the foundation of the castle. The Hossan Major went around the south side of the castle, forming a swift and deep current that protected from that side. It was originally thought that most of Stonelands' enemies would come from that direction. All number of dangerous humanoids claimed the jungles to the south as their homes. On the north side of the castle ran Hossan Minor, more of a wide stream than a river. This smaller body of water had two crossing points. One was a wooden bridge that would support a couple horses side-by-side, the other was a ferry built to carry wagons across. A long bowshot could reach either from the castle ramparts.

At the base of the plateau, the two branches of the river fell, mingled, and converged into wetlands. The whole of Pilgrim's Bay was built north of this area for presumed safety from anything in the south. With the threat of the tribes massing in the north, there seemed to be little protection for the village from such a threat. Fortress Stone prepared to house the entire village, as well as shelter all the armies coming to assist.

The Stonelands' army was split between helping people move in an orderly fashion to the castle, as well as find a place for all the arriving warriors to stay. It seemed the locals accommodated their villagers in the castle first, then tried figuring how they would handle all the extra fighters. Not everyone was abandoning their homes and shops as yet, but the streets were packed with families moving in a rush of preparation.

In the confusion, Trestan and Katressa found time to get away and have a moment to themselves. They walked around Pilgrim's Bay, casting glances up at the castle they would defend.

Cat saw something and paused, putting a hand on Trestan's shoulder. She pointed out the sign of a newly-built inn. "The Temple of Ale!"

Trestan looked at the sign. It displayed the image of a hammer, ready to tap a keg, which rested on a temple. "That's Salgor's crest!"

The companions hurriedly entered the inn. There were no customers at this hour, yet they saw their familiar dwarf friend behind the bar. His back faced them as he set a keg in place. His sleeve was rolled up to reveal the fist-holding-hammer-in-flames tattoo that signified his worship of Daerkfyre, dwarven God of Valor. Trestan was about to announce a greeting, yet Cat halted him silently, putting a hand in front of him.

Adopting a deep, almost growling voice, she barked out. "I hear your swill isn't strong enough for a cowardly mage's belly!"

Salgor immediately jumped around, his face flashing a deep red. He seemed ready to grab his axe, but he halted as he saw who stood in his inn. He came very close to cracking a smile. As it was, he kept his mean look and declared, "You heard wrong! See if you can down a bellyful o' this and still be walking!"

Salgor filled a tankard with mock anger. He purposefully chose a very strong vintage. He slid it down the bar for the half-elf to catch. Cat, having to face her own medicine, caught it and began to slam the drink down her throat. Trestan didn't miss a wince flitting across her features. He was glad he hadn't chosen to greet the dwarf in such manner. However much the concoction burned her throat and made her head swim, Cat finished the challenge and slammed the tankard down empty. The infiltrator was well-skilled in keeping any discomfort or weakness hidden. Trestan had a feeling that she would probably be walking a crooked path soon.

Cat cleared her throat of the burning before answering. "I heard wrong, Salgor Bandago. Your ale is as tough as your axe!"

"That better be a compliment!" He shook one thick finger at her.

"Aye, it was," Cat said, "For I have nay intention of testing your axe next."

Salgor let loose a boisterous laugh and walked up to them. "Good to see ol' friends pay me a visit."

Trestan found himself on the receiving end of a strong handshake. "Old friends…but we've hardly heard a word from you since you left Troutbrook! Well, I haven't anyway."

"Think again if you think I want to visit a human holy school!" Salgor said, hugging Katressa next. "Meaning nay disrespect though, they seem to have filled out yer muscles well. Besides, I had a few adventures with Cat."

"One adventure…and you nearly got me killed!"

Salgor shrugged away the thought. "Ah, we didn't bite off more than we could chew up and spit out! Anyway, 'twas worth enough that I had the gold to build my dream. What brings you to my doorstep anyway?"

Trestan exhaled. "Those tribes that have gathered to attack the castle…"

Salgor waved a dismissive hand. "Bah, that scraggly lot? They don't even have decent weapons 'cept what folks here traded to them. I have a mind to charge into them, smack some manners into their poor skulls, and tell my patrons they can come back out o' hiding."

Just then, Mel Bellringer walked in, followed by Petrow. The gnome was, of course, the first to speak. "Trestan! You can't sneak away from your aide-de-camp like that!"

They both realized they were in the presence of an old friend. Petrow nodded to Salgor. "Good to see you again after so many years."

The dwarf looked over the man, noting the old woodcutter's axe he carried. "Keeping up your skills, lad? You're still using that ol' axe?"

Petrow spun the old weapon in his hands. "I've kept up a few things in between raising a family. As far as this thing goes, well, it has been dependable for any job I put to it." Petrow omitted the portion about his axe being relegated to chopping wood for the past several years.

"A dependable weapon is always the best weapon!" Salgor went over to greet Mel. "Are you still honoring Daerkfyre the Valorous, gnome?"

"I am! Good to see you, Salgor. Daerkfyre told me to come fight alongside my friends, so here I am! I brought the love of my life with me! Her name is Aijak, and she's the best thing to ever happen in my heart. I should introduce you…"

The dwarf waved off any further words before Mel rambled too much, "Can I get you something to drink first?"

Mel glanced at the bar, noticing the Cat's tankard. "I'll have what she's having."

Trestan, Cat and Salgor hid their conspiring grins as the dwarf went back to the strong keg. He filled a smaller tankard and brought it over to the gnome. Salgor motioned a thumb towards the half-elf as he said, "She finished hers in one swig. Can you beat that?"

The gnome raised it in a brief salute to the others. "Oh, I'll try."

Mel thrust his head back and drank deep from the tankard. Before long he was coughing and spilled some. "Good stuff," he exclaimed amidst tears.

Salgor peeked at his remaining liquid. "You can't out-drink a woman, gnome?"

The small figure protested as he looked up to Cat's height. "Well, I can't help it; her stomach is taller than me!"

Salgor let out a belly-shaking laugh. Mel tried to clarify what he said. "I mean her stomach is taller than my stomach…not taller than me. Am I turning red?"

After being apart for so long, the Companions of the Relics shared a good laugh together.

*   *   *   *   *

Hebden and Petrow found themselves in an unusual situation. As the army from Kashmer was being situated around the castle, those who were deemed more as laborers or craftsmen rather than fighters were sent to Fortress Stone to be assigned a support role. Hebden was a smith for Abriana's forces, so he was sent to be reassigned for whatever task Fortress Stone needed him. Petrow wasn't directly connected to the army, Katressa's privateers, or Trestan's church, thus he followed Hebden to find out where he would fit. As the two of them stood in a line of laborers, Petrow seemed to be the only one that stood out as wearing armor, even if it was mostly leather.

Hebden and Petrow looked out at the grounds between the castle and Hossan Minor. They noticed a number of men digging trenches or setting logs to make breastworks. Rocks and sand were being hauled around, while donkeys dragged logs to their assigned spots. As the two men from Troutbrook looked over the terrain, they saw tents being erected near the walls.

Petrow motioned toward the tents as he talked to Hebden. "What do you make of that? Someone camping out here?"

The blacksmith looked from the tents to the castle, before swinging his gaze back over Pilgrim's Bay below the plateau. "I'm wondering, have they run out of room inside? Looks like they will have soldiers camped out in these barricades, maybe defending the river."

Petrow considered the castle walls beyond the tents. "I'm amazed they don't just stand behind the walls. Putting men down here seems a big risk."

Hebden shrugged. "Seems that way to me too, but who knows? The enemy will have to cross this wide stream, carrying armor and weapons, under a rain of arrows and spells. Looks like whoever is in charge of the Fortress Stone decided to make that their first line of defense."

The line moved to a sergeant who was making the list of names and professions, assigning men to their positions. Hebden answered his questions. "Hebden Karok, blacksmith."

Petrow was looking over the ground as the man answered. "I'm sending you to the Carpenter Guild. They'll find a forge for you."

Hebden moved a few steps away, but paused to hear where Petrow would be assigned. The sergeant spoke to Petrow, but the young man barely registered the words. "Young man, what is your profession?"

Petrow, still distracted, replied. "Farmer."

It took a moment for the blue-eyed man to realize the soldier was having a chuckle at his expense. Petrow turned his eyes to focus on the man. The sergeant spoke. "Farmer? Dressed like that? We don't have much use for farmers. Can you handle that axe well?"

"Aye, I can. My name is Petrow."

The man nodded, "Fine, Petrow the farmer. Ok, I'll send you over to the Carpenter Guild as well. Don't be surprised if the first job they ask is to send you back here to build these barricades. Now move along."

Another man known by Hebden and Petrow walked past the line without stopping. Lindon Taleweaver was also in a position where he was not directly connected with any force, despite his assistance to Cat and the privateers. As far as he felt, that was the perfect arrangement. The minstrel had his own plans for how he intended to stay in Stonelands. He had gathered his instruments and belongings, before striding confidently up to the castle. By nightfall, he was living off the generosity of the nobles he entertained.

*   *   *   *   *

Two days later, the ships from Orlaun arrived after circling around the southern end of Shard. Stonelands began to sort through a new wave of fresh faces offering their support.

The banners of the Brotherhood of the Circles as well as the symbols of Ganden waved their greeting.

Trestan and Katressa were in Pilgrim's Bay when the ships docked, along with a few privateers who were willing to help Salgor stash some of his untainted supplies. They were rewarded with what drinks could be offered, while the dwarf's most prized brewing items were hidden from sight. All feared that Pilgrim's Bay would be ransacked. It had been rumored that Commander Ormiz, who was the front-line general of Stonelands' troops, had wanted to actively defend the town. The lord marshal and the king rejected the plan, fearing that the size of the nomad army could easily trap those defenders away from the castle. Thus, a number of valuables were hidden, buried or smuggled by their owners. A line of refugees, carrying goods they hoped with futility they could keep, dragged their feet up the incline to the castle.

Before the day was out, Cat had gotten a messenger to the docked ships and informed Korrelothar of their whereabouts. The wizard arrived bearing a few packages, bringing a few other familiar faces in tow. His guests included his wife Floranue, the cleric Sondra Oskires, and the chiaso Montanya. The old friends were happy to have a reunion at Temple of Ale, rather than in the cramped camp conditions up at the castle.

During the greetings, Trestan took note of a new holy symbol around Sondra's neck. He engaged her in a conversation in order to learn more. "How have your duties changed with your new office as cleric?"

Sondra offered a tiny smile between her full, red lips, "It has been busy, with lots more work with paper and less work with people. I knew some of the chores ahead of time, so it was not unexpected."

The paladin inquired, "You seem to have a new symbol around your neck, worn openly."

She blushed, but one hand reached down to lift the pendant higher for a better look. She had abandoned her dog-shaped symbol for one that looked like a lantern. "As my faith in Ganden has shifted in a new direction, I have also adopted a different set of his tenets. The old symbol was my humble sacrifice to man, but I realized I was sacrificing too much. This lantern is the 'light against the darkness' symbol. It represents my willingness to journey forth, guarding against the darkness using Ganden's spiritual light."

Trestan offered a gentle pat on her shoulder. "I have a feeling this will be a good change, for you and Ganden."

Across the inn, Korrelothar and Floranue were leaving the packages for Cat. Within moments, Trestan noticed Cat had disappeared with the packages in tow. The companions continued to talk and share rumors for several minutes. Eventually, Cat reappeared from the stairs to the vacant rooms on the second floor. Trestan noticed slight changes to her garb as the half-elf thanked the wizard.

Cat bowed. "These fit well. I already had fun trying out the boots upstairs! I most graciously thank you and your helpers for making them."

Korrelothar returned the gesture. "It was a pleasure to craft such interesting items. I hope they serve your purpose well."

The champion of Abriana reached out and felt the light leather of Cat's new cloak. The material was very soft, but even more impressive was the lack of weight. "This is new."

Cat smiled and spun in place, allowing the cloak to float in a circle around her. Her response was simple and yet non-revealing, "Aye, isn't it a lovely cloak?"

Trestan glanced down at her boots. They were certainly of good quality. He wondered what she had referred to when she mentioned having fun 'trying out the boots'. He did note some arcane runes etched into the leather. "And the boots?"

The paladin threw a glance at Korrelothar, but the wizard was doing his best to act occupied with other conversations and pointedly ignoring the conversation between his customer and her inquisitive man. Cat took Trestan's arm in her own and pressed herself close.

"Why, they are good for dancing!"

She whirled him around the room. Stepping to some tune only she heard. Trestan was only half into the effort, pondering the changes in her attire. Even as he looked down at the boots, he noticed an emerald gem buckle on a new belt about her waist. The belt had loops which held three potions, and a holster holding a bone dagger.

Cat's movements pulled him with more force into the dance. Trestan tried to keep up when suddenly one foot couldn't find the ground. He was weightless! It lasted one brief moment before his foot hit the ground and he stumbled slightly.

Cat finished the dance and swept out of his arms, commenting as she did. "Careful of the floor here, it seems to be uneven."

Trestan Karok knew he hadn't imagined that brief moment of weightlessness. He narrowed his eyes at Cat, wondering what tricks she was hiding. She offered an innocent smile and walked back to talk to the others. The half-elf was up to something, and as usual she was flaunting her secrecy without giving it away.

Salgor could be overheard yelling, "Who said my new floor was uneven?"

*　　　　*　　　　*　　　　*　　　　*

While Korrelothar visited Cat and Trestan at the Temple of Ale, Mel and Aijak rode Cathag across the Stonelands' countryside. The sorcerer knew that his lover needed time away from the small town and its large castle. The druid always wanted to explore the vastness of the world. Aijak loved to take nature rides on Cathag daily. Mel suggested they do so today. While away from the others, it gave him time to talk to her.

Aijak remained unconvinced of the sorcerer's reasons for making this trip. Although she respected his views, she still wondered what it meant to worship a dwarven battle god. She thought he was doing something dangerous that didn't really concern them.

During the ride, Mel talked to her at great length, (as always), trying to convince her of the nobility of their cause. Since she was a woman of the land, as apparent by her tree-tattoo on her cheek, he did not need to go into detail on the evil inherent in demons. Druids normally despised the taraz due to their corrupt and twisted nature. It was harder for Mel to convince her that they had to travel hundreds of miles to this place, only to be tangled between massive armies. The sorcerer tried to persuade her with stories of gnomish heroes.

"…and we know what happened. Tullo of the Longnose stood in that gap, facing the ogre, and readied his last spell. He didn't know the gnomes he defended, but he knew the evil that would befall them…"

Mel tried to downplay the upcoming battle at one time, making it sound like it would be easy. "…they won't ever get close to those walls anyway. How do the tribes expect to win? Nevertheless, I have to stand by my friends and make sure they don't get hurt…"

For all that Mel talked, it wasn't his words that had the most impact. Aijak listened but her eyes were on the stricken fields before them. Revwar's use of the Earthrin Stones had drained the land of its life. Trees should have been changing color, yet the leaves had fallen weeks ago. Bushes and grass had become dried and brown. The druid felt the sabotage of the earth all around her. Birds proved rare. A cow corpse rotted at the edge of a farmer's pasture. Barren fields replaced crops. Aijak felt the absence of life in the soil. Her throat felt dried up witnessing the parched fields. Entire farms were abandoned by the families they had once sheltered and nurtured. Cathag also walked with his ears and tail low, saddened by the smells reaching his nose. In the distance, Aijak saw an abnormally lean dog trying to claw the ground for something it smelled below. Unable to claim the morsel, it whined pitifully.

Aijak halted Cathag. Mel's stories stopped at the same time as the dog. He noted the druid's shoulders shaking as she sobbed. He put his small, comforting hand on her back. The sorcerer believed his words must have gotten through.

"I'm sorry, maybe I went into too much detail. You know why we must fight, don't you?"

She half-turned her teary face to Mel. She nodded, knowing why they were needed here.

CHAPTER 17 "Touring Fortress Stone"

A trio of companions made their way through the wall passages of Fortress Stone. They had gone to look for some of their friends; instead, the walk turned into one of aimless exploration of the large fortification. Salgor Bandago led them on their meandering course. Petrow followed the sturdy dwarf, half-listening to the warrior's ramblings as his mind tried to digest the amount of work that had gone into erecting these walls. Accompanying them was Trestan's friend, Sir Leander Swordbreaker, dressed in Abriana's colors. Magical sconces and external arrow ports lit their path.

They had set out to find Trestan and other familiar faces. Although unsuccessful in that regard, Petrow had the chance to introduce his new friend to his old friend. Both Salgor and Leander had trained Petrow at one time or another in the art of combat. They spoke of old fights, though Salgor had many more tales to share than the young men possessed. In truth, Petrow had very little that he could or would contribute. Conversations shifted as they walked about the halls. They couldn't believe that such a network of tunnels traveled within the outer fortifications.

Salgor explained his excitement about a recent development; some new combatants had arrived to aid the defenders. "I may have mentioned a dwarven clan nearby. They hail as the Fardiggers clan, led by King Bromodar. Their ore is durable; a very good quality. It makes dependable weapons that can hold a good edge. Many stones that make these walls came from the quarry just outside o' Drocham. That's the name o' their home. It translates to humans as Deephollow."

Petrow absently nodded as the bearded innkeeper continued. "More to the point, however, a company o' their fighters came to assist the people o' Stonelands. There weren't many o' my distant kinfolk that came. They don't need many! Just sixteen arrived, calling themselves 'Thornbeards', and carrying so many weapons 'round their middle that you can't tackle them without impaling yourself! Ha!"

"You know them well?" Asked Leander.

The three of them walked towards a dark alcove near an intersection. Salgor answered, "As much as any dwarves that have chatted for a few months. The ties between members o' my race take longer to grow compared to humans. I know they appreciate good ale! They lent a hand building the inn and helped fill my pouch with some o' their drink money."

Petrow's mind stalled on something else Salgor had mentioned. "Only sixteen warriors? It seems like a handful compared to the force camped here."

"The Fardiggers have got their own home to worry about. They've had to struggle with feeding their people and seeing to their own defenses. One company o' veteran warriors is generous enough. Don't forget, you have me as well. That makes seventeen dwarves, plus a few in the privateers, which by my guess is more than enough."

The men came to the alcove and paused to glance inside. "What's this?" A startled Leander exclaimed. "There is nay floor in there!"

Salgor and Leander seemed perplexed. Petrow noticed handholds built just inside the alcove. The opening lead to a vertical shaft within the wall, up and down, with no ladder rungs inside. The farmer from Troutbrook felt there was something familiar about it. He ventured a peek down the shaft. Comprehension dawned on his face in the form of an evil grin.

Petrow couldn't hide his mirth. "This castle has all the perks! Salgor, look down there. Recognize that?"

The dwarf had one hand on his axe as he stuck his head over the opening below. He only needed a glance. His knuckles went white as he jumped back from the alcove. "Cracks in the stone!" He cursed, "I'll have to move the inn several miles down the coast just to get away from that gnomish atrocity!"

His movement caused Leander to jump back; the paladin even laid a hand on the hilt of his sword out of reflex. "What devilry is enough to make a dwarf jump like that?"

Petrow had a good laugh at Salgor's expense. He recalled how much Salgor had hated the item the first time they had seen one. His laughter stopped long enough to retrieve a copper coin from his purse. Petrow made a show of displaying the simple coin before Leander, before throwing it into the shaft. They had to be at least on the second floor of the walls, yet when Petrow shouted "Two!" the coin was tossed back up and hovered on air for a second. The man from Troutbrook dipped his hand under the hovering coin, and the metal fell back into his palm.

Puzzled, Leander finally decided to have a look for himself down the shaft. His ponytail hung down as he spotted a circular disk of metal laying on the ground floor. Straightening up, he pointed down the shaft. "And that is…?"

Petrow looked ready to make the grand announcement, but his memory of the exact term failed him. He turned to Salgor, who had moved further down the hall. "What was the name of it? I forgot what Mel said."

"Gnomish catapult!" Salgor spat.

"Nay, that was your name for it. What did Mel call it?"

"A curse?"

Petrow snorted at Salgor. "You're nay help." He turned to Leander. "I guess most call it a lift…since the gnomes gave it some awkwardly long name that changes depending on how you use it."

Leander prompted for more. "What does it do?"

"It uses a magical cushion of air to lift a person or an object to the desired level of a structure. The most you can go is fifteen gnomish-equivalent levels. If the ceiling is actually lower than that, you can get quite hurt. If you go splat into the ceiling, it's your own fault. After all, these devices were made portable and gnomish engineers expect customers to use them properly."

Salgor rolled his eyes. Leander scratched his head.

Petrow went on, imitating Mel Bellringer's voice, "You stand on the disk and call out a number corresponding to how many floors up you want to go. For instance, calling out 'two' will get you to the first floor."

He did his best to hold a smile from his face as Leander puzzled over that explanation. The paladin asked, "Why would I be on the first floor after asking for two?"

"Simple," Petrow stated, though it obviously wasn't, "You have to convert for size. Gnome structures go up two floors for every one floor that humans build. In order to go up a floor, you have to ask for twice the number of floors that you wish to ascend."

Petrow was enjoying his game; Salgor obviously wasn't. The dwarf let out a sigh as he watched Abriana's champion trying to grasp gnomish logic.

The paladin glanced back down at the disk, "But why would I still be on the ground floor?"

"You wouldn't, you would be on the first floor. The ground floor would be below you."

Leander asked, "The ground floor isn't the first floor?"

Petrow shook his head as if he was lecturing a child. "Oh, you're talking about the backwards method humans have of numbering their floors; gnomes have a much better system!"

Salgor turned away. He made an announcement as he began walking down the hall. "I'm going to get ale!"

Petrow responded, "Don't you have some in a flask somewhere on you?"

The dwarf clarified, "I'm going to get ale that is farther away from gnomish contraptions."

*　　　　*　　　　*　　　　*　　　　*

Trestan had the feeling that Lindon Taleweaver wasn't new to the Stonelands. It seemed unlikely that, amidst such new faces and chaos planning for war, Lindon had been able to procure a tour of the castle for a few select people. It wasn't just any tour; their guide was no less than Cardinal Methlen Foresight. The cleric was a spiritual advisor to the king, and therefore the country's highest-ranking religious leader. Cardinal Methlen represented the church of The Codex; a religion that didn't so much depend on a single patron as much as a compendium of morals and philosophies that had been a joint venture of a few gods. He would have seemed unapproachable to most any strangers, yet the balding gentleman laughed and joked with Lindon.

Trestan realized he shouldn't be too surprised. Lindon had mentioned spending a year touring much of the known world, and the minstrel educated himself on the local politics of any region. Lindon made it possible for his companions, such as Trestan, to follow along. The young champion dressed in his best red-and-gold of Abriana to represent her well as he got to see the inner hallways of the keep.

Lindon would have made it possible for Katressa to attend, but she found her duties with the privateers very demanding. She had already used many liberties spending time with Trestan and visiting Salgor's inn, yet she had to help keep the privateers from aggravating Sir Theros Lightshield as well as the hosting castle. The infiltrator was setting her assigned charges into their respective defensive positions. The companions had already noted that the privateers were among those stationed outside the castle walls. Their campsite sat among the barricades facing the northern river. If the tribes attacked from there as expected, the privateers would be among the first to face them.

For reasons similar to Katressa's, Lindon failed to get Sir Penvos "The Steady" from the church of Ganden to attend. The cleric leader cited responsibilities to his people. Instead, he sent priestess Sondra Oskires in his stead. Trestan had to wonder if this wasn't somehow planned by Lindon in the first place. It seemed unusual that out of all the experienced clerics and paladins of Ganden that were available, their friend Sondra got the invite.

The party included a wizard to whom Lindon felt he owed a great amount of appreciation. Korrelothar Balshav, "The Highwater Conjuror", walked beside Lindon and the cardinal, speaking often. Floranue Balshav humbly bowed out, deciding to put her cooking skills to use feeding the large army.

Trestan wondered if Lindon had tried to get Montanya invited, since she was another close friend. The paladin could not know that Lindon had invited her, only to be turned down. Montanya was still coping with uncertainties about her future. She had been very prejudiced against the churches at an early age. Her time in Ganden's sanctuaries had done much to make her reevaluate her views. Lindon almost convinced her to come, but her stubborn streak rejected the invite. Their party did happen to get a glimpse of Montanya during the tour. She was on the banks of the Hossan Minor, doing the Butterfly in the Windmill motions. The chiaso was preparing her mind and body for the battle.

As Trestan listened to the cardinal point out various constructions and share tales of their history, he watched the disposition of the holy leader. If the cardinal felt unduly obligated to be giving a tour, he certainly didn't show it. In fact, he seemed to enjoy the walk. Lindon had met the cardinal earlier and suggested it as a healthy distraction. Trestan began to presume as much.

Generations of royal families had lived here before Pilgrim's Bay was born. In that time, it seemed there had been numerous periods of building and rebuilding to strengthen the fortress. The touring group was shown the interior layers of stone walls and the parapets among the towers. Trestan had to admit to himself that it would take an army of epic scale to break in and take the various sections of the fortress. Unfortunately, the power of the Earthrin Stones would make them vulnerable. All it took was a powerful relic to bring the walls crashing down. Trestan suspected that was why the river was considered the first line, in case the walls would prove useless. The young man tried to hide such concerns as he marveled at some of the tales Cardinal Methlen shared. The priest boasted about failed attempts to conquer the castle in the past.

They were interrupted as a gnome sorcerer finally tracked down Trestan's whereabouts. "Trestan! You're not supposed to leave your aide-de-camp without word of where I can find you! How am I supposed to know your orders if I'm in the dark?"

As Mel Bellringer jogged his small legs to catch up with the group, Trestan turned to the cardinal apologetically. "My pardon. Mel is a good friend of mine. He's my aide."

The cardinal politely offered a hand in greeting to the gnome. "A pleasure to meet you. I am Cardinal Methlen Foresight, advisor to King Legard Brontere the First, and his lady, Queen Jinla."

Mel eagerly shook hands. "The honor is mine! In human settlements I am known as Mel Bellringer, of the Bellringer family: makers of fine bells, chimes, gongs and other acoustical instruments. Given the current circumstances, I present myself to you as a sorcerer and traveler."

Trestan doubted that many kings had an introduction as long as Mel's.

The gnome fell in step with them as the cardinal guided them onward. Since the priest had just mentioned the royal family, he pointed out their portion of Fortress Stone. "The king and queen reside in that palace. It has changed its appearance many times as

136

generations added more decorations. It is almost the center of the fortress. I say 'almost' because the masons built it on a slight hill, and the rest of the battlements filled up the rest of this area later. No matter how an army attacked, they would have to go through at least two rings of walls to get to the king's throne."

The man paused, turning back around to look towards the plains. "Assuming they ever do attack. The tribes are taking too much time. They will doom themselves because of it."

Sondra got up the courage to interrupt his thoughts by asking, "What do you mean?"

The cardinal opined. "There are two ways to take a castle. The first is by brute force. If they attempt to take us by that route, they will suffer many losses upon our walls. They don't seem to have siege towers or catapults…only magic. The second method is by a slow siege. Since they believe our food supply to be sabotaged, I would expect this to happen. On the other hand, they will be encircling this keep with an army that is too big to feed while just sitting here, especially with colder winds on the way. Whatever they do, they missed their most opportune chance to hit us during warmer days. We can warm ourselves indoors by the fires while they sit exposed to the wind."

Trestan looked out over the men camped on the banks of the river. "It will get crowded inside the castle if we have to endure a siege."

Cardinal Methlen proceeded to walk along his tour. "You are correct. People are already bumping too closely and inflaming tempers while we sit and wait in nervous anticipation. We must take care that we don't have a bunch of fistfights among our own soldiers before they are needed on the walls. The king and queen came up with a solution…actually, I think Lindon put the idea in their minds."

Trestan and Sondra looked with some surprise at Lindon. The minstrel tried to shrug off the attention. "Oh, I might have made a little suggestion. Their Highnesses took it from there."

Mel had been preoccupied with his own self-discussion, which the others had ignored, on siege warfare. His head popped up, "How did you get an audience with the king and queen?"

Lindon answered. "I like to travel and make myself known. Sometimes, my journeys take me into throne rooms where my mandolin entertains royalty."

When Lindon said no more, the priest continued. "They decreed to hold a ball. There will be entertainment and dancing. This will help liven spirits and put people in a better mood. It is a lot better than waiting for an enemy to march to one's doorstep. They will even serve a greater share of rations, so that the people will enjoy filling their stomachs. I think it was a grand suggestion."

Korrelothar smiled and praised Lindon. "I think you're right, a very grand idea. It will give the armies a chance to mingle, eat well, and drop their cares for a time. Lindon, you are to be commended for your thinking."

Mel spoke up. "Oh aye, this is very good indeed! Aijak and I could take this opportunity to teach all of you the gnomish leap-frog dance."

This seemed to give everyone pause, as if they were unsure how to comment next. Lindon broke the silence. "This will be a good chance for us all to watch and be entertained by new things."

The tour continued, with everyone thinking of the dance and looking forward to the event. The cardinal led them to his personal favorite portion of the sprawling fortress. They saw a tower marked with many religious symbols. Although it seemed devoted mostly to The Codex, there were other gods and symbols inscribed upon the doorways and walls. The inner walls of the castle ran up to the tower. As the companions entered, they were three floors up.

"This tower was simply called Tuampor…and old word for temple. As you can see, many gods are represented here. This houses most of the priesthood that resides in the castle. It has chambers designed for many aspects of faith. We preach to assemblies in the large sanctuary on the ground level. It also has meditation chambers and a library stacked with scrolls."

He led them into a large chamber near the top of the tower. There were no windows to be found in the room. Sparse light from torches cast flickering shadows across decorative patterns. A golden arch in the center dominated the large room. Circles of runes on the floor surrounded the arch, covering both sides of it. It looked to have some holy purpose, yet the companions noted that several beds were arranged inside the room.

Cardinal Methlen explained. "The beds are being set up to use this room as an infirmary. Normally they wouldn't be here. This chamber appeared suitable as a ward for the sick and injured, and can be accessed easily from the inner ramparts. If you spot any wounded near this place, you can bring them here for healing spells or bandages."

Trestan and Sondra studied all the religious décor on the walls and the arch. Mel and Korrelothar examined the runes on the floor near the arch. Mel wrinkled his nose at something, "You have these drawn out as wards against something not of this world?"

"Indeed," Foresight nodded, "This is the Gate of Issundor. It is used as a means of passing knowledge from one world to another. We can summon in creatures from other planes and speak with them. Sometimes we receive a summons from another world, and we allow passage into this plane to hear what they say."

Trestan was trying to remember his arcane lessons. It wasn't a field through which he excelled. "Now, I know it takes someone on both sides of a gate to open it, correct?"

"Aye. If someone on the other side wants to open this gate, we'll know. This gate was built to make communication between worlds rather easy. It is a permanent, stable gateway, though it still obeys the laws of transdimensional bridges. Normally the summoning of extraplanar creatures involves a lot of power. The exertion is often more than a single person could bear. The gate was designed to work as a smooth conduit for just such a purpose. It can bear the burden of lengthy contact."

Mel piped up, echoing Trestan's next thoughts but finding the words faster, "Once open, a party on either side could keep it open, correct? What if someone doesn't want to close it?"

"There is nay purpose in keeping it open." The cardinal explained things so that those in the room who weren't familiar with the laws of transdimensional portals might understand him. "It is true that once opened, only one party needs to continue concentration to hold open the portal. We have spoken to beings who would like nothing more than free entrance into this world, perhaps to wreak havoc. The taraz are a good example. However, all those runes on the floor bar them from our world. There are runes on the other side of the gate, in their world, that bar us from stepping too far into theirs. You can stand within that inner circle once exiting the gate from the other world, but trying to pass those runes would end up in death. For that reason, there is nay purpose for anyone to hold open the portal; they couldn't pass any farther than that threshold."

An ugly thought came to the paladin. Trestan asked, "There are taraz among the tribes coming here. What if they approach the gate from this side?"

An uneasy silence descended. Trestan watched as his words caused Korrelothar, Mel and Cardinal Methlen to frown at some inner thoughts.

Mel's response was simply, "Uh oh, that wouldn't be good for us."

The cardinal's shoulders sagged, "A demon on this side could open the gate from here only if he was powerful enough. He could simply walk over the runes from this side, but then he would be trapped with only the gate as his exit. Although…"

"He could destroy the runes, couldn't he?" The elf wizard offered.

"Aye." The priest offered a nod. "He could destroy the safeguards that would keep the rest of the demons from crossing over. Our priests will have to guard this gate. We can't afford to let any demons have access to it."

Korrelothar looked uneasy about this revelation. "If they open this mighty gate, they need only maintain it from the other side while sending their own army to hit us from behind. We would need to close it from their side as well as ours, while faced with a powerful host of foes."

In that instant, they each realized the depth of the danger approaching their doorstep. Trestan recalled the image inside Savannah's mind. He remembered seeing that if this keep fell, a greater darkness would spew forth from inside it. It wasn't easy to summon a few demons into this world, yet the gate in this tower would allow easy access for a horde of demons. Abriana's champion looked upon the golden arch with unease. Now he knew why this land was chosen by Mothrok and DeLaris. The demons who had worshipped them during the Godswars of Ibleu Taraz were coming to claim this gate between worlds.

CHAPTER 18 "A Meal and a Dance"

The day arrived when Fortress Stone held the ball for all their guests. Colorful pennants of every variety adorned the walls and buildings. Kitchens throughout the stronghold prepared a meal that was, at worst, better than the standard rations; at best, it was perhaps the largest meal many of the Stonelands' folk enjoyed all year. Not everyone had fancy clothes to wear, especially since some had come only prepared for war and others were refuges from abandoned homes. The occasion did accomplish its intended purpose: it raised the spirits of the people even as it eased tensions between the factions within the armies.

As dusk fell and the lanterns were lit, the festivities truly began. It had been a challenge just designating the space to set aside for the diversion. Much of the inner courtyard was crowded with tables and banquet tents. An abundance of lights from the overlooking structures gave a hint of the nobility having their own party indoors. Though some poor souls still had to walk the walls on guard duty, there were carts wheeled around the ramparts that offered a good, warm meal for those men. There was an extra surprise for some. Both Commander Ormiz and Lord Marshal Aden "Three-Finger" Brocht, the highest-ranking military men of the Stonelands, walked the walls offering drinks. The two men toasted the wall sentries, offering thanks that those soldiers served their kingdom by remaining vigilant on a night of festivities.

Folks partying in the courtyard were greedier with their drinks. Salgor Bandago did his best to raise spirits by offering up the only kegs of alcohol he had brought to the castle. His special, "Bandago's Brew", flowed freely down several throats and more than a few tunics.

There had already been much excitement earlier in the day as another ship from Kashmer pulled into the deserted harbor in Pilgrim's Bay. The disciples of Abriana noted the banners of their seminary flying from the masts. Trestan and Leander watched from Stone's battlements as distant figures were seen wearing the red-and-gold colors of their goddess. The newly-arrived combatants were the students of the seminary who had just passed the tests of their Embarking. The two men eventually saw the person they had most hoped to see. The young cleric with the short, curly, brown hair…Rhijin…smiled with pride as she marched towards them. She held up one hand, displaying the ring known as Faithful's Companion for them to witness. All of the men and women beside her were wearing their rings; instruments of Abriana that would inform them when and if their quests would earn them the right to be a full paladin or cleric in her calling. They were all eager to take up this quest in Abriana's service.

Trestan and Leander greeted all their friends, though they chatted with Rhijin during the party as they got in line for some food. The woman remarked on her most feared challenge: that of the beast.

"It was scary to enter that pit again and wonder if I would fail. I reminded myself of your words, Trestan, and it helped calm my nerves. Whatever beast approached me was a soul in need of my help. I did have a moment of hesitation when those eyes glared at me from the dark."

The trio grabbed plates and walked before cooks. They talked amongst themselves, paying no attention to the food being offered. They had to move along with the line while illuminated by torches and mage-lights, for it had become dark.

"What animal did you face?" Leander asked.

Rhijin responded. "A wolf. The alpha female of its pack. It was in such pain."

They carried their plates over to one of the less-crowded tables. Rhijin continued to elaborate on her challenge. "As I delved into its mind, I was surprised to find that its pain echoed my own…in a way. Who knew that a wolf could have such doubts and fears nagging at her soul? Its agony mirrored some of my own personal worries. We were both comforted by our brief contact. For me, it was an amazing transition. One moment I'm scared of setting foot in that pit, the next I discover a kinship with a woman in fur. Even if I had failed every other test of that Embarking, I would have been proud of my connection with that wolf."

Trestan and Leander nodded, remembering their own experiences at their challenge. Rhijin added. "The experience will have lasting impact on my life."

Leander and Rhijin both turned to their food. Trestan was still watching Rhijin as an odd thing happened. The woman looked down at her plate, preparing to dig in with fork and knife. Her body locked rigid as she stared at the food before her. Trestan's brow wrinkled as he tried to guess why she froze. He watched as her face showed repulsion at the generous dinner. It took a moment for Trestan to remember some of the side-effects of the challenge she faced.

He asked, "You've lost the taste for meat, haven't you?"

Rhijin nodded, unsure she wanted to open her mouth at that moment with the nausea she felt. She sat back from the slab of cooked meat set before her. Trestan knew that some of Abriana's disciples lost their taste for animal-based food after the challenge of the beast. That brief look into an animal's soul could poison the taste of meat for life. Rhijin seemed to be one of them.

She said, quietly, "I can't look at a piece of meat without wondering how that animal felt as it died. It makes me sick even to consider eating it."

Leander paused in mid-bite. Trestan offered. "We can put it aside. I'll put mine aside for you, too. I don't need any tonight."

Rhijin protested, "You don't have to do that."

She soon found that Leander felt the same. They would both put their meat aside for her, settling for the vegetables, soup, and bread they were given. They wondered how they might get rid of the meat when they were joined by a friend. Salgor sat down heavily, carrying a plate in one hand, a sloshing mug in the other, and with a piece of meat sticking out of his mouth. He noisily slurped the strip of mutton into the recesses of his covering beard as he grumbled an unintelligible greeting.

Trestan motioned to their dishes. "Salgor, we can't eat this meat due to…an observance for Abriana. Do you have room on your plate?"

"This circle o' wood isn't big enough to hold enough food for a dwarf! Go ahead and load up whatever will fit o' it!"

Trestan stabbed Rhijin's meat, then his own, and piled it on Salgor's plate. Leander did the same with his portion. Salgor started to assault his food when he realized all three were silently watching him out of the corners of their eyes. Specifically, they seemed to peek at the roasts he was eating.

Feeling uncomfortable, the dwarf announced, "Speakin' o' religious observances, that reminds me, I have to have a talk with that gnome."

The dwarf left the table without further goodbyes. Salgor moved about the tents until he saw Mel and Aijak sitting together. He arrived as some kind of unpleasant discussion was going on between them. The sorcerer turned to him and pleaded, "Salgor, Aijak is unhappy with the meat they served. She found a broken bone in hers and said that they treated the animals badly. Will you take our shares away?"

The dwarf glanced down at his pile. He held the plate forward and said, "See if you can load me up without topplin' the whole mess."

After he had a king's portions balanced on his plate, he looked about for somewhere else to sit. He saw the red-haired chiaso that had been hanging around his old friends. Salgor walked over to her. "Are you religious at all?"

Montanya looked over to the dwarf. "Only when someone has poisoned me, other than that I haven't had much use for praying."

"Well enough!" Salgor dropped his rear on the bench next to her. "Help me get to the bottom o' this stack."

Salgor and Montanya had the chance to get acquainted as they ate. They traded stories of their respective journeys relating to the relics. At different times, they found reason to laugh at their misadventures.

By the time Katressa arrived to enjoy some food, she ran into Petrow. She was accompanied by a tall, muscular warrior wearing shades of forest green and sporting some gray in his hair. The two of them stopped and shared whispers before she dismissed him to join the festivities. Cat dropped into a seat across from Petrow. The blue-eyed man was toying with his portion more than eating it. Even in the dim light, he noticed the angry look on her face.

Petrow spoke first. "What happened? Trestan was looking for you."

Cat began muttering, throwing a thumb over her shoulder to indicate the departing warrior. "Thamin and I had to settle a drunken fight involving some of the privateers. Damn Kashmer! I trained in a lifestyle they refer to as an infiltrator. I make a pretty smile while I steal important evidence or work quietly in the night breaking into places by myself. I scout alone out in the wilderness where larger patrols don't dare go. In fact, that warrior I was with, Thamin, could say the same. At least he's had experience leading troops before. I've had to rely on a few good veterans like him to handle the others. But, I'm just not skilled in running an army! I'm not the type to lead troops."

This brought some amusement to Petrow's expression. "You did a good job leading us years ago. Oh, I know I didn't do a good job listening to you, but you watched over us well."

"How many times did we nearly get killed in that adventure?"

"Well now…" Petrow accentuated his point by holding his spoon aloft, waving it in her direction. "The key word there is *nearly*. You reminded us about armor and spent your own coins to protect us. You were always concerned about our welfare. I think you make a great leader."

Whether Cat believed him or not she switched subjects. Her face and tone softened. "How are you tonight? You don't seem to be enjoying the festive atmosphere."

Petrow sighed. "My mind keeps wandering back home. I miss my wife and children. I worry about whether or not I'll see them again."

"Weren't you the one that once told Trestan to not lose himself in worry? He said you told him something like…he shouldn't dwell on worries that he can't change…that he should enjoy the good moments when they come. I think you should follow that advice. We'll have few enough chances to dance and eat before our real worries finally get to our doorstep."

Petrow nodded, "Alright, but one condition. You also pay heed to your own words. Calm yourself and enjoy the night, don't fret much about what Kashmer expects of you."

Cat chuckled at that. The mage-lights captured the gleam in her emerald eyes. "I fell into my own trap, didn't I?"

He laughed, "I guess we both have our worries. I suppose the situation is better than that of our first trip. Back then, we just had ourselves out in the wilderness. Here, we have warriors from far around making a stand with us."

The half-elf looked out to the crowd. The courtyard was filled with soldiers and magic users waiting for the day to prove themselves. "I better find Trestan." She no sooner took a couple steps before she half-turned back to him. "Did you take my advice and find yourself a good waraxe?"

The farmer from Troutbrook shook his head. "Every time I got a new axe, I lost it. I'll keep my old axe. I am familiar with the balance and where the blade will hit when I swing. It's comfortable for me."

Cat had one more afterthought before she walked away. "Since you don't have a dance partner, I expect you to give me the honor of a dance later!"

"I will!"

As the meals on the plates diminished, a number of people helped move tables aside for some dancing. Lindon and a few other minstrels helped clear a large area. As soon as they had space for entertainment, the red-bearded man bounded onto a makeshift stage. He called out to the assembly. The growing crowd hushed to hear his words.

Lindon's words carried far, bolstered by magic. "I've been told by some that their meal was more than they could hold. The entertainers here are more than willing to put off our songs for another day if you need time for the food to settle."

The throng of soldiers, adventurers, mages, merchants, settlers, farmers, and children voiced their disagreement. Many shouted their desire for a song. Lindon pretended that he was having trouble hearing them, even going so far as to cup a hand behind one ear to listen better. This caused the crowd to shout that much louder. "A song! Play for us!" They eagerly anticipated the first tunes of the night.

The minstrel nodded. "So you are ready for some merriment?"

At their continued excitement, Lindon pulled forth his mandolin. This caused a lot of cheers and clapping to engulf the crowd.

"My name is Lindon Taleweaver, and I have traveled many places far from my home in Orlaun. I won't make any introductions longer than that, for it is best for a minstrel to make himself known through his music."

Lindon began to play vigorously. The first song he performed was "Around We Swing Before the Hearthfire". It was the kind of song that got people clapping or stomping to the rhythm. No one actually got up the courage to dance to it, but several joined in on the lyrics.

Floranue Balshav heard the music playing outside an open window. It did put a bounce in her step but otherwise didn't distract her from her cooking. The pudgy elf was busy working with a number of other kitchen hands. The main course had been served to those outside, yet they had been ordered to provide some trays of desserts. Although she missed enjoying the dance in the courtyard, she was happy to be providing a meal to those suffering from hunger. She hummed along merrily as she bounced from oven to table.

She was surprised as a pair of arms encircled her waist from behind. A voice spoke to her in Elvish, "Oh, how I wish we could be dancing together under the stars, my love! How I hate being surrounded by haughty nobles and their stuffy mannerisms. I would much prefer to sweep you away to the dance!"

Floranue found enough freedom to turn and face Korrelothar. "I wish the same, though it feels good to commit this effort to others…Korrel! You're getting this flour on your good robe!"

The Highwater Conjuror looked down at the white sprinkles on his expensive garb. "This is nay concern. I would singe myself in fire to hold you so close."

"Easy for you to say," She remarked as she attempted to slap some of the powder from his robes…only making it worse, "You never do the laundry more than once a decade!"

"*Faunlessa*, I'm wounded."

Floranue finally gave up. She wrapped her arms around her love. "I am glad you came to see me. You still remember how long it has been?"

Korrelothar smiled, "I have the date written in my hatband in case I ever forget. Two weeks from now will be our hundred-and-ninety-seventh anniversary."

"Happy early anniversary, man of my heart."

Korrelothar hugged her closely. In the beat of the tunes heard from the outside, the couple had a moment to swing their hips together in the kitchen.

The songs and dancing continued out in the courtyard, as well as in other chambers of the castle. The companions were glad to be enjoying the revelry alongside those common folks in the courtyard. They felt that the invisible royalty likely were playing a game of politics while they moved their feet. Sometimes they danced to Lindon's performances, yet often he made way for other musicians.

One song request was made by a pair of gnomes. Mel and Aijak proved true to their word as they taught the others the gnomish leap-frog dance. A number of children giggled as they danced to this new, fun dance. Few adults joined in, preferring to watch and laugh. Mel and Aijak were experts, although the children attempting the dance took a few gentle spills on the ground as they tried it. As the dance ended, the gnomes did receive some applause. Some of the children received some harsh words from parents who noticed the new stains on their good clothes.

The leap-frog dance wasn't the only new dance introduced to the humans. Salgor and the company of Thornbeards marched in dwarvish fashion to the dance area. They formed ranks holding filled mugs in one hand and their crested shields in the other. Shouting in their own language, they moved about waving both. At times they seemed to alternate between toasting each other and smashing shields together. Somehow, not a drop was spilled from the mugs. At the conclusion, they gave a loud shout and slammed the drinks down their throats.

Trestan chatted with his father at one point. "How do you like your adventure? After all, this time *you* ran off from Troutbrook into trouble."

Hebden Karok's undertone was serious, even though he forced a smile. "We haven't gotten to the real adventure yet, have we? The clash of swords…the screams of the wounded…I'm not eager for that part. I do feel some pride that I helped in what little ways I could. Whenever I see a man walk by with sword or armor crafted by my hands, I think that I've already worked my share to make a difference."

"I'm glad you're here," Trestan Karok/Spiritblade ventured, "But I hope you keep safe when things get dangerous. Keep your head down. I know you wouldn't want me to worry for you, but I do."

The older smith waved off his concerns. "They assigned me to help load the catapults on the walls. I'll be safe on top of the defenses, so worry about your own skin out on the battlefield."

Cat and Petrow finished their dance together, letting the music carry them back to the father and son. The two smiths from Troutbrook made room for them to sit. Cat shared a bit of news. "I found out where Lindon keeps disappearing to every now and then."

Trestan swept an open hand across, "Please tell."

The half-elf pointed a slender finger to the nearest keep overlooking the yard. "He keeps bouncing between stages. When he isn't performing down here, he goes up and entertains the royalty in the hall up there."

Trestan said, "Crafty, isn't he? He's making a name for himself amongst common men and rulers. Lindon's probably performing twice as much as any entertainer here. Hope he isn't letting his throat get too parched."

As they talked, another lively tune started up from the stage. Cat smiled, "I'm ready for my next dance!"

"If I may?" Hebden asked of his son and Cat, "I would like to dance with my future daughter-in-law."

"I know she will enjoy it." Trestan promised.

Cat allowed the elder Karok to escort her to the dance area. They both laughed as he twirled her around.

One companion did not indulge herself at the dance. Montanya's greenish-blue eyes watched the people having fun as if she was detached from the event. She felt lonely and separated…and a part of her wanted to stay that way.

The young chiaso had never danced in her life. Her mind had been so focused on serious thoughts for so long, she had trouble letting go of some of her concerns. The woman convinced her emotions that she would be happy just sitting aside and watching the others dance. The music conjured images in her mind, and she was satisfied to let that be her entertainment for the evening.

Her mind began to betray her even as she tried to distract herself. Montanya remembered a fleeting image from Sondra's memory where a young man had whisked her into a dance when she was young. Someone played an instrument in a Sanctuary, a young man grabbed the acolyte without permission, and once it was over, Sondra fled in embarrassment. Montanya found herself fascinated with that foreign memory, even dreamed of it some nights. She wanted to see an image of herself in the arms of a man on the dance floor. Wanting something was different from the reality of pursuing it. She liked to think about it, but she feared such a thing becoming a reality.

The young woman watched the dance with indecision. She had purposefully avoided men who moved about looking for dance partners. Her stomach seemed filled with fairies as she watched all the others having their fun. Montanya thought about going to the kitchen and offering help, since she had done her time in the sanctuary kitchens, just to get away from the dance. She couldn't leave the music and the sights. Part of her wanted to distract herself, the other part felt the need to be invited to the dance by some man. What would she do if someone found her and asked her to dance? She continued to hover at the fringes, unable to leave and yet unwilling to join in.

As the woman watched, she spotted a familiar face moving about the dance area. It was Sondra! The normally shy cleric was dancing with a young man, and laughing along with something he said! The chiaso stood transfixed as she watched the blonde woman and her partner spinning to the pace of the music. Montanya's lips parted in open astonishment as she watched her friend having the time of her life. She had never seen Sondra laugh so hard at anything!

Montanya felt a twinge of jealousy. She wished she could get up the courage to either leave the dance floor or make her way out to it. It was too late. In that brief distraction, the hunter set upon her.

"Fair lady, may I have the honor of this dance?"

Montanya turned her greenish-blue eyes to the man who had found her. Dark-haired, handsome, even if a bit rough at the cheeks. She could see the nearby mage-lights reflected in his dark eyes. He stood before her as a proper gentleman might. His body straightened in good posture as he awaited her response. She looked over his clothing. He wore an outfit that she had seen among a few of the Stonelands' garrison. It was a simple thing, lacking ornamentation. It featured a black tunic tied at the waist with a white sash. A white headband peeked out from his dark hair. He wore a small sword at his side. Montanya had seen only a small number of men dressed that way, figuring them to be some kind of militia unit. They were all lightly armed with very little armor; just joint pads and shields. She looked back to his face and was lost in his eyes. He had cornered her with the question, and he was handsome too. His polite request impaled her feelings like an arrow.

"Aye…I would be honored." Montanya's outward response was different than her inner urge to scream. *I agreed to a dance? Why did I do that?*

Some of her sense returned, and she made an excuse which sounded too much to her own ears like an admission. "I must apologize; I'm not a good dancer. I've never danced before."

Why did I tell him the truth? Am I trying to look like a foolish girl?

To her surprise, he took her hand even as he admitted his own inexperience, "That's alright. I've never danced either. This way, we can learn together."

He has never danced with a woman?

"I am Dern. How may I address you?"

"I'm Montanya…from Orlaun."

"Pleased to make your acquaintance." He smiled. His glowing expression caused her to smile in return.

Montanya allowed her feet to be led to the dance area. Her stride, honed by years of training to adopt a perfect balance, suddenly took on the aspects of a clumsy lope. Montanya hoped she wouldn't trip and make a fool of herself. She took a second look at the man as they walked. He looked about her age, but he could be younger by a couple years. The rough whiskers on his cheeks probably made him seem older than he was. He picked a spot near some the other dancers. They turned towards each other.

The music originated from Lindon's metal pipe. The dance had most of the partners at arm's length and kicking to a routine. Montanya and the stranger talked only a little at first, as they looked to the other dancers and tried to mimic them. The movements were easier for Montanya, who was jumping about in her loose Serud'Thanil outfit. As they tried copying the other dancers amidst attempting their own conversation, she couldn't repress a smile. Nervous. Giddy. Montanya let escape an unforgivable blush.

They arrived at the end of the song. The pipe notes finished with a flourish and a round of applause. Dern didn't relinquish Montanya's hands, and she felt duty-bound to complete a whole dance, despite her nerves.

An announcement came from the performers' stage, as Lindon heralded. "And now to respect the request from fellow redhead, we shall slow things down."

The young martial artist threw a glare Lindon's way, but the minstrel was pointedly not looking at her. He started playing some slow notes on his mandolin. Another entertainer with a flute knew the song and joined in. The couples began to hug closer for a slow, intimate waltz.

Montanya took a deep breath to steady herself as she looked to Dern's face. He was a bit unsure of himself, but he did his best to hide it as he copied what the other men were doing. While tenderly holding Montanya's hand, he slipped his other arm around her waist and pulled her in closer. She raised her free arm up around his muscular shoulder. Their eyes were much closer now, sharing a private look before he led the first tentative step and she followed. They both were a bit clumsy at first, watching others and going by their motions. The couple soon settled into a rhythm and began to chat.

"You honor me, Montanya. I find myself embarrassed by my lack of dance practice."

Montanya wasn't sure what to say. She was self-conscious of her breathing since they were dancing so closely. "Let's not apologize over our clumsiness. You can hold me more firmly than you are; I'm far from fragile."

She meant that he could hold her hand more firmly, but to her surprise, he misunderstood and held her tighter to him. Montanya guided him by tightening her grip on their extended hands, even though something distracted her even more. Her elvish attire was made from thin cloth. In their close embrace, their dance resulted in Montanya's bust brushing across his hard chest. The pleasurable jolt that went through her body helped throw her emotions into more of a tumble.

It was too much sensation for Montanya to maintain her mental wall. The ceiling of stars and the sweet melodies of the music put a romance to the setting that Montanya had never sought. The almost-forgotten danger of the approaching tribesmen gave the evening some urgency to enjoy the moment. Some alcohol she had indulged made her head light. In the middle of this emotional night was someone who wanted to hold her. She had never been so near to any man's arms. She had never given thought of what the sensation would be like.

Montanya tried to voice something to distract her senses from the feeling of this male body holding her close. "You are from Stonelands, are you not?"

Dern nodded, his eyes hovering close to hers. "Aye. I have lived in Pilgrim's Bay all my life. I might have moved to Orlaun years ago if I knew they grew such pretty flowers there."

Montanya was definitely blushing now. "You're shamelessly flattering me. I doubt I have done much to earn such praise. Is it just because I was the first one who said I would dance tonight?"

"You are the only one worthy enough for me to ask." He replied.

Now Montanya's emotions did twirl. Was he playing games with her? All of these women present and she was the only one he asked?

Dern seemed to know her thoughts. "I wanted my first dance to be special. I saw you standing alone for the longest time, waiting for someone to ask you out here. It took me a bit to work up the courage to walk over and ask. A first dance is something you always remember."

Montanya's mind flitted back to Sondra's memories. "Aye, it is." The red-haired woman swayed in lazy circles with the Stonelands' soldier. "I'm glad you came over and asked me."

Although Montanya said it, a part of her pondered if things would have been easier if she'd ducked into the kitchen earlier and thus never been asked to dance. Now her emotions were in a turmoil that she'd never experienced. Even trying to do little things to distance herself from this man only provoked more thoughts. One example was when she tried to withdraw her enfolding arm slightly. Her hand went from resting on his well-defined shoulder to sliding down the top of his upper arm muscle. This was a man used to hard work.

Dern smiled down to her, she helplessly smiled back. A face that was used to handling a variety of emotions with a furious scowl was now returning the warmth of his look. She had never paid much attention to men before, except how to use her martial arts abilities against their inherent strength. This man held her like she was the most valuable thing in his life. It left her disciplined mind feeling scattered. She couldn't escape his touch, and she felt naked under his close scrutiny.

"So," she asked, "this is some type of uniform you are wearing?"

"Aye, all of my company is forced to wear this. Keeps us visible to the guards on the training grounds."

Montanya furrowed her brow, "Forced?"

He suddenly seemed hesitant, "Oh, you didn't know?"

A bit of alarm crept into her voice, "Didn't know what?"

Dern sighed. "Everyone wearing this uniform is from Convict Company."

Montanya felt her troubled heart dangling at the edge of a pit. The song was coming to an end, but not as quickly as Montanya's feet. They still held each other, but the woman stood immobile as she looked at him. "What is Convict Company?"

Dern looked down in shame. "Every one of us was serving time for a crime. They were all minor crimes, nay killers or rapists or such in our ranks. Yet all of us were imprisoned for some wrongdoing or facing punishment. They gave us a choice: face justice or stand alongside the army and help defend against this attack. I chose to protect my home."

Montanya's face was blank. She forced herself to look into his eyes as she asked, "What crime did you commit?"

He dipped his head in shame, "I stole something."

The chiaso reverted to her old scowl. She forced her eyes away from his, staring into his chest instead. Her breathing increased, and steel entered her tone. "So you're a thief?"

Dern was silent a moment. "Not usually, but aye, I did steal something and I'm being punished for it." His tone became soft. He loosened his arms from Montanya as he felt the anger building within her. "I'm sorry you didn't know; I wasn't trying to fool you. I'll understand if you don't feel like dancing."

"I have to go." With that brief response, Montanya turned from him and marched briskly away.

A damn thief! Montanya repeated his admission in her mind. Her own thoughts tortured her as she imagined that handsome man committing all sorts of vile thefts. She mused on whether his thievery had spilt any blood. Her mind even conjured up a delusion of herself, as a young child, looking into Dern's face as he stole from her without compassion. It shamed her to realize that while her heart fluttered dancing with that handsome man; she had actually been entreating the devil. All sorts of phantoms that thieves had implanted in her past seemed to resurface.

Although, he did admit that he had stolen something. There didn't seem to be any intended deceit upon her. He had admitted his shame readily enough for her judgment.

Montanya shook her head as if shaking the thought in anger. He had told her nothing more than she would have learned anyways. Most of the people there probably knew what the uniform represented. Worst of all, some primitive feelings in her longed to feel that touch again…that closeness and comfort in the embrace of a handsome man. She felt at odds with herself. She felt used.

Montanya thought she had moved away to a quiet space separate from the festive dancers. She realized otherwise as some low, musical notes came from some shapes ahead. The lights and sounds of the party were behind her. Staring into the dark, the woman realized she was in a small garden. The plants were mostly withered or dead. Bare branches rose up from the roots that no longer nurtured them.

She saw where the notes originated. The gnome woman who accompanied Mel sat alone in the garden. Montanya recognized Aijak by the tree tattoo on her face, but could not recall the name. The gnome noticed her observer and dipped her head in greeting. The music went on uninterrupted as she blew into a small instrument. Montanya was puzzled until she realized that the gnome druid's spot was the only one in the garden with leaves on the branches. Small flowers were blooming, as their pretty insides came out to enjoy the sounds. Aijak was bringing some life back into the ground.

Montanya nodded as well, but moved on. She didn't want to intrude. She passed a dark alcove and heard more noises. This time it was a couple taking refuge in the shadows. They were standing, still clothed, and embraced in a hug.

The chiaso heard Trestan's voice, "I'm glad we have a moment to ourselves, *faunlessa*." It was followed by Cat whispering something back in Elvish.

Not wanting to interrupt that scene, and stunned to realize that it inflamed her own recent emotions concerning Dern, she moved on. Montanya decided to climb away from the rest of the courtyard. She went into a tower and up some steps. Her mind continued to buzz with thoughts of the man's touch, even as her mind rebelled at his admission.

Just a thief. One more stinking thief in the world! He would steal my heart if I let my guard down!

Montanya finished climbing and stepped onto a wall. The noise of the party dimmed to a low murmur behind her. She stepped out to the outer parapets and tried extricating her mind from her emotions. Even as she did so, she noticed the wall sentries paid her no heed. In fact, their attention was focused on something beyond the walls. The chiaso snapped back to the present situation as she looked over the northern ramparts.

Massed on the horizon, not too far distant, were the vast campfires of the gathered tribes' army.

CHAPTER 19 "Sondra's Star"

Under the rising sun, the wall sentries watched the distant cloud herald the advance of the tribal army. The dust cloud kicked up by thousands crossing the plains became a constant encroaching nightmare. From the first moments of that dawn, few souls within the fortress got any rest. The enemy would be at the river that very day. Officers and soldiers rushed around trying to finish carrying out frantic orders. Everything that wasn't done or didn't need to be done was now ordered to be finished at the last second. Nervous energy saturated the air as each man was called to expend every last effort to get things completed, moved, dug out, stacked up or placed elsewhere. A few runners were the last to exit the fortress, carrying notes to the nearby dwarf community and to the hidden ships holding the remaining food stores. A few last stragglers ran from the countryside to get into the fortress before it closed. These late farmers and their families crossed the bridge and the ferry with burdened mules carrying all their possessions.

The companions kept as busy as everyone else. Cat finished preparing the ground that the privateers would defend. Trestan, Leander and Rhijin were separated among Stonelands' armies. Most of the paladins and clerics sent by Ganden and Abriana were scattered among the soldiers to assist as healers. Likewise, Sondra received an assignment to aid others with her miracles. Since Montanya had nowhere else to go, she worked to improve the fortifications around Sondra's assigned spot. Salgor took up his weapons near the Thornbeards, who accepted his company as one of their own. Petrow and Hebden worked to gather a few last piles of stones onto the walls for the catapult crews. Mel and Aijak could seldom be found. The story told to the others was that the gnome sorcerer prepared some special surprises for the demons. Lindon wandered the walls and trenches, inspiring with his songs. Often, he would join a labor force still throwing defenses into place, and during those times he provided a cadence to give a rhythm to their work.

During a water break, Montanya had time to pause and reflect on a militia company positioned closer to the banks of the river. She watched as the men, adorned in black tunics and white headbands, worked to improve their assigned spot. The leaders of the Stonelands had placed Convict Company in a frontline position. Although the company was backed by veteran soldiers, their casualty rate would likely be high. She looked for one specific member, but couldn't see him. Her body remembered the feeling of his warmth close to hers...even as her mind wished him ill.

"Just a bunch of thieves," Montanya mumbled as she scowled, "At least they can die for a purpose instead of being hanged outright."

As the day passed, something unusual happened in the skies. The sunlight always beamed down on the advancing tribes. Elsewhere, dark clouds rolled in. Those few who knew of the Earthrin Stones guessed it was those same stones affecting the weather. The power of Yestreal was being used by his foes to blot out the sun over Stonelands, yet illuminate the tribal army. As if that was not enough, the noise of thunder shook the air above the fortress.

Sentries spotted the first scouts of the tribes in the nearby fields. The command came from Lord Marshall Aden "Three-Finger" Brocht to torch the ferry and bridge crossing the Hossan Minor. Soldiers left their barricades, torches in hand, and set about destroying the only two means of crossing over to the keep. They dragged the ferry onto the fortress' shoreline as the ropes holding it were cut away. Soldiers doused the bridge with oil and let it be devoured by flames. A group of wizards from the Brotherhood of the Circles hastened the destruction of the bridge with a few spectacular spell-blasts. The two forks of the Hossan River now became a barricade to the enemy even as it walled in the defenders.

After the fate of the fortress had been sealed, the being controlling the Earthrin Stones called forth a lightning storm to assail the keep. Defenders took cover as lightning flashed into the tower spires and hailstones rained down. The tribes cheered the signs that their nature spirits were with them. The sun stayed forever over their heads, lighting their path. Its rays warmed the air around them, while the cold winds of the late season chilled the fortress. They watched as darkness consumed the land around the castle, unbroken except by lightning bolts.

The defenders took cover as best they could as they endured the heavenly onslaught. Some privileged few were able to enjoy the protection of a good roof and a warm fire. Most were rather exposed as they manned breastworks of wood and earth. The elements pounded relentlessly.

It was around the early evening hours, (though it was hard to tell the exact hour except for the angle of the sun shining through the clouds on the tribes), when the invading army arrived at the banks of the river. The defenders waited in tense anticipation. Some placed arrows to their bowstrings, awaiting the command to fire. Spell-casters reached into pouches, ready to unleash their destruction. Some merely shivered in the cold storm.

No command to fire was given, for the enemy stopped their advance. The tribes fanned out across the northern bank of the Hossan Minor. The storm ceased, though it remained dark over the fortress. The defenders watched as the nomads began to set up their camp. Tents were pitched well out of range of the catapults on the fortress walls. Some of the tribes' vanguard warriors shouted taunts over the width of the flowing river, but taunts were all they hurled. It became apparent that the nomads were content to hold off their attack for one evening.

*　　　*　　　*　　　*　　　*

Even in the gloom of night the defenders worked. They took the opportunity offered in the aftermath of the storm to move around once again. They worked with only small, scattered storm lamps to aid them as they went about their chores. Petrow and Hebden worked among those who would not get much sleep. Ropes and counterweights lifted stones from the ground. The two men loaded the rocks into their wheelbarrow and delivered it down the wall to the silent catapults. They did their best to guide the wheelbarrow past obstructions in the dark.

Sondra, well-rested though energetically nervous, happened to be wandering the walls. She had been allowed a few hours of uneasy sleep indoors as the priests tried to rotate rest periods. She paused upon seeing the difficulties the men endured under the dark sky. The priestess of Ganden mused on the similarities of her newest tenet, "light against the darkness", and the realities of this night. She glanced down at the lantern pendant displayed openly on her breast. Sondra Oskires had a moment of amusement as she realized she could uphold her tenet rather literally this night.

The priestess looked around for a suitable receptacle to hold her spell. She found one in the form of a flagpole bearing the Stonelands' banner. A golden orb capped the pole. It seemed to be in the perfect position and height to lend a beneficial light up and down the ramparts.

Sondra Oskires prayed to Ganden for her miracle. The orb at the top of the pole began to radiate light. It was enough to help the men see their surroundings a little better. Hebden and Petrow nodded their thanks to her as they pushed the wheelbarrow past.

Revwar exited the tent in which he had just finished a discussion with Norzal. The elf was having resentful thoughts about his relationship with the demon. The wizard had long been a master of arcane power, yet his service to Norzal felt like bearing a yoke that would better fit someone inferior. The demon showed him little respect, and yet the taraz was his link to immortality and power under Mothrok. The two minds did agree on the overall aspects of the siege. They knew they could knock holes in the walls easily, yet they had to restrain themselves so that the tribes would be greatly weakened as well. What galled Revwar was Norzal's occasional treatment of him as nothing more than a lackey. They both seemed to be unwilling partners whose goals were intertwined.

Revwar paid little heed to the nearby tribe members who bowed and prostrated to him as their prophet. The elf's straight face hid any amusement he felt at knowing he would only be leading them to a slaughter. He turned his attention towards the fortress, and stopped in his tracks at the sight on the walls.

The elf wizard noted the bright glow illuminating the banner of the Stonelands. The Earthrin Stones had worked to keep the fortress bathed in darkness and the earlier storms, yet now this one defiant light pierced the gloom. The radiance seemed to spotlight the banner of resistance. The bottom third of the Stonelands' banner, a crystal blue, represented the water they had crossed to come to this land. The top two thirds signified the green backdrop of the fertile land outlining a black ship. The ship represented the vessels which delivered the people to this free land.

The light seemed nothing more than an insult to those who would conquer them. With an angry gesture, Revwar sent forth his magic and snuffed it out.

Sondra was about to go on her way when her light miracle dispelled. Darkness covered the walls again, punctuated by a solitary sound as some soldier banged his shinguard into an obstacle. The priestess of Ganden looked across at the tribal army camped on the other side of the river. Apparently, someone didn't like her little light spell.

Her first reaction might have been shocking to those who had witnessed her growing up. Sondra became very annoyed. All her life, she found difficulties speaking her mind to people or offering her opinions. The young woman felt that she had just been rebuked by some callous person who was, in effect, silencing her by cutting off her light. Thinking of her outspoken friend Montanya, Sondra decided it was time to be "heard" more. Another prayer to Ganden went up, illuminating the flagpole again. The soldiers on the wall gave a small cheer to the woman.

A second magical wave came from the tribes. Her new light had barely flared to life before it was snuffed. Darkness once again shrouded the banner.

Sondra had set her mind to this challenge; she wasn't about to back down. She even adopted a Montanya-like scowl on her face as she stared back at the tribes. Raising her voice to a shout, her prayers ignited a stronger light over the banner.

She whispered at her unseen adversary down below, "It takes a lot less energy for me to create a light over my head than it does for you to banish it from hundreds of meters away. Let's see who wears out first."

Her efforts had not gone unnoticed by other magic-users on the walls. Korrelothar lent an arcane spell to boost the light. Likewise, Mel Bellringer walked over to see what was going on, and he added his strength to the spell.

Revwar quickly tired of this game. He had other things to do and plan rather than deal with this upstart caster on the walls. The tribesmen around him had already noted his efforts in trying to dispel the distant light. Backing down now might lose needed respect and adoration later.

Revwar shook his length of braided silver hair in disgust, before calling forth another disruptive wave. He hurled his magical onslaught against the distant light once again.

This time, bolstered by more than one person, the light wavered but did not disappear. The elf angrily called to the nearby mystics and shamans. "Put out that eyesore! They light their banner in defiance of you!"

A stronger wave of dispelling magic slammed the flagpole into darkness again. In reply, Sondra called forth another light. Korrelothar and Mel once again joined in. Other priests and wizards along the wall noticed the exchange and began to add their support to the light. Men on the ramparts cheered once again at the stubborn woman and her miracles.

Numbers of observers from the riverside barricades and the tribes began to take note of the back-and-forth exchange. The banner dimmed or completely blacked out again and again, only to relight. Many paused to look up at the duel of spells. Some hastened to get what work could be done while they had the light available. As more magic-users put their efforts into the light, it began to glow all the more. Meanwhile, the tribal casters hastened to the call of their prophet to blot out the insolent spell. Those who knew only the sword or bow just watched as the struggle went back and forth.

Since more defenders than Sondra started reigniting the light on their own, inspiration dawned on her to try something new. With so many allies aiding her cause, it brought to mind one of Ganden's hymns. The young priestess put one foot atop the wall, raised one hand to grab the banner pole, and let loose her voice in song. If she stopped to think of what she was doing, she might have faltered out of embarrassment.

The shy priestess found strength in her voice and shouted forth in song. "...And for the call of burdened men we *rise* up, bringing them light to guide them through dark *forests*. And to bear the weight of their souls we *rise* up, hoisting high a light against the *darkness*..."

As Sondra sang, other faithful of Ganden heard one of their treasured hymns and joined their voices. Scattered amongst the defending forces as they were, Ganden's song took root and sprouted along the lines.

The light wavered under another assault, and then was bolstered again. Missiles of blackness streaked from the tribes to the banner to snuff it. The light of the flagpole flickered momentarily before redoubling its intensity. Sondra stood beside it, head raised high, one arm on the flagstaff, her voice singing louder than she had ever allowed in all her life.

In front of the castle walls, a figure crawled through the breastworks to one of his friends. "Rhijin?"

"I'm over here." The reply came from a shadowed figure.

Trestan crawled over to where she crouched behind breastworks. He pointed to the light on the walls. "I can add some strength to that, but not much. You would be able to help keep that light going better than I could."

Trestan could see the outline of her curly hair as she glanced up to the wall. "It could be a waste. Expending our energy to keep a light going?"

He nodded. "Maybe, but don't underestimate the power it may have on morale. Look at the effect it is having on everyone."

Even as he spoke, the conversations from the men around them reflected interest in seeing the light hold. The light was once again dimmed by an attack. Moments later, it flared back to life. The warriors cheered it every time it stayed lit. When the light darkened, a roar of victory would go up from the tribes across the river.

Amidst the backdrop of voices and shouts, one constant remained as followers of Ganden bellowed their song to the world.

Thamin, one of Cat's privateer commanders, turned to the half-elf. "Listen to that call. It rallies our men's strength and rekindles the fires in their terrified hearts."

Cat tilted her head. "I'm amazed that such a simple display moves soldiers' passions as such."

Thamin glanced meaningfully at a mage sitting nearby. "Never underestimate the power of a standard. Am I correct, Bannermaiden of Kaigal?" He jutted his chin towards the young mage, his own daughter. "Thomena's staff was born as a flagstaff. Let's join them in our magic and our hearts."

Cat nodded, she spoke so that the other privateers, all holed up in their bunkers, could hear her call. "Raise your voices! Lend your energy to either song or illumination! Let them hear your defiance!"

The young mage, Thomena, stood up from her bunker and raised her staff. Her energy conjoined with so many others to keep the banner lit.

Sir Theros Lightshield of Abriana's forces stood on high ground not far from Trestan and Rhijin. After listening to the tunes of Ganden's hymn, Theros voiced one of Abriana's. The tone and rhythm matched perfectly with Ganden's song. Followers of Abriana, likewise scattered around the defenders, joined their voices and blended songs with Ganden's faithful. Even common folk who knew either song added their voices.

Rhijin turned around to rest her back against their barricade while Trestan did likewise. Both looked up and chanted prayers to Abriana. Across the field, others did the same. Priests of Ganden, Abriana, The Codex and Yestreal joined prayers with spellcasters from the Brotherhood of the Circles. Together, they gave strength to the stubborn star burning above Stonelands' banner. The nomads called upon their natura to assault the brightness time and again. From all across the grand tribal encampment, the nomads witnessed the beacon of hope lit by the fortress defenders, they heard the multitude of singing voices. The green and blue banner of the Stonelands stood prominently for every eye within a mile. Even the invaders in the process of looting Pilgrim's Bay began to take notice of the flickering illumination atop the fortress. For all the effort of the natura users in the tribes, Sondra's earlier perceptions proved true. It was easier for those standing close to the banner to support the light than for those far away to destroy it. Despite assault after assault, the banner remained lit.

Lindon Taleweaver made his way up to the wall to witness the deed up close. He asked around to see who had started the light, and Petrow pointed out Sondra. Before long, Lindon started to strum a few strings on his mandolin. He tried out a few verses as the notes left his instrument, matching the blend of hymns but narrating the current scene. The song forming on his mind praised Sondra for the star she created out of the darkness.

Soldiers on the ramparts listened to his melody as they watched the young priestess stand defiantly beside the banner. Among them was an artist of brush and canvas. The painter listened to Lindon's words, studied the scene around him, and made a promise to himself that if he lived out the battle, he would remember this moment.

Sondra got little rest that night. Her superiors made sure that she received some time to sleep. When she did, others kept the light lit for her and sang her hymn. All through that worrisome night, the defenders were bolstered by a light against the darkness.

*   *   *   *   *

The defenders allowed the banner's light to expire when the first rays of sunlight were seen to the east. The dawning sun failed to warm the battlements under the relentless oppression of darkness offered by the Earthrin Stones. The only sunlight viewed by the defenders was that which illuminated the enemy camp.

The day opened to reveal rows and rows of tribesmen lined up across the Hossan Minor River. They stood arranged by their tribal totems. In the east part of the defenses, Montanya offered a scowl across the river at a band of humans with decorative feathered armor. In the middle of the earthen barricades, Trestan kneeled before his inverted sword. He offered a morning prayer to Abriana in view of a hostile line of Raulgan spearmen. In the western portion of the Stonelands' defenses, Katressa rode Eyfan around the bunkers covering the Kashmer privateers. She shouted a few final words of encouragement while being taunted by distant orc berserkers. Above it all, viewing the whole panorama of the battlefield from the vantage of the walls, Petrow and Hebden shared somber looks.

Hebden confided to Petrow. "This is a little more adventure than I expected."

After a moment of contemplation, Petrow replied. "Aye. I feel that way every time I set out from Troutbrook."

The army guarding the perimeter around Fortress Stone noted that the tribesmen, for the most part, carried more weapons and armor than would be easy to bear while swimming. The Hossan Minor ran deep and swift enough that any burden would take a swimmer down to the falls. The tribes seemed undaunted by the presence of the water's flow. They stood as if ready to charge across open grasslands. The defenders prepared to use bows and spells to assault any swimmers who attempted to cross.

Trestan offered words to Abriana as he viewed the lines of men gathered for war. "Abriana, I kneel on ground that may signify the end of the path; one started years ago in my village. I never thought my first steps outside my home would carry me so far. I hope to walk many more roads and paths alongside my love, my *faunlessa*, Katressa. The world as I have seen it is filled with wonder and hidden treasures. With your blessings, I would like to see more of them.

"Alas, today is not for me. All my dreams are mere whims compared to the evil that must be ended on this field. If anything, my glance at the wonders I have experienced…the tree paradise of Serud'Thanil, the spires of Orlaun, the grace of *Doranil Star*, and the open freedom of the plains on this horizon…give me strength to bolster my resolve. Today is for all mortals who would call this world their home. The evil that Revwar organized must be thwarted for good."

The paladin who chose the name Spiritblade paused to look at the dirt embedded in his own hands. Those same hands had worked through sweat and ash at a forge, now they were needed to wield this wondrous sword. He recalled how reluctant he had been to use the sword of Sir Wilhelm Jareth when it came to him. The veteran's grave rested far away, yet the presence of his teachings still weighed on Trestan's mind.

"What did you see in me that you accepted me as your own, Queen of Hearts? I shied at your calling, yet fate finds me here. I wondered what price I would pay for pledging myself to you. Now, I have discovered the high price. It is one I gladly pay. My sacrifice is to put my sword into the teeth of danger, in order to ensure that if I survive to be old alongside Cat, the world will still be a beautiful place to share our love.

"Give me the strength of arms and indomitable will to see to the protection of this plane of existence. Let me be a shield so that the tide of evil may be turned aside from the innocents of this world. For the good of every loving couple and pure child of Dhea Loral, bestow upon me the aid I will need to see victory."

The pounding of several drums interrupted the morning. The tribes began their own dance to the rhythm. Warriors thumped their spears or feet into the ground as they yelled war cries. The increasing pace of the drumbeat helped bring the waiting tribesmen to a fever pitch. It worked to help unnerve some of the defenders.

Not all were so easily dissuaded, thanks to minstrels like Lindon. The entertainer was striding along the barricades behind Convict Company when the drums started. He decided to deflate the enemies' scare tactics. He called out to the men around him.

"They brought all those drums and they can't even keep a decent tempo? How am I supposed to join in such a bland performance?"

With that pronouncement, he drew out his metal pipe and began to play along. His rendition was altogether comical…even more so when he commenced his interpretation of a "jungle dance" in tune with the music. The rowdies of Convict Company, a disagreeable lot by most standards, found amusement in his antics and joined him.

Even those good spirits ended when the drums silenced on cue. Lindon shrugged to his audience, bemused as them, at the sudden cessation of music. A new song came to their ears, plucked from hundreds of bowstrings. Lindon's eyes went wide as he saw the host of arrows arcing through the sky.

"Take cover!" Someone shouted.

"Heads down!" Cried another.

Lindon dove for the closest hole in the ground he could find. He landed hard enough to collapse some of the sand onto his wide-brimmed hat. Arrows whistled from the blotted sky, thudding all around. Lindon and dozens of others hoped they had tucked their hindquarters and all other body parts out of danger. As much as any man might have been curious to look about, the continual arrow impacts kept many heads down.

Petrow, Hebden, Mel, and all the others up on the walls were safe enough to view the whole spectacle as it unfolded. They watched the rain of deadly sticks shower the men below. Many had already built up a lot of cover where they were posted. Despite the protective barricades, cries of pain reached the ears of those on the walls.

Commander Ormiz of the Stonelands sent out the order, "Return volley!"

A messenger on the walls relayed his order by waving a banner to the men below. In the defensible trenches, archers took up their bows and laid arrows nearby. Activity picked up around Petrow and Hebden as the catapult crews, already loaded, prepared to fire. A horn on the walls cued the procedure to let loose. The catapults snapped their loads forward. A mass of arrows launched from the barricades.

The tribal warriors on the far shore were less protected from the assault than the defenders taking cover behind packed ground. A number of magic-users among the nomads, some still controlled by demons, offered limited protection from the barrage. Stones and arrows alike rained into the mass of nomadic warriors with enough intensity to put gaps in the lines. Tribal elders forced the back ranks of the warriors forward. The holes filled soon after they formed.

From a tent positioned well away from the range of the fortress, Norzal watched events unfold behind hood and veil. The demon smiled at the carnage. He encouraged his followers to continue the assault. He promised that their faith in the face of such danger would stir the elements to aid them.

After another exchange of arrows and boulders, the magic-users began to get involved. For the tribes, the mystics proved to be the deadliest at long range. They commanded the elements in the purest form. Their control of the wind had already deflected many arrows, yet now they unleashed their fires. Pejena Cloud Whisperer walked among the tribes, even as her mind stayed a prisoner inside her own body. War paint decorated her face. This day her breasts were not bared, instead they were protected with a beaded tunic adorned with symbols of the elements. The demon controlling her used her command of natura to summon her deadliest weapon.

The phoenix formed out of her incantations. The bird sprang away from her, seeking a target in the mass of defenders. It trailed fire as it soared. Pejena, and thus the demon controlling her, watched through eyes of fire, guiding it towards the enemy. They found a target: a group of men huddled too closely. The phoenix swerved around their wall of dirt to explode into them from the side. Pejena's eyes snapped back to her own perspective as she watched the smoke curling up from where it had struck.

Other mystics sent forth their fire elementals as well. In retaliation, the Brotherhood of the Circles and other magic-users targeted the spots where the flame-trails originated and let loose their spells. Arcane hands unleashed balls of exploding fire, ice, and lightning into the tribes. One such spell nearly killed Pejena. A druid bearing a large shield of living, writhing vines stepped in the way and deflected the assault. The vines of the shield, burned by flames, flailed and died immediately.

Another druid used his connection with the energies of lightning to send a bolt at the distant catapults. His spell failed to burn the catapult, though it left a man charred within a few steps of Hebden. A wizard among the Kashmer privateers returned the favor in the form of a comet of ice. It exploded, killing the druid and injuring several tribesmen.

Some spells struck with more subtlety than others. A druid from the tribes sent a bird around the side of the castle. The combatants paid it no mind as they fought. Eventually, the flying avian found a caster on the walls and dove in. The bird succeeded in taking one eye from the man, before a defensive spell smote the animal in return. Meanwhile, a necromancer among the privateers noted a downed tribesman. The spellcaster took control of the body from a distance, causing it to stab a nearby companion. As the corpse struck down its former fellows, the tribe members closest to it reacted with alarm. They tore apart the corpse's ability to fight, then did the same to a nearby corpse for good measure.

The tribes had more magic-users among their numbers, even though many could not match the power of some of the wizards defending Fortress Stone. While the practitioners of magic dueled, the waves of arrows killed indiscriminately. The nomads fared worse for their lack of cover, as bodies piled on their side of the river.

Perhaps the most powerful wielder of magic on the tribes' side chose not to get involved. Revwar stayed near Norzal, partially shaded under a withered tree. The elf wizard saw no reason to make himself a target when their goal was to slaughter members from both armies. He enjoyed witnessing the display of bloodshed alongside the coldast. For the most part, he had to keep his real feelings hidden. The tribes regarded him as their prophet…it would not serve him to appear any different. Nevertheless, he enjoyed the spectacle as he listened to the screams of the dying.

He did have one private thought that he kept unspoken. *Savannah, you would have enjoyed seeing Death rule this day. I will never understand what made you leave and miss seeing this tribute to DeLaris' domain.*

Norzal turned to Revwar. The taraz whispered in its rough voice. "I think it is time. The earth calls to me."

Of course, the taraz could not talk to the earth. It was communicating amongst any eavesdropping ears that it was time for the next phase. The coldast strode forward a few paces, and announced to some guards.

"The earth is stirring. I feel the spirits crying out for our sacrifice of dead. A sign is about to come upon us."

Excited whispers spread among the tribes as their messiah spoke. No one paid heed to the fact that one hand dropped inside his robe. The undead demon touched surface of one of the Earthrin Stones with his own rocky fingers. A spark lit within the relic as the taraz called forth its power.

CHAPTER 20 "The First Waves of the Assault"

Norzal exerted his will into the hidden Earthrin Stone. The messiah of the tribes pointed to the river, guiding the eyes of his people towards the promised miracle. He tapped into Mothrok's energies, calling to the ground under the Hossan Minor.

An earthquake began to draw the attention of all the combatants. The ground rumbled along the length of the river. Sand slid off the barricades and into the trenches as tremors rocked them. The defenders, for the most part, did not know what to think of the interruption. Some were too busy healing the wounded to bother with the warnings coming from under their feet. Aijak started speaking passionately to Mel as she realized something dreadful was happening to the land. Trestan and Cat knew right away that it must be the Earthrin Stones. Both did their best to look for the source, but the robed coldast and his elf wizard accomplice were not easily visible in the mass of tribesmen.

All eyes began to take note of changes erupting upstream of the Hossan Minor. The earth shifted, sending solid rock jutting upwards where the smaller river split from the source. The Hossan Major, running south of the keep, began overflowing even as the Hossan Minor was choked from its supply. More earth rose, cutting off the Hossan Minor completely. The remaining water continued to empty into the wetlands below the plateau. The river became a stream, and then was reduced to a muddy expanse with some standing pools of water. Fish, turtles, and frogs splashed around the remains of their home. The already-grounded ferry marked the edge of a field of muck. The rumblings of the ground ceased now that the damage had been done.

Witnesses felt as if they had revisited the Godswars of old, when the land and seas shifted and maps were made obsolete in seconds. The defenders simply stood astonished at the power that diverted the flow of the river. Trestan felt a hint of despair, fearing that Revwar would simply use the Earthrin Stones to throw apart all their defenses. The paladin's heart longed for a more offensive action, hoping to find and recover the stones. Of course, he knew such a tactic likely wouldn't work against so many attackers.

Norzal sent word to allow the first assault on the castle's network of barricades. The mass of tribal warriors called out in triumph as they received the signal from their leader. Another volley of arrows preceded them across the muddy expanse, followed only by scattered bowshots as some fired on the run. The soldiers around Fortress Stone had to duck the missile onslaught as the wave surged forward. Officers on the walls called for the catapults and the bowmen to focus on the riverbed.

The first wave of tribal warriors yelled blood-curdling cries as they attacked. Moving forward in a long line, they charged until slowed by the muck in the riverbed. Men slid on wet rocks; others bogged down to their knees. Some who were stalled became trampled by the press of warriors behind them. As they slowly sloshed their way across, the arrows and rocks from the defenders focused fire on those open targets. Along the line, defenders watched as tribal berserkers with little armor died trying to force their numbers past the obstacle. Rocks from the catapults splashed mud over those who were lucky enough to avoid a direct hit. Barbed arrows caused mortal injuries; felling wounded men into the path of others who would climb over them. Bodies became solid surfaces for the feet of those behind.

Trestan felt helpless to do anything until a man next to him dropped from tribal volleys. The soldier died before Trestan could offer a healing miracle. The young paladin resorted to grabbing the man's crossbow and delivering shots at the approaching mass.

Revwar was the only one among the tribes that sensed Norzal's mirth at the carnage. The taraz was fully capable of making the riverbed as firm as solid stone, yet he left it as a mud pit to help provoke more slaughter. The elf wizard assisted the tribesmen in only one regard: he encouraged them to continue flinging themselves into the fray.

The center of the tribal lines received the most punishment. Most of the weapons of the castle were pointed their way. As they struggled, the flanks of their line began to see warriors clambering up the far slope.

In the east, a red-haired woman in the defender's trenches taunted feathered human warriors. Montanya had learned to keep a good measure of calm in battle; however, she was well-educated in the way rage could lead to mistakes in a fight. The chiaso called to them, taunting them. After a number of well-placed insults, a small band of nomads jumped from what little cover they possessed, unwilling to wait for more fellows to join them, and made a futile attack. They came onward in a rage, and died as fast as the archers could fire. One only came close enough that Montanya hit him with a thrown rock before other missiles cut him down. More tribesmen replaced those who had just died.

A larger mass of warriors looked like they would reach Montanya's position. A fairy, seemingly made of light, danced in front of the field to meet the oncoming numbers. Montanya glanced to the side to see Lindon Taleweaver smiling as he watched his creation do its work. The flash from the enemy made her look back. The fairy was no more, having exploded into a stunning display of light and sound. The human tribesmen staggered around, temporarily blinded and dazed. Lindon's crossbow joined a number of others in thinning the weakened ranks. Even though the defending soldiers had an advantage, Sondra still kept busy administering miracles from her leather satchel to men struck by arrows and spells.

In the west, orcs assaulting Katressa's privateers thought they had found the weakest link in the defenses. Unlike the rest of the breastworks constructed near the river, the privateers had erected a small maze of bunkers. To the orc warriors, it appeared as if they could just run around or between bunkers and penetrate fast and deep into the enemy defenses. There was lots of space between bunkers, farther than polearms would reach. It tempted the first few groups of orcs to bypass the prickly front of the bunkers and simply run straight to the back through the gaps.

Just as Katressa Bilil had planned.

Cat had found that the scattered privateers under her command weren't good for shoulder-to-shoulder defense in a customary line. Their adventuring careers made them more comfortable in their own small parties and sometimes solo. Many were not heavily armored knights; they tended to be mages, archers, backstabbers, and wild fighters. Her design of the battlefield allowed them to fight in their respective companies…though a few "solo" types were forced to fill in bunkers. Behind all of them stretched a trench that wasn't very visible from the riverbed. A steep drop led to a spiked floor except for a few small planks bridging the gap. Of course, Cat's finest killers manned the far side of those narrow bridges.

The tribal warriors took the "easy" route to the back rather than head-on rushes at the protected bunkers themselves. They yelled their victory cries as they ran past bunkers, knowing they were penetrating deeper into the defenders than any of their compatriots. The orc berserkers found out how deceitfully deadly it truly was. At first, they paid little heed to the numbers of bows hitting them at point blank range as they ran past the defenders' strongpoints. One group rushed into an open space between two bunkers, only to be caught in the crossfire of mage spells. Another group ran over a trap set in the ground, causing a number of launched spikes to thin their numbers. During all of this, Cat's privateers suffered very few casualties. The orcs' tactic of rushing to the back rather than assaulting the bunkers allowed the defenders to get in their best shots while unhindered by reprisals.

One group of berserkers, escorted by a shaman, succeeded in reaching the spiked trench at the back. The spirits harnessed through the shaman helped shield them from many attacks. As the archers across the bridge saw them approach, they called out their targets and let loose. A few orcs lost their ability to charge as steel points lanced through them. The shaman called upon his spirits anew. Ghostly forms rose up against the archers. Of course, someone noted the shaman and called out, "Caster!"

Although the archers were distracted, a bolt of energy fired from a bunker lit the shaman from behind. Both the shaman and his spirits ceased to fight. The lead orc warrior thought he had the opportunity he needed to get across a wooden plank stretched over the trench. He didn't know that the "bridge" rested on a singular bar which only supported the middle and rotated easy. His foot hit one side and caused the plank to spin out from under his weight. The pain of dropping crotch-first on the spinning bridge didn't compare to the pain felt when dumped into the spike pit. Without the shaman, the other orcs died shortly afterward.

Trestan had rarely seen a raulgan before this battle. He witnessed scores of them butchered in front of the center. His borrowed crossbow lay abandoned as he and Rhijin tended their wounded. There was little the paladin could add to the devastation raking the enemy lines. A few determined warriors succeeded in reaching the barricades. Injured and weary, their bravado wasn't enough to swarm over the defenders' lines. Even in the face of death, they held to their customs regarding courage in battle. They rushed until there were none left. Every male and female of appropriate warrior age in that tribe died.

The first assault ended as a failure. Norzal was neither surprised nor displeased by the losses. He began organizing the next wave as some survivors slogged their way back. Some orcs feared re-crossing the open riverbed. They used the marooned ferry for cover, piling the bodies of former tribesmen for further protection. The lull in the action continued past midday. The churches of Abriana and Ganden used their healing sparingly. Those wounded who weren't in mortal distress were moved to the infirmary inside Fortress Stone. Some defenders were given heals on the battlefield until they could be moved. Likewise, the tribes removed some of their wounded and dead from the riverbed.

*   *   *   *   *

The second assault started much like the first one. A few volleys of arrows and aimed spells launched between armies. At least one tactic had changed. The tribes had a number of horsemen saddled behind their front lines. Among their numbers, Kor Strongarm, (more accurately, the demon inside of Kor), rallied his Spear Riders. Since the river was no longer much of a deterrent, the defenders had to be ready to meet this challenge. The Stonelands brought out their own cavalry of mounted knights, stationed on both sides of the castle. Since many of these horses had been underfed in the many weeks of famine, Trestan and Belgard were a welcome addition to the weakened force. Abriana's champion rested a borrowed lance in a holder on the saddle. This was Belgard's testing moment of battle. Trestan had trained in combat with this magnificent steed, yet this would be their first time together for the real thing.

Norzal used more of the Earthrin Stones' abilities in a slow, subtle way during the lull. He helped solidify the riverbed surface. The tribesmen would have an easier time getting past that obstacle, though they would also be trampling their allies' half-buried corpses. Revwar did little of anything. The use of his magic would only make him a target. He merely observed and let others do the hard work.

As the arrows rained in both directions, a green light struck the ground in several places along the tribal lines. "Let the land come forth and lead us!" Norzal shouted triumphantly.

Everywhere the beam struck, a new threat emerged from the ground. The Earthrin Stone summoned its stone defenders, courtesy of Mothrok. Rocks and dirt erupted from the soil and took humanoid shape. The elemental warriors charged across the riverbed, unimpeded by the muddy areas that remained.

The defenders focused on these earthen constructs. Volleys of arrows came down with no effect. The missiles either bounced off the rocks or stuck between the hard parts of the monsters with no harmful effects. Petrow and Hebden cheered when one of their catapults slammed one into the ground. The rock creature got back up, undaunted by the loss of a limb, and kept advancing. Mages focused their spells on the creatures with mixed results, but they became targets for the tribal spellcasters.

One of the defending companies abandoned their position to challenge this threat head-on. The Thornbeards, Salgor among them, charged with their axes, picks, maces, and hammers. Salgor had faced these constructs before when Revwar had used them. He yelled to the others the trick of fighting the constructs. "In the center o' their chests is a green gem! Smash that gem and they fall apart!"

The earth elementals bashed their way into the defending barricades as the dwarves fanned out to take care of them. The soldiers around Montanya and Sondra were at a loss for how to fight these monsters. A pair of earth spirits began to throw men as easily as dolls. Sondra barely got off a protective miracle on Montanya before the chiaso moved to strike the creature. The woman's training proved inadequate to smash stone. Instead, Montanya got backhanded several feet away. Sondra's protective miracle absorbed the damage from what would have been a deadly impact.

Down by the privateers, the elementals didn't take the seemingly easy routes as the orcs had done. These creatures were only interested in killing men. They charged right into the first bunkers. The first barricades and the men defending them were ripped apart. The earth spirits only became hindered as the magic users in those bunkers found ways to slow them down. Cat rallied some of her men who possessed magical weapons. While Cat's own rapier lacked the bite of the larger blades, she wasn't shy about using herself as a target to distract the creatures.

Trestan watched the center of the line, his former position, as an elemental spirit got into the trench with the defenders. Rhijin cast a protective spell on Leander as he charged. The paladin called forth a shield in his left hand even as he struck. Bits of rock were chipped from the monster. Enraged, it slammed a stone arm down on Leander's shield. Trestan could only watch in terror as Leander was knocked to his knees, the miracle shield shattered by the blow.

Salgor appeared out of nowhere. The warrior and his dwarven compatriots arrived at the elementals up and down the line. He vaulted into the fray using Leander's hunched back. The blessed axe provided by his family cleaved into the chest of the elemental. The axe's head cracked the rock, but stopped just short of the green gem inside. Salgor's other arm was still coming forward even as the elemental focused on this newest target. The dwarf's mace pounded squarely into the back of the axe, driving the wedged blade through the underlying gem. The elemental fell apart in a shower of rocks.

Along the length of the defenders' line, the dwarves pounded their foes. The stout fighters relished excavating stones, whether the stones walked on their own or not. Hammers and picks achieved more effect on the monsters than the swords and arrows. Word went out about the weak spot within the chest cavities, and soldiers rallied to deliver the critical strikes. The attempt did not go easy for many. More bodies were torn and tossed as the earth spirits fought.

Lindon used his magic to send a disruptive vibration into the rocks of the one near Sondra. The woman's mail armor and protective miracles would not shield her any more than the former defenders who had already fallen victim. The creature was stunned by the auditory assault, yet it struggled to advance. Lindon's magic moved away the covering of rocks to expose the green heart. The minstrel tried to use his music to shatter the gem, but he lacked the strength to damage it. The creature turned to face him when Sondra intervened. Her mace aglow with some enchanting miracle, she struck. The woman's mace cracked the gem. As the heart fell to pieces, so did the monster.

The defending men and women were beginning to think they had won their safety…only to see the next threat charging up to the barricades. Under the distraction provided by the earth spirits, the next wave of tribesmen had crossed the riverbed. War cries went unvoiced as the mass of bodies surged toward the injured lines. The soldiers of the Stonelands were too focused on the fighting elementals and the cries of their own wounded; some turned back northward only in time to see a painted, grinning face or a thrown spear coming at them. As alarms went up from the trenches, the tribes finally found their voices: an energetic and unruly thunder of curses and oaths. The wave of nomads crashed over the barricades, hacking blades against Stonelands' shields.

Belgard pranced in place as it sensed the nervous energy from its rider. Trestan wanted to bolt down the slope and assist his friends, but the cavalry was held back. Other commands were given, which included launching new waves of arrows and catapult loads. The volley felled many tribesmen, but could not attempt to target the ones already fighting in close quarters with the defenders.

Once again, the field defended by the Kashmer privateers seemed to be overrun as tribes flowed through the openings between bunkers. The front bunkers were also attacked directly, since the elementals had created gaps in the defenses. Tribesman assaulted those gaps, charging into the maw of devastating spells cast by desperate privateer mages. For those nomads threading between the bunkers, they began to recognize the officer who led this area. The half-elf with the raven-black hair flowing from under her golden *Taef' Adorina* rode her horse through those gaps, rallying her men. She offered herself as a target, and the tribes tried to catch her. Their eyes were so intent on their prize that they allowed themselves to be caught in crossfires as the first orcs did. Cat led them into trap after trap. The open avenues became choked with bodies…yet they still came. Cat worried that many of her privateers would be trapped in islands of their own creation.

Mel had been casting spells from the castle walls. Upon seeing the disorganized fighting taking shape below, he left that post to find Aijak. He found her focusing on a spell that had hawks dropping nasty surprises onto the tribesmen below. When he got her attention, he said, "Let's get to Cathag! I think we're going to be needed out there soon and I have an idea."

The center of the defending line buckled under pressure from orcs holding a pure black banner. The Black Maw tribe preferred heavy, two-handed weapons such as mauls and primitive halberds. They pounded their way past the soldiers. The center line seemed sure to collapse until the Thornbeards reformed into a wedge and chopped their formation into the assault. Salgor went headlong into the orcs as well, pitting his muscle against theirs. Leander and Rhijin grabbed a number of healthy defenders to reinforce the sides of the charge. The lines shifted back to the front barricades, then held again while the orcs tried to regain their momentum.

In the east, Montanya and Sondra fought a struggle of their own when they heard a voice call out, "They are overrunning our left side!"

The redhead chiaso looked left. She saw a mixed group of Black Maw orcs and some human tribesmen scrambling over those barricades. A few stopped to hack aside some of the long, wooden stakes keeping other attackers at bay. The men who had been defending that position were being trampled under the boots of those nomads. Beyond, tribal horsemen were waiting for those obstacles to be removed so they could charge through the gap. The line on Montanya's left would not hold for long, and the chiaso planned to do something about it. Other soldiers were aware of the problem on their flank, but none reacted as fast as Montanya.

The teenage warrior sprinted away from Sondra's side without even a word. The blonde cleric saw her go, but was too occupied to follow.

The armed tribesmen paid little heed to the young wench with the long stick that charged them. She aimed at an orc who was about to deliver a killing blow to a defender squirming on the ground. The fearsome attacker had a large, two-handed maul raised over his head. The orc either didn't notice her approach or didn't consider her a threat.

The young fighter briefly envisioned the training routine "Butterfly in the Windmill" in her mind. She focused her chi into the center of her body. Her mind and body joined harmony as she lashed out with a kick.

The kick to the gut drove the wind from the orc's attack. His arms reflexively dropped, allowing his own maul to drop on his head. The stunned orc went down. The man he had been about to kill ended up taking a sword to the orc's throat instead, but by that time Montanya had moved on to the next goal.

She snapped a kick to another foe wielding a massive bone-blade. The orc's elbow cracked and bent the wrong way. Even as it dropped its sword, the woman's quarterstaff caved in one green-skinned cheek. Montanya spun around the defeated opponent, braided hair flying out wide, and jabbed the end of her staff into the face of a different fighter. She knocked the newest victim down, but didn't try to finish the kill.

Montanya clambered up the barricade, where other nomads still tried to dismantle the stakes. One orc took her seriously. His heavy weapon was too slow for the agile figure. The chiaso's kick found his crotch, then her fist helped his face find the ground. A human woman wielding a dagger came at her next. Montanya spun into a foot sweep that attacked her legs. The tribeswoman fell only to impale herself on one of the stakes.

A roar of yelling figures came from behind the chiaso, originating between her and Fortress Stone. Montanya chanced a glance backward…and the sight stunned her.

The defenders of this portion of the trenches…the men being trampled beneath these nomads…were none other than Convict Company! She was rescuing the robbers and knaves that she most despised. The black tunics had almost been routed; now, they rushed back to reclaim their spot on the line. Rallying them forward was that thief, Dern. His white headband and sash were already splashed with blood. He raised his sword high, calling for them to retake their spot. The men cheered the woman who seemed to be single-handedly saving their hides, rushing to her aid.

Montanya didn't have time to puzzle over her mixed emotions. She stood like a guardian angel between the nomadic hordes and the scum of society. Montanya would have preferred a different place to fight, but she was already trapped by her choice. She guarded the narrow gap where the defenses had been broken. Nomad warriors converged towards her while defenders rallied to hold the spot.

Tribesmen jumped aside as a horseman from their ranks tried to break through. He charged the young woman with spear in hand. When he jabbed it forward, his target was not to be found. Montanya used her staff to jump several feet in the air. Her sweeping roundhouse kick sent the man flying from his saddle. As they landed, one more graceful than the other, her staff came down on his neck.

Orcs and humans in deer leathers came at her with all manner of crude weapons. Montanya's staff snapped the jaw of one orc sideways…she danced to the side as a rock hurled past…kicked a human onto the stakes…hopped into a kick which collapsed the earlier orc. A topless female orc attacked with a sword, only to be intercepted by one of the convicts. His black tunic was torn by the blade, yet as he fell one of his fellows killed the orc instead. Montanya turned her lethal hands to another attacker. She sent forth a powerful chop. Whether or not it would have dropped the opponent, Dern's sword found a home in the same enemy's chest.

Montanya shared brief eye contact with the young man who had danced with her. She could see he was smitten by her. For her part, Montanya did not know how to feel or speak. They simply broke eye contact as more enemies tried to create a new gap.

With so many threats before her, Montanya missed seeing a thrown spear until the head sank into her torso. She dropped to the ground as pain rendered her helpless.

CHAPTER 21 "Holding the Lines"

The wave of tribesmen stalled along their advance, at a great cost of lives. The ranks of the defenders had also been thinned. No definitive line marked the boundaries between armies as Stonelands defenders and plains tribesmen danced the chaos of battle.

Just as Montanya fell to the ground, the tribes sent their largest wave of horsemen into battle, led by the Spear Riders. Kor Strongarm, still a prisoner in his own body, waved his men forward. The men and women of his tribe were quick to obey their Com'der. A drumbeat of hooves announced the charge of a few hundred riders.

In response, an instrument on the walls signaled the Stonelands cavalry to advance. Trestan recognized the call as one similar to a tune played in his homeland. The short, blaring piece of music was called "Muster of Heroes" in Kashmer. The long line of armored men and steeds moved. Trestan readjusted his lance and urged Belgard along. He could see the wave of horsemen coming, yet between the cavalry and the horsemen were trenches, breastworks, spell blasts, and a shifting mass of fighting men. Trestan didn't know how they would find a proper route to meet the enemy. He worried that they would only clash after the plainsmen had ridden over the weak spots in their lines.

In the middle of it all, the oddest sight was seen by only a few. A large dog, running fast, carried two gnomes into a no-man's-land by the riverbed. They had raced through the tribes' footmen, exiting into the path of the approaching horsemen. Cathag turned abruptly, veering along the riverbed and across the route the horsemen would take. Aijak didn't even need to guide Cathag…she had already told him where she needed him to go. The druid and her passenger tapped into their respective magic. Aijak called to the plants in the ground. Much of the Stonelands had withered, but along the course of the Hossan Minor many plants still slept in the mud. The plants grew, forming vines with thorns that began to curl and spread.

From Cathag's back, Mel Bellringer worked his own magic. He threw pieces of clay while intoning words of magic. The seeds of his plot scattered across the riverbed.

Kor Strongarm, close to the front of the ranks, had a glimpse of the two gnomes riding past. The demon in his mind sent a telepathic message to the one controlling Pejena. The demon inside Pejena used the mystic's knowledge of nature to discern the gnomes' strategy. As soon as it realized Aijak's purpose, Pejena called to nearby druids to reverse the growth before it was too late. The demon controlling Kor forced him redirect his course.

It was too late, in more ways than one.

The horsemen began realizing the danger of the vines snaking across the surface of the riverbed. While this caused some distraction, it was nothing compared to Mel's surprise. The tribal warriors were either preparing to jump the tangle or shy and run around it when Mel's spell went off. The timed explosive pellets along the riverbed went up in a series of popping explosions. Concussive blasts knocked the front horses down, throwing their riders. Mud splashed across others as their horses reared in fear. The entire advance of the horsemen halted as the spells wreaked havoc. Thorn-covered vines whipped about, slashing men and beasts. The vines did little real damage…Aijak did not want to hurt the horses…but they scared many.

The two gnomes set back the entire attack. They rode fast to escape retaliatory spells, turning back toward the fortress near the privateers' end of the line in the west. Despite the effectiveness of their surprise, Kor and a horde of others made it past the riverbed. The giant warrior-leader fixed both brown eye and blue on this quarry. The nomad horses chased after Cathag, gaining on him with every step.

*   *   *   *   *

"Release!"

The commander's order came when Petrow was still finishing loading the rocks in the basket. The catapult's arm snapped forward, brushing Petrow's fingertips as he stumbled backward. Heedless of such small interference, the rocks soared onward to their destination.

Petrow landed hard on his butt. If the commander of the catapult felt any remorse of the near-tragedy, he didn't show it. Instead, he continued to yell orders.

"Crank and reload…faster! Those poor souls down there need us to thin the ranks!"

Hebden reached down and help pull Petrow to his feet. "You're alright?"

Petrow nodded, "Just close."

The older man reached for a large rock that lie near the catapult. He offered brief encouragement to the younger farmer. "It may be closer for our friends below. Try not to dwell on it. Keep loading rocks."

Hebden moved away, and Petrow spared a glance over the wall as he reached for more catapult loads. Such a confusing mess swarmed in front of the fortress! He couldn't tell where the one army stopped and the other began. Petrow had no way of knowing how his friends fared in that mix of blades, arrows, and fireballs.

As he watched, he noticed a fiery bird streaking toward the walls from the tribal mystics. There was no time to shout a warning as the phoenix dove into a catapult crew. A wave of heat washed over Petrow, carrying with it the sounds of screams.

Petrow turned to see Hebden rolling on the ramparts. Flaming embers drifted from his tunic. The younger man went to help, even as Hebden smothered the sparks.

"I'm alright," the elder Karok shouted. "I've had worse accidents at the forge."

Not all of the crew could say the same. The catapult caught fire, and another officer shouted for water to put it out. Petrow grabbed a bucketful, hoping to save the war machine.

*   *   *   *   *

Montanya writhed in agony. The red-haired chiaso wanted to get away from the fighting, but every movement jarred the spear in her torso. She witnessed her own blood painting the ground. Dern led Convict Company as they tried to plug the gap in the stakes. The nomads fought every bit as fierce to bust through. Bodies stepped around or fell down beside the wounded woman. She heard someone calling for a priest.

Unable to do anything, except wait for death, she watched the young man in the bloody, black tunic. Dern fought with all the heart of a man defending his home, whether he was a thief or not. When any tribesmen got too close, his sword chopped them down. With

168

all the action at the barricade, even Dern was sent reeling from a cut. It sent him stumbling back into the defenders' trench.

He recovered, but didn't jump back into the fierce fighting. His eyes fell upon Montanya, briefly glancing at the spear draining her life. There were enough men fighting that he went to save the woman. He called to some others, asking them to help him move her further from the action.

Several arms grabbed Montanya. Pain shot through her body as they lifted her out of the trench. Voices still cried for a priest to tend to those stricken. Montanya's focus descended into pain as every movement jostled her wound. The men worked slowly as they lowered her onto a tarp and moved her away from the heavy fighting.

A nomad who had gotten behind their lines went for the easy kills. His two-handed blade chopped into the grouped men holding Montanya. She saw the blade cut across Dern's back before burying itself in the next man. The group dropped Montanya, causing her excruciating pain, as they defended themselves. They killed the nomad, but the fighting distracted them from their former charge. When the pain eased from the chiaso enough that she could see and hear, her world narrowed to Dern and herself.

The young man, perhaps no older than she, lie a mere foot from her. He reached one arm to feel the wound in his back, grimacing as he did so. His hand and sleeve came back dripping blood. He turned from his injury to look into her eyes. Their faces were as close as they had been during their dance. There was no pain or disappointment on his face…just the calm of acceptance. In the background, voices still begged for priests to heal the wounded. With all the bodies writhing on the ground, many would not live to be saved.

Dern looked into Montanya's eyes. "I'm glad you danced with me, Montanya. Of any woman that could have shared my first dance…my only dance…I'm glad 'twas you who honored me."

Her greenish-blue eyes looked back at him softly. She wasn't sure what to say, or how to feel. Her hesitation allowed him to continue.

"I'm sorry I frightened you by revealing that I was branded a thief. I was too ashamed to tell you the whole story…"

Dern hissed in pain. He wanted to hang on long enough to deliver his thoughts. "I stole bread to feed my niece and nephew. Since my brother's untimely death, and the unusual famine this season, their mother struggles to keep them fed. I was caught…but the magistrate showed mercy. I served a few weeks on a work crew as my sentence."

Montanya's eyes went wide as she listened. "I didn't even have to sign up for Convict Company; I would have been free to go in a few days. But I couldn't…couldn't…"

He drew a deep breath, "…wouldn't turn my back on my country…my kin."

As those words rattled out, so did the last of his breath. His eyes dulled as they lost focus. He made no effort to draw in more air.

"Dern?" Montanya whispered.

There was no answer.

"Dern?! Dern!" She pleaded to ears that would hear no more.

Montanya could not stop the tears that began rolling from her eyes. The sobs that escaped her lips were even more pained by the torturous spear.

"How dare you?" She demanded in a whisper, crying as she did. "How can you reveal yourself like that, and then die on me? Don't steal my emotions and then hide where I can't find you."

No response came from the young man. It had been his choice to join Convict Company. Now he lie dead, wearing the black tunic and bloodied white sash. His own blood ran no more. No longer would he bear the concerns of this world.

In the distance, a voice cried out. "Montanya! Can you hear me?"

Montanya had no strength to answer. Her hand moved to touch Dern's unmoving hand. Feet ran past, war cries split the air, weapons clanged. Montanya felt the lingering warmth of his strong hand. She watched a red pool stain the ground between their bodies, unsure from which of them it originated.

"Montanya!"

"There she is! Sondra, hurry."

Sondra and Lindon found Montanya. She tried to wave them to heal Dern. Sondra gave the dead man a glance and then paid him no more heed. He was beyond her help.

Lindon turned a nervous eye towards the line of black tunics. "It's not safe here. Is there any way we can move her?"

Sondra shook her head. The sweat of her exertions all day left her wheat-blonde hair matted to her face. "I can't do anything to help her as long as the spear remains in place. Even now, her condition is worsening. We have to pull the spear out to mend the wound."

Montanya made a sound that could only be described as a whimper at the thought of what Sondra planned. Lindon had to move Montanya slightly to check if the spearhead had passed through. The pain was becoming more than the young woman could bear. The bearded minstrel saw barbed points jutting from her back. Sondra prepared her healing spell as Lindon used his talents on the spear. He focused on a portion of the shaft at Montanya's front. His voice took on an irritating hum as magical sound waves issued forth. The wooden pole of the spear vibrated before it snapped cleanly. Montanya could only moan.

"When you turn her over," Sondra instructed him, "I will start my healing prayer. Pull the spearhead out of her back as fast as you can."

Montanya was too frail to protest her treatment. She feared the pain. The youth wondered if she could even voice her goodbyes to her friends. Firm hands, from those she loved, grabbed her and rolled her on her side. She screamed loud enough to drown the sounds of Sondra's voice. The healing miracle was just forming as Lindon grabbed the spearhead and pulled. Montanya lost consciousness before Sondra completed the prayer.

*   *   *   *   *

Aijak guided Cathag into the maze of privateer bunkers. It seemed their easiest escape route and the one path where they wouldn't be leading the nomads directly at defenders. This brought them amongst other tribal warriors who weren't watching behind them. Kor Strongarm and mostly Spear Rider horsemen were hot on their heels. The demon inhabiting Kor allowed others to lead the pursuit out of its own preservation.

They wove between pockets of fighting. Cathag nimbly forged a course between men, slipping around legs and carrying his small passengers with relative ease through the throng. The nomad riders were slowed as they tried to avoid running down their own warriors. The first several bunkers had been overrun, with some defenders fighting their way to the rear. Further in, Mel and Aijak got assistance from more entrenched adventurers. The horse warriors were attacked on the sides as protected privateers made the open areas kill zones.

They came to an intersection. Aijak and Mel turned left. Just as the nomads turned, a half-elf riding in the opposite direction cut across their path. Cat let loose a thrown dagger, causing one stricken rider to break away from pursuit. Before passing, she drew her rapier and slashed across the upraised arm of another. The second rider's arm dropped uselessly to his side. Cat continued to guide Eyfan in the opposite direction of the gnomes. For the most part, the tribal horsemen continued their dogged pursuit of the druid and sorcerer. A few did change direction and attempt to retaliate against the half-elf woman. She led them into the heart of her remaining defenders.

Kor looked over his numbers as they began to close on the gnomes. Scores of horsemen still bolstered him, winding around bunkers as far as could be seen in a glance. He turned back only to see Mel Bellringer throw a large ball of clay into their path. The ball exploded in front of the horsemen. It caused mounts to shy away from the pursuit. It also left a cloud of dust hanging in the air. Kor yelled to the front men, trying to reorganize their efforts. It was impossible to see ahead while the dust rained down.

Through that curtain of debris came men wearing the Stonelands' livery, atop horses of their own. The defending cavalry formed a line of lances. They charged right into the disorganized, scattered horsemen. Lances snapped upon striking through the animal hide armor of the tribesmen, horses collided despite the efforts of the riders and the mounts to avoid it, and pandemonium swept down the line as men drew and swung melee weapons. The lanes between privateer earthworks were choked with men fighting on horseback. Riders who were thrown to the ground faced the prospect of being trampled by either side.

Kor's large maul was strapped over his back. It would not be safe to use both hands on it while guiding with his knees in this fight. Instead, he stabbed with a spear. The cavalrymen that came too close to him and his personal guards suffered greatly. Many Stonelands horses went riderless after passing by Kor's finest warriors. The giant Com'der shouted commands to one of his men as a new opponent rode past. The man to whom he gave orders never saw the blade coming. The sword's wielder, a paladin dressed in the armor of Abriana, swung a mighty blow as he passed. Trestan's magical sword sliced easily through the tribesman's neck and severed the upraised arm. Reacting fast, Kor stabbed out with his spear. The strike glanced off the paladin's armor as the young assailant used his riding skills to lean out of the way.

Another of the Spear Riders took up the chase of the young paladin. Kor was too busy trying to keep his men intact to worry about one man. Trestan took a few more riders from their horses before he realized the pursuit. Looking ahead, Abriana's champion saw no place where he could easily turn without exposing himself to a blow in the back. He had ridden so far that he seemed outnumbered by tribesmen. More of the nomads began to take up the chase. Trestan needed to find an escape from the trap he had entered.

A slight turn put Belgard in line with one of the bridges spanning the spike trench. Trestan didn't have to look back to know that he had just allowed his pursuer to gain several feet on him. The warrior behind him roared a battle cry, trying to shake the paladin's confidence. Trestan knew the enemy was almost on Belgard's hooves as the trench came within sight.

Trestan urged his warhorse to jump the span of the trench, instead of galloping over the wood planks serving as a bridge. It was not an easy jump for a horse bearing armor and a rider. Belgard made it to the far side, landing hard but continuing forward.

The tribesman was almost within weapon's reach. The man laughed as he realized the paladin's risky jump would only cause his horse to slow. The tribesman didn't try to make his own horse jump. He urged his mount to cross the bridge.

The bridge, as Trestan had known, was one of those which rotated on its center.

The nomad's mount found the solid surface drop away, and it fell. The horse's torso rammed the far side of the trench rather than clearing the gap. The rider might have been thrown clear across to the far side…had he not decided to tie himself to the saddle for stability during the fight. His horse toppled into the spike pit, taking rider with it. Several other horsemen involved in the pursuit reined up hard. Some stayed in the saddle, some didn't. All of them suddenly came under archer fire from breastworks across the trench.

*   *   *   *   *

Rhijin's curly locks dripped with sweat. She moved behind the center of the defending line, guarded by Sir Leander. She healed those who needed it, and simply used cloth wraps for those who were far from death's portal. She had run out of the bandages she had been issued. She administered using torn cloaks and even strips from banners.

Sir Theros Lightshield, commander of Abriana's followers, rode to her position. The old knight motioned to Leander, Rhijin, and the other chosen of Abriana.

"The field may be won or lost by our actions here." The warrior gestured around the battle. "Both sides are being pushed hard. We must remain stubborn at this spot. If the defenders can't hold, then we must keep the enemy from the main gates so that others may escape. If any have minor wounds, send them back into the fight. If any need to be carried…we don't have the members to spare as litter-bearers. Leave them lie unless we are reinforced."

The reality of their situation sank in for the young friends. Every hand was needed to fight. If someone fell here, they would not be moved unless the day was won.

Sir Theros addressed Leander directly. "I need you over there. We lost some of our brethren, and they need our holy protections to shield them."

Leander obeyed orders, running to a different group of defenders. Sir Theros continued riding in the other direction, passing orders up and down the line. Rhijin resumed her grim task. The young healer tended men unable to move themselves from the battle. She whispered encouragement to their ears, even as she realized they would be dead men if the tribes pushed forward.

*   *   *   *   *

Norzal watched the battle in silence. He used magic to see pockets of the fighting more clearly than most without risking himself. Revwar was never far away, yet never too close…in case the defenders sent some attack in their direction. The coldast demon judged the effects of the last attack. He tried to weigh the strength of the tribes against the stubbornness of the defenders. With a slight motion, he summoned the wizard closer.

172

Revwar and the imposing, cloaked demon shared words in private. They both agreed to the same conclusion: unless the tribes received extra help, the latest wave would likely fall apart. The defenders had been moved from many positions, yet it seemed unlikely that the nomad warriors would keep the territory they had gained. Another attack would secure the ground across the riverbed, but still leave the attackers at the mercy of ranged attacks from the walls. Even if the attackers won this round, the catapults and archers would be staring down at their lines.

Norzal could accept the latter easily, as could Revwar. They wanted the tribes to suffer great losses. The trick was to mold the battle so that it would be a close outcome. The elf wizard asked the demon, in a cautious manner lest they be overheard, how he intended to shape things to their liking. Norzal turned his hooded face towards Revwar. The elf's eyes could just make out the ethereal mists cloaking the face, and a slight flash of blue from sockets that lacked eyes of flesh. The coldast reached up to its collar. It absently fingered the necklace hidden under the shadows of the hood. Revwar did well to hide his disagreement.

Apparently, Norzal had no suitable use from the Earthrin Stones to easily influence their plight. Instead, he was considering the powers of the Gitouro necklace…risking its limited number of uses.

Revwar's opinions were of no further consequence. The elf wizard resumed his stance a safe distance from the proclaimed Messiah of the tribes. Norzal considered how to phrase his request. The powers of Kelor, God of Luck, were at his behest. He wasn't sure how well the concept of luck would affect the entire battlefield to the degree he wanted. He did know that the artifact was built at a time when it had to combat the wishes of other gods. It was likely that no will on the battlefield would be sufficient to overturn the relic…but how strong of a miracle did he require?

Norzal uttered his wish, and the Gitouro necklace responded. He limited his request to the efforts of the tribesmen engaging the defenders in close combat.

Along the line, the effects became immediate and brutal. The luck of Kelor fell upon every tribesman, while misfortune hung about the necks of every defender they faced. For the tribesmen, blows that would have missed the defenders found a way to strike, deflected arrows still managed to hit enemies, and attacks that should have maimed the nomads somehow never connected. For the Stonelands, everything seemed to go wrong. A defender that was going to cleave a tribesman tripped and fell victim to someone else. A cavalry horse reared at a bad moment and dropped its rider beneath the hooves of the nomad horsemen. A privateer archer had an enemy in his sights, but during the release a friend happened to stumble into the path of the arrow. Sir Theros Lightshield, carrying a summoned miracle-shield to protect him from harm, was nevertheless hit with a stray magical assault from a different direction. The paladin of Abriana toppled over to lay motionless beside a surprised Rhijin. Sondra had just carried a litter bearing her unconscious chiaso friend to some priests stationed at the gate. When the woman released Montanya into their care, she turned only to witness the entire line of men she had shielded fall dead under a rush of nomads. Lindon missed the event. After helping with Montanya, the minstrel bounded up a set of stairs to get closer to the Stonelands' leaders.

A diviner from the Brotherhood of the Circles approached Korrelothar on the ramparts. "I sense a great imbalance. He must have used the necklace."

Muster of Heroes

Even as the mage relayed this information, Korrelothar realized the truth with his own eyes. The defenders were rolled back before the tide of nomad warriors. Korrelothar spoke quickly with Lord Marshall Brocht and his aides. They could see that the battlefield was a lost cause. Tribesmen under the aid of Kelor's relic were unstoppable as they advanced. Every defender that tried to hold his ground fought a losing battle with fate.

Some warriors had the skill to defy luck. Salgor Bandago found himself nearly alone in the path of the advance. The dwarf went back and forth with his axe, while using his shield to intercept attacks. Kelor affected his fight, but Salgor stayed ahead of disaster. The dwarf began to feel the stings of sword swipes and spear stabs. He returned in kind, knocking aside tribesmen and lopping limbs. Some of Kelor's luck served only to keep the nomad warriors alive, though not always with all parts intact. Defenders on both sides of the strong innkeeper fell. Tribesmen thrust forward despite the Salgor's stand. The dwarf was resigned to walk backwards as he fought, rather than tempt fate from all sides.

From the walls, a metal pipe carried a tune to the far corners of the battlefield. Lindon Taleweaver had been assigned to bring the ill news. His command of magic amplified his musical message to be heard by all. The order to retreat had been given. All across the battlefield, the defenders tried to make their way to the fortress gates alive. The tribes surged ahead to block their escape.

CHAPTER 22 "Farewell, Friend"

Trestan rode with Katressa behind the privateer lines. The half-elf had one prevailing duty to her company now: get them to safety. She called out commands as scattered groups of men made their way past the confusing melee. Stonelands' cavalrymen assisted with the escape by harassing nomad riders. Under the pall of misfortune cast by the Gitouro necklace, the cavalry suffered heavy losses. Those who had time to watch from the walls saw a great scramble of men moving in disarray. Both army banners and tribal standards mixed in the large fight, but all of them began converging toward the fortress.

The situation seemed just as confused on the opposite end of the line. All sense of orderly fighting dissolved into a mix of individual contests. The only constant was the slow push of tribesmen towards the walls.

"Cover the center as best we can." Korrelothar pronounced to a gathered number of mages. "If the center goes, the rest of those defenders may be trapped away from the gate. We must keep the line strong."

The Brotherhood of the Circles rained destructive spells down. The assault centered on a group of trolls from one of the smaller breeds. These monstrous nomads had massed to break the center, but fire and lightening killed them as easily as other men. Kelor could grant luck to the masses, but not indestructibility. Tribesmen who slashed down defenders were hindered as all sorts of imaginative spells took them down. The spellcasters of the castle expended their last-ditch efforts to do what they could. Meanwhile, the tribal mystics and shamans could target the mages on the walls without much retribution.

The defenders filled the entry gate as they retreated. Mel and Aijak somehow squeezed through the throng of legs on Cathag. As soon as they were in the courtyard, the sorcerer dismounted and headed for the walls. Sondra fled just ahead of pursuing tribesmen. The cleric limped along, yet she dared not slow to heal the wound. She had protections from Ganden in place, but they would not last. A blast of spells from Korrelothar's guildmates cleared the men at her back. The blonde woman escaped immediate danger as she limped past the gate.

Hebden and Petrow worked as best they could to keep the catapults firing. They watched the desperate situation below them with worried eyes. They barely contained their impulse to look over the walls for their friends. Even as they worked, they became more of a target for the enemy magic-users. A close burst of fire sent Hebden tumbling to the ground for a second time. The aging smith got back to his feet, but fear gripped him when he tried to return to the catapult. He hated to admit it to himself, but he was becoming fearful of standing near the war machines due to all the close calls that day. As he hesitated, he finally glanced over the walls at the battlefield.

He saw his son and Cat, still alive! They rode among the fleeing defenders, calling out orders and trying to keep the retreat from turning into a stampede of men. A coat of red stained the elf-forged blade. Any fatherly pride Hebden felt at that moment was overshadowed by fear for his boy. Trestan was right in the thick of the action. Emboldened by his son's vulnerability, the old smith resumed his duties with more vigor.

Salgor and the Thornbeards formed a wall of steel on right side. They grudgingly gave ground as the tribes surged onward. Kelor's luck had done its job, but the effects began to fade. Berserkers died against the dwarven line, yet still forced the stout defenders back.

Even as Kelor's misfortune lifted, the left side collapsed to nothing. The majority of privateers rushed inside the gate as Trestan and Cat appraised the situation. The Spear Riders and the rest of the horsemen could not charge into the gate itself. They gave way to a number of foot warriors. A gap opened, leaving an empty killing ground that no one wanted to cross. Nomads fired bows or threw spears, but archers from the walls kept them pinned back. Despite the defenders from the left vacating the field, it seemed the tribes needed to catch their breath. A few privateers remained at the gate, shielding the escape.

On the right, only Salgor and the Thornbeards remained to keep the wall of attackers at bay. They were almost pushed back to the gate. Trestan noted a pair of humans carrying Leander, unconscious but alive, off the field.

That left a small number of defenders stubbornly holding to the center of the line. They manned barricades only a short run from the gate. Trestan was shocked to see Rhijin among the handful of fighters. Though no nomads were in close melee, the defenders faced a barrage of missiles. The reformed tribes slowly advanced up the hill, launching a spear or arrow at every step. One man, then another, fell while protecting the barricade. Rhijin paid little heed, trying to use her blessings to save Sir Theros Lightshield. The leader of Abriana's faithful lay wounded and unconscious.

"Rhijin! Fall back!" Trestan called out. "Everyone else is clear!"

With all the noise and distractions on the field, his voice failed to carry to her. Cat yelled also. There was no reason for the center line to remain stubborn any longer. The gates would close soon. The defenders had to run for safety or be slaughtered outside.

Trestan turned to Cat, "I'm going." Even as he said it, she was kicking Eyfan into action.

With Salgor and the dwarves left behind, Trestan and Cat rode into a vulnerable area to help the center. Cat got there ahead of her lover. Rhijin looked up in surprise as she realized her situation. The priestess seemed drained of energy. Cat tried to get the group to leave, but they hesitated due to their wounded.

Rhijin implored, "Take this man back on your horse. He can't walk."

Cat hoisted the limping man up behind her. She agreed with Rhijin's reasoning; that man needed a ride to get to safety. An arrow buried harmlessly in one saddlebag as she made for the gate.

Trestan let his heart rule his emotions. He was more worried about his friend. He held out a hand from atop Belgard. "Rhijin, take my hand. We need to go. All of you get to the gate."

Rhijin refused his help. She gestured to the stricken paladin of Abriana. "You need to get Sir Theros to safety. I can run on my own."

As worried as he was for his friend's life, he couldn't deny her words. Trestan ducked a few arrows while Rhijin and another man hoisted Sir Theros over Belgard. As soon as the paladin leader was secured, Trestan looked into Rhijin's eyes. "I expect you right behind me."

She nodded, "I'll be behind you, now go!"

Trestan bore the unconscious man from the barricade. A glance behind him revealed another man drop from a volley. Rhijin paused to offer a healing miracle to the wound. As the champion of Abriana looked back to the gate, he saw Cat galloping back to help out.

"Lightning speed, Cat," he called to her as she flew past him. Trestan continued up to the gate. As soon as he was safely inside, he summoned a few clerics to help Sir Theros. Precious seconds ticked by as he felt the need to ride back before things got worse.

Cat was almost upon the barricade as Rhijin finished healing the man beside her. The veteran privateer knew time was nearly up. Tribesmen were charging up the slope within easy target range of the defenders. The nomads focused on that last pocket of resistance before the gates.

Rhijin stood, turning towards Cat. During that brief moment of eye contact, a hail of missiles assailed the group. Rhijin shuddered as the impacts were felt in her back. The few men around her were likewise pierced under the onslaught. Cat could only watch helplessly as the life fled from Rhijin's eyes. The woman crumpled to the ground, revealing more than one arrow in her back.

There was no one left to save.

Cat regretted she didn't make more of a difference. All she could do now was get herself out of danger. Eyfan barely turned when more spears and arrows came down. Cat heard the missiles thumping into horseflesh, followed by Eyfan's scream. Cat barely threw her own body free of the saddle as the horse toppled down hard. She came down in a rough landing on the castle side of stricken Eyfan.

"Cat!" Trestan shouted from the gate, but she was too far to hear him. The champion of Abriana wanted to bolt through the gate but was unable. The dwarves had been backed up to the gate, with a wall of nomad warriors trying to force their way in. Even if Cat got up, she would find no easy way to get into the fortress. Trestan dismounted so he could assist the dwarven line.

As soon as Cat gathered her senses, she heard a rattling breath escaping Eyfan's nostrils. The half-elf remained vulnerable in the open. Archers and spearmen moved in too close. A glance back revealed the gate surrounded by enemies. She crawled closer to Eyfan, partly for cover, but also to be by her friend's side. Sometimes the oddest distractions haunt one's mind in times such as that. The words spoken to Lindon outside Barkan's Crossing came back to her thoughts as she listened to the horse breathe its last.

"I was there when she was born; I taught her the reins and saddle. If she is ever parted from me in death, I'll be there to pray as her soul leaves."

Cat placed one hand on the side of the animal. "Farewell, friend. We covered a lot of miles. You must take this journey without me. Eyfan…my traveler."

Her friend died while she touched the fur and gave Eyfan a final kiss.

The noise of battle and the threat of death prevented her from wasting any more time. Looking back, she tried to find a safe way to the fortress. The gate was a lost cause. Nomads were packed around the entry, pushing the dwarves at the expense of heavy losses. Cat noted Mel Bellringer looking down on her from the walls. He cast spells at the men approaching her. The other mages tried to impede the advance as best as they could. The infiltrator from Kashmer knew that Mel would be her best hope. She started to unbutton a special bracer on her wrist. It contained a grapple hook that could be launched by a miniature version of the gnomish lift.

Cat rose from her position and sprinted haphazardly towards the walls. The first ten running paces were safe. As she approached twenty paces, arrows started to zip past her. A crossfire of spells flew overhead: brotherhood mages targeting archers, and tribal mystics targeting mages. A streak of fire from Korrelothar shook the ground behind her.

Cat yelled, "MEL! GRAB THE ROPE!"

The gnome watched her run as she lifted her bracer to the walls.

"Fifteen!" She commanded, launching the grapple hook on a thin tether up fifteen gnomish-equivalent levels.

She recalled Mel Bellringer on the shores of an isle out at sea, more than four years previous. She remembered how he had snaked a rope into the water to pull her and Petrow to safety. She needed Mel to be as quick now as he was then.

Mel started casting. The tether pulled taut even as it hung in midair. Cat mentally commanded her mage-crafted boots to achieve their magical effect. She began to fall upward even as Mel's magic pulled at the rope. Mel's spell rushed her to the top, aided by the special effect of the boots. Even the tribesmen watched in awe as it seemed that the half-elf jumped over a thirty-foot wall. Cat went flying above the arrows until she settled safely beside Mel.

Down below, Salgor delivered a few more swings as he backed under the closing gate. He spared a brief glance above his right shoulder, watching the heavy gate lowering into place. While even the Thornbeards backed away, this lone dwarf refused to yield any ground until forced to do so. Salgor Bandago, owner of the Temple of Ale, used his axe and shield in tandem to litter the ground with tribesmen. A final pair of nomads were thrown back, (one suffering a broken nose from the shield, the other mortified by the opening in his belly), before the dwarf stepped back under the closing aperture.

In his usual defiant manner, Salgor shouted one more taunt at the closest nomads before the gate shut. He motioned at them with his bloody axe and scowled, "You realize this gate just saved the rest o' you from being slaughtered! I'll be back for you once I clean your friends off my blade!"

Salgor was the last defender to retreat into the fortress as the gate sealed away the outside.

*   *   *   *   *

Once the gate closed, the fighting waned. Arrows and spells continued back and forth, becoming more sporadic as it became apparent the nomads weren't going to push the attack any farther. The tribes displayed no means to breach the walls, though their natura would certainly offer possibilities. The commanders of the castle's defense limited the amount of magic and archery they were willing to unleash at the enemy on the field. The king and queen expected a siege; thus, they expressed a desire to the lord marshal to conserve resources.

The bows and catapults of the ramparts fell silent as the vanguard of the tribes set up positions close to the walls. Druids and mystics aided the strong backs of their tribesmen to rebuild the barricades in a way more fitting for their side. Despite the concerns of supplies, the fortress commanders still let loose an occasional volley, perhaps only once an hour, into the men moving below. The tribesmen replied likewise, though such engagements added few casualties in the face of those lost earlier that day.

178

A relative calm settled, broken only by the rogue spells, occasional surprise volleys, and a few shouted insults. The defenders tried to rest but few accomplished that goal.

Sondra joined many of the other clerics at the tower called Tuampor, assisting the wounded under the presence of the Gate of Issundor. There, she found her friend Montanya. The chiaso was not well enough to accept any duties except rest, so Sondra administered to her injury. Montanya wept as the cleric of Ganden approached her. The young woman would not reveal the source of her sorrow. Sondra looked for more wounds under the heavily stained garb, but was told only that she would not find a physical source of the pain. Montanya would say no more, but Sondra's presence seemed to bring some relief to the youth. The cleric did the best she could for her friend, without knowing the images of the dead man who commanded her patient's thoughts. Sondra stayed nearby and helped others as the tears flowed from Montanya.

Trestan spent a few hours on the wall. His eyes sought and found the body of Rhijin where she fell. The young man would have appreciated comfort from Cat, but the half-elf was reorganizing the remnants of her privateers. Leander was likewise absent, recovering from minor injuries. Likely, he didn't know of Rhijin's death, but Trestan couldn't go to him yet. Petrow and Hebden both found Trestan staring out at the field. The young paladin did not share his pain with them, though they felt his burden. Instead, Trestan offered them refreshing words to ease their minds after the bleakness of that day. While they could not know what ailed him, their presence helped bolster Trestan's heart.

Trestan stood vigil due to the actions of the tribes. The nomads were clearing bodies from the field in preparation for the next day of fighting. After a long wait, Trestan watched as a pair of tribesmen picked up the body of his young friend. Rhijin's limp form jostled between them as they made their way to the cliff overlooking Pilgrim's Bay. They heaved the body over the edge. Trestan watched through blurred eyes as her form dropped from sight, aimed for the wetlands at the base of the falls. He vowed to recall the spot she was thrown as well as he could, in case he had the chance to recover the body later.

*   *   *   *   *

Night was fast approaching. For those guarding the fortress, the unnatural blight upon Yestreal's sunlight brought on an early evening. Dark clouds continued to hover over the castle, while sunlight streamed into the enemy camp. Since the tribes seemed to be settled into their camps for the night, the defenders allowed themselves some rest.

Trestan, Cat, Salgor and Lindon happened to find their way to Korrelothar's grand tent. The Highwater Conjuror had been offered better quarters, but he politely refused in order that refugees might use the shelter. Instead, he camped with many of his fellow guildmates in a courtyard. They found him entertaining company at a campfire. The elf wizard offered the companions a greeting and proceeded to pull out some extra chairs…little more than carved stumps…for them to sit. The seasonal night air and cloud cover sent a cold chill to rob strength from already weary fighters. As they took their seats, they leaned close to the campfire to catch its warmth.

Their arrival did not interrupt Mel Bellringer. The gnome was already smoking his pipe at the tent while Aijak busily brushed Cathag. When the other Companions of the Relics arrived, Mel barely nodded to them as he continued his line of conversation with the elf.

"…which has had me wondering about the manner in which they are aligned against us. How is it that Revwar and this other individual have come about such domination over these people? The tribes have become fanatics; deeply devoted."

Korrelothar interrupted, catching the companions' attention and motioning towards his tent. "Please try to keep conversation low. Floranue is sleeping inside." He turned to the gnome. "My worries mirror your own. This messiah is likely a demon. We can't tell how many more may be hidden."

Trestan spoke up, "Messiah?"

Korrelothar was quick to offer an explanation before Mel launched into the subject. "Some tribesmen we captured spoke of a prophet and their messiah. They are fiercely loyal to both, citing miracles and effects that make it seem as if the gods were behind this duo. From the descriptions, it may be safe to assume the prophet is Revwar. I have nay guess as to the identity of their messiah."

Salgor huffed, "So, are you saying someone may be yanking that cursed wizard's strings?"

Mel nodded, Korrelothar answered, "Well, Revwar seems to be deferring leadership to this messiah. I don't know if the puppet master is Revwar or this new person."

Mel offered, "But we are guessing this new threat may be a demon. I have nay idea how a demon came to hold such power over so many, there could be ways I am sure…"

Cat grasped at something, "Mel said they show a fanatical devotion to this one? So, he may be the knot that holds the net together."

Lindon held his tongue, quietly observing the conversation without taking much part in it. The minstrel seemed to be focusing on everything at once. The set of faces, the arm motions, the tone of the voices. As always, the trained storyteller of the group seemed to soak up every detail.

"Well, we can't be sure," Korrelothar admitted. He cast a nervous glance back at his tent, hoping their conversation wasn't waking Floranue. "There is utter devotion displayed for this messiah fellow. That much we could all see on the field. The prisoners confirmed it. We just don't know who he is, whether he is a demon, or what part he plays in all this."

Cat was sitting in the shadows of the flickering fire, but her emerald eyes lit up, "We could use some more information. If possible…we might even find a way to chisel into that faith they hold."

"That's easy!" Salgor bellowed, bringing a wince from Korrelothar at the noise. The dwarf lifted his axe, "We just go out there, find him, and cleave him. A little more action would satisfy my bones more than resting and waiting. Let's see how they show faith in a messiah who has innards dangling outwards."

Korrelothar looked alarmed as he cautioned, "That could have the opposite effect that you intend."

Mel interrupted, "Violence would please Daerkfyre, but that's not what we need right now. We have all these questions and would like some light shed on them. They will likely have more surprises tomorrow. Will the walls hold?"

"Unlikely," Trestan sighed. As eyes turned to him, he explained, "With the stones they could shatter these walls at any time."

"And yet the stones have their own limitations." Cat pointed out, "They had the stones when we beat them in that castle in the sea. If we can find the means for this fanatic devotion and cause some dissent, the odds may change."

"The stones may have limits," Korrelothar half-agreed, "but the Gitouro necklace is only limited by the number of times it can be used. With any given wish made of that necklace, miracles can be unleashed that have nay counter. It was used once today. It affected fate across the battlefield, allowing the tribesmen to roll over our defenses. It would be a stretch of optimism that the necklace has used its last charge."

A silent moment of contemplation passed. Lindon's eyes went from person to person, watching their facial expressions. Mel translated part of the conversation to Aijak as she tended Cathag, and she spoke back. The gnome sorcerer turned to the others.

"Aijak suggested that we don't know enough about the necklace. Does Revwar still hold it, or does this messiah?"

"More questions and less answers," the elf wizard muttered as he took a drink.

Mel beamed, "Kind of like the gnome game 'moogetta'. It starts out with a person envisioning a fictional story, and then people guess…"

Cat interrupted before Mel could swing the conversation away from the topic. "I think I'll go out and get some answers."

Salgor practically jumped off his seat, "Finally! We make enough of them lose limbs, then they will talk!"

Cat turned a glare towards the dwarf, "I'm going quietly."

The dwarf's brow lowered and he turned to the half-elf. "Quiet tends to defeat the purpose o' putting fear into your enemies."

The black-clad infiltrator smoothly arose to her full height. "Salgor, will you never learn the benefits of the subtle approach?"

He shrugged. "What? People don't fear an axe coming at their face?"

"With a thousand friends backing them up, they won't. However, if their friends hear nothing while a dagger is pressed against their throats, they will talk." Cat assured him.

Korrelothar felt that Cat planned to go regardless of what was said. He had previous knowledge in this respect, since her and Trestan habitually broke rules regarding a wizard's flying craft and off-limit magical exhibits in order to do what they felt needed doing.

The elf wizard stood and stretched. "Very well, I'll have to clear a scouting mission with the lord marshal."

"Don't bother," Cat stated. "He may say nay, so I'll be gone before you get to him." Cat didn't bother to reveal that her privateers had been placed in charge with guarding a sally port at the rear of the castle, facing the Hossan Major. She had an easy ticket to slip out and scout.

She paused as she realized there might be a favor that either Korrelothar or Mel could grant. "The only trouble I will have is getting up the river to where their biggest tents are camped. I don't suppose either of you might have a potion?"

Mel started to go fishing through his bandolier of bags. "I think I have a levitation nut. We could fire you with a catapult, and you break the nut as you fall…"

Cat turned pale as she put her hands up, "Nay, that's quite alright. I'll be fine."

Lindon cleared his throat. As the half-elf turned to him, he said. "I believe I can help a boat safely across that river. We could hike north and paddle back across, coming at them where they least expect."

Korrelothar recalled seeing how quickly the Hossan Major's current raged since the Hossan Minor was diverted. "That river has a strong pull. I doubt a few rowers could handle it."

Lindon patted the mandolin at his side. "I have a plan which will work, and is safer than catapults. We could use one more rower."

Trestan and Mel volunteered at the same time. Cat turned towards Mel and disappointed him. "If I didn't allow Salgor along due to the noise he would make, I'm not taking you either."

Trestan was glad she didn't argue his own attempt to volunteer. Although, worry crept into his mind as he remembered they would be going behind enemy lines.

Mel would not be put off so easy. He removed some vials from a pouch. "You need me to go along and deal with any demons down there. I've been working on this surprise since Kashmer!"

Cat's eyebrows rose. "What surprise?"

The gnome threw a hurt look at the half-elf. "The surprise I told you about before! It is the results of my attempts to create an alchemical agent that would be toxic to those foreign to this plane, yet not harm anyone indigenous to Dhea Loral."

Cat's eyes almost glazed over as she tried to deconstruct the gnome's words. The woman couldn't recall any such conversation with the sorcerer. Then again, she frequently just nodded her head to Mel's words while her attention was on other things.

She pulled her composure together and asked, "Remind me about what you have been researching."

The gnome sighed, holding out some vials for her to see. "This is a catalyst made from reagents natural to our world. It is safe for us," to accentuate his point, Mel's finger dabbed some of the substance on his tongue. "However, it will be poisonous to the taraz. It may only slow them, but it could kill them. You need me with you so that I can use this against any threatening demon."

She refused to give in, tipping her head towards Trestan and saying, "He can dispel demonic presences just as he can repel undead." Cat turned to look at Trestan, "Can't you?"

Abriana's champion wasn't so sure his miracles would work as well on demons, though he knew he would have some effect on them. He could attempt to banish a demon, but he wasn't sure how successful such an attempt would be. He was about to give an honest reply when he realized Cat wanted him to answer Mel's concerns in her own way.

Trestan tried his best to look confident as he spoke. "Aye. I can take care of any demon that comes after us."

Cat thought she had convinced Mel. However, the gnome played one more card. "But how about you? Can you take care of a demon as easily if something happens to him?"

She thought for a moment, and then snatched the vial out of Mel's hand. The grab earned a slight growl from Cathag, but nothing more. "Now I can. I can just coat a bolt or my rapier with this, right?"

Mel's little shoulders slumped. "Aye. A little dab will have great effect on any demon. If you find someone who may be possessed, you can stab them with the weapon too. The poison will cause the demon to flee the host." She was about to turn away, when he sheepishly added, "Well, as long as you don't kill the person while doing it."

CHAPTER 23 "Nighttime Excursion"

A trio of forms slipped out the back gate of the castle. The fortress shielded them from the eyes of the tribes to the north. Only a narrow, rocky strip of land bordered between the fortress and the Hossan Major. There were small boats available behind the castle, pulled up on shore. Trestan, Lindon and Katressa grabbed one and brought it to the rushing water. Friends watched from the walls.

Trestan hesitated, casting an eye down the river toward the falls. He looked back to Lindon. "That's a strong current. You're sure we can get across ok?"

The minstrel smiled, patting his mandolin. "Well, I've never tried this particular trick before, but I'm sure it will work. I thought of a constructive new way I could use sound. You'll be impressed."

The paladin froze in place. His expression clearly showed his anxiety. "You've never tried this before, and if it fails, we'll be dropping over a raging waterfall?"

Cat decided to hide her own worries. If this was the only way to get her scouting trip done, then this was her only choice. She forced a smile for his sake. "*Faunlessa*, since when have we hesitated in doing something risky for the first time? Remember how we trusted Mel to fly *Dovewing* even though he didn't know how? Have some faith."

"*Dovewing* crashed," Trestan muttered. Nevertheless, he threw his supplies in the boat.

They pushed their vessel into the water and took their positions in the seats. Almost immediately, the current tugged them towards the plunge. Cat worked the front, Trestan took the rear, paddling for all they were worth. The red-bearded minstrel sat in the middle, offering no help with the rowing at all. Lindon flexed his fingers over the strings of the instrument before plucking away. A strange sound sprang forth from his mandolin. It wasn't so much a tune as it was some kind of rhythmic cadence.

"What happens when water encounters a boulder in the stream?" Lindon asked.

Cat answered, "The water splits and bends around it."

The minstrel continued his tune. Trestan and Cat felt the boat begin to move with their paddling. It wasn't just their efforts that seemed to pull the boat across the river. Somehow, the flow of the water pushed them to the other shore instead of downstream.

"Indeed," Taleweaver said. "In other words, that portion of water flows sideways instead of downstream, at least until it gets around the boulder."

Trestan's mouth dropped as he spotted something which could only have been attributed to the minstrel. "Cat, look to your right."

The half-elf turned and gasped, slowing her rowing as she saw it.

At first glance, a whirlpool appeared to be floating just to the side. As Trestan examined it, he realized it was more like an impression of sorts. Some invisible force acted as if a huge boulder positioned next to them. He could see down into the depression of water, as the current split around the open spot. The force of sound coming from Lindon's magic sat in the river and split the flow of water. This formed a current which pushed their boat towards the opposite shore. As they moved, so did the empty space in the river, so that the current would continue to flow with them.

Lindon reminded the two of them to keep rowing. "Please continue paddling. This is a strain on my concentration."

Cat and Trestan redoubled their efforts, in awe of the empty space in the water. They could hear excited voices drifting from sentries on the castle walls. Lindon's artificial current sped them to the far shore. Without it, the two of them wondered if they would have been swept down to the falls. They reached the other shore and made preparations to portage the boat upriver. Lindon's balance, gifted as it usually was, suffered when he finally tried to walk. He fell on the beach and momentarily lost his wide-brimmed hat. The effect had indeed been very taxing on his strength. Trestan and Cat did most of the work moving the boat upriver while Lindon just walked.

Across the Hossan Major, they saw the enemy campfires and tents. Cat's eyes spotted better details in the dark. She looked over the far bank and picked a point at which she intended for them to land. They allowed themselves to get plenty of room upriver for paddling. The threat of the waterfall was gone, though they feared to let Lindon try his magic again. They didn't want him exhausted when arriving at the enemy camp. Cat tried to find a launch where she figured the current would bring them to the right place.

They pushed away from shore once again. Fortress Stone loomed as a pale image reflected by fires in the distance. They were a long way from anyone who might help them if something happened. A couple tribesmen wandered the water's edge as the companions approached the camp. Sentries or not, they were not very alert. Lindon began a tune on the metal pipe he retrieved from his magical pocket. The companions watched one guard fall asleep on the riverbank. The second one just yawned. Lindon switched songs. As Trestan and Cat silently paddled into the shadow of a dead tree, the other guard simply seemed preoccupied with some magical distraction Lindon placed in his mind. The sentry lazily walked downriver for some inexplicable reason, though it seemed to have something to do with Lindon's efforts.

"Relatively speaking, that was easy," Lindon whispered. "They weren't really expecting to see anything. It wasn't hard to lull their minds.

The companions hid their boat in the tangle of roots from the tree. There was little enough cover amongst the famine's sparse vegetation. One trade-off blessing included a mostly dry creek bed that wound towards the camp.

Cat grabbed their attention before crawling far. "The common warrior won't offer us anything knowledgeable. We need to find a place where we can get to a leader of some kind." As she talked, she cocked and loaded her crossbow. She dabbed some of Mel's concoction on the tip. "Silence is essential. If we are found, we will likely be killed or tortured. Lindon, your songs will likely be very valuable, I'll have you come right after me. Trestan, follow Lindon and keep an eye behind us."

Trestan nodded. He would never argue Cat's commands in which stealth was concerned. He had done so when younger and more naïve, but had learned that this was her job. She had survived years as an infiltrator sneaking into unwelcome places. As much as Trestan might fear for her safety, he would better serve her health by following her commands out here. She dabbed Mel's poison on all of her weapons.

Lindon offered a comment, "I can usually help distort sound, and sometimes vision, to help hide our movements. I will make that my priority if anything comes up."

Cat thought about it, "You mean, even if we get into a fight, you might be able to prevent a general alarm from being raised."

"That is my hope."

She nodded. With no more words between them, they crawled forward. The tribes seemed to favor camping away from the ravine, preferring more level ground where possible. Despite having some space, the camp still extended to both sides. Very few nomads wandered around in the dark. A number of campfires burned within sight, attracting those still awake. Cat navigated a few turns and branches as she went. The ravine had been partially dug into a larger irrigation system. The famine had destroyed whatever crop had grown here.

They bypassed a spot where a number of horses were tied. Cat disliked going too close due to the alert guards watching over the animals. Their course shifted toward a hub of tents and tribesmen. Human men and women held a mix of conversations while huddled near fires. They spoke some dialect of the human tongue that left some words unintelligible. Some drank toasts to fallen friends, some tended wounds, others boasted of their feats during the fighting. Tribesmen moved about in the firelight, causing shadows to dance around objects. The tents marked the center of this tribe's encampment.

In the midst of this excitement, there stood a tent more impressive than the rest. Cat pointed a dexterous finger in that direction. Trestan and Lindon noted two sentries wandering around near the entry flap.

Cat leaned in close to the two men. She turned an inquisitive eye towards Lindon, still pointing at the sentries.

Lindon nodded, whispering, "When they walk away at their farthest points, we should try. I am confident in my skills, but there is always a chance we could be spotted."

Cat considered her course. In the dark, her emerald eyes swept back to Trestan. "Have your sword ready. If they see us, we have to kill them before they make the slightest twitch."

Trestan returned a grim nod. He hoped he would not have to kill either of the men, but he recognized the gravity of their situation.

Lindon began whistling a song on the breeze. Fingers lightly brushed his mandolin strings, causing the softest music to escape. The noise seemed quite obvious to Trestan and Cat, but the invaders near the campfire didn't show cause for alarm. It made the couple uneasy as they followed Lindon's motions, urging them onward. Trestan stood, drawing his sword. He wore no armor for this trip, favoring stealth over its protection. Cat still had her dark leathers. She smoothly rose to a crouch as they advanced. They slipped between a pair of tents, making use of every bit of cover. The sentries wouldn't notice them until they were close, and hopefully not even then.

Lindon happened to spot a small animal hiding beside the tents. The poor rabbit had an army camped on its burrow. The minstrel changed his tune, allowing the rabbit to see the figures creeping close to it. The rabbit bolted in fright. Its feet sent it hopping into the edge of the firelight, where nomads took notice. Excitement erupted, as two of them tried to get it for dinner. One tossed a hatchet; the other actually took a dive for it. The nimble creature evaded all these attempts.

The distraction turned the eyes of the sentries. The companions crept past their backs while they had the opening. Trestan felt so uneasy. He walked only a couple feet behind a stranger, sword cocked back and ready to take the man's life.

The tent flap beckoned nearby. Cat reached out and began to slide through the divider. Lindon stepped lightly behind her, keeping his constant whistling. Trestan backed towards them, but kept his eye on the sentry. The sentry began to turn in a lazy circle. His eyes were coming back towards the tent entry. Trestan nervously flexed the fingers on his sword handle as he took a steadying breath.

The man's vision swiveled past Trestan with the slightest pause. The nomad blinked his eyes, as if bothered by something. Abriana's champion was ready to swing, but the guard continued to turn his eyes, rubbing them as if he thought he had a speck of dust. Trestan was about to sigh in relief when a hand grabbed him from behind.

It was Cat, guiding him back into the tent opening. He stepped through the flap, and let it close behind him. They were past the danger from the sentries, even if only to face whatever lay within this commanding tent.

*   *   *   *   *

It took a moment for the eyes of the companions to adjust to the interior of the tent. The inside was nearly as dark as outside; the dim setting interrupted by only a few lit candles within. Even as Trestan entered with his sword, he sensed a flurry of movement. Cat launched herself away from him; her right arm pumped forward to launch a dagger. Lindon began to sing of walls and soundless nights. The notes from his mandolin seemed to wrap around the tent, tugging it until the sides quivered from some unseen force. The minstrel's tune provided a wall of sound to hide the noise. Trestan moved forward with his sword.

The young man spotted two forms inside the tent. A man and a woman had been kneeling on a fur carpet. The woman wore a prayer bead necklace, as well as a medicine bag about her neck. That was the only thing she wore above the waist. The man was similarly undressed up top. His bulging muscles flexed as the tribesman jumped to his feet. Trestan was awed by his physique. The man loomed big and dangerous, thus Trestan had to focus on him first.

The woman fell victim to Cat's assault before she could get to her feet. The thrown dagger buried itself in her side, painful yet not immediately life-threatening. Trestan knew Cat hoped to talk to prisoners, the only reason that the throw hadn't been deadlier.

Now, if Trestan could only convince the six-foot-six mountain of muscle to talk instead of fight. The tribesman edged towards a nearby maul.

Lindon continued to pour efforts into his song. Likely he could assist his friends to end the fight sooner, yet his concentration was focused on keeping sound from leaving the tent. If that hold was shaken, the companions would be swarmed by angry tribesmen.

Trestan attacked with his sword. He hoped to try wounding the man so that they might have two prisoners to question. The tribal leader barely avoided the strike. In return, the burly man reached out and grabbed Trestan by the sleeve of his swordarm. The paladin tried to grab the hilt with his left and twist away, but the bigger man was the better wrestler. The young man found himself staring into mismatched eyes: one brown and another blue. They turned and tugged. The magical elvish blade sliced blood from the tribesman, serving

186

only to enrage him. With his arm caught in the giant man's grip, Trestan lacked sufficient control to inflict any deep wounds.

The woman tried to rise and give voice to a spell. Cat promptly kicked her in the jaw. The Kashmer privateer grabbed a cloth to use as a gag. The woman on the ground was in pain, but something began to tear a scream from the depths of her throat. Even Lindon winced at the noise, putting more effort into his sound shield. Trestan struggled with the larger man, but Cat could not spare him a hand. The half-elf jumped onto the other woman and tried to subdue her.

Another sound came from the downed woman, seemingly out of place for her frame. A noise belched from her mouth, sounding sickly and inhuman. One of her hands tried to pull the dagger from her side, but Cat was wrestling with her arms. Finally, the demon inside her could stand Mel's poison no longer. It bubbled up from her throat, sliding between her lips like a brackish slug. Lindon barely held his concentration as it appeared. Trestan and the demon controlling the bigger man were temporarily distracted as they saw the creature appear. The dark, slimy form emitted a noxious vapor as it writhed free of its host.

Pejena Cloud Whisperer finally had control of her body for the first time in months. "Kill it," her strained voice croaked to Cat.

The half-elf was wise enough to understand the threat and react with speed. The demon barely sloshed onto the floor of the tent before Cat stabbed into it with her rapier. This particular taraz was only dangerous when it cowered within the safety of a possessed victim. Outside of the host, it proved as vulnerable as any creature in Dhea Loral. Cat soon had the thing writhing from several poisonous, mortal punctures.

The one controlling Kor began to fear its own fate. Trestan had released one hand from the sword, so the creature bent its will to controlling the path of the magical blade. With Kor's strength, the Sword of the Spirit began to slide towards the paladin's throat.

By that time Trestan had a hand on the coraross dangling from his neck. He held the holy symbol forth as he prayed to Abriana. He hoped his gamble paid off, and that this person was also possessed.

"By Abriana's will, begone demon!" Trestan's words wracked the taraz with pain.

Abriana's power ejected the demon from its host. The slimy, black monster spewed from Kor's throat, dripping a repugnant slime over Trestan. Even as it fully left Kor's mouth, the giant of a man reached out and grabbed it. The thing continued to squirm under Trestan's miracle. The words of Abriana hurt it, but fell short of lethal damage. Nonetheless, Kor suddenly sliced it from maw to tail with Trestan's sword. The big man hacked it twice more for good measure, until its insides splattered among the fur carpets.

The Com'der, still unsure whether Trestan intended more harm or not, had no trouble putting the blade to Trestan's throat in case the young man tried anything else.

"I wouldn't do that."

Kor glanced over, only to see Cat's rapier against Pejena's unprotected throat. Cat's left hand clamped firmly over the mouth of the mystic. The half-elf remained calm as she stated. "We just came to talk."

*   *   *   *   *

While Kor may have praised Pejena's skills at negotetin above his own, he and Cat had carried out enough discussions under tense situations that they soon spoke relatively calmly about their predicament. Cat assumed that their will had been forced by the demons inside them, and Kor's agreement seemed sincere. The tribal leader spoke openly about the demon conversion of the tribes. He revealed that demons inhabited all the leaders and many of the tribes' natura users. Cat established their mutual hatred of the demons. Lindon could not keep his song going endlessly, so Cat verified, as best she could, that she could trust the two nomads in order to relax their stalemate. Kor released Trestan, along with his sword. Cat allowed Pejena to go free. The first thing that the female mystic did was to find a leather top to make herself modest. Lindon finally relaxed the song that kept them audibly isolated from the outside. Kor or Pejena could have shouted an alarm at that moment, but they held true to their trust. Cat had been more nervous than she would have cared to admit that they could have brought the wrath of the tribes down on them at that moment.

They sat facing each other across the spoiled furs.

At Cat's urging, Kor gave an account of the subjugation of the tribes by the demons. His words smoldered with the anger borne from months of being used by them. The Com'der did not part with all of his information easily. He wanted to know the companions' involvement, and how they suspected the demons' presence. The answer to that was a complicated one; therefore, the entire story fell into place from a convoluted timeline. The matter of the story improved as the subject came to the prophet that visited the tribes.

"At the time he arrived, many of the people of the plains were already under his demons. The other leaders and I must have seemed like fanatics. People who asked questions disappeared…others began to accept the lies we fed them rather than risk their lives by worrying over the same questions." Kor told them. "The demons staged a show when Revwar arrived. They used their magic to make miracles appear at his command."

Trestan and Cat both perked up. In his excitement, Trestan spoke out of turn. "We thought that this so-called prophet was Revwar. The details matched him perfectly."

Kor would not continue until Cat explained their history with that elf. Cat did a remarkable job condensing their tale yet leaving Kor no doubt as to how troubling Revwar had been for them in the past.

The nomad leader commented. "Why does this elf aid the demons? Nay good will come from such involvement."

Katressa had no answer. "We don't know his motives. Regardless, he does act in partnership with them."

Kor's unequally-colored eyes stared at them, "If you know of this false prophet, then you must know of this false messiah."

Cat showed her disappointment. "We were hoping you could tell us more about him…or it. Every known accomplice of Revwar has been killed."

Kor seemed to be willing to share some of his thoughts, but he paused. The companions could not know how just the specter of this messiah figure could send cold fear into the giant's spine.

Pejena found the words for him. "I'm a mystic. My interests dwell in the currents of air, the depths of the water, the heat of flames, and the solidity of rock. This 'thing' we have seen, it's partly a creature of rock…"

Pejena's eyes lost their focus, looking inward toward her feelings as she tried placing her horror into words. "It's a cold rock. Mists of the dead flit about an iron husk. Few demons are greater in power, or more lacking in heart. It's an affront to this world."

She refused to say more. Her frame bent towards Kor for support, and he hugged her close with one powerful arm.

Trestan stroked his mustache in thought. "So, Revwar serves a powerful demon."

"Serves?" Cat inquired with on raised eyebrow, "Although I would not know that a demon would ever prostate itself to an elf, we have to be careful in what we assume. The important thing has been learned. Our messiah is a demon, worshipped by an ignorant flock, blind to his true menace."

Kor stirred, "I have seen them both through my enslaved eyes. Revwar hopes to gain something from this demon, so for now he follows that monster."

As always, Lindon stayed a quiet background observer as events went on around him. The minstrel tried to memorize details rather than add to the conversation. Trestan thought about the situation and came to an idea. He wanted to ask Cat about it, but wasn't sure what to say that might not give away some information to these strangers. She finally noticed his subtle hand motions.

"What?"

"Well, I was thinking…" he hesitated. "If we could try to ambush that demon using Mel's stuff."

"Oh," Cat shook her head. "I doubt it. It's a poison, and this creature is made of solid rock?" She ended it like a question, turning to the nomads.

Pejena added, "And a mist that reeks of graves."

The half-elf returned her gaze to her lover. "I don't think the poison will do much to it."

The female mystic asked, "Was that what you used on me? Did this poison coat your blade?"

She motioned to the spot where Cat's dagger had harmed her. The area had been healed by Pejena's own hands. At Cat's nod, the woman prompted, "What does it do?"

Cat hid her emotions well, but Trestan knew how her thoughts worked. On the outside she presented a friendly face, but inside her mind could be plotting tricks. She was probably trying to think of an answer she could offer that wouldn't give too much away.

"It harms the demons. If a person is possessed, such as you were, it drives them out." Cat knew they should be able to figure that on their own.

Kor had been too quiet until this subject sparked his thinking. He looked at Cat. "If used on the other possessed leaders, it will drive the demons from them?"

"Aye."

After she answered, she began to wonder why he asked. This nomad chief seemed as if he wanted to use it on the other leaders and set them free, but in doing so it might unravel the tribes. The results would be welcome to the Stonelands, but not to tribes such as his own. She took a chance and voiced her thoughts.

Kor swept his hands around, indicating the unseen encampments outside their tent. "This is not a tribal army; it is a band of slaves under the demons' whips. We are people who like to ride free. The horizon is our territory. I may have disagreements with some, I may go to war with others. Either way, we always had our freedom."

The giant clenched a fist as Pejena looked up to him. Anger fueled his words. "I have been humiliated and denied my freedom for too many turns of the moons. When you freed us, a part of me was cowardly enough to consider trying to get my tribe to simply flee this fight."

Pejena interjected. "It is not so cowardly. If we stay, they will find out that they nay longer hold us. We should flee east along the river. They have their own concerns and will not follow."

Lindon watched Kor shake his head in disagreement. The minstrel considered the wisdom that Kor and Pejena had shown during the conversation. He realized how much of a mistake it could be for potential enemies to miscalculate their primitive ways for stupidity. On even ground, the nomads of the plains could be every bit as cunning as their enemies…possibly even more so in order to face threats that hid behind stone walls.

Kor explained. "Out here, we are surrounded. If we try to leave, they will notice and many of our spears will be broken. We can't get to safety before they will be alerted. I do not wish to help them in battle tomorrow, but if we stay, they will surely drive us forward."

"What path do you propose?" The mystic asked.

"How much of that demon venom do you carry?" The Com'der asked Cat.

"A lot," She answered, though she wasn't sure how far Mel's poison could be stretched. The gnome had mixed an impressive amount of it in preparation.

The discussion in the tent concluded shortly afterward. The companions found out what a rare man Kor truly was. The nomad leader was willing to take a risk for the people of the Stonelands, and his own warriors, though perhaps influenced a good bit by revenge. Regardless of his reasons, Trestan, Cat, and Lindon got the info they had sought, and perhaps arranged a surprise for the demon army. Kor and Pejena's tribe would be carrying the risk, but it was one they accepted gladly. The tribal couple also hoped that when all was said and done, they could resume a peaceful relationship with the Stonelands again.

*   *   *   *   *

An hour later, Mel, Korrelothar, and Salgor raced down to the small gate on the south side of the fortress. They could still hear wizards and archers on the wall trading death with tribesmen in the night. The three stopped short as guards pulled open the gate. Cat, Trestan, and Lindon hurried into the castle before the small portal slammed shut. Arrows and burn marks marred their canoe.

"Daerkfyre will be pleased indeed at that show!" Mel looked exuberant upon seeing his friends returned safely. "Those spellfires sure lit up the night! Some of those tribesmen weren't expecting such hell to rain down on them, I imagine…"

Cat thanked the mage and sorcerer. "We're grateful for that cover. Getting out was sure easier than trying to paddle back."

Korrelothar shrugged. "We knew you'd likely come back with trouble, so we kept watch."

Mel continued his own version, "…Illusionists giving the appearance of six canoes instead of one, that druid privateer calling up the mists to help shield their view, and I think I used up most of this wand keeping their heads low…"

Trestan nodded. As with Cat, he just talked over Mel as the gnome bantered on. "When that first phoenix zipped in against my spell-shield, we were far enough away that I thought we'd never make it. We owe you our lives. Oh, and Lindon…"

Trestan turned around to congratulate the minstrel. "You are to be congratulated all the same for that wall of wind that deflected those arrows."

The red-bearded minstrel bowed. "And to think, I could have waited until today and adopted the surname of 'Windbag', or such. A proper name indeed for a minstrel!"

Salgor examined their clothes with a critical eye. "There is nay blood on you at all! Did you kill any of them while you had the chance?"

Cat's hands went out to her side. "Sorry, Salgor. I told you it was a quiet raid. You would have been bored with the trip."

Salgor let out a huff, blowing his beard out for a moment. "Well, that was a disappointment. I stayed up this late and wasted some good sleep hoping for more excitement than this."

An imposing figure parted the crowd. Aden "Three-Finger" Brocht made his way towards the gate. Korrelothar noted the approach and turned to the companions.

"The Lord Marshal approved of your venture…"

"Approved *after* they had already left the gate, it seems." Aden Brocht marched up to them with a serious gaze. He didn't look angry, but he certainly meant business. "Was your venture fruitful? Did you find anything useful about the enemy?"

"Aye sir," Cat responded, "including some unexpected helpers for the battle tomorrow."

CHAPTER 24 "The Second Day Begins"

Even inside the tower of Tuampor, a windowless room housing the Gate of Issundor, and despite the dark clouds directly over the fortress, one could see the outside sky lighten through the adjacent hallway archer slits. Morning rose and hope still survived. Those who had died during the night were being removed to make room for the waves of wounded that would take their place today. Scattered items on the floor gave clues to the struggle from the previous day. Blood-soaked scraps of cloth hugged corners next to snapped arrow shafts. The healing miracles supplied by the gods could do wondrous things to mend a wound. Unfortunately, with so many wounded, even the energies of the priests could be taxed to the point that more primitive aid had to be rendered. More than a few of the younger faithful had passed out from the exhaustion of the aid given.

Montanya paid little attention to the details of the room. Even after her sleep ended, (much too early), Dern's face haunted her emotions. She should hate him for being a thief, yet she couldn't forget that he chose to fight to protect his home. Whatever food he had stolen for his family, it cost him his life. She tried to get him out of her head as she attempted to sit up, but he just wouldn't leave her thoughts.

She almost couldn't raise her body from the cot. A twinge of pain gripped her gut and caused her to gasp. The wound had been visibly healed, but Montanya still felt the tenderness stabbing through her.

Sondra hadn't been far away. The cleric had her head buried in her hands; knees tucked to her chest while she sat against a wall. It had been a long night for the priestess of Ganden. The young woman tried to get any scrap of rest before the battle resumed. Upon hearing Montanya moving, Sondra looked up with concern in her eyes. The blonde woman jumped to her feet and was at her friend's side in an instant.

Sondra hadn't missed Montanya's gasp of pain. "Please, don't get up yet."

"I'm not that breakable," Montanya tried to reassure her. "Besides, I need to find the chamber pot."

From somewhere outside, they heard a horn calling. Sondra left her side while Montanya relieved herself. The priestess couldn't see much from the hallway arrow ports, but she heard a few more horn calls and the rush of feet as men found their positions on the walls outside. She feared that the armies were rousing their numbers for the next fight. Ganden's worshipper went back to the cot only to find Montanya looking over her piled armor pieces.

The priestess rebuked, "You're not that well yet."

"I'll be fine. I fought that halfling after an arrow passed through my hand."

Sondra didn't want to physically get in the way of her friend, but she did situate herself in front of Montanya's eyes. "That was a simple wound, cured easily by a healing draught. Your spear wound went much deeper."

Montanya started to scowl, "Don't treat me like a kid. I know what I can handle."

Before the chiaso could say more, Sondra reached over and poked her belly. Montanya gasped and flinched.

"It's not totally healed," Sondra declared.

Montanya lost her temper; she threw down a leather guard and yelled at Sondra. "Well then, fix me up so I can fight normally!"

Sondra stared back into those greenish-blue eyes. "Even if I did, my healing isn't good enough to regenerate lost blood. You lost a lot. I can't justify wasting efforts on an inconvenience when men will need my limited powers as they lay dying."

Montanya crossed her arms over her chest. She wore her old scowl upon her expression. Her tone softened, yet her eyes turned serious as she stated, "You just don't want me to fight."

Silence hung in the air for a moment. The priestess leaned back from her friend and averted her eyes. "Maybe. I certainly don't want you to get hurt. On the other hand, I was truthful in regards to your injury. You are still injured, but not badly enough that I should waste energy that could save another's life today."

"And what if you need me? What if some demon breaks through?"

Sondra gave a sigh. "Then you will see them in battle anyway." The woman motioned to the arch that dominated the room. "They are after the Gate of Issundor. With a demon on this side to destroy the protective wards and open it, they can easily travel in mass numbers to our world."

Montanya glanced over at the arch. Her face softened and her shoulders sagged. Her eyes went down to the floor. "I don't like the thought of sitting here while my friends are fighting."

The chiaso had a forlorn look upon her. Sondra came closer to her friend and put a hand on each shoulder. Their eyes met again.

"In my youth, at the sanctuaries, there were days that I worked much longer than I should have." Sondra spoke softly. She never took her eyes off Montanya's. "There were always wounded, there were always hungry, and I owed the church my life. I worked until I was ready to drop…and sometimes I did. In emergencies, I would heal until my strength gave out, then I would stay and bandage until Mother Evine forced me to get rest. I guess that's really why I'm such a talented healer. I pushed myself to my limits again and again, and found ways to extend my limits."

Sondra paused, "Nay matter what I did, there were always more wounded. I wasn't much help when more came in and I hadn't rested since casting all my available energy. Mother Evine was right; I needed to get my rest so that I could assist later. I tried to take on everyone's job by myself, and I was too shy to ask for help when I should have done so."

Montanya sighed. "So, you're saying to just wait here and trust in hundreds of people to get along fine without me for a bit."

A smile and a nod answered her. Montanya hugged her friend. "Well, just remember I came to fight. If I think someone needs me then I'm coming."

"But you'll rest for a bit?"

Montanya nodded. "I'll try."

The healer helped her friend back into the cot. Montanya grunted again as her abdomen complained. Sondra gathered up her own belongings, including her mace and healer's satchel. The woman donned her chain shirt over her unwashed robes. She looked tired but resolute. The priestess turned towards the hallway.

Halfway there, she stopped and turned around. "Friends forever?" She asked.

Montanya, lying on the cot, smiled back. Montanya's smiles were still few enough that Sondra treasured each one. The red-haired youth replied, "Friends forever."

*   *   *   *   *

Inside a tent among the tribal army, Norzal pulled on his cloak to conceal his stone body. Revwar stood ready by his side. They had just finished talking at length about the numbers of casualties and estimates of the strength of both sides. The demon was ready to step outside and give instructions to a number of possessed tribal leaders.

The taraz spoke in his usual deep, rumbling voice. "The defenders held better than I predicted yesterday. I disliked using the Gitouro necklace to obtain the ground we did."

Revwar nodded, "Neither of us expected them to try defending outside the keep. The tactic delayed us, but probably brought about more of their casualties than they planned. We will have to breach their walls and throw down their defenses today, or too little might be left of the tribes to win tomorrow."

"Perceptive, and I agree." The coldast hid its face under the cowl. "I'll use the stones at the start. That will give us the opening we need. I also have plans in motion to silence their catapults as we charge. Once the catapult crews are dead, the mystics can use the wind spirits to deflect arrows. We will be able to get right up into their midst unhindered."

Norzal threw aside the tent flap. The demon's ghostly blue eyeballs lifted enough to make out the tower Tuampor, rising above the outer walls. The tribal leaders were amassed outside the tent. Somewhere in the back of the gathering stood Kor and Pejena, keeping as quiet as possible around the other demons.

The demon's eyes went from the tower to Revwar. "We all know our objective."

*   *   *   *   *

"Loaded and ready, sir!" Echoed down the line.

Shouts went up along the catapult crews as they aimed at the throng of tribesmen. Their hands poised near release levers, awaiting the order to fire. The tribes had assembled in large numbers on the other side of the riverbed. Many groups of warriors were standing a lot closer. Several had camped overnight under the occasional catapult and bow volleys. Those numbers were hiding under meager cover near the walls, waiting for some sign. Above them, the walls were thick with defenders. Lines of castle archers stood on the inner walls, bolstering the numbers.

Hebden smoothed back his hair, more gray than dark. In doing so, his soot-blackened hands only deposited more rock grit into his sweaty strands. He looked over the edge of the wall. "How do they plan to get up here? I don't see any ladders."

Petrow squatted next to him. With the catapults loaded and ready, they had nothing else to do at the moment. Petrow examined the enemy army under the shade of his straw hat. The hat looked out of place from his armor and good leather boots, but he wanted it for comfort.

The blue-eyed man opined, "Likely they have something magical planned. Cat jumped over the wall yesterday. She didn't need a ladder!"

The old smith nodded, "Hopefully those folks didn't learn that trick by watching her."

Activity increased among the catapult crews. Petrow looked over and saw men swarming around the releases of the weapons. "They're about to fire."

"Finally!" Hebden declared, "If it was up to me, I'd have been firing since first light and kept firing as long as they're standing."

The first volley of arrows and boulders rained down. Those tribesmen directly under the wall were relatively safe as the missiles arced overhead. Their fellows by the riverbed started losing warriors. Unbeknownst to the defenders, Norzal disallowed the natura users from shielding their friends. The demon wanted the tribes to appear more vulnerable until the catapults were rendered useless. He did allow the tribesmen to attack the walls with their spells. Fire-streaking phoenixes and lightning bolts flew up at the Stonelands' archers.

Lindon moved along the walls as the first spells tore apart some defenders. The minstrel's weapons were of little use to the fight in this situation. His crossbow would only have been one among hundreds. Instead, he raised the morale and energy of those who heard his magical tunes. Men fought as if they'd had a restful night's sleep. Their fear was tucked away while his songs bolstered their courage.

A few of the companions milled about in the various courtyards. They had to be ready if the tribes used magic to breach the door or the walls. Leander and Trestan shared a brief conversation as the first screams went up from those stricken. Both were saddened by the loss of Rhijin, yet they kept their minds on the coming day. In the next yard over, Cat discussed some last-minute strategy with Mel, Aijak, Thamin, and her other privateer officers. Near the front gate, Salgor and the Thornbeards waited with tense anticipation. If they had their way, they would just open the door and invite the tribes to try getting past them.

*   *   *   *   *

The giant of a man returned to his tent. The best of his warriors gathered there, awaiting his words. Faces painted for war, they all looked to their beloved Com'der. In the distance, they heard the exchanges between catapults and spells.

Kor addressed them, "You all know what to do. As the army moves forward and lines get disorganized, I need you to seek out your targets. The risk to your own lives will be great, but you carry the future of our tribe with you."

The men nodded solemnly. At his dismissive nod, the warriors exited the tent with blades coated with a surprise.

*   *   *   *   *

Petrow and Hebden assisted the loading of the catapults, unaware that they were the first targets of Norzal. They didn't see several forms burst from the water behind the fortress. The forms changed in midair, becoming large raptors. With all the attention on the tribal army on one side, there were few eyes watching for an attack from the back. Guards couldn't relay the warnings in time. The unnaturally large and seemingly intelligent birds dropped leaf-wrapped packages on the wall.

Bombs landed all around the catapult crews. Their contents puffed out in a mix of poisonous gasses and smoke. A number of men immediately went ill and vomited. Few could hold back their stomachs as the gas choked them. Officers tried to shout orders between gagging. Hebden stumbled out of one gas cloud, choking and retching. Petrow hadn't been hit directly, though the smell assaulted his nose. He went over to give Hebden a hand in escaping to clearer air.

Tribal druids in raptor shape descended to finish off the job. Their magic allowed them to breathe in their poisonous attack as if it was nothing. The avian forms clawed at throats and gouged eyes with their beaks. The artillerists were unable to fight effectively. Arms flailed to keep the attackers from them as men stumbled and gagged at the same time. The druids began to revert to their humanoid forms. Humans, elves, and even small gliel appeared among the ranks. Any of the crews that seemed able to offer any defense were quickly cut down. Others who could only crawl or gasp for air were left alone as the druids switched to their goal.

"We need help over here!" Petrow aided a stumbling Hebden to a pile of rocks, whereupon the smith collapsed. The former farmer was uncomfortably close to the attacking druids. He shouted for the others further down the wall. "We're being attacked!"

The druids swarmed over the catapults and used their magic on the wood. Firing levers began to grow new sprouts until hardened branches wrapped around the frame. Another catapult's ropes writhed and untangled themselves, letting several pieces of the siege engine fall to the ramparts. One druid simply set fire to his target. Within moments an inferno whipped around it. The entire arsenal of rock-throwers was quickly sabotaged. Helpless catapult crews could only attempt to escape amidst their own infirmity.

Petrow's yells attracted both sides. The closest druid, an elf, turned towards his voice. A staff elongated in the druid's hands as he took a step towards the defender. Petrow reached down, untying his old woodsman's axe from his side. The young man hoped the armor recovered from that aging castle would protect him as well as it had preserved itself during the long years in the cellar. Both antagonists commenced to swing with all the strength they had. The druid was skilled, though Petrow's own abilities had increased with his time training under Leander. Weapons cracked together as the druid drove Petrow back.

A smith's hammer came in unexpectedly from one side, smashing against the druid's knee. The elf barely spared Hebden a pained glance before Petrow took advantage of the shot. The axe came around and chopped the elf in the chest. The force of the swing knocked the elf over the fortress wall. The fall likely finished the job, but Petrow had no time to look.

As soon as one threat was handled, another approached. A male, human druid, wearing a cloak of feathers, brandished a bone-bladed scythe as he spun near Petrow. Troutbrook's hero realized that the blade was nothing more than the jawbone of some huge carnivore. The sizeable jaw and teeth could bite a large chunk out of the side of a horse.

Petrow switched his grip on his axe, spinning it in a circle to match the druid's movements. When the druid swung, Petrow aimed his axe's arc to catch the bone blade. Weapons collided and locked together. The farmer from Troutbrook used leverage to keep the scythe to the side, while rolling his body closer to its owner. The druid tried using his muscles to disarm Petrow. He wasn't quick enough. Petrow came close enough to his opponent to try a desperate move.

196

Petrow head-butted the druid…or tried to. In all the excitement, Petrow managed to collide face-to-face with his enemy. The druid stumbled back even more surprised than Petrow. The farmer recovered quicker, finding his axe freed of the jaw-scythe and plowing a valley into the druid's skull.

"Another…there!" Hebden managed to croak out between coughs.

Petrow turned to see a small gliel facing the two men. The diminutive humanoid began to raise his hands and utter words of magic, rather than try matching the two men physically. The farmer had no time to worry about the blood flowing from his own nose. His face stung from his contact with the human druid. Petrow hefted his axe in both hands. He was prepared to throw the axe in order to stop the creature in time…something he thought he'd never be desperate enough to try again.

A bolt of energy flew past the two men, slamming the gliel back against the catapult that was already an inferno. The druid became a ball of flames.

"Pick on someone your own size!" called Mel's voice.

The two men turned to see the gnome sorcerer arriving with a smoking wand. Behind him, several more archers and wizards came to their aid. Arrows and spells launched into the druids. Those who survived resumed winged form and went over the wall to their friends. Few made it.

The intended damage was done. All of the catapults and ballistae on that side of the fortress were destroyed.

*   *   *   *   *

As the druids were seen taking flight, Norzal ordered the tribesmen forward. Those few warriors standing in the shadow of the fortress walls fired their bows almost straight up. Arrows came back down on the ramparts. A spell battle resumed as the tribes charged. This time, the natura users had their defenses up. Spellcasters from both sides targeted each other with explosive bursts as the line moved forward. Archers atop the fortress walls let loose volleys as the nomads came onward. The lack of catapult fire, and the protection from the tribes' magic-users, allowed the nomads to cross the terrain with greater ease.

The first lines of tribesmen still suffered many casualties. Warriors went down and were trampled by the numbers behind them. The army continued to surge forward, throwing themselves toward a wall of stone too thick and high to be breached by anything short of magic.

The coldast touched his frigid fingers to the Earthrin Stones. He gestured at the wall with his other arm. While his mind commanded the stones, his voice called out for the sake of showmanship to the tribes. There were many elders near him, preparing to shield him with their spells. Revwar was close and already had his protections in place.

Norzal commanded, "Spirits of the earth! Carve a path to the enemy! Let stone melt before our might."

Green rays shot from his frame, illuminating several points along the fortress wall. The tribesmen shifted the course of their charge to funnel towards those spots. The wall began to quake in several areas. Defenders on the ramparts stumbled as the stone trembled.

Korrelothar, stationed alongside his guild brothers on the wall, saw the threat and recognized it. "The stones! He's attacking the wall. Focus on the origin!"

Mages sent energy crackling back at the coldast. The force of their magic thundered against the shields of the shamans and mystics. Even subtle magics, such as swarms and disease clouds, touched the line of defensive fields but did not pass. A few magic-users around Norzal fell over in death from the strain, but the coldast and Revwar remained protected by their efforts.

Within the walls, Cat, Trestan, Leander, and Salgor saw the thick stone walls growing cracks, illuminated by a green shine. They knew the significance of the attack. The cracks widened, throwing slabs of stone to the ground. Sondra happened to be on the walls with the archers when the tremors threw her off her feet. Lindon jumped away from an unstable section that crumbled away. The nomads charged unhindered as the defenders on the walls fought to keep their balance. Fortress Stone was soon plagued with breaches along the outer walls.

Salgor ran over to the closest hole, hefting axe and shield high. "Open the door if you crave death! I'm here waiting to punch a few holes also!"

All the soldiers in the courtyards tried to recover their shock. Officers pushed them at the walls. Cat commanded her strongest privateers forward. Trestan and Leander stood side-by-side as they picked a section of fallen wall to defend. Instead of standing behind solid protection, all of the inner defenders found themselves forming a new line that faced their attackers on even ground. The first wave of fanatical tribesmen yelled war cries. Holding a mix of flint spears, metal-studded cudgels, leather flails, copper axes and modern steel swords, they thundered like a storm up to the walls. A last flurry of deadly spells sent flames dancing around the mass of men. Tribal orcs, raulgans, elves, and humans alike fell to the magic, only to be replaced by the numbers behind.

The first breach to be approached was next to the fortress' main door. At this portal, Salgor stood in line with his dwarven kin. They gave fierce cries of their own, calling to their gods and hurling insults at the approaching mob. The dwarves stood in a line, locking shields together in anticipation of the strong push they were about to receive. Five across and three deep, their wide bodies plugged the gap in that section. The last two dwarves, clerics of Taekbol, offered miracles from behind.

With both sides roaring in anger, the mass of the leading tribesmen crashed into the stubborn dwarf barricade.

CHAPTER 25 "Defending the Breaches"

Hebden and Petrow felt helpless atop the damaged wall. The siege machines were destroyed. Some of the catapult crews picked up smaller stones to drop on the heads of those below. Hebden chose to attempt the same. The aging smith huffed as he hoisted a heavy rock onto the lip of the wall and then shoved it over. It thudded onto a tribesman attempting to get into a gap, dropping the man into the crush of his kinfolk. For his efforts, Trestan's father had to duck a thrown hatchet.

"This is pointless," he declared. "I wish they'd left us one working catapult."

They noticed a number of tribal warriors forcing their way into the courtyards. Archers on the inner walls opened fire, even as defenders tried to push the invaders back.

Petrow was also looking over the battle when he gave pause at Hebden's words. "That's it!"

"What's it?"

Petrow turned the smith to indicate the top of a staircase. A door led from the stairs into one of the towers. "Get a bucket of rocks hauled over there! It's a perfect firing position to hit those orcs."

"Firing? All we got to throw these with is our bare arms!"

"Trust me," Petrow yelled, turning to run towards the tower. "I'm getting another catapult!"

"What catapult?" An exasperated Hebden yelled. He got no answer as Petrow kept running.

*   *   *   *   *

Montanya listened to the commotion outside while she sat. She heard the thunder as the walls split, but could only wonder at what had happened. The orphaned noble retied the braid in her hair, securing it with the elven clasp. She figured that if a fight was coming, she needed her hair out of her face.

There was no mistaking the sound of arms clashing in melee. From the tower of Tuampor, she could hear angry curses and mournful wails with equal clarity, echoing through the arrow ports. She reached down to tie her leather shinguards in place. More screams originated from outside. Montanya slipped her chest piece over her torso, wincing as she stretched. Montanya wanted her sparse armor on for when swords came seeking her.

The first wounded were carried into the chamber. Clerics descended on them with prayers and miracles even as the men screamed unashamedly over the pain in their wounds. Blood drops landed with bright splotches among the dark stains from yesterday. Wounded men despaired that the walls were broken. They cried out the absence of hope. Montanya grabbed her staff and twirled it to test its balance. She abandoned her cot to those who truly needed it.

The fighting heard outside pulled at her stronger than her will to resist. She touched the chi inside her, willing the pain to fade behind a door of her own mind. She moved out of the tower altogether, offering it back to the priests and those who were truly wounded. No longer waiting for a fight, Montanya sought one.

*   *   *   *   *

A company of nomads moved too late to rush one of the openings in the walls. A few that got into the crack found themselves victim to an unusual plant growth. Vines sprouted from barren ground, wrapping around their legs. The ones in the rear tried to help hack through the tangle, though some of them were suddenly pulled into the trap. One berserk human at the forefront saw the reason for the wild plant growth.

Their tormentor held her ground, standing an imposing two feet and five inches over the soil. Aijak's dark eyes and tanned face stared ahead as she motioned for nature's flora to blossom. The berserker thought he imagined the tree tattoo on her cheek moving as she concentrated on the spell. She stood in her raggedly-cut leather, holding back a number of tough attackers through her control of natura.

The berserker screamed, calling her a witch as he flew into a rage. His arm pumped wildly, using a copper axe to chop at the vines. His left arm worked in tandem. Strapped to that hand was the claw of some fearsome animal…now affixed to his knuckles for his own use. His companions tried to assist him, but they quickly lost all control of their bound limbs. The warrior of the plains finally released the last of his bonds with a primal scream. He barreled across the fortress grounds, intent upon that small foe.

Cathag caught him by surprise. The dark gray mastiff clamped down on his axe arm and thrashed its body wildly. The big dog's weight turned him around. Cathag continued to yank, using all its weight to tear the man's limb. The berserker, maddened in his rage, punched the dog with his clawed hand. Cathag fell free at least, taking the nomad's right forearm with it. The mastiff continued to jerk the severed arm around, as if it could cause the former owner any more harm. The berserker roared in rage and agony as he stumbled. He drew the attention of an archer who finished him.

As Aijak's plants continued to fill the opening, Mel arrived by her side. The gnome sorcerer threw a handful of clay balls over the heads of the men stuck in the gap. Those trying to hack the vines from the outside looked around as they heard small objects landing next to them.

BOOM! BOOM! BOOM!

Men and weapons went flying as the growing vines finally obscured them from view. A few plant pieces flew back through the crack as well. The tribesmen stuck within the branches could no longer help themselves as they became trapped. Aijak finished her magic. At least for the moment, one gap in the defenses had been sealed. The druid was able to turn her attentions to Cathag. The dog had been hurt by the berserker's claw-weapon, but not beyond her magic's ability to mend the wound.

*   *   *   *   *

Trestan and Leander, friends all through their ascension to paladins, fought nearly side-by-side from one courtyard into the next. They steadily lost ground against swarms of enemies. Assistance came in the form of Korrelothar and his most talented mages. The spellcasters stood on the walls, raining death at those below. The nomads had their own spell-casters trying to either shield them or strike back. The tribes knew they were on the verge of gaining a firm foothold within the walls of the fortress, so they pushed forward recklessly. Leander had been using shields found among the dead. He was now on his third shield; the rest having been hacked to splinters. Trestan refused shields, preferring to fight in his two-handed style. His method allowed him to conjure miracle shields to deflect spells when needed.

Leander reflected a foul mood. Despite the callings of Abriana to show love and compassion, even for enemies, the fair-haired paladin felt anger inside him over the loss of Rhijin yesterday. The warrior threw all his efforts into beating back many foes in repayment for that loss.

Trestan understood his friend's emotions, but could not share in the anger. The loss of a close friend hurt him, yet he had glimpsed into the enemy camp and understood them. They were victims as much as the people here. All had been manipulated by Revwar and his allies. Trestan could not afford to carry hatred in his heart for those who had been tricked. He fought, but his fight was only to keep the demons away from Tuampor.

"Tres, we have to do something about feather-head."

Leander pointed at a shaman wearing a feathered headdress. The old nomad deflected the spells cast at his tribesmen, allowing his followers to carve a path ahead of the other warriors. Korrelothar and the mages were laying waste to many lives, but that group moved undeterred due to the protection of their elder. Spells could not get to the man…perhaps swords could.

Trestan got an idea. "Leander, come with me."

The paladins withdrew behind the defenders into the arch leading to the next courtyard. A small guardroom held a rack with crossbows. Trestan whispered his plan to his friend. Immediately, both men sheathed their swords and loaded the crossbows.

As the group of tribesmen around the mystic broke past another line of defenders, they began to see the arch ahead. Their elder called out directions, aiming them to take that strategic spot between courtyards. A surprise attack came from their flanks. Two armored men charged at their side from behind the broken line of defenders.

Leander and Trestan supported loaded crossbows in each hand. Almost as soon as the nomads on that side spotted them, the young men both fired the left-hand bows. Two nomads dropped in pain. The paladins continued to run straight into the group of men. At close range, Trestan and Leander fired their right-hand bows. Two more tribesmen went down. Their rush hit so fast that the inner ring of warriors hadn't realized the danger before two insane youths were running through them. Thrown, empty crossbows caused some to flinch aside. Trestan brought his remaining spent crossbow up and shoved it into an opponent's face as he ran him over. The shaman was before them at last, arms waving as he tried to bring magic against them. Leander went for his sword, Trestan brought up his left arm. A few brief words of prayer, and Trestan formed a magical shield. The shaman threw the force of his summoned spirits at them, only to witness the energies absorbed by Trestan's miracle. Leander took the lead, coming around Trestan with his sword. The elder's howl of rage turned to pain as the weapon hit its mark.

The shaman fell with a mortal wound as the two paladins were swept up in the retaliations from his kin. Trestan and Leander danced in the midst of furious swordplay. They realized they would probably die for their bold move. Trestan tried to summon one image of Cat in his mind before he died; however, his concentration strained to block all the swings coming at him.

With the protection of the elder gone, the mage guild began to pummel the group. Korrelothar didn't miss the danger to the two young men. The elf lobbed fireballs close enough that he almost singed their hairs. Brotherhood mages along the wall loosed deadly beams and crackling bolts that sent men reeling.

The shock waves from exploding spells knocked Trestan and Leander down. Korrelothar watched with a nervous stomach as castle defenders rolled back over the staggering tribesmen. Armored troops wearing the heraldry of the Stonelands drove the leather-clad nomads back from the arch. The elf on the wall looked down upon the smoking forms of men left behind.

Korrelothar felt relief a moment later, when Leander and Trestan sat up amidst a score of dead men. The hurts that they had suffered were quickly mended by their own healing prayers.

*   *   *   *   *

Cat cursed as she shoved some of her privateers forward. A couple breaches had opened in the span of walls before her. The fighters from Kashmer thought they would be held in a reserve position, but Norzal's plan changed that. Adventurers, rogues, and mercenaries brandishing magical weapons, positioned themselves to withstand the surge of sparsely-armored nomads. Cat's voice screamed above the din, directing her forces as best she could. Her hands worked her bow as she added her arrows to the defense.

The half-elf had little time to reflect on how costly the battle had been for her forces. A number of Kashmer-renowned companies and solo adventurers fought under her command. Songs and tales had spread the length of Quoros involving some of them. Now they fought in a battle that would either open or prevent another Godswars. Figures who were already heroic in lore added to their tale, sometimes writing only an ending to their story.

On her right fought the Redcloaks: a famed company of seven who had defeated a rowdy bunch of giants in Kashmer's southern provinces. Now they numbered five, having lost their leader and one other when their bunker was overrun the previous day. The remainders of their group handed out vengeance for their losses.

On Cat's left was a priest called "Saint of Toresco" due to his reputed efforts to save that small community from a magical malady. For all the man suffered then, it wasn't until the previous day's fighting that he had lost an arm to an orc's axe. Despite Cat's request, the man stayed on the lines offering healing from his remaining arm.

One figure missing from the courtyard fight was a woman known by the name of a constellation, Saphydie. The woman was a mage of mixed repute who had no other name known to men. She identified by the constellation she used as her personal symbol. Her true name was likely as lost as her head…which had gone missing since the Spear Riders charged through the privateers' bunkers the day before.

A few feet away struggled the Agrend Brothers, noted warriors who frequented every tavern in Kashmer with rowdy tales. They had helped Cat whip her volunteers into a fighting force. Now, one lay dying while the other tried to keep the enemy back long enough for a healer to arrive.

One of her other officers, Thamin of Kaigal, wielded weapons in both hands as he stood stubborn in the face of tribesman trying to reach his storm-mage daughter. The youth, Thomena, mounted a broken wagon. She used the added height to throw lightning and lethal icicles at attackers. Together, they made the tribes pay in blood for every patch of ground.

Cat was fighting alongside living legends…and watching them die. Though many of the fighters from Kashmer were just beginning their reputations, other heroes reached their conclusion. The minstrels would have a lot of tales to sing once this was done, most of them tragedies.

The half-elf had almost spent her entire stock of arrows. One enemy after another would tempt her aim. The sheer numbers of the tribes were overwhelming better armed defenders. Suddenly, her bow began to twist in her hand. The wooden portion began to bend in odd angles. Cat dropped her valuable, misshapen Serud'Thanil bow as she tried to understand what was happening. She finally spotted the source of her problems: a druid who had ruined her weapon from afar. Cat moved to draw a throwing dagger.

A companion beat her to her opponent. It began with a bright fairy, seemingly composed of colors, hopping towards the druid. The fairy exploded into a boggling array of sight and sound. The druid staggered…deaf and blind from the assault. Lindon quickly followed his musical creation. The minstrel from Orlaun danced in and delivered a skillful thrust from his smallsword, bringing a finale to the troublesome druid.

Lindon danced back to Cat's side, sparing a glance at the useless bow. "Can't have a menace like that around in case I use my bamboo flute. It's priceless to me!"

Lindon and Cat fought together for awhile. The half-elf noticed that the minstrel wasn't the only help to arrive. Sondra Oskires attended to the wounded Agrend Brother with an acolyte of Ganden. It was surprising how well the young cleric performed during the fight. Sondra had gained both courage and confidence in her travels. Her acolyte was flinching from every noise, yet Sondra kept a calm voice directing the younger healer. Only a few months ago, the blonde priestess would have been as nervous as her student. When the action came close enough that the acolyte cowered, Sondra whipped out her mace and assisted in driving their enemies back.

Those who faced life head-on often learn more than all the teachings of schools and seminaries.

*   *   *   *   *

Salgor and the Thornbeards gave a rowdy cheer as the latest wave of tribesmen melted away from their shield-wall. The stout defenders watched their opponents' rout over a growing mound of bodies. Each rush of the nomads proved fruitless against the dwarves.

The elation from the dwarves died as the retreating enemies revealed the next wave. A line of shapeshifting nomads, druids and greenmen, were pawing the ground in anticipation of their turn. Each one assumed the guise and properties of a tough animal. Bison, bears, and an elephant stood among the chosen forms.

Salgor spit at the ground in front of him, "Looks like they pulled a whole herd at us boys! The smokehouse will be full o' meat tonight!"

The dwarves grunted and returned their shields to a guard position. Arm against arm, feet set to receive any charge, they called out insults. The shapeshifters charged as one, letting loose animal growls even as the elephant trumpeted the assault. The ground shook under their hooves and paws. The dwarves wouldn't even consider shying away.

Warriors fighting distant from the gap still heard the tumult as the two forces clashed. Animal grunts and screams mixed with the same from the dwarves. The stampede busted through the first rank, rolled over the second rank, and finally began to founder as it breached the third. Trampled dwarves still hacked at legs and bellies from underneath. Gutted animal-men yet kept charging. As long as life clung to the trampled fallen, they butchered all their enemies as they passed. Pick heads and axes swung from below. The nomad animals bit into arms, gored shields with their horns, and kicked at flailing limbs. Dwarves tried but failed to rise as more and more forms stepped on them.

The dwarves were thrown from the breach or crushed to death. The elephant's trunk tossed Salgor aside. Cheering tribesmen surged through the hard-won gap. Arrows began to rain from the walls, felling several invaders. The tribes stubbornly remained in control of that entrance.

Many of the shapeshifters paid for their victory. Several were grievously wounded or permanently maimed. They dropped dead even as they won the entry into the courtyard. As for the elephant…

"We're not finished yet!" Salgor came in head-on, planting his axe into the thick skull. The shapeshifter joined the growing pile of dead.

*   *   *   *   *

The warriors of the tribes mixed together as they funneled toward the narrow gaps. In all the confusion, raulgans elbowed orcs for position, and gliel tried not to be trampled by their allies.

In such disorder, few paused to consider the occasional, stray Spear Rider making his way on foot through the masses. The nomad horsemen moved in singles and pairs, but never more than that. They spread out among the entire tribal army. Each one sought an elder and began to shadow their movements. Tribal leaders and wise men took little notice of the Riders that happened to trail them.

*   *   *   *   *

Norzal and Revwar watched the distant battle. They could not tell how the courtyard fight progressed. The only hints offered as to the tribes' successes were that many still flowed in through the gaps, and the spells launched from the defending wizards were aimed inside the walls.

The coldast beckoned Revwar closer. "The time has come. The defenders seem appropriately distracted. If the tribes get too close to Tuampor, it will make it harder to carry out our plan."

Revwar spared a second glance at the fortress with his golden eyes. He could not refute the demon's claim. They were about to pick a dangerous path, but no less dangerous than the service which had brought them to this pinnacle.

The elf wizard joined the taraz, whispering spells. The elders around them, (all demons), tried to block the view of any non-possessed bystanders. Revwar's cloak began to rise against the wind, flapping out to his sides. Norzal's cloak began to flutter of its own volition as well. The rocks and mist forming his true shape were briefly visible, but only to those in the immediate vicinity. Revwar drank a potion, while the demon continued to chant. Both turned invisible.

Hidden from the eyes of all, they took to flight. Elf and demon soared high above the field of battle. They flew hand-in-hand, for they could not see each other. No catapults were left to catch them by accident. No random spells burst in the sky. The archers on the fortress walls aimed down, not up, allowing them to fly free of volleys. Even if they had been visible, few looked up to the darkened sky above the fortress. The Earthrin Stones still commanded Yestreal's power, blotting the sun from above the defenders. It was without hindrance that the evil pair flew towards the tower Tuampor.

Revwar examined the structure, commenting, "The upper windows are all narrow arrow-ports. We'll have to go in from a wall entrance."

"Any high windows would be warded," The unseen taraz snapped back. "It has to be a wall or courtyard entrance."

Descending past the structure, they suddenly encountered one such ward. Neither had figured the wards extended so far beyond the upper portions of the structure. Even in peaceful times, the magical barrier defended against an enemy approaching in the way they currently attempted. It only protected certain areas of the fortress, but Tuampor was of such importance. In a heartbeat, the wizard and demon became visible and lost their ability of flight. A few eyes spotted the two as they fell toward a courtyard.

CHAPTER 26 "Demons near the Temple"

Revwar had only a few seconds to cast a spell or hit the ground. One hand had been holding Norzal's in order to keep them together. He jerked it back, requiring both to reenable his flight spell. The elf began a fast incantation, dependent on years of arcane practice to deliver the spell in haste without mistake. His robes flapped to life again, diverting him from the plunge in time, but soaring quite visible to the many combatants.

Norzal spared no such time for a flight spell. The demon's body was made of stone, strengthened by Mothrok herself. He blasted an impression into the ground as he hit. To the amazement of all who saw, he got back to his feet almost immediately. He calmly stepped out of the small crater. No human could bounce back so easily from such a plunge. The coldast suffered nothing, having never felt pain since Mothrok's powers raised him into this form. His robes cloaking his true form again, he took in his surroundings. The battle raged in all directions as tribesmen and Stonelands defenders engaged in a great melee.

The wizard did not see Norzal's landing, but knew the demon would survive it. Revwar's immediate concern was to get out of the air, before attracting the attention of the archers and mages. The silver-haired elf darted towards a balcony supporting two archers. They witnessed his approach and raised their bows. Before they could release the arrows, a blast of fire threw them apart. The men writhed in flames as the wizard flew past them. Revwar stuck his head back outside briefly, only to orient himself with Tuampor's direction before going inside again.

The coldast on the ground saw defenders situated between him and Tuampor. He called tribesmen to his side. They were surprised to see their messiah taking such a direct hand in the fight. His presence inspired them to lay down their lives if needed for him to advance safely. The mass charged towards one of the doors of the interior tower system. Heavily armored men from the Stonelands guarded the way. Weapons collided with flesh as the forces met. Progress was made, but it only attracted the attention of the mages on the walls. Spells began to explode among the tribesmen. Norzal shrugged off blows that tore his cloak asunder, but his ring of protectors began to thin. He reached into a bag and touched the Earthrin Stones. This time, a band of undead clawed their way up from the earth. The animated bones put a scare into the defenders. The diversion offered Norzal what he needed to gain entry into the door. His protectors and the men of the Stonelands were left behind to their own fight.

From above, the entry of those two foes was noted by a young chiaso. Montanya's greenish-blue eyes recognized the wizard who had once pulled her parents' locket from her neck. She realized both enemies were trying to get to the Gate of Issundor. The youth had been moving towards stairs set in the walls; instead, she turned and ran back inside. She would have to try intercepting either foe before they got to the wounded.

Another Companion of the Relics spotted the wizard. "That cowardly cur! Flying o'er a fight instead o' partaking in it!" With that, Salgor broke free of his latest challenger.

The dwarf pumped his legs as he charged the closest door. His axe brought him past knots of tribesmen who plugged the way.

*   *   *   *   *

Hebden felt foolish dragging a heavy bucket of rocks since he didn't have a use for them. He arrived at the stairs Petrow had indicated. The latest bucket joined a group of buckets, already loaded with stones. Looking down, the aging smith saw the current yard filling with tribesmen. A glance over his shoulder told him that the next section fared just as badly.

Petrow came running down the wall. "I got it! Don't say a word!"

The former farmer was carrying a shiny metal disk by a strap fitted to it.

Hebden had to wonder, "What is that…"

Petrow waved his free hand frantically to stop Hebden from saying more. "Don't say anything!"

The blue-eyed human, still wearing his straw hat, glanced at the courtyard. He kneeled next to Hebden's bucket. With the disk now pointing towards the courtyard, he felt more comfortable speaking. "It may take me a few tries to learn to aim this."

Seeing that Petrow seemed to relax, the smith dared ask, "What is that thing?"

"Salgor would call it a gnomish catapult," Petrow grinned as he attempted to align the gnomish lift to face a group of tribesmen. "In this case, he'd be right. Now, take one of those stones. Hold it over the front of this. When I say a number, drop it. Don't get in front of this surface when you do."

Hebden hoisted a heavy rock, which seemed to weigh close to twenty pounds. He held it over the front of the lift, while keeping himself safely to the side. Petrow voiced a number.

"Fifteen."

Hebden Karok dropped the rock, fully expecting it to land at the base of the wall. Instead, the rock was stopped by a moment of hesitation in mid-air. An awed look came over the smith as he watched the rock suddenly shoot out from them at a high rate of speed. The gnomish lift threw the rock with the force that would normally carry it upwards more than seven human-sized floors off the ground. Petrow and Hebden were only on top of a two-story wall. The rock angled into a mass of tribal warriors. Somehow, it missed all of them before ricocheting off the hard ground. The two men from Troutbrook watched it bounce a second time amidst the many targets below. After that second bounce, it slammed the leg from beneath a tribesman, collapsing him to the ground in agony.

"My word!" Hebden breathed in wonder.

Petrow grinned like a mad fool as he nodded his head towards the closest bucket. "Don't stop! Keep 'em coming as fast as you can!"

A moment later, after another call of "fifteen", a second rock landed with precision on an unsuspecting warrior. A third rock caromed through without much harm other than making two men dive out of the way.

As nervous as Petrow should have been, he couldn't help but laugh at his own ingenuity. "I hope Salgor can see this! Fifteen!"

A fourth rock dashed into a group of warriors, clipping the antler helmet on one and spinning him senseless.

*   *   *   *   *

The half-elf's exotic green eyes did not miss much from her surroundings. She certainly did not miss the fall of two beings near the tower Tuampor. Katressa even recognized Revwar's black-and-red magical cloak as the wizard blasted his way past the two archers. She glanced toward his cohort, a robed man who stood head and shoulders above everyone else. It had to be a demon. She could not intervene in time before the second cloaked figure was winning his way toward an entry.

Cat called for two of her officers, spitting out commands as fast as could still be understood. She gave them a few final orders before turning towards Tuampor. Thamin asked where she was going.

Her brief answer, "A couple got past us. I'm headed to Issundor to protect it."

The lead privateer raced for Tuampor. The remaining privateers from Kashmer rallied under her officers as she departed from the fight. Random arrows and spells struck near as Cat ran, but nothing slowed her from her objective. She had never really considered trying to grab a few of the privateers to assist her. They were hard-pressed in a losing battle. Possibly, though Cat couldn't admit it to herself, she had left them because she felt she was the only one who could catch Revwar. Her heart burned for vengeance left unfulfilled since the loss of her father.

Sondra Oskires had been tending the wounded near Cat when she overheard the woman's last statement. In the time it took for the woman to give some advice to her acolyte, the half-elf was already a distant figure in the relative closeness of the melee.

"Wait! Katressa!" Sondra's call went unheard above the din of battle.

The priestess of Ganden knew a faster way through the keep, accessible only by the clergy. As a stretcher-bearer, she already used the secret route many times with wounded, ferrying them into the tower. She worried about the Gate of Issundor also, but it was too late to guide Cat up the quick way.

She turned to her acolyte, "As soon as you heal this man, find one of the other priests. Don't stay here by yourself."

"Sister Sondra?" The acolyte's hesitant call failed to recall Sondra, for the woman was already running towards the clergy entry.

*   *   *   *   *

Trestan fought alone in a confusing sea of battle, carried along as the currents of men swept him around. The Sword of the Spirit dripped blood, adding more as Trestan used the magically keen blade to sever the weapon-arm of an attacker. He could have finished his opponent, but it would not have been Abriana's will. Trestan knew that the man was not his real enemy. The man's dismemberment would remove him from the battle, even if he survived the injury. The paladin let his course be carried along among the other defenders.

He did not know where Leander had gone. They had been fighting together before a mass of combatants pushed them apart. Trestan had a last glimpse of his friend at a distance. Since then, Trestan fought among strangers. It left him feeling lonely and vulnerable, wishing Cat or Salgor were around to help guard his back.

In his head, Trestan tried to remember the many courtyards and sections of Fortress Stone. He had already fought in three different areas. The tribesmen were claiming more and more as their own. The outer areas had mostly fallen. The invaders were beginning to press against inner passageways, using makeshift rams or magic to break through sectional gates. Abriana's champion was funneled into one of the few outer sections that still held. In one of the former gaps created by the stones, he saw the reason. A thick wall of vegetation had been raised to block that entry.

Trestan joined a number of defenders. He set his back against the wall, watching a few Stonelands' soldiers go by, and allowed himself a moment to catch his breath. He couldn't deny that his sword felt several pounds heavier. Some of his muscles still ached from yesterday's action.

His vision passed across the wall of vines and noticed something odd. The plants began to shrivel and turn brown. Someone from the tribes was withering the plants from the outside.

Trestan gave a yell to warn others even as the dead vines began to crumble. Axes appeared, chopping through the tangle. Aijak had noticed her creation falling apart. Even as Trestan moved towards the gap, Mel and Aijak rode past him on Cathag. The first tribal warrior burst forth, only to be jolted by a blast from the sorcerer's wand. More followed, thrusting into the flank of the defending force.

Abriana's champion advanced in the midst of battle again, slashing at the warriors who faced him. Somewhere near, he heard the gnomes intoning spells to stem the flow of attackers. From above, Korrelothar dropped a fireball that blew a hole in the nomads' rush. Trestan noticed that some of the men fighting alongside him were Kashmer privateers. He wandered if Cat might be close, but there was no free time to search for her. He was enmeshed in a fight for his life.

*   *   *   *   *

Norzal's passage through the inner corridors of the fortress started uneventful. The occasional guard or messenger stumbled into his path, yet each became a smear on the wall without causing the demon much distraction. None of his enamored nomads were there to guard him, nor witness the reality of his appearance through his torn cloak. The hood had been ripped down, exposing his rocky face. The coldast assumed a skeletal form, allowing his fiery blue eyes to float in their sockets. The fighting had torn loose the cloak's front clasps. It revealed the wide leather straps that displayed the ears of his enemies, slung over a stone chest branded with the symbol of Mothrok. The gems of the Gitouro necklace continued to gleam from his neck, despite the cold, ghostly mist hugging his form.

The taraz freely explored behind the defenders' lines. Markings on the walls indicated that he had entered the holy tower Tuampor. Symbols composed of fine metals pronounced the holy domain of goodly gods, gilded on the doorways and halls. Soon enough, he would be opening the Gate of Issundor for the sake of his brothers. Of course, the coldast knew the way would be guarded. Norzal had been bred for war, living in constant conflict for many centuries. The undead, elemental demon from Ibleu Taraz held no fear from these pitiful, mortal foes.

He entered a foyer which gave testament to the many gods worshipped within the structure. Along one side, a number of statues depicted various deities. Across from the statues were stained glass windows, each depicting scenes or deeds related to the corresponding god. Normally, the smitten sun would cast the glow from the windows across the marble busts. Norzal's use of the relics intended that no sunlight shine on the Stonelands defenders for the rest of their short lives. He passed over the floor, made from polished tiles, his eyes noticed recent trails of blood. The taraz wondered about the reasons for it. Of course, Norzal did not know that Tuampor was being used as an infirmary.

The far door swung open when the demon was halfway across the chamber. The demon's hard claws flexed involuntarily, expecting to deliver another quick death. The small figure that walked out and blocked his path brought amusement to its dead face. The plaything actually seemed to think it stood a chance against him.

Indeed, it frightened Montanya to see this huge…thing…advancing straight towards her. She began to spin her staff in practice patterns. The chiaso had been expecting to meet a more 'human' opponent. Fate had delivered this menace to her footsteps, so she resolved to meet it with courage. Few fighters of any kind stood between her and the gate, and the priests might be unprepared for a threat such as this. Montanya had to protect them any way that she could. Numerous disciplines passed through her mind, as she tried to think of lessons that might allow her to shatter rocks. Envisioning them and putting them into practice were two different things. She had only broken a caleocht board once, months ago.

They closed within a few paces, staff raised against stone claws, when a voice boomed from a side entrance. "Pardon me, have you seen a cowardly elf wizard pass this way?"

At the calm demeanor of this new arrival, Norzal stopped and turned his gaze. He saw a short, stout dwarf. The impudent figure walked at a deliberately slow pace towards the posturing figures. The brown, partly-braided beard swept from one side to the other as he looked between the two. His arms flexed, stretching the tattoo honoring Daerkfyre on his left bicep. His metal shield hung from that forearm, displaying the ferocity of his fighting by the many scratches and dents that marred his personal crest. The right hand gripped his waraxe tighter.

Dark eyes rolled up to stare at the coldast, towering at twice the dwarf's height. Salgor spoke casually, "Silver hair, braided, has chicken-yellow eyeballs." The dwarf paused to spread his hands wide apart, "Has an ego this large…" Salgor brought his hands to within an inch of each other, "…and manners this small."

Even Norzal was amused by this depiction of the elf. "You mean Revwar?"

Salgor raised one eyebrow, smirking under his beard. "Aye, that's the weasel. I bet you're a friend o' his!"

The coldast's amusement came to an end. The blue lights in his eye sockets flared. "What do I look like to you, dwarf?"

Salgor casually stepped to Montanya's side. The young warrior grinned as this unexpected ally joined her. Montanya readjusted the grip on her staff, taunting the taraz with her eyes. Salgor hefted his axe and answered the demon's question.

"A future gravel pit."

*   *   *   *   *

The group of demon-possessed elders watched the battle from afar. In voices too low for other tribesmen to hear, they took amusement at the deaths of so many Dhea Loral natives. None of the other tribes had paid much attention to the fact that their messiah and his prophet were missing. The elders kept the others busy, until the moment their brothers would break free from Tuampor.

They saw two of their acquaintances returning, despite having orders to assault the fortress. The possessed elders made way, hoping to inquire as to the change in plans. Even as they did, the taraz began to get the feeling that something was unusually wrong.

Kor and Pejena walked among them. The six-foot-six Com'der of the Spear Riders looked ready for war, which was expected. The demons could only ponder at why the battle led him back here, instead of among his men in the assault. Strongarm wore hides except for his chest, revealing the presence of war paint on his body. His eyes, brown and blue, swept around in his search for Norzal. The strip of leather, branded with a spear symbol, held his whitish-gray hair back. The massive maul he normally used was strapped over his back. In his hands, he carried a long, double-headed spear.

Pejena Cloud Whisperer walked by her husband's side. None of the other demons paid much attention to the fact that she wore coverings which hid the view of her chest. She walked with her staff held close. Her free hand reached up and idly fidgeted with her prayer bead necklace. The mystic also looked for any sign of Norzal or Revwar.

The two had known the full extent of the demons' plans while under their control. Kor surmised that they had arrived at the camp too late to catch their targets.

"What brings you here? What news of the front?" An elder asked.

Kor turned to face him. The elder was one of the higher-ranking demons. Its influence had allowed it possession of one of the most fearsome mystics in all of the tribes. When the fight started, this one would be their most dangerous adversary.

The Com'der asked, "Has Norzal already headed to the fortress?"

A couple of the other elders nodded, but the suspicious one facing Kor said something in a language native to Ibleu Taraz. Of course, Kor could not understand what was said; not without a demon translator inside him. The other taraz began to suspect that the two humans in their midst possessed free minds.

The foremost elder began a wicked laugh. "Foolish human! What madness led you back into our midst?"

Kor gave a final glance around, lingering his gaze on Pejena. They spoke no words, but the woman he loved gave a knowing nod to him. Their primary enemy was gone, but the other demons were within easy reach. The leaders of the Spear Rider tribe held no delusions about their odds. Despite Kor's double-headed spear coated with Mel's poison, there stood no less than twenty demon-possessed elders around them. Given the chance, Kor would free all of them, but he simply had to settle for stabbing as many as he could. Some would be freed, some would be dead.

Pejena began channeling her natura. The elements rushed to her call.

Kor finally answered the demon. "Vengeance!"

Strongarm's spear shot forward. The sharpened tip thrust through the elder's guts even as Pejena's elemental winds whipped up a small sandstorm around them. The other demons were just reacting even as the wind and dust obscured their vision.

*   *   *   *   *

An explosion of flames sent a group of guards flying backward. The smoke quickly settled, revealing twitching, blackened forms that would never rise again. The door beyond them, displaying holy symbols marking it as an entry to Tuampor, stood accessible to the wizard.

"Peons." Revwar remarked in a calm demeanor, stepping past his latest victims.

The elf waved his hand before the door, checking for wards such as those placed outside the tower. He found some barring the way for demons, but not elf wizards. He used his magic to remove the wards. Revwar worried about entering the tower without Norzal by his side, yet he had no choice. The wizard had come this far and his magic was formidable. Let any priest who came before him pray for mercy before he sent them to their gods.

He opened the door cautiously. The wizard was in no hurry to place himself in unnecessary danger. The demon would likely get through with less resistance. Either one of them, demon or wizard, could open the Gate of Issundor from this side. Revwar would not be disappointed if the taraz cleared the way for him. It was one thing to be confident in one's abilities, but another thing to actively test them out. As many chances as Revwar had taken for his goals, he preferred to strike from secrecy. Let the coldast face any priests in the tower. The elf wizard might pass as an ally until he chose to strike.

The smoking men behind him had strictly followed their orders that none should pass unless accompanied by a healer. They paid for their arrogance.

His golden eyes examined the long hall before him. It was likely contained within a wall leading to Tuampor's central rooms. In peacetime, it might be a nice, quiet place to read and relax. The left side had an unbroken wall of stone, covered in tapestries. A few religious tomes sat on small bookshelves. Near the shelves sat benches made of wood, padded for comfort. Across from the benches, colored-glass windows interspersed the right side along its length. The glass did not allow one to see out, nor were they made to open. There would be wards outside the glass to prevent entry from flying opponents, like he had discovered earlier. Between colored sections, a few panes normally allowed plenty of bright sunshine. It looked like it could be set up as a pleasant study hall, or perhaps a reception area where guests could pause and reflect before entering the temple. Four men could easily walk abreast down the hall.

With a last glance behind him, he closed the door. As an afterthought, he began to work a spell around the edges. Revwar magically sealed the door against anything except a demon trying to pass through. Of course, another mage could undo the spell, but it would still slow them. He was just finishing his incantation when he heard the door on the far side of the hall open. The wizard remained calm as he prepared to turn and confront the surprise intruder. If they simply asked him questions, he could talk his way past without a fight. If the unknown person was exiting, he would have to finish them, since they would raise an alarm upon finding the warded door or the bodies beyond.

Revwar turned. His golden eyes widened as he recognized an unmistakable figure at the other end of the hall. The edge of his mouth twitched upwards in a slight grin as he realized that the long hallway between them was a wizard's ideal killing ground.

Returning his intent stare through emerald eyes, Cat met the gaze of her prey. She paused partway through the doorway opposite the wizard. Her black leather made no noise as her hips swayed forward another couple steps. One hand moved beneath her new cloak, drawing out the magical silver rapier. The wizard almost chuckled at seeing neither bow nor crossbow visible on her. Cat's prized Serud'Thanil bow was now a useless piece of twisted wood.

The elf wizard held all the advantages here. No living mortal could succeed in getting down this hall to him before his spells could finish them. Of course, Cat could simply slip back beyond the door and ambush him later. He had to try to goad her forward. Revwar felt it wouldn't be a hard task.

"Your stubbornness is matched only by your foolishness, agora." Revwar spoke. As always, his voice stayed calm, yet clear enough to carry down the hall. "You hold much hatred for the one blamed for your father's death."

His words baited her forward a step. Cat's face didn't show anger, or unfulfilled rage; instead, she offered Revwar a smile. For an infiltrator, a smile was usually their first means to lower the defenses of an opponent.

"I said I'd hunt you and be the death of you. I like to keep my oaths." Cat's words echoed down the hall.

Revwar kept his voice calm, as if he was discussing the flavor of soup, "You should take up your gripe with Norzal. He is the one who wears your father's ear as a trophy."

Cat was not so easily lured into rage. Her left hand rose up to brush the raven tresses away from her eyes. "My concern is you. My heart tells me that my father has some words for you. He'd like me to send you to him."

It amazed Revwar that his longtime foe, one who's specialty was a stab in the back, would instigate a challenge in which he held every advantage. The elf made an offer, "Reach me over here, and you can kill me."

"Deal." Cat answered. The half-elf turned to the door behind her. To Revwar's surprise, she had the audacity to slam it shut before turning to face him. Her meaning was clear, but she gave voice to it anyway. "Only one of us will leave this hall alive."

Revwar stretched his arms, making sure that his robe would not hinder his spells. The wizard watched his half-elf opponent assume a guard position. He held a smile of his own as he mimicked Cat's earlier response.

"Deal."

CHAPTER 27 "Three Different Duels"

Norzal swung his heavy, stone arm at the impudent dwarf. His claws swiped air as Salgor ducked and charged. Salgor's blessed axe scraped across the rock of the coldast's body, sweeping around a vortex of tendrils from the demon's spiritual form. The imposing monster turned to track the more dangerous foe. Montanya, seemingly ignored, used her opportunity. The chiaso tried to focus her energy into a thrusting jab with her staff. She hit the coldast in the side; causing no more damage than if she had jabbed a castle wall.

Salgor's weapon left a mark, scraping along the side of the chest that bore Mothrok's symbol.

The taraz recovered with amazing speed. One stony claw raked at Salgor, sending sparks flying from the raised shield. Norzal turned to keep facing the moving dwarf, when another push came from the woman behind it. Her wooden weapon caused no damage, but it irritated the coldast. Her shove led to Salgor's axe leaving another scratch on a stony arm.

Norzal used magic: a type that came naturally to his artificial body. Its ghostly tendrils reached outward, causing the temperature of whatever they touched to drop dramatically. The undead side of him acted out, draining the life of the living. Both Salgor and Montanya got a taste of it. They retreated with chills shaking their bodies.

The demon singled out his more dangerous adversary. Norzal's claws raked at Salgor time and again as the dwarf stumbled back. Salgor's teeth were rattling from the cold effect. More often than not, his shield blocked the claws. Little by little, Salgor began to lose some blood as some of its attacks scored hits. The bare hands of the demon could rend armor.

Montanya launched into the demon, giving it everything she had. Her staff cracked across his head. A foot protected by soft leather kicked uselessly at the taraz's leg. The painful impact hurt the chiaso more than the demon. The red-haired fighter caught a glimpse of the priceless Gitouro necklace. She recalled her companions telling her of the item, giving a proper warning about if she ever came across it. The necklace became her goal. With it in her possession, she could change fate.

The taraz continued focusing on the dwarf fighter. The demon's unnatural speed and fortitude allowed it to rip the shield from Salgor's arm. Norzal raised the shield, then bent it over his own knee in a show of strength. Priest-blessed metal warped, as wood layers cracked apart. The dwarf backed against one of the many busts of gods adorning the room. A rumble escaped Norzal's maw as it tossed the broken shield aside.

Salgor's mouth never backed down any more than his arms. "Poor 'sandstone' here got scratched by my little axe! Imagine if I had a chisel handy!"

The coldast prepared to clamp down on Salgor's windpipe, until interrupted from behind. Montanya's staff stabbed between the necklace and the taraz's stone neck. Using the demon's own leg as a launching point, the chiaso leapt up in a way that used her staff as a lever. The caleocht staff strained against the relic's chain. As finely crafted as the necklace was, having once been destined for the necks of immortals during the Godswars, Montanya's staff slipped free before it could break the chain.

The maneuver gave Norzal pause. It turned its cold blue orbs towards the woman. It knew her attack couldn't have been random. Somehow, she knew the importance of that treasure. The demon stepped towards Montanya so fast that he reminded her of trying to catch an arrow. Sharp stone claws sliced a trail that sent blood flowing from her side. Montanya screamed as she fell. The demon reached for her neck to finish her…

A marble likeness of the god Kelor soared through the air, only to dash against the coldast's head. As painful as it was to move, with her new wound as well as her previous day's pain, Montanya scrambled out from the demon amid a shower of marble shards. Norzal half-turned back to the dwarf. Salgor was charging, but not with his axe. The dwarf held a pillar, (which, until seconds ago, had supported a bust of Kelor), and used it like a battering ram. The bearded follower of Daerkfyre timed his attack perfectly. He hit Norzal's weight-bearing leg as the demon twisted at an odd angle. The momentum sent the demon into a cartwheel as Salgor's bulky frame thundered past.

Montanya tried regaining her feet as she saw the results. The floor cracked outward from Norzal's impact. Salgor came to the end of his rush, noting with disappointment the remains of his shattered pillar falling apart. The demon raised his torso off the damaged floor.

"You broke my ram!" Salgor shouted, before shrugging as if it didn't matter. He retrieved his axe from his belt, while nodding to the rows of god statues. "Good thing there are a lot more around!"

Norzal screamed curses in his native tongue. Despite all the damage hurled at him, he barely looked harmed.

*   *   *   *   *

Within the duststorm, fueled by months of dried farmland, Kor's spear stabbed relentlessly. Demon-possessed elders who knew nothing about the nature of the Com'der's poisoned weapon went heedlessly into battle. They refused to submit to two inferior humans. One or two at a time, they found him. They wielded the magical knowledge or battle skills of those they possessed. Normal wounds meant little to the demons as long as the weapon didn't happen to hit their physical bodies, hidden deep within their hosts. On the contrary, Kor began hurting from his wounds. He ignored his pain even as drops of blood whipped about when he turned. The giant of a man seemed indomitable despite the efforts of the demons. He arced his double-ended spear at all angles, stabbing repeatedly at shadows and noises. Soon those who were hit realized the danger of his weapon. All it took was one scratch and the poison drove them out of their hosts.

He had little chance of harming Pejena in the blinding conditions. As soon as her duststorm whirled into being, she rode the winds to float above his head. Hovering above all, she was able to use the elements to stall his attackers. Stones would roll and trip elders, while wind currents blinded them.

Kor began tripping over writhing bodies. Possessed elders who were moving out of the cloud witnessed their taraz allies being ejected from their former hosts. A demon-possessed mystic finally released his own magic into the cloud. A phoenix exploded into a column of flames, fed by the whirling winds. Pejena was almost enveloped. She cut her flow of energy into the storm, dropping as she did so. The dust unveiled Kor as it settled. A shaman elder used spirit magic to weaken him. More than one possessed warrior descended upon Kor and Pejena to capture them. Several worked together to pin his spear-arm. Pejena struggled next to him, wielding only her staff. She tried to voice another spell, but another mystic countered her efforts with his own concentration.

Many enemies charged in and brought the couple down. Some possessed men held down Kor's dangerous spear while another demon prepared to slay him with a dagger. Breathless Pejena struggled under the weight of adversaries.

Suddenly, the possessed man who was bringing the dagger to Kor's throat was beheaded by a stone axe. A druid in wolf form bowled one attacker off of Pejena. The wolf's fangs devoured his throat. A number of writhing demons, naked to the world after being ejected from their hosts, lay mortally wounded from their previous victims. The possessed elders were accosted by their former captives, men and women who had been freed from control by the poison taint of Kor's spear. The freed tribesmen loosed their vengeance after being slaves to the demons for many months. Kor and Pejena suddenly had allies. The couple struggled for freedom as both the possessed and freed elders began to unleash death at one another.

*   *   *   *   *

Cat was never one for battle cries. The long hallway granted the wizard a couple chances to cast spells before she could reach him. She didn't waste time or breath. Her athletic legs propelled her toward the elf who had been responsible for countless deaths.

Revwar didn't even bother to spend the time on something extravagant. He brought up the ring on one hand. From this distance, he could use its cutting beam and simply swing it back and forth to slice her down. A quick magical command and the ring let loose its destructive ray.

The half-elf had expected something more along the lines of fireballs and such. As the wizard pointed his fist at her, she realized he would use the beam he'd used to wound her in the past. A touch of that spell nearly ended her life, and would have if it wasn't for Trestan finding his faith. Cat sent out a mental thought to the boots she'd commissioned from Korrelothar's guild.

Yesterday, they assisted her in jumping the wall. With them, she could affect gravity, even change its direction temporarily…at least for her. She jumped as the beam struck out. Revwar's ray burned a hole in the far door. He expected her to fall back into the beam, but she gave him her first surprise. Cat was running on the ceiling! Revwar brought his hand up, slicing burns into the far wall as he attempted to chase her with his spell. The half-elf bent gravity to her will, somersaulting to a wall, then flipping to the opposite wall, running towards the wizard on every surface. Revwar only managed to burn a trail along the walls, as well as slice a tapestry in half.

With disgust, the elf dismissed the beam. Keeping his outward calm, he began the motions of a different spell. A set of flaming swords launched down the hall. Cat had seen this spell before, but the wizard had improved upon it. This time, four swords stretched like an X through the air. They cut a path in such a way that Cat could not evade all of them.

The half-elf had little time to prepare a defense against this magic. She jumped to a portion of the wall that would only put her at risk of one of the swords. Her nimble left hand reached down and twisted a portion of the belt buckle. This was another item from the magic of the mage guild, a one-use trick. A shield formed in front of the adventuress. Designed the same way as Trestan's miracle, it would deflect one magical attack and then fade. The flaming sword clashed against the shield, canceling both. The other three swords went past the half-elf, creating burnt gouges in the far walls before fading.

Revwar started feeling desperate. Every spell of his had been countered, and the Kashmer privateer would be upon him soon. He flicked a strand of silver hair out of his eyes as he briefly considered his next move. Keeping a calm face, he began a spell that would likely knock her backwards if it didn't kill her outright. His hands moved until a blue light coalesced between them. He threw the spell down the hall.

Cat raced to get to the wizard's throat. Most of the hallway was behind her, but too much space existed between her and her target. There would be little time to react to anything Revwar sent her direction. The blue light streaked towards Cat, trailing a cold tail like a comet. Her emerald eyes went wide as she recalled the same spell assaulting her and Trestan on Wilder continent. One hand went to one of three potions at her belt, as she twisted to get behind a bookcase.

The comet of ice exploded, sending icy shards in all directions. Icicles punctured walls, windows, tapestries, ceiling, and floor. A layer of frost settled about the area. Revwar watched as some of the projectiles went Cat's direction. She was partly behind a bookcase, but the spell knocked her back. The half-elf dropped, twitching, upon the floor.

Cat's pain was the same sensation she had felt when healing Trestan of a similar wound. She felt this version more directly. Breathing brought forth agony, along with a taste of blood. *You have to get up.* She cried out inside her mind. *You knew this would happen. That's why you made sure you had these.*

Her hand came up, holding one of the healing vials from her belt. She fought the pain and forced herself to drink.

Revwar watched as the half-elf drank a draught. He reached into a pocket to grab some reagents as Cat regained her feet. Strands of raven hair matted to her face by blood, but Cat's wounds were closing. She stood, displaying holes in her dark leather armor. The flow of blood stopped as the flesh healed. The wizard stretched his arms, loosening his sleeves in preparation for the next spell. He needed something that could not be so easily healed by miracle draughts.

Cat's legs drove her towards him at a run. She still held the silver rapier forth, offering him no mercy if he failed this duel. She ran past icicles buried in the floor.

The golden eyes of the wizard reflected the fires springing from his spell. The heat rolled over his hands and down the hall. An inferno of searing flames expanded outwards; wall-to-wall, floor-to-ceiling, rushing out to envelop everything that stood before him.

The half-elf grabbed the edge of her new cloak. She continued to advance, but spun to put her back to the flames. Her hood fell over her head, and the edges of the cloak wrapped around her as the wall of fire roared past. The explosive heat surged far beyond her. It consumed tapestries, bookcases burst into pyres, and tongues of flame shot out from under the far door of the hall. The force of the spell blew out all the windows, allowing the heat to dissipate into the outside sky. The wizard continued to cast his firestorm for a few breaths. He poured his mounting frustration into blackening the stone along the hall.

The golden-eyed elf released the flow of energy. He felt like his magic was nearly spent in all that effort. A moment of lightheadedness caused him to lean back against the door. Fires gave way to air and smoke. Bookcases still burned, while the embers from the tapestries still swirled in the air currents. The dark clouds hovering over the fortress could be seen through the shattered glass.

The Kashmer privateer was still standing.

Cat turned to get her bearings. Smoke wisped from the ends of her hair, as well as her boots. Her cloak had been crafted for just that sort of attack in mind. Flames simply slid right off of it. Despite its protection, the woman had still been injured by the intense heat. As her cloak opened up again, a second drained bottle dropped from her hands and clattered on the floor. Her rapier caught the glow of reflected fires as it came ever closer to the wizard.

There was little room left between the wizard and the infiltrator. Revwar needed a spell that would give him some time. He had one spell that he knew could batter the woman as well as force her to give ground.

The wizard called upon another of the elements: wind. He made the motions of flinging the half-elf away from him. A wind fury kicked up, causing strong winds to hammer at Cat. Her progress halted in the face of all the wind resistance. It would have been enough to fling her body back down the hall, or even out a window, but the privateer used her gravity-defying boots in reverse. She added weight to her form, sealing her feet against the floor. Stubbornly, she gritted her teeth in the face of the gale Revwar hurled. Objects in the room became missiles. Flaming books were stripped from a collapsing bookcase and tossed her direction. One fiery book after another hit her torso before crumbling to ash and drifting behind her. Hot cinders struck her exposed skin. She transferred her rapier to her left hand, as bits and pieces swirled around her head. Her emptied right hand slid along her torso to find the dagger tucked in her belt.

The last item purchased from the Brotherhood of the Circles mage guild was also the most expensive item, due to its unique properties.

With the wind hammering at her resistance, she pulled forth the bone-bladed dagger. Cat suddenly found that her throwing arm could move normally, even if the rest of her body was stymied by the gale. She opened her emerald eyes and locked gazes with the wizard. Her arm whipped forward, sending the dagger into flight.

The wizard's first instinct upon seeing the half-elf's action was amusement. She offered his spell a dagger by which to toss back at her. As the dagger went into the air, the wizard tried to affect the flow of winds to redirect it. To his dismay, the weapon seemed unaffected by his spell.

As a bone weapon, it could easily be broken or destroyed by many non-magical means. However, this particular bone was from a monster called a dhuanid. When the goddess Dawn had given life to this particular race of creatures, she blessed it with one unique defense: any magical force would bend around it. In a world filled with magic, this one property gave the creature an uncommonly helpful means of self-preservation. Thus, Cat's dagger might be vulnerable in many ways…but it nullified magic.

The dagger not only flew unhindered through the wind, it stabbed right through Revwar's protective robe as if it was plain cloth.

The elf's spell fell apart as he staggered back against the door. He looked down in surprise, and delayed understanding, as he viewed the bone dagger sticking out of his chest.

Revwar winced as the first breath brought an onslaught of pain. His golden eyes looked up as Cat's third and final healing draught took effect. The many new wounds he inflicted were fading away.

Rapier led the way as she came for him yet again. A few mere strides separated them. Revwar began casting the one spell he had already cast which he felt could stop the daughter of Reatheneus Bilil with any finality. Cold temperatures centered on his hands as another blue orb of ice formed. It was the one spell which she could not avoid, one which could possibly kill her outright. He would have to practically throw the spell at his own feet, but his magical robe should protect him from the frozen shards…hopefully.

In the last moments, Revwar realized he would not get the spell completed in time. The tip of the rapier was drawing too close to his mortality. At the final second, he switched to one last desperate action. He could only hope that his enhanced magical strength would be enough.

Katressa Bilil thrust her magical rapier as she came within reach. The elf's enchanted robes would still deflect it, so she aimed high. The tip went through Revwar's soft-spoken, conniving tongue. It carved a path to the back of his throat, stabbing up through his brain before spiking itself in the door beyond.

An infinite moment of silence, as Cat's emerald eyes noted the dying denial in the elf's golden orbs. Her face offered no sympathy for the elf that had caused her family and her friends so much hurt.

"Give my regards to my father." She said, as the wizard slid into death's embrace.

The wizard's body did not fall, pinned as he was by the rapier to the door behind him. As death took him, his lifeless hand did fall from the handle of his planted dagger. The slim dagger Revwar always carried at his side, was a last, pitiful means of defense if all other measures had failed.

Cat staggered back one step, looking down at the slim dagger buried to the hilt under her left breast. Her weakened fingers slipped off the handle. Her magical weapon remained impaled in the elf and the door. A rational part of her mind wondered if the wizard had run it through her heart, and with that thought her legs gave out.

Even after she dropped to the floor, she remained conscious. A number of thoughts passed through her head. All three healing draughts had been used up. Even all their strength hadn't been enough to totally heal her wounds before the wizard's dagger stabbed its way past her leather. The door next to her had been locked by magic, so no escape would be found there. The door on the other end of the hall could be opened, if she could crawl all the way across that ash-strewn passage with a dagger inside her. No one was likely to simply find her there if she stayed still. The battle still raged elsewhere in the keep; she could be found by enemies instead of friends. Probably not until after death.

She raised her left forearm, staring at the jeweled caleocht band Trestan had given her as their engagement present. Cat wanted to live to see their wedding day. She wanted to bear his children. She imagined that Trestan would be a wonderful father.

None of that would come to pass unless she put forth the effort to help herself. She was lying on her back, the exit door up past her head. Cat tenderly bent one knee up, then the other. She willed the boots to make her lighter than she was, for she had lost a lot of strength. Cat pushed with her limbs, moving herself a little closer to the other door.

The half-elf kept thinking of her wedding day. She hoped that by holding onto that vision, she might have the strength to actually make it.

CHAPTER 28 "How Does It Feel to Face Your Own Death?"

Petrow had just fired another rock into the mass of warriors. He couldn't miss all the tribesmen bunched below, and Petrow's aim was rewarded by a warrior dropping to the ground. Hebden didn't fail to notice a danger to their situation. While Petrow waited for the next rock to drop, the smith tugged at his shoulder. They had stood on the walls in one place for too long. Nomads had taken notice of them and were closing fast. The courtyards on either side of their wall had more invaders than defenders.

"We've got trouble!" Hebden pointed with his hammer.

Petrow looked over his shoulder to the opposite stairs. He turned in time to see a spear-wielding raulgan emerge at the top. A second one followed on the heels of the first. Hebden was already trying to assume a ready stance. His arm pumped a few times as he tested the heft of his hammer. Petrow went to reach for his axe, but changed his mind in a last moment of inspiration. He swiveled around, bringing the gnomish lift up in front of him like a shield. He made a quick sidestep in order to line up both attackers.

"Fifteen!"

The lift caught the first raulgan in its influence and stopped him in his tracks. He had a moment of confusion register on his face, before the energies of the lift tossed him backward. His body became a missile which rammed his companion off the stairs. Both dropped into the courtyard below, one of them moving a lot faster than the other one. Hebden winced upon witnessing the painful departure, though he couldn't help but chuckle a moment later.

He patted Petrow on the back, "Nice thinking, now let's go somewhere else."

Petrow grabbed his axe in his right hand, kept the gnomish lift supported on his left arm, and began to retreat further into the interior layout of the fortress. Their first few steps proved dangerous, as more tribesmen closed in. A few more had gained the top of the walls and closed hand-to-hand with the archers stationed there. There were no organized lines of defense, only a number of individual duels for survival. Even in such duels there was no sense of honor. Men were stabbed in the back if they didn't keep their wits about them. Hebden and Petrow played by the same game as everyone else. They had no qualms about blindsiding a nomad to save a Stonelands' defender. Their own survival was at stake.

Before they knew it, a few other tribesmen swarmed into the fray, following the calls for help from their fellows. Hebden felt the sickening crunch as his hammer caught one man in the head. The smith couldn't dwell on it before dealing with more action around him. Petrow nearly injured an archer as his axe swings kept a few attackers at bay. Suddenly, Petrow had a wall of tribesmen in front of him, threatening to bring him down under their numbers.

The young farmer from Troutbrook brought up the lift and sent command after command into it. In rapid succession, bodies went flying through the air. Nomads soared across courtyards: some catapulted back outside the fortress' outer wall, others landed with bone-shattering impact into the crowds below.

A Stonelands' archer, who seemed to have some rank inscribed on his tabard, caught Petrow's attention. The man commanded, "We need to fall back…regroup with them." He pointed along a portion of the wall near Tuampor. "Lead with your magic!"

There was little Petrow could argue before he was pushed at the head of a charge. Bowmen drew swords before taking up positions to either side of him. Hebden contentedly lagged behind the line of men as they ran down the wall. Nomads stood between them and their destination, forming a barrier of weapons directly in their path. The young farmer had a brief image of how horrified Inedra would be if she could have seen him in that moment. He was actually leading a charge toward a line of men ready to take his own life. Petrow started to heft his axe, but then realized that the safe bet for him was to keep abusing the lift's magic. As a number of launched weapons were thrown between the closing groups, Petrow lifted the disk and kept chanting away.

"Fifteen! Fifteen! Fifteen!"

In at least one case, the lift did little more than redirect an arrow that might have harmed the group. As the two sides closed, the lift began to focus on the men before Petrow. Shielded behind its repeated energy waves, the young farmer spearheaded the wedge that began to split the tribesmen apart.

Some of the people fighting in a courtyard took note as bodies flew over their heads. Mel Bellringer was just sorting through now-empty bags on his bandolier, searching for any surprises he had left. The gnome saw a nomad flying through the air with limbs flailing, before the poor victim dropped into a well.

"What possessed that man to think he could fly?"

A second body passed overhead, only to break upon a stone wall.

"This is peculiar. Men from the skies?"

Mel turned about, looking for the source. It wasn't easy seeing above all the large humans fighting nearby. The gnome set eyes upon the action atop the walls. He saw Petrow in the middle of a desperate fight. Mel was not one to display worry, yet he did feel nervous about his good friend facing so many tribesmen.

Suddenly, Petrow raised a circular disk, and shouted a number. The gnome's lip and mustache twitched as he saw a tribesman catapulted like a rag doll. Before the gnome could react, and before Petrow could utter another phrase, the Troutbrook native had to shield-slam the next tribesman with the arcane device. With an axeman gripping the disk, Petrow spoke the number again, followed by the axeman being turned into a missile.

Mel saw the man launched into a crowd of warriors. With a bit of a stutter, the sorcerer tried to yell at his friend. "Y..y..you're not using that responsibly! That's…oh my!...an improper use of that device!"

Of course, Petrow couldn't hear the irritated gnome in the noise of battle. With Hebden and others nearby, he created a path to unite with another group of archers. Mel still voiced complaints as Petrow stooped to grab a sword. The farmer tucked his axe under his shield arm. As enemies in front of him hesitated, Petrow yelled the number fifteen and tossed the sword into the lift's field. The blade shot into the body of a tribesman several steps away, piercing the hide armor and shoving him over the ramparts.

It really upset Mel. The gnome yelled, "You're going to give gnomish magic a bad name!"

*   *   *   *   *

Trestan fell back against a wall after stabbing a skilled opponent. The tribesman sagged to the ground, likely for good. Abriana's champion raised his left hand to see the damage done by a bad parry. The blow had rendered his gauntlet useless. A deep cut went across two fingers, but neither was severed. His hand shook as he looked his wound. Wincing, he drove his magical sword into the ground, then brought up that other hand to heal. The energies of the miracle flowed into his digits, tiring him even as he closed the gash. He flexed his fingers, satisfied they were well again.

Trestan plucked the sword from the ground. He noticed Thamin, a man whom Cat had deferred some rank among the privateers. The paladin shouldered through reinforcements to reach the fighter.

"Have you seen Katressa?" he asked.

Thamin glanced over, recognizing Trestan. "She put me in charge here before running to Tuampor."

The Kashmer privateer had his hands busy directing the fight, so Trestan stumbled back towards the tower. He looked up at its full height. What could drive Cat to run there? Inside, he began to worry about the safety of the Gate of Issundor. Perhaps Cat had discovered something important.

In that instant, a firestorm burst through a row of windows on one side of Tuampor. Flames roared into the sky as glass fragments showered fighters below. Trestan stood dumbstruck as his mind tried to comprehend what it could mean. The young man could not know that his beloved was the target of that assault from Revwar.

Only a moment later, a glass window on the opposite side of the tower burst outward. This time, the cause was a figure who had been thrown through it. Trestan watched as the body thrashed in mid-air a second before it crashed through the thatched roof of a stable. The paladin thought that the person looked very familiar.

Trestan sprinted towards the stable. Through the open front, he saw movement from the person within. A muscular arm threw aside the handle of the broken cart he had landed on. Trestan recognized the thick brown beard, as well as the tattoo on one arm. The situation had the young man confused. What was happening on opposite sides of Tuampor? And what could possibly throw Salgor Bandago out of a window?

A cleric of The Codex reached the dwarf first, lending him her healing powers. Salgor struggled to get up on his own, despite the severe injuries that must have been caused by the fall. Trestan heard the words shouted by the angry dwarf.

"Cursed pile o' rock! Demon o' nay, I'm gonna turn him into a doorstep in front o' my inn! Ooohhh…I think I fell o' my flask."

Trestan nearly shuddered. A demon inside Tuampor! With all the fighting in the courtyard, the taraz had somehow passed by them. As much as Trestan wanted to help his friend, the dwarf already had a cleric tending to him. The Gate of Issundor mattered most. If the demons opened it, there may be no stopping the legions that would come forth. Abriana's champion veered for the closest door to the tower.

On the way, he stopped a man wearing arcane robes. Trestan didn't know if the mage was a member of the Brotherhood of Circles or not. He could only hope. "Find Korrelothar! Tell him there are demons in Tuampor!"

The young paladin spared not a moment for the shocked face of the caster. Trestan Spiritblade left his earlier exhaustion behind as he sped for the tower. He prayed he could make a difference in time.

*   *   *   *   *

Montanya tried to rise. Her broken staff lent her some support, but one leg would not cooperate. Any attempt to use her bad knee at all brought more pain than that suffered by the gash in her side. She struggled to stand, to breathe, to hide her pain from the glowing blue orbs leering at her.

Norzal offered a skeletal grin while looming over the red-haired, young chiaso. Montanya brushed a strand of hair, wet from either her sweat or her blood, to the side. She looked for an exit from this nightmare. She found no escape except those beyond the demon. The creature moved too fast and proved too tough for her. She couldn't even run with the hurt suffered by her leg. Montanya wasn't willing to die, yet she faced the nonexistent mercy of this killer.

It spoke to her, in a voice that sounded like rocks rubbing together. "How does it feel to face your own death? To know that your life is seconds from ending?"

To Montanya, it seemed mere gloating. A haughty statement from the vilest of creatures. She reasoned that the demons must indeed be a tortured society, so much so that they took pleasure in returning the pain to others.

Its words did find a resonating chord within Montanya's thoughts. How did it feel to die? Montanya knew the answer. She'd known it all too well since she was a small girl. She remembered when she was forced to watch her parents die while trapped within a crate. A wound from the attackers had nearly ended her life, yet the memories of the night were deadly to the mind of a young child.

She remembered the night she had first battled Kemora. It was the first time she had sought to fulfill some destiny other than that of a victim. The halfling had stabbed her with poison. Montanya recalled how frail she had felt as the poison ran through her system. She recalled how helpless she had been as the substance had incapacitated her.

Weeks later, she had fought Kemora again, only to be poisoned a second time. Montanya still succeeded in killing the rogue. Once the halfling was dead, Montanya saw only emptiness in the way she had lived her own life. She had been willing to surrender to the poison and end the shallow existence she had led.

Montanya scowled up at the demon looming over her. What right did it have to ask her how she felt? Norzal, watching the angry expression, paused. He seemed to like the reaction. The demon approved of the fire still burning in one who should have lost all hope.

As if reading her thoughts, Norzal said more, "I like to ask that of my prey sometimes. I have seen many die by my hands or my command. I died once, though Mothrok's rebirth," the demon indicated its stone body, "left me nay memory of the incident." Its eyes narrowed at the woman, "Sometimes I hear an answer that intrigues me, but usually I am disappointed. Do you have wisdom for me? How does it feel to face death?"

For a silent moment, Montanya said nothing. She just scowled and stared unflinchingly at the demon's visage. Norzal resigned himself to the fact that no answer would be forthcoming. He readied his arms to crush her, when a response emerged.

"I have died three times already." She declared.

Norzal paused, hoping to hear more. It would not change his mind about his decision to kill her, yet the final words of an enemy were one of the few amusements left to this taraz.

Montanya sorted out the memories of the last few months of her life. She did it for her sake, not the demon's. She remembered offering help to the poor and homeless of Orlaun. Her ears could still hear the applause and delight when she had walked on her hands with bowls balanced on her feet.

Montanya remembered sneaking food to the fat cat that strayed into the sanctuary many nights. She recalled hearing that it had given birth to kittens. She wished she could have had the one extra day to go see those kittens.

She thought of her friend…her best friend. Montanya and Sondra had shared memories, even though it had happened unwillingly. Sondra knew the darkest places in Montanya's heart, and had accepted her as her best friend. *Friends forever.*

Of course, Montanya couldn't forget the dance. If she closed her eyes, she could feel Dern moving against her. She remembered the jolt as his chest brushed hers. How could she hate a man tried to feed his family and eventually died protecting them? His image wouldn't leave her thoughts.

Norzal seemed to be losing his patience awaiting a response. Montanya's eyes rose to meet those blue demon orbs. As she lifted her gaze, she saw the countless dried ears of his enemies displayed across a portion of his chest. She could almost feel sorry for this wretch. The coldast had lived in a world without joy; a world where no pleasure could be gained. His only life relished the pursuit and death of his rivals. It was a world Montanya left behind when she gave up her life of vengeance.

She stared unflinchingly into his eyes. "After the last death, I finally found the enjoyment in life. It was then that I truly began to live."

Her unwavering look dared him to disagree with her. She didn't wait for an answer. His claws poised to take her life. The door was an eternity away. Montanya fought the pain to stand erect in a combat pose. She still leaned on her broken staff, but forced her body to stretch as tall as possible. In her mind, she danced the Butterfly in the Windmill. The martial artist had never cracked stone, but she was willing to give it a try. As the dance of the butterfly counted down in her head, she dropped her scowl for good. Her greenish-blue eyes challenged the demon.

"May I have this next dance?"

The taraz seemed to approve of her answer even as it offered one of its own. Its claws swiped in fast. The butterfly dance came to a conclusion as Montanya entered a fight she could not win.

*   *   *   *   *

In the midst of cracking weapons and grunts of exertion, one man's voice rang clear with song. Lindon's throat felt sore from the amount of singing offered in the last two days. He kept a few skins of water handy and drank often when he could to keep his voice going strong. The minstrel offered the soldiers encouragement and protection through the harmonic web. His strongest asset, that melodious voice, also made him a target for the tribes. Lindon had barely escaped a few arrows and blasts of natura magic, but he'd seen men next to him get caught up in those same attacks due to the misfortune of standing too near to him. He had his smallsword out for defense, but it was his voice that contributed the most to his fellows.

The minstrel inspired those hearing him. Many could not actively listen, but the messages of hope and bravery entered their minds regardless of their attention. He was sure to intertwine some aspects, such as the Stonelands' name and "defending the fortress", so that his words would only affect those who identified with the Stonelands. With those words, only those on his side could benefit from bolstered courage. Lindon's inspirations were only interrupted when he was forced to use the power of sound as a shield or a windstorm in the face of the enemy.

One familiar ally drew closer to the singing. Leander's armor marked him as a paladin of Abriana even before Lindon recognized the face. The young man's hair was no longer confined to a neat ponytail. The battle wore on him, making him tired and dirty. The champion followed the notes of Lindon's song since it seemed to draw his mind to a calmer place. The courtyard was a far cry from calm, yet the musical voice made things more bearable.

When he got close enough, he ventured a query to the singing human. "Seen anyone else from Kashmer around here?"

Without interruption, Lindon shook his head. They were fighting amongst Stonelands' militia. The minstrel had seen the occasional Kashmer privateer, but he knew that the paladin was searching for his friends. The red-bearded minstrel offered a question of his own, using only his eyes.

Leander knew his thoughts. "Nay, I haven't seen anyone I recognize either."

As they turned to their enemies, a voice from some commander called for them to rally around a gate. This courtyard was also succumbing to the invaders. They had to try holding the portal to the next area. There were fewer and fewer places to retreat.

On the walls above them, Korrelothar stood protectively with Aijak. Some gnome casters from his guild helped communicate with the druid. The elf wizard tried to gauge the strength of his remaining guild members, and post them along the walls according to need. Aijak was cooperating, but her attention and spells focused around Mel, who was still down in one of the yards.

In the midst of the chaos, a mage wearing the robes of his brotherhood came running through the haze caused by fires. The man caught Korrelothar's attention, screaming something about Tuampor before a tribal arrow came from below and pierced him. The elf wizard shouted for a cleric, sending one from Ganden's flock to tend the man.

Korrelothar's gaze drew to Tuampor. He immediately noticed the tendrils of smoke rising from a line of shattered windows, remnant of Cat and Revwar's duel. Suddenly, the elf wizard had one more important thing to worry about.

*　　　*　　　*　　　*　　　*

Sondra Oskires patrolled the halls of Tuampor. She had been to the gate room and cautioned the clergy that some enemies may be approaching from within. The wheat-blonde woman didn't care to stay there once she noticed that Montanya had gone missing. Sondra began a lone search of the tower, looking for anything amiss. She marched with mace in hand. Sweat trickled down her brow, and not all of it from the earlier struggles. The priestess was alone and frightened about what she might find. Nervous energy made her breathe hard as she envisioned any number of bad things that could happen to her or her friends.

A faint scrabbling noise at a door caught her attention. Curiosity and fear mixed within her. Quiet as she could, her feet moved further along. She had detected smoke in the air from the battle, but it was stronger here. Something burned nearby.

Sondra moved up to the door. For a moment, all she could do was stare at its aged, decorative handle. Since all of Tuampor was dedicated to a number of gods, every little piece of the décor reflected it. The handle curved in a shape that reflected a dolphin on one side, and a shark on the other. It paid homage to the two greatest symbols of Krakus. Despite its beauty, Sondra paid more attention to the scratching, clawing noises on the other side.

The priestess of Ganden spent a moment deciding her course of action. Did she dare just throw open the door, and be ready to strike? Was there a miracle she should utter to shield herself, even though the thing on the other side might hear? Should she not touch the door at all?

Sondra decided to call out to the other side. Her mace poised ready to swing at anything that thrust the door open. "Who goes there?"

A faint cry whimpered from the other side. "Help."

It had to be a wounded person! They must be unable to reach the handle and pull it open. The cleric still had her mace in hand as she reached out and opened the door. In the hall beyond, Sondra had quite a shock.

She recognized the dying person at her feet as Katressa Bilil. The half-elf's black leathers had holes, burn marks and wet blood. A dagger was stuck just under her ribs. The woman had crawled from the other end of the hall, leaving a bloody trail amidst the ashes of books. Wind blew through shattered windows on one side. At the far end of the hall, an evil wizard that Sondra had seen before was pinned to the opposite door by Cat's rapier.

A phrase escaped Sondra's mouth as she looked over the situation. It was a popular one that arose from the God of Storms and Cataclysms, though it usually referred to the mess in children's play areas. "Did Juliustan himself throw a fit in here?"

Her words brought a glimmer of amusement to Cat's face, though Sondra wore a serious expression as she moved to tend the wounds. She eyed the dagger hilt, but refused to tackle that problem as of yet. Cat's other pains had to be alleviated before she tried to add to the trauma by plucking out the blade. The priestess moved her hands over the largest wounds. A chant went up to Ganden, requesting the channeling of healing miracles. There was some relief to Cat immediately as her blood loss lessened and skin healed over.

Sondra paused a moment, once again considering the dagger. It would possibly cost her the rest of the energy she had; however, if she didn't attempt to heal it, Cat's life would still be hanging in the balance. Sondra put a comforting hand on Cat's head.

"I have to pull this out."

Cat nodded. The adventuress knew what was coming, so she gritted her teeth. Sondra pulled the dagger out as fast as she could. The half-elf didn't scream; the pain made her shudder and gasp for air. Ganden's favored daughter attempted to seal the loss of blood from this most dangerous wound as Cat sucked in pain with every breath. By the time the miracle expired, Sondra was spent. Cat could breathe easily, yet her lingering wounds left her no strength to move on her own.

When Sondra had the chance to recover her own breath, she set about trying to get Cat moved to the center of Tuampor. The wounded woman could get more healing there. For now, she was stable enough to recover on her own, given time and rest. Sondra used the cloak Cat rested on as a stretcher. The young human hunched over, pulling the cloak with weary Cat on it back to the main healing chamber.

Thankfully, she didn't have far to go. They arrived in the room with the gate, where an acolyte helped Sondra lift Cat onto a cot. Even that motion caused pain, but the half-elf's condition was not life-threatening. They were just exchanging a few words, with Sondra offering comfort, when screams pulled at their attention. They looked across the room to see what had caused the commotion.

They witnessed the large, stony demon, its robes shredded and blood staining its form, enter the chamber.

CHAPTER 29 "The Gate of Issundor"

It shocked Sondra to see such a powerful taraz standing within the midst of this divine place. Her hands fumbled as she pulled out her mace. Her weapon seemed to be a pitiful threat to such an evil presence. Everyone standing close to the demon's entry went running for their life; even healers ran despite the worried screams of their patients. Many of the injured defenders had no ability to run from the nightmare.

Clerics across the chamber began to pray for miracles. The mere utterance of the holy devotions, none of which were offered to Mothrok, irritated the demon. Norzal had entered the chamber ready to give as well as receive. Both Cat and Sondra saw the green stone held in one of its clawed hands. It held the stone aloft, calling on its powers. A green light illuminated the chamber. Some clerics shielded their eyes from the unknown assault, others tried finishing protective miracles.

A host of figures arose, some melted upward from the slabs making up the floor. The earth spirits took shape and sent tremors with every step. Magic-users hastily prepared spells to combat the summoned elementals. The recent dead fell sway under the control of the relics borne from DeLaris' alliance. Deceased soldiers, who had not yet been removed, stirred under their death shrouds. Priests and stretcher-bearers were paying more attention to things other than the dead men. The undead rose up to seize the living. Some wounded soldiers found the strength to fight, though they faced unnatural adversaries.

The large chamber became a battleground.

Clerics of many different faiths fought back. While some focused spells on immediate threats, such as the walking dead, most focused on the taraz as their key enemy. Cardinal Methlen Foresight of the Stonelands rallied many priests to target the creature. Norzal looked unsurprised and unworried as the might of several clerics focused toward him. Cat caught sight of the magic necklace the demon wore. Norzal spoke to it, calling for the aid from Kelor.

The Kashmer infiltrator reached over to Sondra, trying to get the woman's attention. Cat spoke through her pain. "Necklace…Gitouro…"

She was too late to warn anyone. The item granted the demon's wishes. As scores of miracles launched to attack Norzal, the power of this other relic from the Godswars reflected the energies back at the owners. Clerics were caught up in their own spells. Cat watched as Sondra threw her own miracle towards the coldast. A flash of light, and Ganden's priestess shuddered from the shock of the misdirected attack. Sondra collapsed beside Cat's bunk. The human woman muttered something, weakly, but she seemed to lack strength.

Norzal relied on his physical prowess to crush some men who tried to scratch his enchanted body with their steel weapons. Around the room, a losing battle played out as the coldast and his summoned allies swept everyone from his path. His obvious goal was the Gate of Issundor. Once he had control of the transdimensional bridge, the host of demons that could pour through would make the coldast's solo assault feel like the breeze before the storm.

*   *   *   *   *

Trestan's heart pumped much faster than his running feet. The sanctity of Tuampor had certainly been violated. Bodies in the halls bore silent witness to the work of a demon inside the holy tower. Each defender that stood in its path had died horribly. Some were burned, others chilled to death by his ghostly mist, and still more were left in a pile of detached limbs. A feeling of mounting dread clutched at Trestan's heart as he realized the ferocity of this opponent. The paladin had the Sword of the Spirit in hand as he entered yet another room that showed signs of a fight. A breeze from a broken window circulated the dust from many shattered statues and podiums.

Trestan's breath caught in his chest, bringing him to a staggering halt as he came across the lone body in the room.

There was no mistaking the broken caleocht staff, the loose Serud'Thanil pantaloons, and a broken elf clasp half-hidden in the tangle of long, red hair. Montanya su Troyeal bara Westonhout lay torn apart on the floor. A glimpse of her was enough to know that his friend's spirit was gone from her body. The blood-soaked clothes and the visible injuries gave testimony to how tortuously she had died.

Wide-eyed Trestan stopped, then collapsed to a kneeling position. His hands held wide in helplessness; all he could do was stare in horror. The paladin began to breathe raggedly as he looked in disbelief over his lost friend. His mind cried out that Montanya should not have fallen in this battle. Trestan could have dealt with his own death easier than the image of this promising youth sprawled amidst a pool of her own blood.

Of all the uncounted men and women who had already met their fate on the field, this young woman should have survived to see better days. Kelor's luck had already cursed her with a lost childhood. Now she would never grow into a woman and explore her full potential. Since Trestan had once melded Sondra's and Montanya's memories together, he had likewise shared in some of those visions. He was aware how much Montanya felt shunned by the gods. Her childhood had been nothing but sorrow and anger, but Trestan had watched her outlook change ever since initiating that contact. Trestan didn't miss the close friendship Sondra and Montanya had formed, despite how much they had argued when they met. He had been pleasantly surprised when Montanya said she would stay in Orlaun to help the poor. The chiaso deserved more than she had gotten. He knew she had finally found a life beyond her thoughts of vengeance…why hadn't the gods seen fit to let her explore more of what life had to offer?

His left hand tenderly reached out to her. After a slight touch of one of her scarlet strands, his fingers recoiled. Trestan wanted to wake up from this bad dream. Rhijin's life had been cut down before she could really begin her devotion to her beliefs. Montanya's view of the world had been blinded by her darker side for too many years; the veil coming free only as her path came to an end. Trestan had seen so many faces of death in the past two days, even now he had no idea how most of his friends fared. How many more young sacrifices had to be made?

His feelings even had Trestan questioning Abriana. In a moment of frustrated denial, Trestan let loose some of his emotions. He swung the magical elvish blade down at the stone floor as hard as he could. He wasn't considering the value of the sword to his heart, or whether his action might actually cause irreparable harm to it. For that moment, his anger surged over his better judgment. The sound of metal striking stone echoed out the window through which Salgor had been thrown.

After that angry release, his calmer, rational mind sought control again. He couldn't dwell here in anger. Montanya was dead and beyond help. A good friend would be forever missed. She wouldn't be the last one taken from him if he let the demon get to the gate. His sword was needed, lest more promising young people meet their death. He cast a worried look to his blade, afraid he had harmed it.

The Sword of the Spirit had gouged a mark in the stone floor. The blade still held its amazing edge.

Trestan forced his legs to allow him to stand. Much as his heart pained over this new loss, he knew he couldn't linger. His living friends were still endangered. Somewhere, a coldast caused trouble, ignorant of the fact that at least one blade in the fortress could cut into stone without dulling. He found himself anxious to try his sword against the body of the demon. The paladin paused only long enough to give a prayer for his fallen companion.

"May the gods grant you the peace in death that so often eluded you in life."

He went forth, leaving a portion of his heart with the friend he left behind.

*   *   *   *   *

For the longest time, the lives of Kor and Pejena hung in a precarious balance. They had been pinned by numerous demon-possessed elders, but those whom they had freed with Mel's poison now fought their former captors. Kor struggled to get his spear arm out from one body, hoping to get in more blows. Pejena tried calling to the winds while underneath the smothering weight of another demon. Elders, who once would not regard themselves as allies to the couple, began to rescue them for the sake of the fight. Demons lashed out with magic, though they sometimes injured the hosts of their brothers.

The tide of battle turned in favor of the freed tribesmen. Kor finally threw off the body trapping him. The tall warrior immediately speared the demon-controlled person that was trying to cut off Pejena's air. The possessed man fell away, writhing as the poison went through his body. Pejena's winds kicked up dust into the eyes of those who stood against them. Axes, spears, magic, and flames brought down each demon host, while the same attacks were returned to the freed people. Brackish taraz slugs erupted from the throats of more elders as the poison took effect. The ejected demons found nowhere to hide. They were slaughtered with a vengeance.

Kor and Pejena stood triumphantly among the freed elders. The Com'der addressed them all once it became apparent that no more possessed stood among them. "We must call back our tribes, our brothers! The demons may be coming in great numbers from the fortress. We have to call away our warriors and be ready for whatever comes."

The freed men and women needed no encouragement. Their tribes were still attacking an enemy that was once their friend in trade. The battle served no one but the taraz. Elders began to search for their clans and families.

During this time, the demon-possessed elders mixed among the nomad army ranks were caught unaware by hunters who knew of their nature. The various Spear Riders, each wielding a weapon coated with poison, had melted into the army until they were stalking close to the demon hosts.

The first Rider calmly moved within range of his target and struck with a dagger. Just as quickly, he turned and nonchalantly got some distance from the convulsing person. Those nomads nearby wondered what sort of magical malady overcame this leader. They all jumped back as a demon spewed forth from him. The slug-like creature almost got away, if not for the same Spear Rider stabbing it directly with the poisoned dagger.

A proud orc shaman, also possessed, felt the stab of a spear in his side. Hot agony flared from the wound. The demon turned to the side and used the magic of its host to burn the attacker…noting with surprise its attacker was a tribesman. The Spear Rider died, but the poison still did its work. Less than a minute later, the orc shaman burned the taraz which once held it captive.

From courtyard to courtyard, and even up on the walls, numerous Spear Riders came up behind the demons leading the attack and promptly backstabbed them.

*　　　　*　　　　*　　　　*　　　　*

Trestan ran closer to the heart of Tuampor, driven by passion and the noise of a battle. He was closing fast when the clamor suddenly dimmed. It ended in a crashing sound as numerous elemental earth spirits fell apart. Abriana's champion threw open a door already ajar, staring into the room housing the Gate of Issundor.

He expected to see a demon, but saw much worse. Wounded soldiers hacked at bodies on the floor. The fright in the eyes of the injured suggested they feared the dead would walk again. Piles of boulders littered the chamber. The clerics were all either dead, dying, frozen by spells, or otherwise unable to perform their duties. Trestan could see some trapped by the effects of miracles that were often used by priests such as themselves. Something happened here, but no taraz were visible.

It was easy to see where any demons went. The Gate of Issundor crackled alive with magical energy. A surface looking like a reflection of water stood vertical, filling the arch of the gate. The connection had been joined between Dhea Loral and Ibleu Taraz. His countenance visibly paled as he realized the danger. Trestan's heart jumped as he spotted his lover, lying wounded on a cot, weakly waving to get his attention.

"Cat!"

Trestan jumped to her side in an instant. As he knelt, he saw Sondra sprawled on the floor. The blonde woman showed no visible injury, yet she lay barely conscious and groaning. Even as Trestan asked Cat what happened, the half-elf strained to answer him. He looked over her wounds as she talked. Trestan could almost feel her pains as his own.

Cat whispered, "It came through…the coldast from my nightmare."

"Nightmare?"

"From my village, years ago. Revwar's demon partner. It just opened the portal and walked through as you came in. We have to get out of here."

Trestan looked back at the arcane structure. "How did it get through?"

She spoke in a weak voice. "It had the Earthrin Stones and the Gitouro necklace. The necklace debilitated the priests, twisted their spells back at them. He called up the guardians of the stones. Once he walked through the portal, the elementals and undead faded."

That explained the injured attacking the dead bodies and the presence of the boulder piles in the room. Trestan was so concerned on his lover's wounds that he wasn't really thinking about the rest. "But, the wards around the gate?"

Sondra answered. She was lying as helpless as Cat on the cold floor as a result of her reflected miracle. Her limbs trembled. "The wards only protect from one direction. He was on the outside. It was easy for him to strip the magic of the ward, like one pulls a stitch loose by grabbing the free end of the thread. There is nay barrier left to restrain the demons of that world."

Trestan glanced over her. "Sondra, what ails you?"

The young priestess offered a weary smile, though she seemed on the verge of tears. "I tried to weaken it. My own miracle debilitated me."

Trestan observed, "Neither of you can walk."

"Nay, I can't." Cat agreed. Her emerald eyes looked beyond Trestan at the shimmering gateway. "But we have to leave…somehow. We have to get away from here before nightmares pour through that portal."

The champion of Abriana looked back at the shimmering gate. He felt hopeless. He knew he couldn't drag Cat and Sondra very far before something nasty arrived. Where would they go even if they could get away from Tuampor? The nomads were winning the battle in the courtyards, and now the demons would emerge and descend upon all.

He looked into Cat's pleading eyes. Couldn't she see the problem as well as he did? "Where would we go in time? Where would we hide?" Trestan's thoughts turned to Petrow's worries. "Even if we got away today, will we find demons playing in the fields of Troutbrook tomorrow?"

Cat reached out and took his hand. She understood the futility of it all. They had failed. Their great last stand would only get them all killed quicker and hand the northern half of the continent Shard over to the taraz. Trestan and Cat would never live to be married. Any hopes of a long life and children blew away like a candle flame in a storm.

Trestan's eyes went back to the gate. He desperately searched for ideas, aware that he had precious little time. Arcane research wasn't one of his stronger points at the seminary. It occurred to him that he had failed this very question when posed by one of the elders during his Embarking. He recalled the words of the elder from that day.

"Once the transdimensional bridge exists, you need only one of the two interested parties to continue holding the gate open, thus they can support the portal from only one side. This party would be henceforth called the gatewarden for simplicity and obvious reasons. They may continue to hold the passage open by continuing the proper spell phrases, or by keeping concentration constant on the aforementioned magically focused device. If a foreign interest seeks to close the gate against the wishes of the party that is still supporting it, they must go through extreme efforts. Usually this requires strong spells of the proper type as one method to close the gate peacefully. If nay such spells or power is available, then the gate must be broken by means of destroying the concentration of the gatewarden, by destroying his magical device, or if all other means fails by killing the gatewarden himself. Remember this, Trestan, for it may benefit you some day."

They could not close the gate with force. A number of powerful clerics in the room were capable of such a task as to force a closure from this side, but all were restrained and incapacitated by their errant miracles. The cardinal from the Stonelands and some high-ranking priests from Ganden and Abriana suffered helplessly in their own predicaments. Trestan had no idea how to free the clergy, but he feared it would take too long.

The next step was to interrupt the source that still held the gate open. This meant attacking the gatewarden in some way. Unfortunately, Trestan knew where the gatewarden *wasn't* located. No demon was needed on this side to hold the portal up. The coldast just had to be on this side to open it and get rid of the restraining wards here. Once activated, the demons could hold it open from their world. Since this was a strong, permanently erected dimensional bridge, it could be held open relatively easy.

He briefly reflected on the wards that had safeguarded the entry. Such protective boundaries could be erected by clerics of Ganden. Trestan didn't need to glance to Sondra to realize that whatever she could summon in her weakened state would not matter to the powers coming through that portal.

That still left the gatewarden…and the gatewarden safely hid on the Ibleu Taraz side of the gate.

Trestan got a cold chill up his spine as he realized what was required. Once the demons marched through that portal, the beleaguered forces of both the Stonelands and the tribes wouldn't be enough to fight back. All of Trestan's dearest friends, even his own father, would be killed. Once the demons finished them, it would only spread from there.

Even worse, as Cardinal Alunetar had stated, the deities of the pantheon might intervene to save their followers. Such a thing would shatter the Covenant, bringing an end to the one thing that held the gods in check. Doing so would trigger an open Godswars once again, likely with no easy end in sight. Dhea Loral faced extermination, either by demon invasion or by the wrath of another Godswars.

"…Abriana sends us…We are her mind and body in this world. We are her only tools."

Trestan once wondered what the price of following a god would be. The bleakest possible outcome threatened to strangle his courage as he faced that prospect. Trestan sighed as he committed his decision to the sacrifice required.

He turned to Cat and knelt at her side. "In order to save us all, the gate has to be closed."

Cat started to say, "How?" Her voice choked mid-word as she saw the sadness in Trestan's eyes.

"I have to kill or interrupt the demon holding it open on the other side."

Her eyes went wide. "Nay. Nay! There will be another way. Perhaps a magic phrase you don't know about will shut it. Maybe Korrelothar? Find Mel! This can't be all on your shoulders!"

Trestan held her hand. "Any moment now, a host of demons will flood out of that gate, and then it will be too late. If even one gets over here, they can reopen the portal easily from this side even if I close it. It has to be done now. There is nay time."

Tears brimmed at the edges of Cat's sparkling eyes. She tried to clasp his hand harder, but she lacked strength. "Don't go through that gate. I can't lose you that way…just like my father. There must be another way."

He could only shake his head. "I wish there was. I don't want to go, but I have to go. That's the choice I agreed to follow when I saved your life in that keep in the sea. There is hope. Once I strike my blow, I will come back before the way is closed."

His words couldn't stop the tears flowing from her eyes. Trestan felt the pain welling up in his own heart as his finger brushed the streaks from her cheek. Even as he did, he felt the wetness roll down his own cheek. He tried to keep a brave face.

"This is what your father tried to tell you. This is why I followed the call of the Goddess of Love. One has to love someone, and something, so much that they have to be willing to risk everything."

Cat whispered to him through trembling lips. "I know. It's why I love you. You never back down from doing what you feel is right. Even when the odds tell you to go back, you keep pushing towards your dreams." She looked at the other wounded men in the room. "Don't go alone. See if anyone will go with you."

Trestan held his blade high and called out the attention of all in the room. "Listen to me! I need some brave men with faith in their gods! Any moment, a horde of demons will come through that portal. If not stopped, your fortress and your country will fall. I need someone to step through the gate with me. If we kill the demon on the other side, your lands and loved ones will be saved!"

A voice asked, "That gate is open to the demons' world right now?"

Trestan looked to the man and answered, "Aye."

"Bloody cesspit! To DeLaris with that idea!" After cursing his opinion, he turned and fled elsewhere. Three others, who could run, did.

None of the rest volunteered. Even if they had been willing, many had their own injuries hindering them. Sondra didn't have the strength to sit up or heal. Her condition wouldn't get worse, but the miracle debilitating her wouldn't wear off soon enough. Abriana's champion turned to his love.

"I have to go, alone if I must." He said, in a mournful manner.

Even after he said it, Trestan still lingered. Despite his claim that hope remained, he knew this was probably the last time he might ever see Cat.

Her eyes looked over him, noting the cuts and bruises from the two days of fighting. She knew he was hiding some of his pain. If Trestan was allowing some of his wounds to go unheeded, that meant his mental reserves for miracles were also almost used up. She had a hard time bringing herself to respect the nobility of his cause when he seemed to be throwing his life away. Her mind came to a decision. Cat could offer him one last bit of help. In doing so, it would also better ensure that if she lost him, she wouldn't have to suffer that pain for long.

"Kiss me," she asked.

She didn't even have to ask. Trestan leaned close, allowing her to wrap her weak arms about his neck. Their lips touched, sweetly caressing each other. Cat lent him her breath, and in return he breathed back into her. His strong, blacksmith hands supported her delicate form, absently twirling some of her raven hair. Cat's perceptive fingers found and traced the symbols of Abriana on his shoulder armor. His faith had saved her, and now it would take him away.

Trestan was about to part from the embrace when he felt a sensation: warm and full of love. It moved like a wave from Cat's hands, rippling over his injuries and healing them. At the same time, he felt his lover's body become tense and rigid. She was in pain!

Cat used the *Taef' Adorina* Trestan had given her to transfer some of her life-force to him!

234

Trestan forced himself from her tight grasp. She fell back to the cot, greatly weakened. "Cat, you can't! You're too wounded!"

If she was weak before, she became crippled now. Some of her wounds reopened. Her breathing wheezed. Cat's eyes rolled around in her sockets, distracted by the pain.

The paladin had very little strength to call on any miracles. Regardless, he needed one now. He knelt back at her side, trying to bring forth a healing prayer.

Her eyes resumed focus. She let loose a weak slap at his hands. "Trestan…nay…think about it."

Trestan paused. Her voice, so labored, brought him sorrow. She continued explaining, "You need…your strength. Must hurry, they will come through at any time."

His brown eyes roamed over her body. "Cat, you gave too much. You'll die if I leave you like this."

"Exactly," she whispered. Her emerald eyes lost him for a moment. They refocused on him, reflecting the beauty in her soul. "If you make it…you can come heal me. If you fail…the demons will make sure I don't live long."

Trestan hung his head. His heart went against leaving her here like she was. He wanted to save her. The young man knew he might not make it back through the closing portal…what would happen then?

"Don't delay." She pleaded. "There's…nay time…love you."

He looked to their friend lying nearby. "Sondra, do what you can for her, alright?"

Sondra gave a weak nod. The woman didn't seem that much better off than Cat.

He turned back to Cat. "I'll be back. Hang in there. I'll be here in maybe a minute. You have to make it."

She loved the way he looked when his dark eyes filled with resolve. Lacking the strength to give a proper verbal reply, she simply nodded. One of the hardest things Trestan ever did was turn away from her at that moment. He walked over to the rippling gateway. The eyes of all the wounded in the room followed him. They would all be running or dead soon and one man's sacrifice didn't seem like it would sway the outcome much. The watery-looking cascade offered him no clue as to what lay beyond the portal. It proved hard to get past that hesitation. Humans don't belong in Ibleu Taraz any more than the demons who visited here. The paladin recalled the stories of how twisted and torn that world had become since the Godswars.

He threw one last look at his beloved. For Cat, it was like watching her father step over to the portal all over again. She remembered how he had looked to her, touched his hand to the unicorn earring, radiated false confidence that she would see him again as he went to his death. She remembered the many years afterward when she felt angry at her father. Cat had often posed her question to the gods: why did he throw his life away and leave her alone?

Now Trestan stood alone but for his magical blade, looking back at her. The wavering light of the portal framed his dark hair and brown eyes. The former blacksmith tried to exude a confidant look which was wasted on Cat.

"I will be back."

He stated it as if the proclamation itself would make it a reality. Katressa Bilil, daughter of Reatheneus, couldn't bring her feelings to match his optimism. She hid too much emotion behind her soft face to offer him a smile or a nod.

Trestan faced the gateway. He filled his lungs with one last treasured breath of Dhea Loral air before stepping through the portal. Once he had disappeared from her sight, Cat didn't have to try holding the tears back anymore; she let them run free.

CHAPTER 30 "Ibleu Taraz"

The courtyards were chaotic enough when tribesmen were fighting defenders, but now the forces of the Stonelands witnessed fighting amongst the tribes. Small pockets of warriors turned against themselves. In each case, the excitement centered on a member of the Spear Riders stabbing their nomad allies. Some of those tribesmen were killed as soon as their treachery was witnessed. Traitorous insults would be hurled at the same time as weapons. Sometimes the attacker was swift enough to stab and retreat during the battle. In each case, witnessed or not, demons were expelled within sight of the tribes. Elders shouted orders that reversed their attitudes of the last several months. Instead of being called to attack, the various tribes were being recalled to attend to their respective leaders. The attack became less unified as nomads gave contradictory orders.

Kor's men and women were slowly taking the heart from the battle. With each tribal leader converted back to his freedom, the rebellion against their demon masters grew. The nomad force began dissolving.

This didn't spare the Stonelands' defenders from retreating to the heart of the fortress. The central castle section and inner walls housing the royalty became the rallying point for the tired men. The various soldiers, privateers, mages and clerics that had come to aid the frontier kingdom fell back to the last position they could defend.

Mel and Aijak were reunited on Cathag's saddle. The two gnomes rode up and down the ramparts offering spells only when needed. Their reserves of energy were nearly sapped. Mel had used up the stored magic within his wand, and Aijak had already blooded her wooden thacca on a couple orcs' feet.

Lindon had no voice for singing. He managed to hum a melody which served only to ease the weariness on his own limbs. The layers of clothes he wore on his chest, typical of Orlaun fashions, were torn open for ease of access to his throwing knives. No knives remained, lost amidst the bodies in the outer yards. He lacked bolts to load the crossbow on his back. The red-bearded man had only his smallsword as he ran messages between officers.

Leander was separated from the rest of those in the inner walls. The young paladin and a handful of cut-off defenders took refuge in a portion of one of the outer towers. They were surrounded by too many attackers to fight their way to the others. They barricaded their lone exit with anything heavy enough to resist the nomads trying to force them open.

Tuampor stood as one of the towers in this inner ring of walls. Salgor had tried to get back inside, but found himself delayed by tribal warriors. The dwarf charged into them with his axe swinging in wild abandon. The healing received after his fall gave him all the energy he needed. Orc berserkers, raulgan fighters, and gliel shamans found it hard to stop the dwarf's progress.

On the opposite side of Tuampor, Korrelothar Balshav and members of his guild were also clearing a path to get inside. They worked desperately even though some overextended their magic. A couple mages tried casting past their endurance, only to lose consciousness instead. Most resorted to the magic stored within wands and staves. An onslaught of spells knocked down those barring their way.

Floranue Balshav stressed about her husband between worrying about her own life. The elf had been sequestered since the fighting began. None in the room really knew how badly things were going for the defenders. Many of the nobles and their retainers were crammed behind barricaded doors. She had been herded along with the rest of the kitchen staff to one such large chamber inside a keep. Guards braced the doors, piling objects that would slow the entry of any attackers. There was nothing for the commoners to do except cower and wait. Many were too old or young to be a threat to seasoned warriors. Floranue's own hand kept a grip on a knife pulled from the kitchen as she had fled, though she feared it would be of little use. She looked at the doors and the poorly armed guards. If the tribes managed to get this far, a slaughter would follow.

On the ramparts, Hebden and Petrow joined several men that were slowly giving ground. They fought desperately as they sensed they were being backed into a corner. Hebden had all the adventure he would ever want for the rest of his life. He struck men a couple times with his tough hammer blows. Arrows flew uncomfortably close. Spells erupted in a show that would have left the smith awestruck, except for the fact that they were trying to take his life. Hebden wondered how long his apparent invincibility would last. His thoughts were brought short as an arrow hit him in the side.

The aging smith went down hard. The initial pain stole his ability to scream. His lungs tried to force in a deep breath. Some tribesmen charged, leaving Hebden to assume the end of his long years as a smith and his few weeks as a warrior.

Petrow stepped over him, partially straddling his body. The young man swung both axe and the gnomish lift. The device on his arm no longer functioned magically. A tribal shaman had somehow drained the magic from it before losing his life to a Stonelands' archer. The lift served as a poor shield, denting easily with every blow. Petrow still used both items in his hands as he stood defiant against the charging enemies. The bent metal disk was finally ripped from his arm by the force of a large club. Petrow put both hands on his axe, sweeping back and forth in large cuts. The desperate farmer knocked down two men before the rest stepped back to regroup.

The young man from Troutbrook left it to the Stonelands' army to do the rest. While he had a moment of opportunity, he hoisted Hebden to his feet. The older man had to lean on him as Petrow walked him away from the tribes. Hebden saw that his wound didn't seem deep, but it still gave him enough pain to make moving difficult. The alternative…lying on the ramparts as the tribes rolled forward…didn't hold any appeal.

"We'll find some help for you," Petrow assured him as they staggered along. "I bet we'll find Tres and he'll fix that up."

*   *   *   *   *

In the darkest pits of Trestan's nightmares, the paladin had never been in such a forlorn place. The coldest fear that left his teeth chattering, the deepest sorrow that had ever lanced his heart, the darkest torment he could ever imagine…all of this described his first glance of Ibleu Taraz. "Forsaken Fruit" could not even begin to come close to the truth. Whatever paradise had once been here had been scoured away by more than a millennium of warfare. Dhea Loral had enjoyed an age of peace and renovation. Ibleu Taraz never had an opportunity to turn back. The twisted denizens of this world were beyond the granting of

238

such benevolence. The changes that had warped their bodies enslaved them to continue the Godswars as if the Covenant had never existed.

Trestan's first experience with this wasteland was shoved down his throat in his first unwilling breath. Smoke from endless fires saturated the air. Toxins burned in his lungs from that first inhalation. He harbored no doubts that any human exposed to this world for too long would be poisoned by the air itself. The acidic taste stung his eyes as he tried focusing on the land before him.

The light illuminating Ibleu Taraz paled in comparison to Yestreal's sun. In fact, Trestan could see no sun at all. The brightness compared with one of those rare nights in which Dhea Loral observed three full moons. The sky over Ibleu Taraz, whether it was day or night, was a far cry from such a romantic vista. In this strange land, a swirling vortex of angry clouds filled the air, thundering against themselves. An uneven light swirled up there, giving bare illumination to the ground. Shadows flickered around as the lighting changed in the clouds. Sometimes bolts of lightning leapt from cloud to cloud or flashed into the ground; sometimes other odd objects would tumble from the sky. Fiery bursts mixed in the air alongside tumbling meteors.

The land looked as dreary as the sky. The few structures Trestan saw looked like they had once been religious in nature. To the last, each one showed signs of being converted to a barricade or fort before deteriorating into a scarred ruin. Even the structure he stood upon was a half-collapsed ziggurat. The pyramid-shaped temple was missing the rear portion behind him, past the wavering portal. In front of him, partly crumbled stones still propped the walls. A few smashed statues gave evidence that the beings who called this place home once had a more humanoid appearance.

Craters pocked the lands between ruins. Crevasses spewing steam ripped across the landscape. There were pools of liquid that looked nothing like water. Trestan witnessed jagged, narrow rocks stretching along the whole length of the land. A second inspection revealed that the rocks were actually bones. The realm had become an enormous graveyard.

As shocking as this world was to Trestan's eyes, it paled next to the fear that stabbed him when he looked upon the demon hosts. Aside from the almost bare structure he stood upon, the land and sky swarmed with thousands of misshapen terrors. This was no random sampling of the taraz; all the demons in sight were part of Mothrok's and DeLaris' loyal minions. The followers of the Earth Goddess were either made of rock or made to carve through rock. They melded with animal forms, spawning nightmarish versions of worms, snakes, moles, rats, and other burrowing creatures. The worm-like demons matched the ones forced from Kor and Pejena. The chosen army of the Death Goddess reeked of decay and disease as they shambled around in skeletal forms. Some were made from a ghostly mist, others seemed to be a mix of body parts and appendages from past opponents. Winged, flesh-eating undead circled high above Trestan.

The paladin of Abriana went weak in the knees as their frightening screeches increased the queasy feelings already taking root in his gut.

The top few floors of the ziggurat were almost free of demons. The stage had been cleared for the coldast addressing the rest of the demon army. Trestan's visit through the portal placed him several steps behind the demon, but within plain sight of the multitude of malicious eyes focused in that direction. The young man spotted a pair of demons kneeling nearby; one on each side of him. Both held glassy orbs to their chests, facing the cracked arch on this side of the portal. Trestan realized there wasn't just one gatewarden: both demons possessed items that allowed them to channel their will into holding the gate open. The pair of taraz that shared the upper tier of the ziggurat with him had bodies of flesh and fur, hunched over. Unfortunately, the coldast lingered only a few steps from either of them.

Norzal had shed his disguising cloak. Trestan witnessed the revealed monstrosity addressing an army of loyal demons. The dark-gray, stone body, wreathed in ethereal mists from his ghostly soul, presented a dual composition. Even if the Sword of the Spirit could chip stone, could the creature still kill him with just a tendril of its ghostly essence? The coldast had no weapon; it needed no weapon aside from its own claws.

In Trestan's moment of hesitation, Norzal swiveled around to face this lone intruder. The paladin saw the mark of Mothrok burned into his chest…among other details. A wide strap crossed the demon's chest, displaying several grisly tokens. The dried ears of many vanquished foes hung there.

The chilling words declared by Revwar to Katressa in Serud'Thanil came to his mind: *"If you ever want to hunt down the coldast demon that killed him, it won't be hard. The creature wears a collection of ears of the people it had killed. I hear Reatheneus' ear had a gold unicorn symbol dangling from it when it was cut off."*

Trestan knew he couldn't get to both gatewardens with the coldast standing so close. Trestan realized that killing the one gatewarden wasn't enough. The glass orbs in their hands seemed to be channeling their concentration. If Trestan killed one without destroying the orb, another demon might take over before he killed the second one or the gate closed. He recalled the vial Korrelothar had given him in Orlaun. The "Blood of Dalios" remained in a pouch at his belt. There were times during the siege that Trestan either forgot about it, or chose to save it for a proper moment. The young man recalled Korrelothar saying it would give him the strength of ten men, as well as endow him with amazing regeneration of his wounds. It seemed as if Trestan would need to drink it soon, or never. While the paladin held his sword before him, failing to present himself as a fearful opponent to the old demon, his other hand reached for the potion.

Norzal turned to the gathered host and roared in laughter. "Look, my brothers! We are foiled! An insect with a toothpick blocks our route to conquest!"

A chilling laughter erupted from hideous maws. The sound came from all around as the sea of taraz ridiculed Abriana's champion. Only the two demons serving as gatewardens limited their mirth. They had to keep their concentration on the portal.

The intimidating coldast faced Trestan, "Come over here and prove yourself a hero."

Trestan unleashed a miracle. The young man hadn't yet drunk the potion. He realized he could attack Norzal in a way that might debilitate him long enough to act. Trestan shouted his prayers to Abriana, calling for the repentance of the demon's soul. Norzal was momentarily shocked as it felt the assault to its core. The ghostly tendrils ringing its body began to blow backward like streamers from Trestan's miracle. Faithful followers of Abriana had a good amount of power to repel undead and demons…and Norzal was both. The paladin poured his faith into rebuking the evil of the creature.

The holy wind tore at the coldast. He felt his ghostly self repelled from the young champion. His consciousness anchored itself to the stone portions of his body. The miracle still attempted to scrape his undead self from his elemental aspects, but he held firm. The demon survived too many years to fall that easily. It willed itself forward despite the pain.

Trestan's eyes grew wide as he realized his banishing miracle would have no effect on a creature with Norzal's dual nature. The paladin released his concentration, his beleaguered spirit already feeling more taxed by the attempt. Watching Norzal recover almost instantly, Trestan broke the seal on the potion.

The dark-red liquid within gave off a nauseating smell. Trestan couldn't afford to hesitate. He slammed the foul liquid down his throat and swallowed despite a reflex to gag on it. It tasted like blood. It oozed its way down his throat, leaving an odd taste on his tongue. His eyes momentarily clouded over with a mist. Just as quickly, his vision sharpened back into amazing clarity, taking in more detail than ever before. He felt a change in all his senses. Up until that moment, it was as if the rest of his life he'd been walking in a daze. Now, the world appeared focused. Even though the air of Ibleu Taraz felt that much more corrupt, it no longer choked his body. He practically smelled the power of the Earthrin Stones, tucked in a bag at the demon's side. His mind saw a magical glow around the Gitouro necklace, as well as a glow surrounding his own sword. Trestan could hear muttered words from demons half a mile away, and could sense their strengths and weaknesses. His body and mind felt reinvigorated. A hidden strength arose in his muscles. He had no doubt that he could throw his bastard sword halfway across the demon ranks if he dared. Every fighting move he had ever learned, (and some that he never knew about), flowed through his thoughts. He perceived the world moving at a different rate than before. Norzal's movements seemed slower than they were a moment ago. Trestan became a champion of Dalios, God of Strength and Courage, also God of War.

The other demons ringing the ziggurat stayed their distance, content to watch as Norzal tore this lone human to pieces.

Trestan had to ignore the stones and the necklace in order to accomplish his goal. He couldn't afford to distract himself with the relics when all those he loved were at stake. He needed to kill the gatewardens and shut down the portal. The coldast loomed too close, but unaware of Trestan's heightened awareness.

Trestan raised his sword in challenge. "For Abriana, and those that I love!"

The young paladin did exactly as Norzal would expect him to do. He charged straight at the demon with his arms raised for an overhead, two-handed chop. Norzal easily sidestepped the sword's intended path. The demon even raked his claws at the empty air where Trestan should have been. Utilizing the amazing speed and strength given to him by the potion, the paladin veered towards his true target. Even as Norzal realized his mistake in judging Trestan, the paladin's magical elvish blade split a path. The Sword of the Spirit cut through the orb of one demon, before halving the creature also. The glass-like object blasted outward into a mist. The first gatewarden gave a weak howl as it tumbled apart.

The other gatewarden kept his concentration, but began jabbering away to its friends as Trestan turned his eyes that way. This one would not be so easy. The coldast moved directly between Trestan and his next target, and now the demon knew his plan. The paladin attacked while he still had the momentum of his surprise; Norzal was prepared to strike back.

The sword stabbed in but was turned aside by the stone claw. Norzal moved fast, but Trestan found himself able to track the movements and respond. As the second claw came around, Trestan used his wrist-over-wrist spinning technique to get his sword back in line. Claw and blade met. Trestan was pushed to the side but he felt the sword leave a cut in the stone arm. Norzal exhaled a roar as the demon felt the sword put its mark on him.

The veteran taraz offered the next trick. It overreacted to its injury, leaving an apparent opening. Trestan launched forward with amazing speed. Norzal failed to stop the sword's tip from knocking a chip from his torso, (only a chip despite Trestan's newfound strength!), but in return, it smashed a fist on top of his head.

He dashed Trestan against the unyielding surface of the temple. Norzal immediately followed up by grabbing him. The paladin swung blindly with his sword, his vision hampered by blood and sweat, leaving another scratch on the coldast's body. The demon was not slowed. It got both hands around Trestan's left leg, then used the strength of the earth to break it. Agony swam over Trestan as he felt the limb snap. Norzal then hoisted Trestan overhead before throwing him into the broken base of a pillar. More bones broke upon impact.

Even as the pain threatened to make him unconscious, Trestan felt something inside him fight back. The effects of the Blood of Dalios surged through his body. His leg twitched and suddenly snapped back in place. The cut above his brow disappeared under fresh skin. His other bones regenerated back together. The rage in Dalios' blood washed the pain away. Even as Norzal stomped over to inflict more pain, Trestan felt almost whole again.

The demon reached down to grab him. Trestan, barely propped up, offered only a punch. The demon's head snapped to the side as the paladin struck. Despite punching solid rock, Trestan's hand didn't hurt that much; the potion quickly healed the bruise. Norzal stepped back to reexamine this uncommonly tough human. By all rights, no mortal man from Dhea Loral should be offering resistance after such punishment. Certainly, no human should be able to punch him like that. Trestan sprang to his feet, still holding his sword.

Both adversaries stared each other down for a moment. Time favored Norzal, so Trestan went on the offensive. Neither wanted to stretch themselves out as before. Paladin and coldast went at each other in a measured way. Both combatants tried to gauge the fighting ability of the other. As they clashed, Trestan still fought at a disadvantage. His muscles and bones had been toughened and regenerated quickly, but were still breakable. The demon's rock-hard body wouldn't heal, but lacked vulnerable spots. The best hits Trestan delivered only scratched the surface. Norzal's torso couldn't be penetrated too far. Trestan refocused on getting around the demon and destroying the second gatewarden.

The other taraz held their faith in their leader. Norzal had fought much worse opponents in his thousand years. They stayed back, enjoying the fight from afar. The conflict gave them an appetizer of what awaited beyond the portal.

Trestan and Norzal finally stopped testing each other as both launched a furious assault at the same time. They both got as close as they ever did. Trestan felt the chill of the ghostly mist wreathing the demon. Arms moved in a blur as both combatants went through several strike-and-parry combos.

One stone finger, separated from its host, flew into the gathered throng of demons. The body of Abriana's champion went flying the other direction.

Trestan's back broke as he bounced over a pile of rubble. He took in a sharp inhale of pain. The shock washed away a moment later as the injury repaired itself. He exhaled a roar as he got back to his feet.

They clashed again, dancing around between the open portal and the kneeling gatewarden. Claws and blade slashed complex patterns trying to evade defenses. Trestan got in one slash across Norzal's torso that cut loose the bag holding the Earthrin Stones. The

242

coldast felt another cut mar its immortal form. It retaliated with a stab of its claws into Trestan's chest.

The paladin dropped to a kneeling position. He worked to take in air as he felt blood running down his front. This time, the wound did not close so quickly.

Trestan blinked as he looked up at the demon. His vision lacked the purity it once held. The stench of this plane began to choke his lungs when he finally drew a breath. Trestan glanced at the bag lying at Norzal's feet. It had spilled open, leaving one of the green relics visible. He could no longer smell its power like before. The wound in his chest healed at a slower rate than his earlier wounds.

Norzal sensed his weakness. The demon leaned in; Trestan spun his sword in response. The coldast suffered another scrape in order to grab Trestan's swordarm. It held the paladin tightly in his grip. The tip of the sword rest at the edge of the mark he had just caused. Norzal brought his other claw around to grab Trestan's right hand. It yanked the sword from his possession as the strength of Mothrok's granted form allowed him to crush the bones in that hand.

The young paladin gasped in pain, falling prostrate before the towering demon. He appeared to be bowing in worship before it. The other denizens of Ibleu Taraz gave a roaring laugh at the sight. Norzal casually tossed the blade aside. Trestan cradled his damaged hand in the shadow of the coldast.

A moment went by that felt like an eternity as Trestan felt the bones in his hand meld back together. They became whole, although a dull ache lingered. The wound may have healed, but it did so with a lethargic energy compared to the rush of feelings earlier. The paladin felt the presence of Dalios slipping away, reducing the potion's effects. His muscles and will became weary from all the fighting that day.

Norzal, finally tiring of the young man at his feet, reached down and pulled Trestan to a kneeling position. The demon suspected his magical strength had gone. Trestan was no more of a threat than the legions of other mortals the coldast had killed over the years.

For Trestan's part, he felt shamed that he could not have done any better. The melee had now put Trestan between Norzal and the gatewarden. The coldast stood between Trestan and the gateway home. The positioning was as Trestan had wanted: a clear shot at the remaining gatewarden. Of course, with the coldast blocking the way back home, Trestan would find no escape even if he disrupted the portal. The paladin couldn't capitalize on the opportunity. His sword lie discarded to one side. The only option running through his head was to try banishing the gatewarden. All he needed was enough time to disrupt its concentration, and then the portal would close. He doubted he would have that luxury. Norzal towered directly over him. Without the Blood of Dalios, the demon possessed more speed and strength than Trestan could hope to match.

Norzal leaned closer to the tired human. Abriana's champion almost flinched away, knowing the end was about to come. Trestan heard the rumbling voice speaking directly into his ear. "How does it feel to face your death?"

Trestan blinked. He looked up at the demon, but Norzal said no more. The demon stood with is claws poised to strike. Trestan knew he wouldn't grace the demon with an answer. Did it ask the same question of Montanya before it killed her? How would she have answered?

Despite his reluctance to voice an answer, he could not stop from envisioning one. He worried for Cat, dying on the other side of the portal. *She was right. At least now we'll die together.* He had given his life in vain, much as Cat believed her father had done years ago. Trestan couldn't help but glance at the dried ears on Norzal's harness. He saw the glint of a gold unicorn on one of the twisted trophies. Horrified, he pulled his gaze away. Trestan stared into the green sparkle of an Earthrin Stone that had rolled out of the fallen bag.

Why had it all come to disaster? What could they have done differently? He could only imagine Petrow's worry about demons in the fields where his children played.

Suddenly, staring into the depths of that old relic, Trestan knew how the coldast could be defeated. He wondered why he hadn't realized it before. Unfortunately, in order to implement his plan, Trestan needed to reach one of the stones. The closest one lay slightly behind Norzal's foot talons. The paladin felt his slight bit of hope fade to despair. Maybe someone else would figure it out after he was gone, for he couldn't reach the stone without dying in the process. By the time someone else figured it out, the demons would already be pouring through in great numbers.

Norzal hadn't missed the glance Trestan offered towards his collection of ears. The demon brought one clawed finger up and touched one. "You have earned a place in my collection, answer or nay. Feel honored!"

Trestan resigned himself to look death in the eye. He voiced the words his predecessor once said. "Thank you, Abriana, for the wonderful life you have given me."

Trestan raised his head. The young man glared at the glowing eyes of the demon. Assuming that was the only answer he would get, Norzal's claws retracted slightly in preparation for the final strike. A great clamor rose among the assembled taraz. Trestan assumed that they were cheering his downfall.

Another possibility became apparent. In the moment he stared death in the face, a movement caught the edge of his vision. An object raised into view behind the coldast's rocky form.

It was nothing other than a simple woodcutter's axe. Useful enough for any farmer. The old axe had a blackened mark on the handle where it had once been scarred in battle. As Trestan spotted it, the axe descended for a strike.

Petrow chopped into the back of Norzal's skull-like head.

The young farmer from Troutbrook registered shock as the axe-head bounced off without leaving a mark on the demon's form. He barely hopped backward before the demon turned on him. A gale blew by Petrow as the coldast's claws shredded past.

Trestan took the opportunity to make his move. Petrow couldn't match the creature. For that one moment, Trestan had the distraction he needed to make his last gambling effort against the demon. The paladin of Abriana dove for the bag of stones. He grabbed one in his hand and rose to one knee. By this time, Norzal's slash dropped Petrow to the surface of the ziggurat. Strips of shredded armor scattered. The coldast glanced back to check on its former adversary. Its glowing blue spheres flared in anger as it saw the human kneeling with the relic held aloft.

Trestan let loose the banishing miracle of Abriana. The holy words pounded against the demon as they did before, straining its ghostly essence. The mist that formed the remainder of its soul stayed anchored to the artificial rock body bestowed by Mothrok. As before, Norzal was too strong to be restrained for long by this miracle. The demon roared as it took a step against the pain.

While maintaining concentration on the miracle, Trestan opened his mind to the Earthrin Stone in his hand. Cat had deciphered the means by which the relics were controlled from the leather scroll. The green light of the relic ignited, burning against the demon. Norzal felt assaulted to his very core. The banishment miracle tore at his spiritual form. His elemental shell erupted from within by the power of the Earthrin Stone. Neither side of his essence could keep a solid hold on this world. Norzal called to Mothrok, beseeching his matron for the strength to hold his body together. Mothrok could do nothing. Her energy was easily accessed by the stones, which held power over her dominion of the element of Earth. Unless she moved to breach the Covenant, which no single god could do, she could not directly interfere in this mortal affair.

The coldast screamed in terror…the first true fear it had felt in over a thousand years. A moment later, the sound cut off as its millions of molecules burst outward. The rock body became nothing more than a spray of dust, pulled apart in the noxious winds of Ibleu Taraz. For a brief second, the ghostly essence hovered in the air, vainly seeking a body. Abriana's banishing miracle dispersed it a moment later. The cloudy tendrils dissolved to nothing.

Trestan ended the miracle, lowering the relic. His eyes frantically sought the welfare of his longtime friend. Petrow lie on his back, though propped up on his elbows. Three scratches had torn through Petrow's steel breastplate, leaving shallow cuts in the enchanted leather underneath. Norzal's claws had stopped just short of leaving a more permanent mark on his skin.

Petrow's eyes reflected his fear, but he kept his voice steady as he examined the rip-marks across his armor. "Whoa, that was close!"

Trestan felt relieved beyond measure at his friend's timing and apparent good health. The paladin thought that he was probably smiling like a village idiot, in the worst setting he would ever expect to find a smile. As the uproar of demons drowned out all noises except his exhausted gasps of air, Trestan quickly bundled the Earthrin Stones in their bag. As he did, he once again noted the leather strap of ears lying in Norzal's dust. Acting on impulse, unsure why he bothered to do it, he reached over and snatched the dried ear adorned with the golden unicorn earring. It was the last remains of Cat's father; Trestan wanted to bring it back from this hell. The paladin tried not to be repulsed by what he was handling. He shoved it into the bag with the relics. Petrow got back to his feet, axe at the ready. His blue eyes were about to launch from their sockets as he saw the army arrayed on that hostile world. While Petrow began realizing how dangerous his trip through the portal truly was, his friend worked to expedite their return.

An awed Petrow began to mumble something as Trestan shoved the bag of relics into his hand, interrupting him. "Get these out of here!"

His childhood friend looked into his brown eyes. Trestan began pushing him backward. "There's nay time, just run back. I'll follow! I'll have the gate closed in seconds." Trestan didn't have to add that if they spent more time than that, the approaching demons would be upon them.

"Gods be with you!" Petrow stumbled back, axe in one hand, bag in the other. "Get it done and flee this hell!"

"As fast as I can!" Trestan reassured him.

Trestan spared no looks backward as he went to grab his fallen sword. Winged demons were diving from the skies. Other taraz with anywhere from two to six legs were charging up the sides of the ziggurat.

Petrow felt a disorienting feeling of weightlessness, a moment of floating in something like water, before his foot touched the floor of Tuampor. He stepped out backwards, watching the demonic world be replaced with the mesmerizing waterfall effect of the portal.

A voice barked out from behind him, "Petrow! What are you…nevermind, stand clear!"

He looked around as Korrelothar stormed into the chamber. A small swarm of mages followed the elf. The wizard waved him to stand off to the side. "We have to attempt to close the portal, no matter the cost."

The look in the elf's eyes suggested he doubted the present members of his guild could easily accomplish such a feat. Petrow scooted to one side as fast as his legs could carry him, but he held up a restraining hand.

"Trestan is on the other side! He's going to close it from there!"

As Korrelothar stopped, surprised at this news, Petrow turned to meet two pairs of eyes. Hebden Karok sat on one cot while a minor cleric tried to heal his wounds. Cat's emerald orbs perked open at the sound of Petrow reemerging from the gateway. Both worried for Trestan, but Cat seemed more in need for some affirmation that he was alright. She viewed Petrow even though her perspective was lying on her side, on what could be her deathbed. He caught her attention, hoping she could hang on to awareness long enough for Trestan to get through.

"He'll be right back!"

Trestan swept up his sword at a run. The remaining gatewarden uttered foreign syllables as it called for its allies to come to the rescue. It held the glass-like orb towards the portal, unable to move from the spot without spoiling its concentration. A dozen paces separated it from the watery surface that would bring Trestan back home. The paladin had to strike a blow that would leave the demon with perhaps a couple seconds of life; whereupon he could then run out just before the portal collapsed. The Sword of the Spirit came level with its throat.

All the howling demons rolling across that fetid plane thundered forward, colliding with each other as they ascended the ziggurat. They had left too much confidence in Norzal, too much distance to intercede. Trestan slashed across for the kill. At the last moment, the gatewarden lifted the orb up to deflect the blow.

The blade managed to deliver a mortal wound…after shattering the glass orb.

Trestan spun in place, bringing his gaze back to the portal. He took one fast step, then another, as he heard a difference in the humming noise emitted by the field. The paladin threw his body forward as fast as he could. Home awaited only a few steps away.

The air shuddered as a vibration rolled from the rift. The form of the watery portal blurred and disappeared. In a heartbeat, it vanished.

Trestan, gasping, teetered to a stop before falling off the far side of the ziggurat. There was no longer any portal to hide the hundreds of demons swarming in from that

246

direction. A pair of flying demons pulled up short over his head, cursing the human that destroyed their route to conquest.

No gateway home. No means to get back to Cat's arms. No hope for any future other than a painful one offered by the taraz. Trestan lamented his loss even as the demons began to cry out over the anger of losing their bid for Dhea Loral.

The defenders in Tuampor could not turn their eyes from the arch. Even as mages moved to assist some of the stricken clerics, they kept the portal in sight. A few tired warriors, who couldn't be moved, held makeshift weapons close as they stared at the gateway. Sondra bandaged Cat's reopened wounds, her movements slow and weary, occasionally sneaking peeks towards the passage between worlds. The young healer lacked the strength for channeling. Any attempt to try a healing miracle would cause her to pass out. The dying half-elf barely kept her eyes focused. Petrow dropped his weight on an empty cot, clutching the bag with the Earthrin Stones close to his chest. Hebden, clutching his own barely-tended wound, reclined next to him.

The humming noise coming from the arch changed. Everyone looked up, fearing the nightmare that might set upon them. Many expected no more or less than their life's end. The watery portal vibrated and blurred in their sight, then flashed out of existence. The gateway had been severed.

There was a moment of absolute silence. People had been caught holding their breath. Men who recalled the warning of demons pouring through the gate felt immense relief that a miracle had delivered them. Petrow, Sondra and Korrelothar stared in shock, knowing the cost at which their deliverance was paid. Hebden's mouth moved, no audible sound, as he failed at mumbling a plea to the gods. And if any others in the room had forgotten the young man who entered the portal alone, they were reminded a moment later.

The one sound that ended the silence, to the point where it pierced the stillness of the adjoining halls, was the scream of inconsolable loss as Katressa Bilil's heart broke.

CHAPTER 31 "The Harvest of the Death Angels"

A rallying call blared outside the fortress walls. The tribe that recognized their retreat signal began to flood out of the holes in the defenses. A different call came to another tribe, and they too responded to their summons. Warriors tasting victory with every conquered courtyard were surprised to be asked to pull back. The number of nomads turning to the rear outnumbered the amount trying to press forward. Stonelands' defenders held their last ring of walls as the enemy seemed to collapse back unto itself. The demon infestation had all been driven out and killed. The freed tribal leaders wanted nothing more than to recollect their survivors and return to the open plains.

Some fortress defenders tried to capitalize on the apparent weakness by rushing the retreating warriors. A few needless deaths occurred before their commanders reined them back. The nobility of the castle realized that the spirit driving the tribes' attack had somehow been broken. Along the lines, fighting men from both sides drew back to their respective leadership. Fortress defenders scrambled to reform their companies and hold their positions. Tribal clans pulled back to the encampment across the dried river.

Kor and Pejena endured the hard moment. Their freedom, and the freedom of their fellow nomads, did not resemble a victory. The two watched the retreat of the plains people with tears brimming in their eyes. As they anxiously called back the Spear Riders, many faces were missing. The only relief was when word had reached their ears that the demon army had failed to launch an attack through the fortress temple.

Across the grounds of this castle on the edge of the frontier, everyone turned to the task of treating their wounded and burying their dead. The battle of Fortress Stone was over.

*   *   *   *   *

Her love was gone, just as her father left her years ago. Cat couldn't bring herself to resist the weakness of her body. She had given much of her life force to Trestan, and he failed to return. Despite the friendly faces surrounding her, Cat felt empty and alone. Her spirit lost the will to fight for breath. Voices grew distant, as did warmth and pain. Katressa could no longer feel breath passing through her. She descended from the world, floating in darkness. Memories faded until she couldn't really remember her name.

After a timeless moment, stars filled her vision. They moved of their own will, thinly veiled by insubstantial bodies which failed to fully cloak them. It was as if the stars had ghostly shells which covered and thus diminished their glow. Cat's essence seemed to be a shining star, shrouded in a similar shell of mist.

She perceived a presence hovering next to her, more substantial than the ethereal figures floating in the starfield. This new presence allowed her to see those other bright lights. Her awareness and memory came back. Katressa remembered dying. The ghost-like image surrounding her star was actually her old body. It became ethereal as she released her grip on life.

With understanding that she was passing into the next world, Cat's essence focused on the luminous being hovering nearby. It had once been a star, like her, but its form had been made into something more complex. A pale skin stretched between all its limbs, flapping like wings. The form was certainly pleasing to the eyes. It had beauty beyond death.

Katressa 'heard' a voice that went unspoken.

"Most souls never recall their passage into the next world. The Karet-Atriul tend to let the soul sleep soundly for the journey through the stars."

It came from the strange form floating alongside her consciousness. Now she identified it as a *Karet-Atriul*, otherwise known as a Death Angel. They were servants of DeLaris who ferried souls of the dead either to a place they would find rest, or be tormented for eternity. Cat heard the voice draw her closer, even as she shed the ethereal cloak of her mortal body.

"It is my honor to bear you to the next world, though I shall not let you sleep peacefully for our journey. You shall remember our long trip across the near-darkness of the nether realm. During our time together, we can discuss your failures."

The Death Angel opened its wings wide, allowing Cat to see its face. Although death had changed the body, there was no mistaking the identity of her otherworldly chaperone. A hint of blue radiated from the eyes, as Savannah offered a wicked smile.

*   *   *   *   *

Trestan stood with his head bowed low, in the place where hope fled. His escape was gone, leaving him alone amidst a diminishing circle of hatred. He could not understand the words of the demons; however, the tones of their voices and growls conveyed their anger. They had been denied the chance to conquer Dhea Loral, after years of working through agents from that world. Trestan had sabotaged their plans and now they surrounded the frail human.

A moment ago, they were all trying to rush him. With the disappearance of the gate, they patiently marched forward. The flying ones would swoop past, offering only spine-tingling shrieks and pulling away. The flyers seemed to be testing him. The others who crawled and slithered up the side of the ziggurat played a game of dominance with their fellows. Their circumference shrunk tighter, forcing some demons to threaten others to back off. Every one of them wanted a piece of the lone human. Even the ones made of stone, other minions of Mothrok, moved forward. They knew the paladin had given away the Earthrin Stones. Without those powerful relics, the formidable sword had limits to how much it could damage creatures of stone. These were intelligent beings, despite their penchant for warfare. The biggest and toughest creatures spawned from the imaginations of both Mothrok and DeLaris made their way to the forefront of their fellows.

Trestan determined to put away his fear. He had no misgivings about how quickly he could die if he resisted. A bigger worry would be how slowly he would die if he didn't put up a fight. Abriana's champion looked for weaknesses to exploit. He might have only two swings before they could bring him down.

As his dark eyes glanced over the terrain, he spotted another item of importance. The Gitouro necklace lay among Norzal's accouterments. With the demons playing their game to demonstrate who was top of the pecking order, Trestan kneeled down and snatched the necklace. He pulled it over his head.

He didn't know how many times he could use it, or even necessarily how he could activate its powers. Such an artifact in the hands of these taraz would be unthinkable. Trestan resolved to drain the necklace of all its magic before they ripped it away.

The taraz stepped within a couple paces from him. The closest few towered over him as Norzal had. They hungered for him, yet they clawed and hissed at each other to determine who would feast first. A flying demon dove down to try stealing the morsel for itself. Trestan flattened against the stone. Another of the towering demons caught the flying one and killed it. Much raucous laughter came from the mouths of others amused by the spectacle. The limp body crashed beside the paladin.

Trestan moved to stand when a strong claw came down on one leg. It trapped him. His sword raised against the monster, only to fail. A claw from one opposite came down on his swordarm. Trestan was pinned as the opposing demons locked stares. Each one wanted to dominate the other; neither wanted to release the hold they had on the helpless human.

"This is it," Trestan mourned in a whisper.

He envisioned his love one final time: long, raven hair, sparkling emerald eyes, slightly pointed ears, perfect legs dancing, soft back under his massaging hands, wonderful kisses.

"I wish I could be home and see you again."

*   *   *   *   *

Sondra felt the remainder of her wits being shaken from her. The voice continued to yell in her ears. Surely Petrow didn't realize how weakened she was or he wouldn't be reacting like this.

She tried to make sense to him. "I tried! I have nay strength to do more. She absorbed my last miracle and there was nay response."

Petrow stuttered as he relaxed his grip on her. "But that doesn't mean…"

"Cat is dead!" Sondra hated to state the obvious, but he couldn't face the truth. Her trembling hand moved to find a blanket with which to cover their friend's sightless eyes. "I'm so sorry! Her will has gone from her body."

Petrow refused to see it. He knelt near the cot with tears forming in his eyes. Korrelothar came from behind and took the farmer's hand from Sondra's shoulder. The elf wizard understood Petrow's pain, but couldn't allow him to injure the weakened cleric. Hebden Karok had even shuffled from his spot of rest to try holding Petrow back. With Petrow's hand removed, Korrelothar looked down upon the black-clad woman. The founding member of the Brotherhood of the Circles recalled the memories tied around Cat and Trestan. They seemed to appoint themselves as guardians of the Earthrin Stones. Both had paid the ultimate sacrifice to see them safe.

The elf broke from his reflections as a familiar voice spoke.

"Dead? Abriana, nay, she can't be gone!"

Sondra, Petrow, and Korrelothar looked up in surprise to see Trestan standing inside the room, right next to them! The three of them jumped back as the dead walked among them.

"Tres!? How?"

"We saw…I mean…"

"We thought you were gone! You weren't there a moment ago."

"My son," Hebden went over to be by his only child. Trestan was relieved to see his father alive, despite the bandage. Father and son shared a brief hug, though Trestan's heart tugged a different direction. The younger man led his father back over to an empty cot so the smith could rest.

Hebden's strong muscles were shaking with relief that his son was alive. "How did you make it back?"

The young paladin wore his scarred armor, sweaty from his exertions during the day. His attention focused on the body of the woman he loved; his eyes had never really left her. A hand rose up, past the coraross symbol on his chest, to touch a jeweled necklace. "It was this. It brought me here."

Korrelothar noted the presence of the Gitouro necklace around Trestan's neck. The elf didn't realize it could cross worlds. Apparently, the god Kelor had more influence across planes than he realized.

Trestan stumbled forward. "She can't be gone!"

The magical elvish blade clanged against the floor as the paladin reached both hands to his lover. He turned Katressa to him, looking into the lifeless green eyes from his dreams. He willed his healing power into her. He called out loud to Abriana, bending all his will into healing her body. Nothing happened. He tried until he swayed with the effort. Korrelothar and Sondra moved to restrain him at the same time.

"You'll kill yourself for naught!" Sondra cried.

"Trestan, you can't heal the dead," the wizard implored.

Trestan collapsed to the floor in a fit of weeping. Petrow shifted closer to his friend. He set down the bag next to the cot, placing a hand on Trestan's back for comfort. As Trestan noticed the bag, his head snapped up.

He exclaimed, "The relics! Remember what Cat told us, Sondra."

The blonde woman remembered the words as Trestan reached for the bag. Ganden's priestess recalled them as translated by Cat. "She said, 'From DeLaris, Goddess of Death and the Dead, the relics stood on the precipice between life and death…they could also be used to restore life to someone who had just died.'"

Cat had instructed Trestan and Sondra on the use of the relics. Even though the half-elf had not understood all the concepts she translated, it provided the two of them with the knowledge in how to summon those powers. Trestan withdrew one of the green stones from the bag. He moved close to Cat's cot. He placed the stone inside the crook of her arm, placing his own hands on opposite sides of it. His head bowed in prayer, even as his mind unlocked the hidden abilities of the relic.

"Hear me, Cat. Let your soul follow this beacon back to your friends. Follow my words back to those you love, who love you in return…"

*   *   *   *   *

The *Karet-Atriul* enfolded Cat into her arms, as Cat's star asked, "Where is my destination?"

Savannah looked down upon the soul with a cold glare. *"Boyal metes out Justice as he weighs it, and decides your course. I don't have to tell you where. My responsibility is simply to see that you get there."* The Death Angel started to flex her wings. They were nothing like the traditional paintings of angels. The wings seemed like flimsy lace catching an invisible breeze. *"It can be a long, cold trip in the dark. It will seem like an eternity for you, though little time will pass for the living. I will be back in time to ferry more souls as the demons destroy your loved ones."*

Cat no longer had a physical body. The ghostly remnants of its outline fell away. The 'star' that was her consciousness wilted at the news. It would be a long journey indeed.

A voice floated to her. "Hear me, Cat."

She strained to listen. More words drifted in the dark, "Let your soul follow this beacon."

Katressa Bilil resisted the flight for a moment, mentally stopping herself as she tried to recognize the voice. It couldn't be Trestan. Or, could it? Wasn't Trestan most likely dead or dying?

Savannah felt the tug at Cat's core. The Death Angel inwardly frowned. She gave a vigorous tug at Cat's soul. *"There is only emptiness back there. You are dead! Accept fate! Everyone you love dies today!"*

The former half-elf didn't give in so easily. She looked back, through the nothingness interrupted by small stars, towards where she had shed her body. She could not see its outline, but she did make out a few cloudy wisps glowing where she had been. The Death Angel tugged at her soul, yet her will…all she had left…resisted.

Words floated in the darkness. "Come back to us. You are loved here. You are needed by my side."

Katressa recognized the stars hovering together, not far away. She saw the souls of her friends. Petrow. Sondra. Hebden. Trestan! She thought she had lost him to the land of the dead. Instead, Trestan was alive somehow, and she was separated by death. As his words came into the darkness, a beacon lit from the ghostly form that had been her physical body. The beacon pulled at her soul, drawing her back.

"You are dead!" Savannah cried out. *"DeLaris has taken your soul to be delivered to your next existence."*

Savannah possessed DeLaris' power to deliver souls across the spiritual realm, but DeLaris was also passively empowering the relic that offered Cat her life back. In the end, it became Cat's decision. She mentally pushed Savannah away. Her star brightened as it drifted down the lights of the beacon. Her body floated there, ready to be reunited.

Cat voiced a message back to Savannah. "If many lifetimes pass in this darkness compared to the mortal world, then it will be a very long time before I see you again. I await our next journey through this dimension. If you keep me awake through it, I will spend the whole time reminding you of your failures."

Savannah's form melted into the shadows, becoming indistinct as Cat's essence returned to the core of her body.

*   *   *   *   *

A breath of the sweetest, freshest air swelled Cat's lungs. Trestan added to the tears shed. Immediately, he called upon Abriana's miracles to heal the wounds of her body. Her green eyes lit with their inner fire once more. She looked upon his face, taking many moments staring at it. The first sensation she experienced upon returning to her body was the warmth of his healing miracle pouring into her. In that moment, nothing Cat had ever seen came close to the beauty felt in Trestan's presence. The half-elf worried that she was becoming delusional, between seeing Savannah and then finding herself in Trestan's arms in this world. She had to prove to herself that he was real.

The others still looked in awe as Cat weakly reached up and drew him into her embrace. They buried their bodies together so that it was hard to tell where one ended and the other began. The others said nothing, mostly turning away as the two lovers enjoyed their moment.

A figure burst through one of the doors of the chamber, crashing it to the floor. All eyes darted over to the new arrival. Salgor Bandago breathed heavily, hefting his axe and ready to cleave the next thing that looked at him crossly. The dwarf had obviously had a recent tangle with another druid, as evidenced by a broken elk antler stuck in one shoulder piece. He seemed utterly unconcerned about it as his rage-filled eyes looked over the room.

"Where is that overgrown chunk o' rock? The blockhead that isn't even fit for skipping 'cross a river? Not that I wouldn't try!"

Trestan grinned. Salgor was not an opponent to be taken lightly. Nothing seemed capable of slowing the dwarf for long. "He's dead. I'd have saved a piece of him for you, but there wasn't anything left but dust."

Salgor stared over at the young man. The paladin got the feeling that the dwarf rankled at the possibility that Trestan killed something which had thrown the dwarf out a window. Salgor huffed through his facial hair.

He shouted for his other adversary. "What about that tongue-waggling, idiot elf wizard?" As his gaze passed over Korrelothar, he decided to clarify, "The one that doesn't mess with flying contraptions?"

Cat raised her arm to get his attention. "I took care of him. If you still want a piece of him, he's pinned to a door down the hall."

This was the first time Trestan and the others learned of Revwar's demise. He looked down at her in admiration. Cat whispered, "Who did you think was the only skilled adversary that could plant me in this cot?"

"A lot of people will sleep safer now that justice has caught up with him." Trestan stated. The paladin had to admit that his dreams would be a lot better without that evil presence in the world.

The couple noticed that Salgor did not share the joyous expression. The dwarf continued to wear the look of wrath upon his brow. He sternly pointed at the two of them. "I thought my friends would understand. Those two were MINE!"

Their smiles fell at his words. They realized he was simply using his dwarven mirth a moment later when, still wearing a grim face, he said: "Although you deprived me o' the chance, I suppose I should still pay your efforts with a few free tankards when the bar reopens."

Korrelothar wasted no time on any levity. The wizard turned to his guildmates and ushered them back out to face the tribes. He was giving them suggestions for their strategy when Trestan came up to him. The paladin had the Gitouro necklace in hand.

"You may need this," he offered, dropping the relic in Korrelothar's surprised grasp. "It was used a couple of times. I don't know how much divinity still resides in it."

The elf wizard was still turning it over in his hands, watching the light play across the gems, when Salgor's voice invaded from the other side of the chamber.

The dwarf motioned with his axe. "There's not much left to fight out there. The other savages grew chicken and retreated back across the riverbed."

Heads all over the room turned at this news. Eyes lit up with hope.

"Their leaders were calling retreats, only a few stubborn ones are still raising a fuss." At those words, the dwarf seemed to notice the elk antler stuck in his armor. He yanked it off and flicked it over his shoulder. "A crying shame! Just when this place was starting to get interesting, everyone lost the belly for fighting."

Cat and Trestan glanced at each other. She whispered, "Kor and Pejena must have done their work."

Moments later, acolytes and fresh wounded entered the chamber, reaffirming the news of the tribal forces scattering back across the riverbed. Rumors of victory swept through the fortress.

Trestan knelt by Cat's side. She thought he was coming over to offer her another hug, but instead he pulled the relic from her arms. She looked into his eyes. Abriana's champion held the green Earthrin Stone, idly turning it over in his hands once, twice, before looking at her. "Since the battle is over, there are more to save."

Trestan raised the stone and began to open his mind to it. Sondra quickly came to an understanding, and she reached for another of the stones to assist him. Trestan and Sondra called upon DeLaris' dominion within the stones. It felt suitable that a goddess that was half guilty for the destruction of the day be forced to make amends. Green light from the stones turned to mist, seeping through the cracks and expanding into the courtyards outside. Trestan and Sondra both called to those who had recently died, asking them to give life another chance. They imparted no distinction between the two sides. Defender or attacker, soldier or shaman, human or raulgan…all the recently departed were called to embrace life once again. The *Karet-Atriul* began losing their grip on the souls currently being ferried. Men of the Stonelands rose once again from the edge of death's domain, alongside tribal warriors who also heard the call. Warriors thought dead a moment ago cried out for healers to mend their partially-healed wounds. Both Trestan and Sondra worshipped gods that saw no division between the two sides. The men and women who had fought the battle, regardless of which faction, were lives worth saving. Many were brought back from the arms of the Death Angels without ever knowing whom they had to thank for their deliverance.

The relics could not restore most of those who had died. It only worked on souls who had not fled far from the mortal remains. This meant that a certain wizard pinned by a rapier, as well as a young woman with long, red hair, were too far gone to be saved.

CHAPTER 32 "Apologies and Negotetin"

Korrelothar's mages, joined by other clergy, worked to restore the priests affected by their reflected spells. Cat and Hebden were left to rest under the care of the recovered healers. Salgor, Petrow and Trestan went back outside to see if they were needed. When Trestan stepped forth from the tower Tuampor, his eyes drank in the bittersweet tidings of the battle's aftermath. No more war cries thundered. The lightning flashes and fiery bursts had ceased. The majority of sounds reaching his ears were the cries from the wounded, or the calls to heal them. A few motes of fire spawned smoke in the ashes of the catapults. Other buildings fed flames, but they would be handled soon enough now that the mages were freed from slaughter.

In the distance, outside the walls, the tribes mingled in disarray. They seemed more like a mob than an army now. Warriors and natura-users began to break camp. Soon enough they would return to their nomadic lifestyle on the Tribal Expanse, minus an untold number of sacrifices for a cause that was never theirs.

Trestan observed the men and women of the keep. Soon enough, he would be among them, lending his weary healing hands to those in need. Abriana's follower wasn't sure that he had enough energy to do anything more than wrap bandages. Trestan felt the need to spend a minute simply observing the aftermath. He lingered on that high perch, pacing while he surveyed everything. Petrow and Salgor seemed to feel the same way. They tarried by his side, each silently holding their own counsel on what they saw.

The paladin lifted his eyes to the sky, even as he closed them. He was content to feel the warmth spread on his face and hands.

"What're you about?" Salgor asked, tugging his beard at the human's strangeness.

With eyes still closed, Trestan said, "I'm just enjoying the feel of it. More than anything, it signifies that everything came out right as could be. There will be a hopeful tomorrow."

Petrow and Salgor shared a confused look. "Tres, feel what?"

Trestan cracked an eye open so he could see Petrow. "The sun. Yestreal is finally shining over the fortress once again. The dark clouds are gone."

With Norzal's departure with the relics into the gate, the storm clouds could no longer hold sway over the people of the Stonelands. The sun lit the shadows between walls and warmed the chill of battle from tired bones. If anything, it was a symbol that the darkness tainting the demons' world would not be saturating Dhea Loral anytime soon.

Petrow enjoyed the symbolism. He stared off at the last remainders of clouds, blowing away on the winds. "Look there," he pointed off to the east. "A rainbow."

The three companions looked at it for a moment. Salgor looked at it longingly, but his gruff nature soon resurfaced. His bluster buried the soft feelings that were upon his face only a wink earlier. "Well, I'm not about to go looking to see if there are unicorns over there. There is always work yet to be done."

With that, the companions descended among the survivors.

   *   *   *   *   *

As the stillness pervaded the fortress, soldiers began to come out from behind their barricades. Lindon Taleweaver climbed the steps of one tower as he sought a better vantage point. He came out at the highest point of the stairs, stepping upon a crenellated turret. He took off his hat to wipe some of the sweat from his brow. The minstrel succeeded only in redistributing the grime on his hands with the same on his face.

His light-blue eyes absorbed every minute detail in the landscape. All the images, all the people, all the damage, implanted into his memory. In his mind, he paired the results with the motivations of the few who brought both sides into the conflict. He felt the weight of the sacrificed dead, the betrayal that misled the tribesmen, the fears of the surviving peasants and the weariness of those who gathered from far and near to defend their way of life.

Lindon felt the tones of the story in his mind. He sheathed his sword and brought the mandolin up to the ready. His fingers hovered over the strings, preparing to be immersed in the music of the moment. He tried to construct a song worthy of the tale.

His hands faltered; his dry voice cracked. The Taleweaver sobbed as the emotions proved too much for him.

   *   *   *   *   *

Evening descended over the fortress flying the Stonelands' pennant. The waving banner overlooked the field where so many had died. A few tents had been hastily thrown up near the old banks of the Hossan Minor. Trestan and Katressa walked from the castle down to the tents. The half-elf, still fragile from her injuries, refused to miss the meeting occurring this night. As one of the field commanders of the battle, representing Kashmer's privateers, she had an invitation.

Trestan informed her, "When the bodies are all collected, we'll use the stones to reconstruct the path of the river. The Hossan Minor will fill this riverbed again."

Cat glanced over at Trestan. His face was almost directly over hers, since he assisted her walk to the riverbed. "What about after?"

The paladin would have shrugged if not for the weight of the woman hanging onto his arm. "Only rumors. We will likely be carrying back the Troutbrook stone and the elf stone to their respective owners. It will be sometime after the winter, however. That's fine by me. It will give time to use the stones to make sure this land will have a fertile harvest next year to atone for this season's famine."

The half-elf spent a moment in quiet contemplation. She voiced her worries a moment later. "Troutbrook doesn't need to be ransacked a third time if someone shows an interest in the relic again."

He nodded. "Nor would I want such a thing to happen. I talked to a priest of Yestreal earlier. He seemed to be someone of importance in their church hierarchy. He promised that when the church is rebuilt in Troutbrook, they will account for the stone's importance. I have the feeling a lot larger structure will be built there. Given the importance of the stones, Yestreal's subjects will take it very seriously from now on."

Cat asked Trestan to halt at a ruined section of breastworks. They were near the tents where the nobility of the Stonelands held audience with several tribal elders that had requested parley. The attending tribes were trying to make atonement for their actions and mend their relations with the Stonelands.

Trestan looked upon Cat with worry. She was taking deep breaths and wincing at the pain. He snuck his hand behind her back and whispered a few healing words. Cat felt some of his healing miracle trickling into her.

"Stop it!" She slapped his hand away. "You aren't much better off than I am. Sometimes it feels like you're leaning on me!"

Trestan did sway a bit, mentally exhausted and depleting his reserves further by attempting to heal her. "It's been a long day."

Cat offered a grim smile, turning her head back towards the tents. "Aye."

She seemed to catch her breath, though she turned to him again. "When you were out healing folks today, did you find our friends?"

Cat had been afraid to ask earlier, and Trestan had not volunteered the information given her weakened state. Trestan started with the easy ones.

"Well, Leander survived with some minor injuries. In the morning, he and I are going to recover Rhijin's body from below the cliffs." Cat nodded, so he continued. "You know Petrow, my father, Salgor, Sondra and Korrelothar survived…oh, and Floranue was safe during the battle. Those two were kissing like they were newlyweds."

Trestan threw Cat a sideways glance to see her giggling. "I found Aijak tending to the wounded. I can't understand her language, but when I asked about Mel, she pointed me in the right direction. Seems Mel helped the wounded better by running errands for her, rather than 'keeping the wounded talking in order to distract them from their wounds,' as Mel tells me."

Emerald eyes glittered in the sinking sunlight. Cat giggled. "Mel is cuter than a baby rabbit, but I don't think his chats would necessarily help the wounded."

Trestan laughed, but his next message took on a somber tone. "I ran across Lindon. I'm worried for him." At Cat's questioning glance, he elaborated. "I caught him in a quiet spot, with ink and parchment, and his mandolin at his side. I asked him what he was doing. He only said, 'composing,' but he just stared at the parchment. It was blank except for a spot of ink directly under where he held the quill."

Half-elf ears can't hear things that don't make noise, yet Cat's hearing picked up on what Trestan wasn't saying when he continued by talking about the privateers. He mentioned the ones who had survived and were playing the leadership role while Cat recovered.

"Aren't you skipping over someone? Montanya?"

Trestan looked uncomfortable. Cat knew the answer before he even spoke just by his reaction. "She didn't make it. She and Salgor delayed Norzal from getting to the arch. Salgor was thrown out a window, which wasn't enough to slow him down for long. That left Montanya alone…you don't want to know."

Cat shuddered. Trestan put his arm around her again, comforting her. Her voice was soft, "Nay, I don't want to know. I've seen a demon attack and what they are capable of doing to their victims. I'd rather not be exposed to it ever again."

Silence passed as both turning their heads to the setting sun. Cat whispered, "She didn't get a chance to enjoy life."

Trestan searched for the right words. "It was too early for her to go; however, she did change a lot. Abriana allows me to sense some things in a person's heart. Montanya's was full of hate when we met her. By the time she landed here, she was a kinder, warmer person. Kelor should have dealt her a better hand in life, but she began to make her own fate at the end."

While they leaned against the breastworks, Trestan considered the bundle in his pocket. Cat had yet to learn of the return of her father's remains. He decided to save it for the morning. It would likely be too much for her to bear right before this meeting.

"I'm rested. Let us continue."

*　　　　*　　　　*　　　　*　　　　*

Trestan and Cat sat, more or less, as witnesses before the meeting between tribes and nobility. Kor and Pejena noticed them, offering them respectful nods. The two companions noted Pejena doing much of the talking on behalf of the tribes. She was very gifted with words, and the art of "negotetin". On the other hand, the nobles of the Stonelands acted quite haughty. They let the tribes feel inferior, having felt they were attacked without warning and won the battle. To Trestan, the posturing seemed a pointless waste. The tribes hadn't requested a meeting to demand any tribute. They were making their apologies and trying to repair relationships.

The talking halted when some treats were brought down to enjoy. Many of those at the table hadn't savored a good meal in two days. The nobles of the Stonelands shared the food with the tribesmen, yet in such a way as to accentuate their 'generosity' to a former enemy. They even flaunted the fact that the food survived the year's famine.

During this break, people mingled in various circles. Trestan and Cat took the opportunity to meet with Kor and Pejena. The companions gave a brief account of the opening and closing of the gate. Kor and Pejena were relieved that the taraz threat was gone. Their worries turned to the future of their tribe. For one thing, their efforts to reestablish friendly ties with the Stonelands seemed like they were being treated as beggars. The proud couple felt as if they were humiliating themselves. Another concern regarded the loss of their hunters and gatherers, and a lot of equipment. The chill winter winds would be upon them too soon. Their food stores would suffer.

Trestan and Cat went about seeing what they could do to remedy things. First, they cornered Korrelothar as he chatted with Sir Theros Lightshield of Abriana's church. Sir Theros had recovered from the injuries received on the first day of fighting. After some diplomacy on their part, Trestan and Cat followed the two influential men as they in turn cornered two others. The next two to be coerced into the plan were Sir Penvos "The Steady" of the church of Ganden, and Cardinal Methlen Foresight of Stonelands. From that point on, other Kashmer and Orlaun representatives began making 'suggestions' to Stonelands' nobility.

The Stonelands' nobility did not favor the plan, but pressure from the foreign dignitaries made them accept it in favor of their own relations. When the representatives next gathered around the tables, the Stonelands put forth a benevolent gesture and made it seem as if it was their idea. A substantial amount of food had been stored on the ships from Kashmer with the knowledge of the famine, the effects of the relics and the coming of winter. After taking stock of what was sent, there seemed to be extra to go around. The nobility made the goodwill offer of some of those stores to the tribes. The nomads felt their first taste of jubilation since their toils. Kor looked over to Trestan and Cat. Seeing the feigned looks of innocence on their faces, he offered them a warm smile.

Relationships between the different people would hopefully heal, although like most wounds it would take time. The Stonelands would remember that the Spear Riders was one of the few tribes to come forth, aid them, and make amends. The Spear Riders would be fed well enough to survive the winter better than some of their rivals.

*   *   *   *   *

Trestan and Leander stopped by the Com'der's tent the next morning. The fair-haired paladin stayed outside while his friend went in for a visit.

"You have become an honored friend in my tent!" Kor declared as Trestan took a seat among the furs. "You brought our freedom and, I would guess, helped ensure that our stomachs are full in the next few months."

Trestan would not comment on the latter, so Pejena spoke. "What brings you to our tent this morn, and without your lady?"

"Oh, she's resting. I came to you because…Abriana granted me a vision last night."

"Ahbri-ahna is your god?" Pejena looked over the symbols on his dented armor.

"Goddess," he corrected. "Aye, she is. Her domain is Love and Healing."

Although Trestan paused, the two nomads bade him to continue. "She gave me a vision concerning both of you." As Pejena and Kor shared a glance, he continued. "She knows that your love has suffered in the months that the demons controlled your bodies. Abriana felt the pain of your hearts being strained."

Kor's eyes went neutral, though his tone suggested anger under the surface. "Speaking about such things will not keep you as an honored friend within my tent."

Trestan took in a breath, but he knew he had to continue. Abriana wanted to help this couple. "Abriana blesses your love and she offers you healing. I assume, despite all that has happened, that both of you are unshaken in your commitment to your partner."

Kor seemed ready for a violent outburst, but Pejena waved him to be calm. "We discussed it. He is the same man I fell in love with years ago. Coming out of the nightmare of these past months, neither of us would keep our sanity without the other to lean on."

Trestan nodded, keeping an eye on Kor. He tried to calm the large man. "That is what Abriana needed to know, so that she might bestow a gift upon you. She wants your love to thrive."

Pejena didn't understand what Trestan wanted to offer. "Neither of us worships Ahbri-ahna."

Trestan touched his coraross. "You don't have to worship her to allow her to bless you with a gift. Your love for each other is reward enough for her."

Trestan moved to place a hand on Pejena's abdomen. Kor immediately reached for his large maul, but the mystic motioned for him not to overreact. The mixed set of eyes on the muscled man fixed on Trestan, awaiting any sign that he was harming Pejena. As Trestan whispered unknown syllables, Pejena felt a warm feeling low in her abdomen. Her eyes widened.

Trestan finished quickly and pulled back from her. Kor sneered at him, "Begone from our tent! Be thankful you are granted your life…"

"Wait!" Pejena implored. "I feel…different…but good. What did you do to me?"

Trestan spoke to her, glancing occasionally at the large man next to her. "Where once you were barren, now you have been healed. Your blood will flow again from your womb. After it does, you will be able to bear children once more."

The wind blew into the tent, rushing around Pejena. It tousled her brown and gray strands. Her tanned, freckled face began to smile. "So it is, for the wind tells me also."

She remembered that her husband still brandished his maul. "Put that away! It is true. He and Ahbri-ahna have given us a wonderful second chance!"

Kor felt shamed for reacting as he had. "I owe you an apology for my insult. You have proved yourself a friend again."

Trestan was too humble and uncomfortable to say much more. He took his leave so that he and Leander could seek out a friend's body among the dead. When he was gone, Kor and Pejena embraced.

Pejena admitted, "I still know fear in my heart, my husband."

Kor asked, "Why? Is it not exciting to be able to explore a dream that was once closed?"

Pejena nodded, "It is…and yet frightening to get my hopes up after how much I hurt when we lost our second child. To find out I could nay longer be the mother who bore your baby…it pained me greatly."

The giant of a man softly caressed her cheeks. "If we never had the ability to raise a child, my life would still be perfect just being with you. I think having a little one of our own will now make things pleasantly unpredictable."

She laughed, and they began to make love as if they could already conceive.

CHAPTER 33 "Goodbyes to Friends Lost"

Days of mourning came, when the bodies of thousands of dead were being recovered and set for burial. They differed in how the Stonelands' dead and the tribes' dead were given a final farewell. Most of the Stonelands' defenders were being put in coffins for an earth burial. A new cemetery was created north of the keep, well across the dried riverbed and yet still overlooking Pilgrim's Bay. A few select people had made known their desires, religious or cultural, to be burned in pyres. The tribesmen, including the remains of the Spear Riders, were often placed atop wooden scaffolds for the birds to carry away. The tribes erected their scaffolds a long walk upriver from the fortress. Even if it was not at the nobles' behests, the tribes wanted their dead honored in lands that felt at least partially theirs. The place where rows upon rows of these stands marked the final transition, (where the bird-spirits of DeLaris would carry away their dead), was eventually given a name and preserved as a holy site for the tribes. Stonelands' farmers wouldn't dare plant there anyway. It gained a name derived from one of the orc tribes: *Kag Arlo*, meaning "Great Sacrifice".

All three burial methods required a lot of wood. Many of the coffins came from nearby barns that had been abandoned by their previous owners. As a result, a lot of old, cheap, and painted boards made up the many coffins lined up to receive the dead. More of the colored boards were made into grave markers.

Even those who did not have someone to mourn, which were few, had the task of trying to repair and reopen their shops in Pilgrim's Bay. A lot of buildings had been looted or sullied during the tribes' visit. The Temple of Ale was emptied of drinks, (except for Salgor's well-hidden personal stash), making the dwarf feel like he should storm into the Tribal Expanse and get every stolen bottle back.

*   *   *   *   *

On the edge of the plateau, in a patch of woods, Cat sat staring across the glimmering waves. The cold did little to chill her any more than how her insides already felt. Not even Trestan was allowed to stay with her on this personal vigil. Cat's strength had returned, thanks to her lover's healing once he had rested. Although, in moments like this, she didn't feel strong. She allowed her emotions to run from laughing at memories to crying at realities during this time of imposed solitude. It was the way of the elves when a loved one had passed on.

Her fingers moved across the bundle in her hands. She had already glanced at the contents. The golden unicorn earring remained in her father's keeping. Katressa hugged the last remains of Reatheneus close, reminiscing about their time in life together.

The wind blew her raven strands, but in her mind, she recalled her father brushing her hair as a child. A slight shift of her position brought a small creak of the leather she wore, her thoughts reminding her of the creak of his leather when he came in the door at the end of the day. She remembered those moments when she knew he would be coming home. The little half-elf would find a hiding place, then pounce on him in surprise when he came close. Of course, he probably knew where she was most of the time, but he always pretended to be surprised.

"There you are!" He would laugh as he found his child wrapped around his leg. "I had a feeling my little hunting cat was around here somewhere."

Katressa sniffled at that thought. His little hunting cat. He had said it enough times that she had grown into the role after his death.

"What is that?" The child asked, seeing him inspecting a rune block in his hands.

Reatheneus quickly tucked the block from view. "It's a great honor. Something I have sworn to keep safe. I am its guardian."

Little Katressa jumped into his arms. She smiled playfully at him. "I thought you were a hunter."

His chuckles made her bounce in his arms. "A person can be a guardian as well as a hunter. In fact, one role can complement the other."

"How so?"

"Well, a guardian protects people and things that mean a lot. Sometimes the person wishing to do harm to them won't show his face so easily, or venture too closely. At times, you have to go out and hunt them down in order to protect what you are guarding."

The memory triggered another one, which occurred years later.

A matured Cat spoke to an adventurer in the port of Kashmer. "So, what is it these privateers do?"

The man answered. "Guard Kashmer's people and treasures…well, trade routes anyways. They get paid to go out and hunt bandits, bringing proof of their deeds to local magistrates."

The raven-haired half-elf considered it. "Guardians as well as hunters? That sounds interesting."

Cat's tears spilled down on the bundle in her arms. It was nothing for which she should feel shame. The elvish way of properly mourning one so dear to their heart included such private moments. Elves filled their mind with the thoughts of the person in question, and cried or laughed as needed until every possible memory had been explored.

Cat needed that time to finally say a meaningful goodbye to her father. With the thwarting of the demons, the death of both Revwar and Savannah, the recovery of her father's remains from that demon plane, it felt as if a long chapter of her life was now closed. Soon enough, a new one would open up beside the man she loved.

But first, she spent the time on a proper farewell to the demons that all people carry inside themselves.

*   *   *   *   *

Cathag's beleaguered pace matched the mood of the druid guiding him. Aijak and Mel had survived the battle with no injuries of concern. While they had cause to feel relief at the outcome, Aijak felt the wounds of the land in her heart. As the two gnomes rode around the fortress grounds, surveying the damage to the people and the land, Aijak felt filled with sympathy for the people who had to pick up the pieces of their lives here. Even Mel's positive attitudes were submerged under the realities of loss.

262

It was impossible to keep Mel from commenting, but the sorcerer remained sensitive to the feelings of his lover. Aijak felt the pain in all aspects of the land. She was attuned to the damage to the soil, the work of rebuilding that faced the farmers, the losses of so many druids in senseless fighting, and the plight that many nomads would face in the coming winter. As Mel watched the sadness in her eyes, he hit upon a solution.

"You know," he said in their gnome language. "When the winter has come and gone, we don't have to sail home right away."

She looked over her shoulder at him inquisitively. Mel continued, waving about his hand like his pipe was lit, (which it wasn't, for fear that Cathag would take offense to burning fur and pin him for a while), "I can see the sadness in you. I may miss a few things from time to time, but I know what you desire. Let's stay a bit. We can help rebuild some farms. You can show me a few tips on planting crops. Ooh, maybe we can journey out with the tribes a bit and see what it is like living out on the plains. Some of those folks could use a druid's help after losing so many of their own. You might learn about new herbs and medicines. Just think of the new magic tricks I might learn out here, new customs…there is lore hidden even in the uncivilized areas of the world. Of course, Salgor has his inn nearby! I would love more chances to trade stories with him."

A hopeful grin momentarily replaced the sadness on her face. She leaned back and gave him a quick peck on the cheek, assuring him she would take him up on that offer. Mel went on about how they both would enjoy exploring this new land together.

Aijak smiled and let him carry on. Even though her heart still felt the pain of loss in the land, at least she could help it recover.

*　　　　*　　　　*　　　　*　　　　*

Trestan held back tears. Beside him, Leander found it hard to stand without leaning on some support. They stood at the foot of one coffin among a long line of coffins just outside the fortress. Wooden boxes ran along both sides of the perimeter walls, even occupying many rooms inside buildings.

The coffin they faced remained unclosed. A shroud covered the body, though the wind tended to tug at the edges of the fabric. So many sheets were being used by other dead that Rhijin's burial shroud was ripped from portions of a sail. Trestan and Leander had been standing in silence for some time. They had recovered her body, carried her from the wetlands back up to the keep, and arranged for the coffin and the shroud. Little more remained to be done, yet both men hesitated to close the lid on Rhijin's life just yet.

"It's just hard to let go of her." Leander's voice cracked when he finally spoke. "I keep thinking of the things she wanted to do and the family she left in Kashmer. I suppose I should deliver her things to them. I don't know what I will say."

Trestan nodded, only because he was unable to find his own voice. He finally choked back a sob and spoke. "I keep thinking of how brave she was on that center line, and yet wishing she had run sooner." He looked like he wanted to say more but no words came.

Leander Swordbreaker reached into the box, feeling the curly, dark strands peeking out from under the shroud. "I remember considering at one point…of courting her. I never did. Even under Abriana's guidance, I have trouble dealing with the way some things happen in life. Especially this."

Leander turned away from the coffin, unable to look upon her form due to his emotions. "She finally got out of the seminary! Rhijin just started her Embarking! She barely served any time to Abriana, much less any room to fulfill her personal dreams."

Trestan moved closer to the coffin. "And yet, in dying under Abriana's care, her Embarking is complete."

He pulled back a corner of the shroud, revealing Rhijin's hand. The two warriors found it hard to observe. Dirt from where her body had lain still sullied her pale, stiff skin. A golden ring unmarked by any symbols adorned her finger. "Behold, Faithful's Companion glows! In death, not a single requirement mars its surface. Abriana has washed the slate of remaining tasks clean and taken her in."

Leander turned and viewed the ring. They knew Rhijin had found her goddess in the next world. Trestan Spiritblade brought his other hand down by hers. He held back personal emotions as he said the words deemed proper by the church in situations such as this. "Bear me witness as I reclaim this relic for the church; mark well that Rhijin has finished her tasks and upon our return to Kashmer will be buried with all due honors."

The two paladins witnessed the religious obligation as Trestan removed the ring from the body. Being divine in its creation, it slipped off easily. Slowly, it reverted to its rough, brown state, marked with symbols, awaiting the next squire to take it upon their Embarking.

Trestan declared, "Abriana has decreed her as a full cleric with her death. We shall bring that news to the seminary."

When the former blacksmith looked to his warrior friend, he noted the depth of sorrow evident in those eyes and cheeks. Trestan barely held more tears in check by trying to not think too much on the deaths of his friends. If he stopped to dwell on it any more, he would likely be drowning in his own tears. Trestan tried to give Leander more support. He stepped closer to the young man and put an arm around his shoulders.

Trestan was hesitant on what to say. Luckily, Leander laid his thoughts out in plain view. "It just...doesn't seem right. Maybe, if we'd helped her study more before her first Embarking...she would have been able to adventure in the world and miss this fight. I know we should think of it as the will of Abriana, or perhaps fate. Why venture forth now only to die? There is nay vindication of this."

Silence befell once again. Leander took a dirty cloth, (there were no clean ones in all the Stonelands at that moment), and tried to wipe the tears from his cheeks. Beside him, his friend had the impossible job of searching for comforting words when likely none existed.

Trestan offered an idea. "Perhaps, if I told you about a conversation we shared before setting sail."

Leander didn't seem to invite the story, but he didn't make a move to refuse it either. Trestan decided to carry on with the memory.

"I was talking to Rhijin, trying to offer encouragement that she would pass her Embarking while we were away." Trestan swallowed the lump in his throat. He worked hard to keep his voice from breaking. "She admitted to me that she wasn't intimidated in any way by the Embarking. With all the effort she put into her studies and her faith, Rhijin knew she could pass any test put before her by the elders."

A breeze wafted past, rustling the sail which draped her still form.

"What she really feared, was the knowledge that upon passing she would be facing this battle. Rhijin had seen injuries before and dealt with it. Despite that experience or maybe because of it, the scale of this fight frightened her. She declared to me that if somehow she still failed her Embarking, she would never know in her heart if her fear of this battle was what poisoned her efforts." Trestan sucked in a breath. "Rhijin told me because she wanted me to know…in case this very thing happened. Meaning, in case she died here. Rhijin said that by passing her Embarking, she would be conquering the requirements of her faith, as well as her fears of dying in this battle. I guess Rhijin tried to comfort me, so that if I mourned over her coffin, she wanted me to know she had accepted this outcome."

Leander thought about his words. "And what did you say to her?"

Trestan saw the trap he had dug for himself when Leander asked that question. The tears rolled down as he admitted, "I told her she wasn't going to die."

Leander gave him a pat on the back. The two paladins continued to stand by the body, consoling themselves and reminiscing about the sweet person who once resided there.

*   *   *   *   *

A hundred coffins down from where Trestan and Leander stood, a couple familiar faces mourned a lost soul under a makeshift overhang. Both mourners heard men with hammers coming down the length of coffins. As the men moved closer, the pounding of their hammers counted the number of souls whose faces were hidden from the light forever. This particular coffin housed a former noble of the Westonhout family of Orlaun. The teenager who had grown up as both orphan and chiaso was being prepared for rest. The wooden box displayed her full name: Montanya su Troyeal bara Westonhout. It included instructions that the body would be sent to the church of Ganden in Orlaun, not buried in the Stonelands. At her feet were two of her closest friends, albeit people whom she had known for only a few months.

The first mourner had his brow buried in one of his hands. He stood in the shade of the overhang. The wide-brimmed, red hat, removed to pay proper respects, dangled limply from the other hand. Lindon Taleweaver's red hair and beard remained unruly from the events of the battle. He wore the many layers of Orlaun clothing in even worse fashion. His light-blue eyes had often sparkled with the music of the world. At this moment, they matched a haggard face.

At his side, Sondra Oskires sat on an upturned barrel. She wore her priestly vestments, without her chain armor, face hidden in the depths of her hood. Sondra knew she should probably say something even if just for Lindon's sake. The woman couldn't bring herself to speak. Like she often had in the past, Sondra easily retreated into her silent world. She couldn't voice her feelings this day. Her throat worked to swallow back all the tears that threatened to rain from her eyes. Sondra had her hands together, allowing mindless, automatic finger movements while the rest of her body formed a statue. Her rigidity only twitched as the banging noise of hammered lids came closer.

The Orlaun minstrel finally sighed in frustration. "I'm sorry," he apologized to Sondra. "I can't just stand here anymore and stare at her. It's too hard on my heart. In my mind, I can hear the song of her life: the tragedies and accomplishments in her short time in this world. There is so much sadness to her abrupt tale, it pulls me to despair."

Sondra nodded, agreeing in his assessment. Montanya had been Sondra's closest friend for the last few months. Before their time together, the youth had been a homeless orphan kept alive only by a need for revenge against a vague enemy. The chiaso could have died a sad death…but then, hadn't she anyway? Montanya had found her way to a better life, a happier outlook, only to have it end suddenly.

Lindon gathered up his mandolin. He turned to regard the still woman in her final bed. The shroud hid the grisly details of the coldast's assault. The curves of the linen still allowed him to see the shape of her face for one final time.

The minstrel adjusted the instrument in his grip. "Goodbye, dear Montanya of house Westonhout. A pity that I shall never again be graced with your rare smiles. Maybe death will be as some playwrights say, 'We're carried off the stage willingly or kicking and screaming, not to be seen during the ensuing acts, yet returning to be reunited with our fans after the final curtain falls'. All I know is this will be the last time, in this world, that I can make out the contours of your face. Let me offer you a last tribute before we part ways."

Lindon put forth a tune on the mandolin. All those who heard it stopped to listen, even though their thoughts filled with their own lost loved ones. Even the men nailing shut the coffin lids paused in respect of the music. The notes had a Tariykan theme to them. Sondra recognized the tune as the one Lindon played while Montanya performed her Dance of the Butterfly routine. The cleric could not help but remember Montanya practicing her chiaso movements. For a time, both companions reflected on their friend in brighter days. Sondra recalled Montanya's grace, defiance, and helpfulness at the Sanctuary for Those in Need. Lindon's melody slowly eased to an end. His head bowed down to the dearly departed. When his head came up, he raised an arm. A rolled-up parchment, containing the notes of that song, dropped into the coffin with Montanya. Lindon turned, patted one hand on Sondra's shoulder as he went by, and walked away.

Sondra appreciated having time alone with Montanya's remains. The cleric wanted to share some words, but her shyness kept her from being open while Lindon was present. She pulled the edges of her robes tighter, unsure if she was feeling the chill of the air or something within herself. Sondra peered out from the side of her cowl, following Lindon with her eyes until sure he could not overhear her. Other friends and families of the departed moved around the coffins, so the shy woman kept her voice low when she spoke.

"I don't know what to say, Montanya." Sondra's throat felt as dry as the cold winds heralding winter. "I've already watched my share of people die in the sanctuaries. A number of times I've been asked to say a few appropriate words at small funerals for unknowns. Sitting here now, looking at you laying there so silently, I've learned something. Pulling a few words from scripture or asking the gods to safeguard a stranger's soul, is a waste of breath compared to an honest attempt to sum up how much you will miss someone who truly put themselves in your heart."

Sondra's hands continued to fidget, underlying her anxiety. "There are priests and acolytes I have known since a young age. I've chatted with them about innumerable small things for years: patterns at the weaver down the street, or tips on hair braids, maybe how cute some boy might be. I've known you maybe half a year? Such a small amount of time, and yet…looking at you…like this…"

The blonde cleric couldn't bear to look at the covered body at that moment. She dropped her eyes to her lap. Her voice, small as it was, began to whine as she continued. "It makes me feel torn! You left me and took something of me with you. I keep thinking of things I want to ask you, or tell you. It reminds me of when we linked memories. I can't help but think that a part of you is still inside me."

She tapped her chest. "You took a piece of me from here. I'm still figuring out how much I've lost. The dumbest things keep tormenting my mind. Some of your valuables were left behind here, and in our room back in Orlaun. Meager, I know. You didn't own much. Just a brief look at your things made me feel numb. What will I say to the homeless in the sanctuary? Who will do handstands with bowls on their feet with you gone?"

Sondra lost her composure. Her shoulders shook as she wept. She dried her face with her own sleeves, casting ashamed looks to both sides. No one paid her any attention. Most were too busy preparing the dead or shedding their own tears over loved ones.

"Why did you have to go out and fight? I asked you to stay and rest." Sondra remembered their last exchange of words together. "I just had a gut feeling that if you went out, I'd never see you again. Now, I keep thinking of those words over and over, wondering what I could have said different."

The young cleric could not help but recall the view she had of her friend before the shroud obscured the details. She kept reliving the memory of Montanya lying in her blood-stained Serud'Thanil outfit. "I have admitted before that maybe I give too much to others. Of course, my faith pulls me in that way. Even if I had been a more selfish person, I still would gladly trade places with you. There is much in this life I have come to appreciate experiencing. Yet, even for all those things I crave, I would have offered every opportunity for you to live it instead. Your star was just beginning to shine."

The cleric nearly jumped as the sound of a pounding hammer started up nearby. Sondra cast a frantic, tear-blurred glance at it. They would be arriving soon to seal Montanya's coffin.

She hurried to find the right words, leaning forward as if Montanya might not hear her whispers. "I want…I need you to know something. I know that you never really considered worship of any god, even Ganden, despite sleeping in his home. It's understandable that you had no love for them after the trauma from your childhood."

A look of urgency came to her eyes as she stared at the contours of Montanya's covered face. "If you ask in the next world, I know Ganden will take you in." Sondra reached under her robe and brought forth the lantern pendant adopted as her holy symbol. "A light against the darkness. You, my friend, were such a light. You committed your life to defending people, even if you went about it selfishly at first, in the way you pursued rogues. In recent times, your antics in the sanctuaries brought laughter to those who so often shed tears. Your hands worked tirelessly for them, and yet you were homeless and poor also! Montanya, you came here and put yourself in danger for many when you could have stayed behind in Orlaun. You even taught me ways in which I hope to improve myself."

The lantern symbol swayed in her outstretched hand. "If that isn't a light against the darkness, I don't know what is."

With tears still streaming, Sondra leaned over the wooden box. The priestess reached under the shroud and tucked the pendant alongside Montanya's cold hand. "Consider what I said. Take this and show it to Ganden. I can always get another one for myself."

Once Sondra sat back on the upturned barrel, she felt a surge of loneliness. She had thought herself ready to deal with her own death or watching the deaths of numerous strangers on the battlefield. Sondra found herself unable to cope with losing this close friend. She turned her watery eyes back to the shroud.

"This is probably the longest conversation I have had with anyone…but you're…you're…"

You're dead.

Sondra couldn't finish it out loud. Her eyes shut even as her upper body collapsed in a fit of sobs. She took sharp, shallow intakes of breath as her breathing gave in to sniffles. Ganden's child no longer wanted to look upon her friend in this way. As she heard the pounding coming closer, she forced her eyes open. The men working on the lids were only a few strides away.

Sondra attempted a couple deep breaths to steady her nerves. Her sleeves became wet and stained in the efforts of trying to keep her cheeks from showing her sorrow.

"They're almost here." She whispered. "This is hard on me, but I'll stay beside you. I'll sit my vigil until the last nail is in place. Goodbye, dear friend. My heart will never forget you."

*   *   *   *   *

Several wooden boxes away from Montanya's, a coffin laid whose occupant had lost his shroud to the cold wind. The laborers who recovered his body from the battlefield had not left a name or designation to mark the coffin. They didn't know him and didn't bother to try identifying him due to his uniform. It didn't matter that he had a handsome face or looked young in years. The black tunic, coupled with the bloodied white sash and headband, identified him as a member of Convict Company. He was just another coffin among a field of coffins.

By some miracle, Dern's face was recognized by those who sought him out. A sister, flanked by the children who had been fed by his theft of food, threw herself across the coffin in grief. The inconsolable woman couldn't understand why the man had joined in the fight instead of hiding with the other citizens. She cried to the gods who took him away, and she dreaded how the children would get along with only her left to care for them.

His story was all too typical of many of the hundreds who fell in that battle. He had fought because war came to his home, without knowing the motives that drove it. The fight ended his life before history had the chance to honor him for any noble deeds. Like the uncounted masses whose bodies littered the field, he would be one of many who wound up forgotten in an unlabeled grave, unknown and unsung by the minstrels in the years to come.

CHAPTER 34 "Homage to the Light"

Winter blew across the continent of Shard, bringing hardships upon all who had fought. None of the ships from Orlaun or Kashmer left port. Although the warm climate in this realm prevented ice from locking the harbor, it did make for bad sailing conditions. Pilgrim's Bay sat on the west side of the continent. Out before them, an endless ocean stretched away to the horizon of the setting sun. A few islands were known to exist in that endless field of blue, yet the westerly winds blasting the shoreline brought forth unimpeded cold air. Even when it didn't snow, freezing rain and hailstorms made any travel dangerous.

The armies assisting the Stonelands reverted from the trade of war to the trade of rebuilding. They repaired the farms destroyed by the tribes. Materials were gathered to prepare for more efforts once the planting season would arrive. Despite the many mouths to feed, the stores sent by the larger cities provided for all. A lot of graves continued to be dug during the cold month of Vientula, breaking up the white landscape.

The Temple of Ale was restored to its former glory. Salgor managed to throw together a few cheap concoctions while he set about trying to renew his supply of drinks. Even before "Salgor's Brew" began erupting from the kegs, the companions had their share of stronger drinks made from a basement still. Mel even offered his own advice on some drink secrets. While Salgor scoffed at first, he did create a drink with Mel's description of a gnomish recipe. Both added a little of their own mix to it, (arguing loudly enough to wake the sleeping guests), until they actually came to a taste that Salgor would trust selling under his roof. "Mel's Boomy" was born, catering to gnome patrons. Like the sorcerer's spell, it went down smooth, then kicked you in the throat shortly after you swallowed it.

The companions spent many nights under Salgor's inn roof, awaiting the next phase of their lives. With all foreseeable threats gone, it left several long nights during which each person thought about which path to take next. Whenever they got together and enjoyed drinks in the bar, the discussion sometimes came up as to where everyone would go. The subject never stayed as a topic for long; the various friends didn't want to consider that their time together would end.

When not socializing, they spent their time in vastly different ways. Sondra Oskires looked to her writing skills, setting her quill into a description of the battle and the people. It was a work intended solely for her own experience. The priestess suffered moments of distraction in which she could not write. Her eyes would stare into the candles, seeing a face that wasn't there. Lindon Taleweaver didn't fare much better. Although a skilled storyteller and composer, there were moments he had trouble grasping the words he sought. The scenes in his memory sometimes proved all too overwhelming to give proper credit upon paper. In the evenings, he would take a break from composing new songs in order to lift the spirits of others. He performed all that winter in Pilgrim's Bay and for the nobles in Fortress Stone.

Petrow had long been a handyman before being a farmer or warrior. He enjoyed spending his time raising barns and chopping wood. In those quiet moments between chores, he looked to the eastern sky and spent his thoughts on his wife and children. The common folk took note of the farmer-hero-wearing-armor who helped them rebuild, and it gave birth to a folk hero legend. Hebden Karok stayed busy working a forge and anvil. Lots of work became available for a blacksmith following the damage to the town. Trestan Karok/Spiritblade donned a leather apron and worked alongside his father. Father and son enjoyed their time together. They knew it was likely the last time they would ever work side-by-side at a smithy. Whenever Trestan's day was done, he found Cat's arms and rested there.

Korrelothar and Floranue Balshav got to stay as guests in the castle, but only along with other members of his guild. They shared some private time together, staring out at the snowy landscape and making small talk about centuries gone by.

"And here I thought my adventuring days were in the past." The elf wizard stated between puffs on a pipe.

"Well now they are!" She giggled jokingly. "You've helped save the world once again, my love. When we get back to the guild, the only adventure will be in keeping arcane students from destroying laboratories."

Korrelothar let out a smoke ring. "I only wish that were true."

Floranue raised her eyebrows and looked directly over to him. "What do you mean? All this running and fighting given you a wild hair?"

Korrelothar reached a hand up and stroked at the wild stubble on his chin. His reply carried a solemn undertone. "After all these years of peace, two goddesses nearly brought us a second Godswars testing the boundaries of the Covenant. Don't think for a moment there won't be repercussions of such an act. Other gods are bound to cause some mischief with their own disciples."

Her shoulders sank. She returned her gaze to the snowfall outside, sipping a warm drink. "You make it sound as if this is only the start of something, instead of the conclusion."

Korrelothar looked over the plains of the Tribal Expanse, but his mind was on all of Dhea Loral. "Aye, I'm afraid this may be just the start." He sighed as he took another puff. "Oh well, it was a peaceful age of rebuilding while it lasted."

*   *   *   *   *

During one particularly snowy day, Trestan pulled his cloak tighter as he walked through town, having volunteered at a delivery task for his church that he could have passed on if he'd wanted. He saw a short figure standing outdoors, also doing his best to conceal himself from the foul weather while smoking a pipe. Apparently, Mel continued to be forced outside for his favorite habit or suffer the wrath of a druidess. Trestan and Mel shared a brief nod and salutations, neither expecting to stop and talk, since they could usually find themselves sharing drinks at Salgor's Inn.

But Trestan's footsteps soon turned around and returned to the gnome. It was rare for the two to have a moment alone together, and a thought struck the young paladin. The gnome looked up, snow resting on his eyebrows, mustache and pointy beard.

"Mel, do you remember that talk you gave me in the wilderness years ago, right after the fight on the bluff?"

The gnome took a puff while he gathered his thoughts. His eyes widened, "Oh! The one when I was on sentry? You were sick from your abdomen wound, and you woke up. Goodness that was so many years ago! I'd forgotten about that night."

"You told me of the troubles with your father back home, when he kicked you out. Do you remember what you said about carving your own destiny? About walking back to your hometown wearing a mantle of victory?"

Mel chuckled, "I did use words like that, didn't I? I barely remember the conversation. I was worried for you. Why do you ask?"

Trestan knelt in the snow, preferring to talk face-to-face with his longtime friend. "You couldn't know it, of course, but I thought about that conversation many times since that night. You said it, 'compelled you'. Well, it did the same for me. Those words helped compel me whenever I struggled, even when I had a hard time studying at the Seminary. I wanted to live my life a special way, and seek my mantle of victory. I helped find my pride because your words helped guide me."

The sorcerer shied away. "Oh! You're going to make these gnome cheeks blush redder than my frostbitten nose! I'm glad I could help you."

Mel was about to go on and on, but Trestan saw the opportunity and stopped him. "But I'm not telling you this today because of me; I'm sharing this for you."

"For me?"

Trestan nodded, "You've gone back home, haven't you? You've faced your father?"

He didn't miss the sad look that came over the gnome. "He won't see me. I live on the other side of the village and he avoids me. So close and yet he acts like I'm a stranger…"

Trestan cupped Mel's free hand in his own. "You don't need his opinion anymore, Mel." At Mel's confused look, he continued. "Some people's opinion is set and will never change. Don't worry about changing something you can't. Instead, realize you no longer have to try."

"I don't?"

"In my travels, I've heard a few stories about *your* legend. The early stories we've told in Troutbrook have grown as they've traveled, but their origin is true. People hail the gnome archmage who destroyed a pirate village and saved a princess. You've been talked about in inns you've never visited, and more than that, you've saved us and been a true friend. The people who care most about you know your good qualities. I'm just trying to say, you've carved your own destiny and can walk proud bearing your own mantle of victory. You can walk with your head held high, no matter what your father thinks."

When they parted, Mel felt a warmth inside him that couldn't be dimmed by the snowfall.

*   *   *   *   *

Late in the month of Icethule, when the snow was beginning to melt, a summons bade Sister Sondra Oskires to appear at Fortress Stone for some ceremony. The reasons were vague, something about a commendation for some effort on her part during the battle. Sondra blushed at the news and wanted to avoid any ceremony for whatever minor favor she had done that earned notice. She was given no choice to refuse. Lindon made sure she accepted with all graciousness and he personally escorted her to the castle. The minstrel made it obvious that he knew the reasons behind the summons, but he made a theatric show of keeping her in the dark. Flustered, Sondra buried her irritation and accepted with as much dignity as she could muster.

Muster of Heroes

She expected some minor, general commendation to the clerics and priests that helped during the battle. Upon her arrival, it became obvious that this was something bigger. The ceremony took place in one of the grandest ballrooms inside the castle. Sondra was glad she wore her best priestly attire, as it was apparent that she was one of only a couple guests of honor. A sea of nobility gathered to witness the presentation, leaving Sondra frantically trying to recall if she had healed some prince during the battle. The king and queen arrived, taking seats close enough to Sondra that she could count the gems circling the crowns. Her friends didn't possess enough affluence to be invited. Only Lindon stood present, dressed in fine Orlaun attire and holding his mandolin handy. Several high clerics of Ganden witnessed, most notably Sir Penvos "The Steady". Of course, no one had bothered to tell the shy cleric why she was being honored. She sat with an embarrassed, uncertain flush on her face as everyone gathered.

A noble took the stand and addressed the crowd. He made a few introductions, one of which indicated a man sitting next to Sondra. They introduced the man as an artist who had served the defense of the castle during the siege. The noble then went on to describe the start of the battle. He spoke of the encroaching army and the terror it created among the starved populace.

"…And before them came dark clouds that blotted the sun. They commanded the weather, using the gods' own relics, to pound us beneath hail and rain. They let the sun shine on their army while ours was made to suffer…"

Sondra's attention drifted several times during the speech. One could trust the nobility to stretch a tale much longer than the actual event.

"…it had to be the darkest night the Stonelands had seen in a long time. Men strained to make last minute preparations whilst staring at their mortal foes across the river." After making a pause for effect, the speaker took an uplifting tone. "Suddenly, a bright star came into being. It lit upon our brave standard and displayed it proudly against our foes."

Understanding dawned on Sondra. She had cast that light spell on the Stonelands' banner during that first evening before blows were exchanged. Of all the efforts Sondra had put forth during the entire fight, she couldn't see why a simple light spell meant so much. Apparently, the gesture was treasured by several.

The speaker continued. "Our brave little star cast a light across the river and announced to our enemies that we did not fear them!"

It was just a little light miracle! Acolytes learn it early on! Sondra thought but wouldn't voice that out loud.

"It lifted our spirits! It gave us a shining moment during a time when despair loomed over many." The speaker used his hands and body language to ramp up the drama of the moment. "Across the dark battlements, under the stormy thunderheads, all could see our banner displayed proudly! The light of hope shined among us.

"The enemy recoiled at this proclamation. They sent magic and snuffed our precious star. Once again, we lingered in darkness. It only lasted for the briefest of moments. A new star reappeared where the old one had been. The beacon of hope emerged rekindled by its creator! She stood bravely in plain sight of the hordes. The second light was snuffed a moment later. We all stood in awe as time and again they assaulted and it renewed. Our light conquered the forces trying to extinguish it. It grew strong and held, despite the shaman spells aimed to destroy it. A star as bright as any in history stood vigil over us during that worrisome night. Within that star we found hope, determination and courage to see our way through the storm!"

The crowd applauded when the storyteller drew his recital to a close. Sondra did as well, although her cheeks burned at the attention she knew she'd receive. She wondered why these nervous moments made one's bladder feel as if it needed to be emptied. As she expected, the ceremony came to the moment where they pointed Sondra out as being the one who originally created the light.

Sondra Oskires stood and bowed at her introduction. The crowd cheered her as if she led their defense. It made her feel very uncomfortable, but she endured it with smiles and nods, betraying none of her inner nervousness. The king and queen thanked her and toasted her long life and health. They even asked her to say something on her behalf. What followed was a simple message interrupted by the occasional stutter. Overall, Sondra simply tried to not embarrass herself further, though she gave one of the shortest speeches in the history of the castle.

Just when Sondra felt she would actually get to the end of the night without fainting from lack of air, the biggest surprise of all was revealed. The "artist" sitting next to her was on the wall that night. He turned out to be a painter named Uvan Refstah. The name meant nothing to her, but Lindon would tell her later that the man's paintings circulated even in distant Orlaun. Apparently, he had been commissioned to create a masterpiece to immortalize that moment in time. After introductions, the artist stood arm-to-arm with Sondra while their attention was called to one side.

A tapestry covered one wall to the side of the ceremony. Sondra had given it little thought until this moment. On cue, the tapestry dropped to the sides and revealed the work which had been keeping Refstah busy since the battle.

The painting covered one wall of the ballroom. It depicted Fortress Stone from a distant perspective, such as the one the tribes might have had. Dark clouds rolled over the castle, as they did on that night before the attack. The centerpiece of the painting showed the glowing banner of the Stonelands, green and blue, with rays of light originating from that point to lance across the horizon. Some tribesmen in the foreground shielded their eyes from the beacon. Although distance made it hard to see figures around the castle, Sondra could make out her image next to the banner in the painting.

The image of an unraveled scroll bordered the bottom of the painting. When Sondra saw it, she knew the painter had researched a bit of her faith. The scroll's painted words, done in such decorative calligraphy, read: "A Light against the Darkness".

Even as the painting revealed itself, Lindon's mandolin began a song that had been prepared for the moment. He sang of Sondra's Star in such lovely melody that she couldn't hold the tears. That was how her light came to be known by many: Sondra's Star. The painting was forever a part of a ballroom in Stonelands. Decades may pass where visitors to the dances would see that moment in time. Even those departing for distant lands, when the planting season came, would share that story of that beacon with others.

After seeing that painting and hearing the hope her star brought to many, Sondra Oskires never again doubted her worth.

*　　　*　　　*　　　*　　　*

The image appeared hazy, yet distinct enough to convey its message. A hawk perched on a bull, walking through plains of grass. The hawk stretched its wings and took flight. It built a nest in the trees, while the bull kept guard. With a squawk of delight, the hawk laid two eggs in the nest. The bird sat contentedly on its new young, while the stronger mate proudly stood guard.

The dream ended as her eyes opened. Too early for the morning sun to interrupt the darkness in the tent. Rumbling snores reminded her of the strong man keeping her bed company. The memory of her vision replayed in her mind. She smiled as she deciphered the message from the winds.

"Twins," Pejena Cloud Whisperer spoke through her smile. "I carry twins."

A snort and some movement behind her marked Kor shifting on the furs. He wasn't awakened by her words. Pejena rested a hand on her abdomen. She didn't need to wake him yet. The mystic would find a proper time to share the good news.

CHAPTER 35 "Spiritbond"

As testament to the Earthrin Stones, the warm season started early that year in Stonelands. The snow retreated faster than usual, while trees began to sprout buds early on. The land recovered as if there never had been a blight infecting it the previous year. As the winter season ended on the calendar, the planting season appeared underway around the fields. Around Pilgrim's Bay and the rest of the Stonelands, the people celebrated the coming of New Season Day on the first of Primus. The day marked the start of the year 1255 After Covenant.

Katressa Bilil reached out to the well-dressed man standing before her. She took in his calloused hand between her small, nimble ones as she expressed her appreciation. "I can't thank you enough for standing in my father's place today. It must seem something of a role-reversal."

Hebden Karok smiled back at his daughter-to-be, "You think it strange that I am giving the bride away to my own son?" He chuckled. "The way I see it, my role verifies the choice he's made. I am honored for you to join our family, even if you're likely going to take him on all sorts of new adventures."

They smiled while hidden from the general gathering inside a tent. Cat chanced a nervous glance outside, catching a glimpse of the many filled chairs next to the restored Hossan Minor. Trestan had used the Earthrin Stones to return the smaller river to its former glory. Now the riverbank flowed with the beauty of the new season, once again fueling a waterflow to the wetlands below.

"I hope I look fine." Hebden whispered to himself.

Of course, Cat's half-elf ears heard every word. She had to stop from laughing at the absurdity of the comment. Hebden had never before worn such an expensive and dressy outfit in all his life. Trestan would have offered to add his own coins into the cost, but the father would not allow himself to be treated by his son. As a result, Hebden dropped a lot of his new earnings to look good for this important day.

The half-elf went up on her tiptoes to give him a kiss on the cheek. "You look great."

"But I still pale beside you," he observed.

In Dhea Loral, only a few wedding gowns limited themselves to plain white. Cat's wedding dress was no exception. White, lacy sleeves ended in two delicately knitted, fingerless gloves. Sewn into the lacy back of each glove were gold coins stamped with symbols belonging to Laedelious. The black, leather bodice displayed decorative ruffles at the edges. She requested that portion due to a statement Trestan made, along the lines of how often Cat wore that material. He had remarked that even her wedding dress wouldn't seem appropriate if it didn't have some element of black leather. The contour-hugging piece constricted her waist while pushing everything up to the top. A number of times, she looked down to make sure nothing peeked out from concealment. The lower portion of the dress was a deep green. Elf embroidery represented symbols of love, fertility, and long life. The *Taef' Adorina* glittered gold on her brow. On one wrist, she displayed the caleocht bracelet given to her by Trestan as an engagement present. She sat still as her maid of honor tied her silky, black strands of hair with emerald ribbons.

"On the earlier subject about the roles we play," Hebden pointed to the woman behind Cat. "Shouldn't she be leading the ceremony?"

Sondra Oskires 'humphed' while trying to work the ribbons around Cat's long hair. She replied while maintaining her concentration on the design. "With the entire church of Abriana gathered out there, it just wouldn't look right. Besides, I've never been a maid of honor before. I'm glad to play an important part without attempting to perform my first marriage with all those veteran priests watching me."

After a few more moments of wrangling things into place, Sondra stepped back to approve her work. Cat checked over her appearance in a large mirror that had been placed in the tent.

Cat took a breath and nodded. "I'm ready as ever to join my soulmate. It's time to let the oathbond become a spiritbond."

Although Trestan or Cat may have preferred a more private affair, crowds of interested parties had blossomed at the first hints of their planning. Now, several rows of chairs from an assortment of designs occupied the riverbank. At the head of the ceremony, the chosen of Abriana garbed in their robes of office. Sir Theros Lightshield had the honor of presiding over the union. While mostly keeping to Abriana's standards, there were a number of things he had been instructed to add in as part of Cat's elf heritage. Other followers of Abriana formed the choir or worked as ushers to the ceremony. Leander stood present, watching Belgard. The bride and groom planned to ride to their honeymoon room at the Temple of Ale upon the back of the warhorse, after the festivities. Trestan could only laugh when he first saw Belgard with colorful streamers tied all over the saddle.

Not to be outdone, a number of members from Ganden's church filled several seats, even if only to be seen at the event. Several privateers that served under Katressa, who had gained much respect for her, imposed on the couple to be present also. Lindon Taleweaver assisted Abriana's choir. His music provided the chief entertainment prior to the ceremony. Korrelothar and Floranue occupied a seat of honor near the front, while dozens of people attached to the mage guild filled seats behind them. Mel and Aijak contented themselves to separate from most of the rest. They spread out a blanket way off to one side and enjoyed some delights next to Cathag. Salgor hosted a pavilion tent, organizing the casks and libations. A number of other people seemed to wander in of their own accord. Some were patrons of Salgor's inn, others were farmers whose homes had been partially rebuilt by Katressa's privateers.

When it first became apparent how the numbers of guests were swelling, Cat had been ashamed to attract so much attention on their special day. Trestan put her at ease when he laughed and shook his head. The young man had taken it with a bit of humor. "Let them have their party. They could use a celebration after what they endured this past year."

Once Trestan and his chosen right hand, Petrow, had taken their place at the front, both men looked back to where Cat would emerge. Two children of Pilgrim's Bay walked down the aisle; a boy and a girl. They were part of a ceremony specific to Abriana's weddings. The boy carried a phial of holy water which would anoint and bless the couple. The girl carried a ribbon that had a coraross attached at both ends. The two children were guided to a spot near Sir Theros, whereupon they proved it was hard to keep two young minds standing still for any length of time at a wedding.

Lindon raised the bamboo flute. He thought of it as an appropriate herald in regards to Cat's woodland racial ties. He played the song used most often by elf families when the bride appeared: "Sweet Flower, We Adore You". At his notes, a curtain pulled back and the bridal procession marched forth.

The maid of honor led the way. In Dhea Loral, it would not do for a bride to carry a weapon; however, during the years of rebuilding, it became a custom that a warrior-bride's maid would carry her weapon. This had developed during harsh times when a wedding ceremony might be raided for the prize of a dowry. The custom of having the maid of honor carry the warrior-bride's weapon and play the part of a guard persevered to this day. Sondra Oskires neither slouched nor lowered her eyes during the trip down the aisle. She stared straight ahead, holding Cat's silver rapier upright before her as if inviting enemies to test her prowess with it. Her step was measured in a way that allowed Cat to walk at a relaxed pace.

Katressa Bilil followed next, escorted by the only living parent of the couple. Hebden presented himself in a more regal manner than any citizen of Troutbrook had ever seen in the old smith. It was possible that none of his neighbors would have recognized him for his clothes and his neatly trimmed hair. He proudly presented his future daughter-in-law to his son.

At the first sight of his bride, Trestan's heart swelled to the point where he thought he might get tears in his eyes. The young paladin never thought he'd deserve to find such a beautiful, strong-willed woman presenting her heart to him. At times he thought they would never even live to see this day. As he watched her glittering emerald eyes look back at him, he knew there may never be another day in his life so filled with joy.

Petrow's mischievous whisper was low enough that only Trestan heard. "When can we expect a baby?"

Trestan's eyes widened at that. He spoke out of the corner of his mouth in reply, "One thing at a time."

As the bridal procession approached the altar area, Trestan's eyes passed over the bouquet in Cat's hand. She had once told him that elf males grew the flowers which they presented to their loved ones. It was fortunate indeed that there was an apothecary in Pilgrim's Bay that grew medicinal herbs in its own greenhouse during the winter months. Trestan found time during the winter to grow the flowers which Cat now held close to her heart…after a lot of helpful effort from Aijak and diverse addendums from Mel.

When bride and groom stood face to face, Trestan saw that he wasn't the only one blinking away tears of joy from his eyes. Hebden removed Cat's arm from his own and placed it in Trestan's. The older man threw Trestan a smile before taking his seat at the front. Petrow and Sondra flanked the couple. Lindon's sweet notes drew to a close. The pair of them turned to Sir Theros as he began the service.

The start of the ceremony involved announcing the couple to the crowd, as well as asking for favor from the divine overseers. The boy brought forth the holy water for Sir Theros to anoint the couple with Abriana's blessings. The girl brought forth the ribbon with the coraross symbols on both ends. With Cat and Trestan holding out their conjoined arms, Sir Theros wrapped the colored material around the limbs twice. The coraross ribbon now tied them loosely, arm to arm.

"This ribbon reminds us, even as Abriana gave half her heart to the world, you are joined because you gave half your heart unto your loved one. May both of you live as two halves of the same heart."

Sir Theros went on to honor the elf portion of the ceremony, calling upon Laedelious and the aspects of nature to look kindly upon the couple. He then went on to share a story relayed to him earlier by Cat, on how the elves view the spiritbond. All who attended were enlightened on the elf customs regarding marriage.

Next, the couple prepared to exchange vows. Sir Theros addressed the crowd. "The bride and groom wish to offer their written vows to one another. Trestan and Katressa, by your own words feel free to express your commitment to your betrothed."

According to an earlier agreement, Trestan went first. They turned to face one another, standing close since the ribbon still encircled one set of arms. Trestan spoke with the tone of authority. He set his voice so that most of those gathered should have no problems hearing his declarations.

"As I once told you, you redefined the qualities I sought in women. None have, nor will ever, match up to you in my eyes. From this day forth, I, Trestan, ask you to be spiritbond with me. As I once took a vow to Abriana, and have been rigorously tested to live up to her expectations, I likewise put my vow before you as your soulmate in this world. I promise to be your best friend and lover if you will have me. I promise to offer comfort in times of woe, enrichment in times of poverty, support when the weight of the world may be too much, healing hands in times of ill health, a watchful eye while you sleep under the stars, and a strong sword to protect your back. I vow to respect your wisdom and encourage your desires. Above all else, I promise that my welfare and happiness will be entwined with yours.

"I give you my hand, my heart, my love and my soul from this day forward."

Katressa needed a moment to wipe her tears as Trestan finished. Sondra furnished a handkerchief, and relieved the half-elf of it when she was done. It took some time for her to get the composure to say her part.

"I still remember your sweet innocence from when we first met. Though time has worked to try and scour your innocence, it has only chipped away the rough edges. The man before me is one of the most caring, passionate, strong-willed and indomitable spirits of anyone I have known.

"I am flattered that you wish to pass the seasons alongside me. I pledge to always honor you, keep you above all others, respect your wishes and build upon our desires together. I cherish everything about you. I will be by your side for all the years that destiny will grant. I declare the spiritbond between us even if nay others do; we are one already."

Trestan was moved to tears again by her compliments and declarations of faith. Sir Theros moved on to the emblems of marriage. Trestan and Katressa had chosen an item they could wear on a necklace. Katressa wore hers on a bejeweled necklace; Trestan slipped his on the same necklace as his coraross. The gold medallion displayed two trees, growing close enough together that the branches of one intertwined with the other.

After a few more words from Sir Theros, he came to the finish. "In the eyes of Abriana, and according to the traditions of the elves, I now pronounce you joined in spiritbond. Remember your vows and treasure your love. Sir Trestan 'Spiritblade' Karok, Lady Katressa Bilil-Karok, you may seal the spoken promises with a kiss."

And so they kissed.

*   *   *   *   *

Trestan and Katressa Karok stood beside a winding line of folks waiting to wish them well. The numerous guests went by the new couple and congratulated them before moving closer to the drink-stocked pavilion tent. Due to the numbers in the crowd, there were many whom the paladin and the infiltrator did not know. The couple offered brief thanks and wished a good day upon the guests. Petrow and Sondra still flanked their friends, offering help for anything that came up.

They were very touched by a short speech Lindon gave. The minstrel seemed to paraphrase words from some play. Though the couple didn't know the source, they resolved to catch Lindon later and make him write the words for them to keep.

Although the attendees mostly spoke of hopeful wishes, one in particular brought a gift that he insisted on giving to the couple. He produced a velvet bag in which a small item rested.

"Korrelothar," Cat spoke, "You don't need to give us a gift now. If you wish, it will be safe under Salgor's watchful eye in the pavilion tent next to the other items. We're just glad to share our day with you."

The wizened old elf wizard broke into a grin. "Well, I wanted to present this myself. It's a rare item. I may need to explain a few things about it."

She started to hold out her hand to accept it, but Korrelothar turned slightly towards Trestan. "Actually, this gift is meant for Trestan to hold, though it benefits you both."

"My sincerest thanks, sir." Trestan accepted the bag. "Any gift is really too much. I still feel as if we owe you due to *Dovewing*."

The wizard waved him off. "Think nay more of it ever again. Don't tarry, look in the bag before you thank me and I'll explain why I chose this."

Trestan dipped a hand into the velvet enclosure. He felt the soft strands of metal mixed with jewels. As he withdrew the item, Cat's jaw dropped in shock. The paladin's eyes went wide as he looked upon the Gitouro necklace. The New Year's sunlight reflected off its many gem facets.

"What? We can't accept this!" Trestan started to sputter.

His free hand dropped to the side, whereupon Cat took it in hers. He looked to her for support. The Gitouro necklace had been worn by champions of Kelor during the Godswars. It was a priceless item. Trestan went to hand it back to the wizard, but the elf held up his hands against such an action.

"I won this prize on my travels. It was I who chose to store it inside the guild, and it is mine to give. It will benefit you now."

Cat shared the same feelings as Trestan. Since Korrelothar had made it clear the gift was for Trestan, she let him handle the argument. The paladin argued, "What about the power of fate? I might abuse a wish accidentally for some insignificant reason. Please, your well-wishes are enough of a gift to us."

Over Trestan's protests, Korrelothar made his words clear. "Just take it. I told you it was limited on the number of times it could affect fate. Kelor's luck has run dry. You and the demon used the last of its miracles. It is not much more than a gaudy display piece for one's neck."

"Gaudy?" Trestan gasped. "This is something a king would wear. Even with just the value of the gems set in it, this is worth more than a chest full of gold coins."

"Gold bars," Cat added.

"Aye, more than a chest full of gold bars! Please, I can't accept." Trestan held the necklace and bag out to Korrelothar while Cat still clung to his other hand.

The elf wizard sighed. "Ah well, a pity. You see, although the luck has run out, the necklace still possesses a passive magical effect. Kelor wanted his followers to stay healthy for however long the Godswars lasted, and not all of them were immortal champions. Therefore, he imbued the necklace to slow down the aging process for the wearer."

Cat's hand suddenly clenched tighter on Trestan's, revealing her excitement.

Korrelothar smiled, "I'd say a human that wore such a necklace would extend his life for a century or two...almost as if he had a bit of elven blood flowing in him.

Abriana's champion turned with wide eyes and an awestruck gaze to look at Cat's response. Those emerald eyes stared back into his. In her gaze, he could see something she had longed for ever since falling in love with him.

Her words cut across urgently, "Put it on right now! I don't want to waste any precious seconds!"

They lost any reason to argue with the priceless gift. Trestan brought the necklace around, and Cat helped him fasten the clasp. They turned and shared a knowing smile. Hopefully, they would be destined for many beautiful years together. It removed a large weight from her heart. She hugged him close, giving in to tears.

Korrelothar tried to discreetly slip away while they were distracted. He got only a step before Cat caught his arm and turned a hug upon him.

"You were mistaken about the necklace. It had one more miracle inside it." Her wet eyes looked up to the wizard's. "Now I can grow old alongside someone."

*   *   *   *   *

Shortly after Korrelothar and Floranue turned to the pavilion tent, they happened across Lindon in their path. The minstrel flourished, "Good day of all days, wouldn't you say? Nothing like music, some drinks, and some fine company to raise one's spirit. Tends to give a person renewed vigor, wouldn't you say?"

"Ah, the lord of weaving tales, it is good to see you!" Korrelothar shook hands with Lindon. "Aye, I feel a good half-century younger today!"

The minstrel inquired, "Hopefully enough cheer to turn those proud-heads among your students as well. Today's generation doesn't seem the type to walk among the Highwater poor, conjuring gifts to improve their lives."

The wizard feigned insult, "Now why spoil a day such as this continuing that discussion? It is inherent in the revelation of magic that some people get a little haughty, and true, I have many students living up to that status. I do feel, however, that the struggle of these lands and the battle they fought has brought their nature to a more grounded level."

Lindon leaned conspiratorially close. "Why not take it a step further? After all, you set the terms of their magical studies, do you not?"

Before Korrelothar could answer, Sondra practically rushed in from the side. "Are we talking about Montanya?"   .

The elf wizard, keen eyes opening to the details, noted both friends were blocking him from the pavilion tent. As he also watched them trade glances, he realized right away the presence of an ulterior motive.

"Timing, Sondra. You must learn timing. I haven't reached that point yet." Lindon admonished.

The elf wizard offered, "You have something to say about that young girl? Pity I didn't know her well. The way she presented herself at the mage guild in Orlaun, you could tell a hot fire burned in her forge."

Sondra interceded, "A fire she displayed in the Sanctuaries for Those in Need. She brought smiles where none existed."

Putting a calming hand in front of his companion, Lindon interjected. "Montanya had a gift for entertaining those who had nay cause to smile. She brought laughter to a house of quiet tears. She motivated people to look beyond their situation. Very similarly, I might add, to the Highwater Conjuror. The very same wizard who brought me from rags to the cultured heights of the world."

Korrelothar bowed at the compliment to his earned title and acknowledgement of the impact he had on Lindon's life. "What are you proposing, my friend?"

Sondra practically jumped at the chance, "For you and your mages to visit the houses of the needy. Stage a show every so often."

Lindon added, "Illusions of wonder, conjured gifts and toys for the children, maybe regale a story or two? I'm going to convince the Artistic Enlightenment College to send students to perform as well."

Sondra nodded enthusiastically, almost as if it wasn't rehearsed. "To empower and lift up Orlaun's lowest citizens. To give them smiles and a better outlook…"

"And help both mages and young minstrels develop their talents in humble surroundings, face to face with the people who will help keep them modest…"

"…maybe even inspire some of those people to find a future they never envisioned…"

"…aspiring higher, seeking the mysteries of the arcane or the harmonic web…"

Even as Korrelothar put his hands up to deflect the rushing words, Floranue stepped to the front. "He says 'aye', and that it's a great idea, and he'll do it."

Korrelothar's eyes went wide as he registered the sudden surprise flank attack from his wife. She stared back and spoke, "Well, you know you're going to do it. The quicker you say aye the faster we get to the food."

The wizard laughed and faced the minstrel, "How many times did you rehearse this before ambushing me?"

Lindon stood up straight, "The best lines are practiced twenty-five times before breakfast, and at least five times during it."

Chuckling, Korrelothar turned to the person who, he realized, actually initiated the idea. "Sondra Oskires? Tell the church the Brotherhood of the Circles guild will do as you ask. We'll have to do it the right way, of course. We don't want a house of the needy to turn into a stage. I will see it done."

Once the elven couple had resumed their walk to the pavilion tent, Lindon and Sondra shared a grin.

"For Montanya," Lindon whispered.

Sondra nodded, "For Montanya."

*   *   *   *   *

Mel returned to Aijak's blanket bearing an armful of treats. The female gnome had been simply enjoying the weather, but her interest shifted to some type of event going on. The wedding party seemed to be clearing a small area, as the bride ascended a table. Katressa held up her bouquet for all to see. Aijak had helped Trestan grow the flowers, so the druid wondered what was coming next. She inquired as much as Mel made himself comfortable.

'What? Oh." The sorcerer looked at the gathering. As Katressa did a little dance on the table, she teased the audience with the bouquet. Mel explained to Aijak in the gnomish language. "It's a custom among human marriages. A bit of a superstition, but a good one. Notice how all the young, single women are gathering near Katressa?"

Aijak had already noticed. A number of women filled the formerly empty space next to the table. They all looked up at Cat expectantly.

Mel continued, "The women are waiting for her to throw the bouquet. Now, keep in mind this is just a ritual, it seems to have nay logic to it. The story is that supposedly the woman who catches the bouquet will be the next one to be married."

Aijak suddenly perked up at this. Mel watched as Cat's maid of honor joined the hopefuls. Sondra still had the silver rapier strapped around her waist as she got up the courage to try for the bouquet. The blonde woman didn't know how she'd feel if she caught it. Succeed or fail, Sondra got up the courage to try. As Mel watched and explained the ritual, Aijak made some whistling noises. The sorcerer continued with his explanation anyway.

"Look at them all gather! It's a silly tradition. How can a bunch of flowers predict the next wedding? I'd have offered you the chance go to up there, my dear, but you might get trampled among those tall people…"

Cat turned her back as all the women got ready to catch. The half-elf threw the bouquet in a high arc. Sondra rushed into a favorable spot with dozens of other women. From the side, they all heard Aijak let loose a piercing whistle. They were suddenly shocked as a hawk dived low and plucked the bouquet in mid-flight. The bird turned towards the druid, releasing its catch as it went over. Several of the women playfully voiced their dismay at being cheated of their chance.

Mel was still chatting about human wedding rituals when he glanced over at his love. Aijak smiled at him, batting her eyelashes suggestively as she cradled the bouquet in her arms.

A rare thing happened…Mel was struck speechless.

CHAPTER 36 "Final Partings"

The fleets from Kashmer and Orlaun were ready to sail back to their home ports. Provisions had already been loaded and sailors set about preparing the ships for the journey.

On one sunny day, a sad procession walked from the castle to the harbor. A repaired catapult on the ramparts of Fortress Stone commenced the march. It threw a fiery projectile out over the wetlands. The missile exploded in a thunderous mix of colors created by an arcane spell stored inside. As the colors and sound died away, the procession moved down the long ramp. Lindon was privileged to take the lead, though saddened by the duty he now performed. He strummed his mandolin in a sad dirge, singing songs to honor those who were forever sleeping in the wood boxes behind him.

Remember my courage, remember my stand;
In this way, learn the measure of man.
Now some may grieve, and some never know;
But this was the path, I chose to go.

Look not for me, to return to my home;
I will die here, in strange lands I have roamed.

Lindon moved at the head of the long trail of coffins bound for the two distant cities. Pallbearers from the armies carried their former friends and acquaintances to the boats that would take them to a final internment. Some coffins rode on carts, but many were carried by former associates. Trestan and Leander were among Abriana's chosen supporting the one that contained Rhijin's remains. Her coffin bore a special decoration given to it by Sir Theros Lightshield. It offered thanks from the man she had died to protect. Abriana's faithful displayed black cloth patches cut in the shape of the coraross and pinned over their hearts. Katressa Karok had the duty of riding with the dead of the Kashmer privateers. Since Trestan marched, Katressa rode Belgard at the head of her company. Petrow and Hebden walked among those bearing Kashmer's departed heroes. Aside from the losses to the privateers, a few of the more influential dead had been members of Kashmer's two adventurers' guilds. The half-elf knew she would have to make a personal appearance to both guilds and give an accounting of their deaths. Cat's mind occasionally wandered back to Sondra, wondering how the young cleric held up. Sondra Oskires did not have any of the Companions of the Relics with her. She had only her brothers and sisters of Ganden alongside her as she carried Montanya away from Stonelands. Korrelothar marched with his guild as they bore their sacrifices.

The long caravan stretched a good portion of the ramp leading to the harbor. Lindon's music led the way, but was not heard as well in the back. Priests of Abriana, Ganden, and a few other sects murmured chants along the way. Prayers summoned miracles which would hopefully protect the dead from unlife, as well as banish any ghosts which refused to leave their shell. The churches carried banners representing their gods. The flag bearers marched with the flags dipped in sorrow, though they made sure that the fabric never touched the muddy road. The road dampened more as they passed, as tears of the mourners consecrated the soil they walked upon.

The procession came to the streets of Pilgrim's Bay. Salgor Bandago left the bar to one of his helpers as he moved to his own window upstairs. He didn't throw open the shutters; however, he stared through a crack at the long parade of mourners. Somewhere in those coffins was a red-haired woman with whom he had shared a meal in one of her last days. He would never admit his weaknesses to friends, but he blamed himself for not being tough enough to put the demon down before it killed her. He felt the sorrows on his face, the dwarven way of referring to tears without actually naming them. Salgor brushed the wetness away as he watched the people pass along beside the inn. He grieved in his own private way, out of sight from his friends.

The townspeople, including young children, watched the long march of foreigners. They were awed to silence at the losses offered by people they didn't know. Despite the famine suffered in the previous year, the families of Pilgrim's Bay brought out seeds to throw for the dead. The seeds seemed to be a repayment for the debt to the fallen. Through blood, the dead defenders had saved the livelihood and future of the people of Stonelands.

Trestan thought it was an odd twist to his quest. When he left Troutbrook that summer to chase after the stones, they showered him with seeds to bless his quest with prosperity. Here, most of a year later, a shower of seeds marked the sorrow of sacrifice.

He also noticed wildflowers being cast out to the coffins. They had colors of lilac, yellow and white, but most seemed to be the same type of flower. As they tramped through town, the many petals were flattened in their path. Those same flowers fell upon Rhijin's coffin, or bounced off him and Leander. That evening, Trestan carried one of those flowers to Cat and asked her what type it was.

"A crocus. There are many different kinds, but these grow early in the season."

For the rest of the days of his life, Trestan could always identify that type of crocus flower. Whenever he did, they reminded him of that sad day.

*   *   *   *   *

It was the last night they would all share together. Some of the ships would set sail in the morning to their respective home ports. Regular customers of the Temple of Ale were turned away at the door by a sign that stated, "Private Party - Invitation Only". Salgor had closed down his establishment to everyone but a limited number friends and their few select friends. The definition blurred as to who all could claim their membership to the "Companions of the Relics".

The original Companions gathered and shared their merriment. Mel Bellringer tried teaching them some foreign dance movements while wobbling from too much drink. Salgor Bandago served the strongest mixes ever concocted in human lands. The former Katressa Bilil intrigued Trestan Karok with the sights they would see when next they traveled. Petrow retold some exaggerated versions of his adventures from when they first set out. When folks weren't paying attention, the farmer cast glances out the darkened windows. Thoughts of home were ever with him.

Scattered about the inn, several others that shared their adventures enjoyed laughter and drinks. Some of these people might be deserving of adding their names to the title of the original group. Lindon Taleweaver provided all the music, and only half the tales that the gnome sorcerer conjured. Sondra Oskires got up the courage to dance when no one else did. The shy cleric did it for the simple reason that she was trying to get past her fears of attention. Her awkward movements brought some laughs, but then she just laughed along with the crowd and enjoyed the moment. Sometimes Petrow or Leander Swordbreaker would join her, bearing some of the attention. Korrelothar Balshav smoked a pipe and provided an audience for whoever jabbered on at any given time. The elf wizard sputtered after tasting something from the kitchen, finding out that Floranue Balshav was teaching Salgor's cook how to spice things up Orlaun-style. Leander entertained Hebden Karok with descriptions of coast cities he had seen during his sea voyages. The aging smith listened intently. Though Hebden Karok felt homesick for the little village of Troutbrook, he felt glad to have gotten away and traveled the world a bit before being too old to consider it. This was as much adventure as he had ever craved when younger! Aijak settled into a corner. The gnome druid didn't understand much of anything that was said. She simply enjoyed the drinks and petted Cathag as the mastiff curled up on a blanket. Occasionally, Lindon's music compelled her to dance.

Near the bar, a small shrine held two candles in memory of those who could not attend. One candle played light across the broken caleocht staff propped against the wall near it. The second candle shed its light on a Faithful's Companion ring that was being returned to the seminary separate from its chosen bearer.

At some points the companions mentioned a friend who would have been welcomed to the party if he had been present. They toasted Cassyli Wessail and hoped he was well in far-off Serud'Thanil.

On this night, the Companions of the Relics took advantage of the last moments they would have together. They tried not to dwell on thoughts of the next day, when their paths would once again scatter. Some would be sailing southward to their homes in Orlaun. Others would be crossing the northern route of Shard before passing by Abriana's seminary in Kashmer. Salgor would stay to tend the inn he had built and defended. Mel and Aijak surprised everyone by stating that they would be exploring the Tribal Expanse. The druid wanted to bring help life recover and prosper across the land. Lindon Taleweaver saddened Sondra by the news that he would not return to Orlaun right away. The minstrel felt he needed more time in Stonelands to properly work on his dedications to those who fought in the battle. He couldn't turn away from the land until his completing his compositions.

They drank for the moment, knowing their paths would soon diverge. Each of them accepted the change, acknowledging that fellows who stood beside them in the darkest of hours would be spread to parts unknown. With every drink and story of their adventures, they tried not to reflect on the fact that memories would soon be all they had to sustain them until such time when they might meet anew. Whenever that day happened, they would likely never be together again as they were now. This was their day of glory. The companions could all be together and toast their victories, feel relief at banishing their old enemies, tease each other lightheartedly about matters which once scared them, and speak hopefully of future plans. The conversations and well-wishes flowed as they stood united in a brotherhood forged in adventures and blood.

Had they not delved into forgotten lands? Didn't they face their fears and leave their enemies shaking? Did they make friends where once they had shown indifference? Did they scrape the skies in glorious flying machines? Hadn't they built a core of trust when their friendships survived some dark days? How much of the map had been filled in by their travels? Wouldn't they trust the person next to them with their back when threatened by the Goddess of Death herself?

The friends talked until repeating their stories; they drank until the casks ran dry; they danced together like they would never do so again. A few of them never even surrendered to sleep. They fought drowsiness with the same ferociousness as they had treated any foe, until the morning sun brought their day of change. They parted when the word goodbye had been expressed so often it had become redundant. They would miss their friends, but each carried with them the warmth of companionship in their hearts and the hopes that they would get a chance to make new memories during some future reunion.

*   *   *   *   *

When the citizens of Troutbrook witnessed the return of their relic, (for the second time), the village filled the streets with another party. Their champions of old had returned anew, creating an enduring legacy that would be spoken for generations to come. Hebden and Petrow enjoyed being honored guests in any house in Troutbrook for the rest of their lives. Trestan and Cat were accorded the same privilege, yet the couple planned to do a lot of traveling. The people of this small fishing and farming community made known their debts to the paladin who looked after their welfare after when own lord had not.

Trestan returned the Earthrin Stone that belonged to Troutbrook. The church of Yestreal grew as the clergy now recognized the stone resting upon the well as a deeply religious site. The history of the stone spread from many voices, and pilgrimages came from neighboring farming communities to see it. Numerous wards once again guarded the relic, but it was never locked away. True to the God of the Sun, it basked in the open air to nurture the croplands for miles around.

However, before the companions delivered the relic to the church, before the people of Troutbrook knew that it was returned, and before the companions set one foot into the village, they had to make one stop on the way…

The four of them journeyed down the road that three of them considered as a road home. Katressa had ridden this way numerous times; Trestan, Petrow, and Hebden had barely traveled it. They had come within two miles of Trestan and Petrow's birth village. The planting season brought the beauty of fresh flowers and green grass. On all the farms they had passed, families worked the fields to prepare for a fresh new season. Kids played in the new year's sun. The friends caught snippets of conversations as they traveled. Farmers were discussing all their worries in life: the health of their mules, whether there would be rain soon, and how to find a husband for their daughters. Hebden listened with mild amusement. His own worries seemed just as simple before his son went chasing a minotaur and its friends in the middle of the night.

The four riders turned down a lane leading off the main road between Kashmer and Troutbrook. Petrow led the way. The closer they got to his destination, the harder it was to match his pace. Of course, it could just be that Petrow wasn't used to guiding a horse and it was picking up on his nervous energy.

They dismounted within sight of a farm. Petrow was almost at a run as he moved. His eyes searched the house and surrounding lands filled with nervous anticipation.

He saw her. Inedra sat on the porch, looking out to the northern horizon at the group as they crested a slight rise. Suddenly, Petrow felt the need to run faster than the horse he led. Trestan noted the body signals and reached out to grab the reins for him. Petrow ran towards the house, straw hat flying from his brow, wearing the leather armor of the battle. The three rending tears in the chest piece had been repaired.

She almost jumped up at the sight of her husband. She spun around and entered the house. Petrow's step slowed in hesitation. He wondered if his absence caused a rift.

His needless worries faded a breath later, as she reemerged from the house carrying a bundle. His mind finally registered the slimness of her waist. From the cloth swaddled in her arms, he could hear a baby's cry. His third child!

Petrow rushed across the farm field to her side. He looked to his new child and saw the face of innocence peeking out into the world. It was as beautiful as he imagined. Moving from one angelic vision to the next, his blue eyes went to Inedra's. He could see the worries of the past winter disappearing from her brow. Petrow and Inedra reached out tenderly to one another. The couple had spent too many months worrying over each other. With the baby between them, they hugged, kissed and spoke reassuringly about their love.

Petrow took his baby in his arms. The tears he shed left drops on the cloth wraps. He finally remembered the friends arriving at the house steps. He turned to them joyously.

"Look! Come see my new…"

"Son." Inedra interjected.

"My new son!"

    *   *   *   *   *

A few weeks after their arrival in Troutbrook, it was time for Katressa and Trestan to go explore the world. The young man had already said his goodbyes to his father. Hebden Karok expressed his sorrow, yet confessed a little envy that he was missing such a journey. Trestan hugged his father and promised to bring back a few mementos of the places they visited. Cat hugged Hebden as well. While he had her in his grasp, he pleaded with her to watch over his son. After all, Trestan tended to run off in the middle of the night to get into trouble. Cat laughed. By the time Trestan and Cat rode out of town, Hebden found that his son left him a few gifts. The aging smith wouldn't have consented to Trestan buying things for him, but Trestan was mindful of the cash his father spent dressing up for his wedding. Trestan left him a number of practical tools for the smithy, things Hebden wanted but never bothered to get or craft, as well as a few more good clothes from Kashmer. By the end of the day, Hebden smoked a pipe with Mikhael, talking about how much he would miss his boy.

Upon leaving Troutbrook, Trestan and Cat rode out to Petrow's farm. Petrow and Inedra once again lived in their old house. Savannah's blood stains were missing, since the floorboards had been ripped out and replaced by the childhood friends. Now the paladin and farmer stood in a private moment inside the house, before the younger of the two planned to leave for parts unknown. Outside, they could hear Inedra chatting with Cat. The farming couple insisted on sending a few provisions for the journey. Inedra was in the process of discussing some of the farewell gifts with the adventuress. It granted Trestan and Petrow a moment together, with the only exception being the two youngest children sleeping the day away.

"I suppose it will be several phases of Aburis before I even hear from you, much less see you again." Petrow sighed. He took off his straw hat and set it on the table. "Where are you thinking of traveling first?"

Trestan stroked his mustache in thought as he spoke. "Thinking of going up through Tariyka first, seeing a few monuments up there that are reportedly wonders to behold."

"That's kind of a war-like empire. I'd be afraid to step on any toes there."

Trestan nodded. "There is danger in all parts of the world, but beauty as well. It had one element that really attracted us."

"Oh?"

"Neither of us has been there before. It will all be new to both our eyes."

Petrow smiled in understanding. In the brief moment of silence that followed, Trestan took a second look at his friend. He wondered if the wanderlust feeling was tugging at Petrow. He knew the man wouldn't leave his family. Still, Trestan sensed there was something on Petrow's mind that couldn't be expressed well.

Trestan offered an opening. "How are you feeling Petrow? You've walked part of the unknown world with me and came back with a few tales to impress our neighbors. What is on your mind?"

The older of the two friends expressed a moment of sadness, perhaps even regret. The question seemed to touch on a sensitive spot.

Petrow sighed, "Sometimes it is hard. I have to live up to an image that others place on me. I don't mind when Inedra tells me I'm her hero. The problem grips me when others give me this hero worship attitude. They come to me with all sorts of questions and ask me to settle disputes. They seem to treat me like I'm the lord and master of this land, not Lord Verantir."

The farmer turned and glanced up at his axe. It hung on the wall, displaying the black scorch mark visited on it by Savannah years ago. The cleansed blade showed no sign of the blood which had coated it during the battle in Stonelands.

Petrow continued, "I feel as if I have a shadow longer than I am tall. I try my best to fit into it. All the time, I keep wishing I could tell them that I'm not a hero."

When Petrow seemed to have aired out his feelings, Trestan walked around to him and put a hand on his shoulder.

"Petrow, always remember that the only person you have to answer to is yourself. If they come to you with advice that you can't give, tell them so. Most people know what their heart wants; they just need someone to tell them to follow their gut feeling. I can get shy of some attention too, but try to think of it as simple respect. They can't know what you have really been through. All you can do is be Petrow, nay more."

Trestan wasn't sure what else he could say on the subject. He started to turn towards the door and begin his journey. Abriana's champion stopped short of opening it. After a glance up at the axe, he turned back to Petrow. "On that other subject, I should make something clear."

Petrow furrowed his brow as he saw Trestan stumble over what to say next. The brown eyes held their indecision for a moment, before he looked up. Trestan had earned Petrow's respect several times over. Next to him, Petrow had begun to feel less important. Where once Petrow had felt superior, Trestan had long since surpassed him in his understanding of the world and how he reacted to it.

Petrow listened as the paladin of Abriana spoke his feelings.

"I don't want you to undervalue yourself. The last time I was here, you said I was the hero, not you. Do you remember back during our first adventure? Who was willing to go with me into the wilds even after he got run over by a horse and stomped by a minotaur?"

Petrow rolled his blue eyes, "Oh, don't remind me…"

Trestan put a hand up. "Wait. Don't answer, just listen. I need to get this out." He took a breath before continuing. "Who was willing to rescue Lady Shauntay all by himself that night on the bluff? Who was it that defended her life the next morning, even though your hands were tied behind your back?"

Petrow tried to look away, but Trestan moved back into his vision. "Who helped steal a magical flying machine from a powerful wizard to make things right for our village? Who trussed up Savannah…how did you say it?…in so much leather that she could be mistaken for a cow?"

Petrow snorted at the memory, "Was that what I said?"

"Aye, and there is more. Who was it that found time to raise a family with someone he loves in those years? You loved them and supported them enough that you turned down friends in need in order to stand with your family. I was sorry that you stayed when we went south, but I agree it was the right decision. It had to have been hard. But, when the time of desperation came, who had the courage to leave his family and come to Kashmer to fight demons? Without training! You stuck with them when they needed you, and left only once the odds required you to make a stand."

The paladin came closer and put his hands on Petrow's shoulders. "Who was the only person who jumped through a portal to the homeworld of demons in order to come to my aid, then had the audacity to hit a coldast demon with a simple woodcutter's axe?"

The farmer took a solemn look into Trestan's eyes. "What are you getting at, Tres?"

Trestan had a look of honest admiration on his face. "I'm telling you, you're one of my heroes, Petrow. I really mean it. I've looked up to you many times and I still do."

Petrow seemed ready to choke up at those words. He turned his head away, but Trestan kept him from turning his body away. The paladin continued. "Just because I can call you my hero, doesn't mean you have to live up to some false image. We're all human. We make mistakes. If we'd been perfect, we would have had this whole affair wrapped up and solved years ago. As it is, we did the best we could do, and it was enough. I just want you to realize you're called a hero for good reason. That doesn't mean you have to be anything other than yourself."

Petrow couldn't bring himself to voice any words. The last thing he expected was Trestan looking up to *him*, admiring him despite living the simple life. The two childhood friends hugged a goodbye. The handyman-turned-warrior-turned-farmer hid his expression by facing away. Trestan took his leave.

Once outside, Trestan found Inedra and Cat loading provisions into the saddlebags. His privateer wife was still getting used to a young, mixed-color horse bartered from the tribes. As she informed him, the nomads of the plains raised good horses with agility and stamina. Katressa even named her Cryssel, after a bright star which usually appeared first after nightfall. The elf name meant 'star of hope'.

As he approached, the two women were trying to hush themselves over something they were giggling about. "Are you conspiring about married life?" He asked them.

"Oh, us? Never." Katressa smiled.

Trestan was content to know he was getting better at knowing when Cat lied, no matter how straight a face she kept. He glanced around, but saw no sign of the child named after his mentor.

"Does this mean you are ready to leave?" She asked, favoring him with the emerald sparkle in her eyes.

"Almost. I had hoped to say one more goodbye. Where is Lil' Willy?"

Inedra ran a hand through her auburn hair as she glanced over to the woods. She pointed him out. Trestan saw the young lad swinging a stick at some trees.

The farmer's wife sighed, "He's been in the mood to play hero and swordsman ever since Petrow went off to war. Right now, he's defending the farm from some giants."

Trestan smiled as he watched the boy play. He recalled his own escapades in the woods, pretending every tree was a potential enemy. In his youth, he had broken a number of play swords defending the village of Troutbrook from imaginary enemies who the people never saw.

Trestan turned to his *faunlessa*. "Do we have time to wait just a bit longer?"

Cat sauntered over to him. She fingered the jeweled Gitouro necklace around his throat, before pulling him in for a kiss. After a sensual dance of lips that left him nearly blushing in front of Inedra, Cat purred, "We have plenty of time."

He didn't want them to pull apart, but after a warm hug he did. Trestan tried to recover from the pleasure received by his senses. "Ok. I'll be back shortly. Don't ride off without me."

She laughed and patted her horse's neck, "If I do, blame Cryssel! I have yet to break her of a few bad habits."

Trestan smiled before turning towards the woods. Halfway across the field, he turned back to look at his love. She stood watching him, only half-listening to Inedra's conversation. Her black, silky tresses floated on every breeze. A reflection of sun sparkled off the *Taef' Adorina* upon her brow.

He briefly thought back to his days in Troutbrook before his adventure. "Ah, the flimsy dreams of youth," he thought. "I once pined for the prettiest girl in Troutbrook as if she was everything. Finally, I have found a woman who *is* everything to me."

Trestan walked into the woods, surprising Lil' Willy as he smacked a tree with his stick. Trestan tried to sum up his deepest imitation of Sir Wilhelm's voice. "And just what are you doing in these woods, my boy?"

Willy spun around to face him, hoisting his 'sword' in the air. "I kiwwing ochs!"

It took Trestan a moment to understand his young words. "Killing orcs? How many have you got so far?"

"A hun'erd!" He proclaimed, holding up five fingers.

Trestan towered over the boy, so he decided to kneel down on the damp grass. "I used to defend Troutbrook against these monsters too. I'm glad that someone took over my duty while I was away."

Willy looked up to him. "Will you play soads wid me?"

Trestan smiled from ear to ear. "I'd love to play swords with you."

He looked around until he found a decent-sized stick. Willy and Trestan clashed their sticks together. Trestan, in order to make things fair, stayed on his knees while he fought. The paladin was constantly parrying wild back-and-forth swings from the child. While they played, Trestan couldn't help but wonder if Willy would ever follow an adventurer's life. Of course, he hoped the lad would never need to go down that road.

Willy spoke. "I heard dem talk about you. Dey say you a warrior!"

The paladin couldn't stifle a laugh. "Some might say that. I've gone on a few adventures."

Willy slacked off his frantic swinging for a moment. "Did you fight any big monstas?"

Trestan remembered the towering, half-ton minotaur. He had barely kept ahead of its axe. In the end, due to some luck, he had managed to kill the creature. The memory of the firbholg also came to mind. It had uprooted trees and caused extensive damage before he freed its mind.

"Aye, I knocked down some big monsters."

In the middle of ducking and swinging, Willy asked another question. "Did you wescue a pwincess?"

Trestan remembered the troubles dragging Lady Shauntay through the wilds on the way back home. He had fulfilled a young man's fantasy, only to realize that she was too spoiled for his tastes.

He nodded in the middle of Willy's vicious back-and-forth, back-and-forth play style. "I rescued a woman of noble heritage from some ruffians that would have harmed her."

The child laughed. Trestan wasn't sure if his words were believed. The boy then asked, "Did you explowe a cass-tel?"

The paladin remembered the four-level keep by the sea. His mind filled with the images of the forest-city of Serud'Thanil. He also thought of the Fortress Stone, which had dwarfed all other fortifications.

Trestan admitted, "I've seen some very big castles. I got to spend a few nights in one."

Willy suddenly took on a look of awe. The child stepped back, lowering his sword. He looked at Trestan with hero worship as he asked his last question.

"Did you slay a dwagon?"

Trestan chuckled, "Nay. I've never seen a dragon, much less slain one."

"Not a warrior!" Willy declared, pointing a finger at the taller man.

"What?!" Trestan looked shocked. "Just because I didn't kill a dragon?"

"Not a warrior!" Willy repeated.

Trestan took on a laugh, "Why you little…"

Across the field, Inedra and Cat listened to the boys as they resumed their swordplay. The laughter and fun cries echoed across the peaceful farmland around Troutbrook. Trestan played for much longer than intended. The knees of his leggings were hopelessly covered with ground stains. By the time they returned to the house, he carried a drowsy young warrior cuddled in his arms.

Trestan carried Lil' Willy into the bedroom. The boy barely fidgeted as he was set down to sleep. The champion of Abriana left him comfortable: head resting on a pillow, dirty shoes placed on the floor, and the practice sword leaning against the wall next to the bed. When he went to leave the room, he paused. He cast back one more look at the young man whose story had yet to be written. Willy was already sleeping.

Trestan offered him a parting wish before turning away. "May all your fantasies come true." With those words, Abriana's hero left.

As many young men of Dhea Loral tend to do, Lil' Willy dreamed of castles, swords, magic, monsters and adventure!

Douglas Van Dyke Jr.

Behind the Scenes…A Few Notes from the Author

Welcome, honored guest, to the world of Dhea Loral! As your host, I have a few things to share with you to give you a better understanding behind the scenes of this fantasy world. Enjoy a fireside chat with me in which I offer you a glimpse into the making of this tale.

THE ORIGINS OF DHEA LORAL

As long as I can remember, I wrote stories that were usually of a fantasy nature, though they did span a number of other interests. My brother and I shared a fascination in role-playing games which helped develop this passion. We started out with books that instruct you to turn to certain pages depending on decisions you choose. The "Dungeons and Dragons" game, (© Wizards of the Coast), was an interest we shared, but our parents were a little leery of some of the bad publicity about the game at that time. We began to make up our own fantasy worlds and rules instead. Eventually, my vision resulted in the creation of Dhea Loral, a world in which gods were limited in how they could affect mortal affairs, and yet recovery of this post-apocalyptic world gave plenty of opportunities for adventure. There were numerous legends that gave hints to the location of hidden cities and forgotten treasures. Growing up during the Cold War definitely molded the setting so that the gods drove campaigns covertly, but couldn't directly interfere without a "world war" exploding.

One day, my brother and I did get the D&D game with our parents' blessing. To this day, we get together with friends when families permit, commencing to smash down dungeon doors and gain levels. I have also gotten involved in a lot of MMORPGs, (Massively Multi-Player Online Role-Playing Games).

During those early homemade adventure days, I began to write an adventure story based on some of our favorite characters. It started out written in pencil, because back then we didn't any kind of typing computer. My typewriter skills were on a par of about four words/minute.

Around the year 2000, I finally set aside the first book I ever wrote. It had taken me fifteen years, in pencil, and was on its third draft. I decided that practice was over. The book was good for my writing experience, but it was time to write something worth trying to share with others.

For a fantasy setting, it was only appropriate that I turned towards my old world of Dhea Loral. I had maps, monster descriptions, bios on famous characters, even notes on the places and important dates in the nations…all pre-made from my days creating the world for our own amusement. Through this opening trilogy, I've had the opportunity to breathe new life into Kashmer's industrious port, Orlaun's maze-like aqueduct and the mysterious elves inhabiting the forests of Wilder.

When my world was born, I told my brother and friends the meaning of the name. "Dhea" meant table or dais. "Loral" was 'of or pertaining to' a hero. In that old language, Dhea Loral was Hero's Table. I considered it a fitting name for a world of adventure.

A FEW NOTES ON THE CHARACTERS

In no particular order...

I'll start with **Salgor Bandago**, my ale-chugging dwarf warrior. He was the first role-playing character I ever made. He has ever been a macho strongman who mocks danger. His hatred for mages developed during a fight in a game which mirrored the story he shared in the first novel. The sturdy dwarf was introduced into one of our home campaigns as a bouncer at a pub. His goal was to spend his time learning the brewing secrets of many, only to save up for his own inn someday. In that, he succeeded. At home, I have a map of the three-story Temple of Ale that he built with the gold from his adventures.

Trestan Karok/Spiritblade started as a name on a piece of paper. It sounded good, but it was some time before the name became attached to a character. He was born in one of the popular MMORPGs that came about in the late 90s. For the longest time, I struggled with the growth of this character in games. There were many things about his paladin nature that fit my own personality directly. In him I also found part of my own real-life religious conflicts. He endures some of my own struggles of faith. The result is a character that in many ways is someone I might-have-been, had I been born into such a fantasy world. To this day he is one of my favorite characters in a popular online game, where you may sometimes find him at a forge developing his craft.

Revwar, Savannah, Bortun, Loung, Jentan and Kemora have been plaguing players in my home game world since Dhea Loral came into existence. From the very start, I decided I wanted an anti-party to compete with the players or even work to cause trouble. Bortun even went one-on-one against a player hero of my world in the great Kashmer coliseum. (Both managed to survive the fight). This group of troublemakers was always set up as a worthy challenge to any adventuring party. Savannah worshipped a goddess whose ethics didn't shy away from murder. Revwar was always a soft-spoken leader who cast terrible spells from behind the protection of his muscular allies. Kemora was the perfect thief to assist with Montanya's story.

Korrelothar Balshav, the "Highwater Conjurer", was tailored specifically for the trilogy. I needed a wise mage not unlike such influential literary predecessors as Merlin, Gandalf, or Aslan. It would be a stretch to compare any of his powers to those icons. He is a stubborn enough 'wise man' that he refuses to shave his unsightly chin stubble due to the respect he feels it should earn him for his age. At the same time, I couldn't allow this elf to take the entire spotlight from my younger heroes. He was there to add many elements which helped either the companions or the reader, without being put in a position where people would depend on him to save them. Mostly. He might be wise and powerful, but even such figures have their flaws.

Montanya su Troyeal bara Westonhout has been an active character of mine in a few games. She is a flawed hero, driven to do the right things for the wrong reasons. She represented a few of my darker aspects. There are too many people in this world who are driven too quickly towards violence in order to justify warped values. Montanya found where this road leads, only to struggle to get back to a life that had been ignored. Part of her was based on a woman I knew who may have held a lot of potential, but was her own greatest enemy.

Petrow was unlike any character I had ever portrayed before, so he had to be tailored for his part in the trilogy. He starts the first book rather cocky and sure of himself in the world. The events of that adventure leave him scarred as much as any war vet. He attempts to secretly hide his pain from those he loves. Petrow may be the most human of them all. He finds his quiet space in the world, hiding from his nightmares, yet fate brings the quest back to his doorstep. He goes into the battle at Fortress Stone with his heart on loved ones he may never see again.

Katressa "Cat" Bilil was born during a dice-rolling role-playing game. I wanted to play a sneaky, thief-type character that was all good at heart. I didn't know that her skills would be tested so early in her creation. During a cold day in Duluth, Minn., she was part of a sanctioned RPG event. Twelve "dungeon masters" and over sixty players were simultaneously involved in a rarely-seen castle siege scenario. Katressa took her part defending the walls as a low-level character huddled among a bunch of heroes with more stature, (and levels!). Her wits kept her alive long enough for the siege to end. When formulating the characters of my trilogy, it seemed she would be a natural pick for a strong female lead. The half-elf introduced the Kashmer privateers and provided the experience of a well-traveled adventuress to those who were less worldly.

Lindon Taleweaver has come a long way from the slums of Orlaun. A part of him inspires me to sprinkle the occasional song verses or historic tales throughout my work. In order for a world to be more believable, it has to have a history and a culture. The minstrel helps expand on descriptions that already seed my pages. As far as Lindon's adventuring career, there is more than what could be revealed here. His story has yet to truly be shared.

Sondra Oskires, like Montanya, tells a story about aspects of my childhood. I was very shy and lacked confidence. Sometimes I found it hard to speak up even when I knew I should. It was an enduring task for me to open up to other people. I feel that I have moved past that portion of my life…Sondra is still struggling to identify it and get past it.

Mel Bellringer's personality was introduced to a new group of role-players outside my family circle during a role-playing weekend in the Twin Cities. Some of the stories he shared in the first book, especially his tearful outpouring to Trestan, were experienced firsthand at a gaming table. The poor gnome had such bad luck at the start of his adventuring career that it seemed his god had abandoned him. Despite his misfortunes, Mel could never be put down for long. He was hopelessly optimistic even in the worst conditions. After an event that developed alongside dwarves, and featured a vision from their god, Mel converted to a dwarf deity. Since then, his adventuring career has been one success after another. Players around the table held a vote for the "best role-player" of the weekend, and the tears and laughter of Mel Bellringer earned me their recognition. Trust this special gnome to bring a smile to the reader when things look bad.

The Gnomish Lift is worth mentioning due to its reasons for being in the story. In my "adventuring career" I have seen too many cases where someone took an item, mundane or magical, and abused it in a way that wasn't intended. I wrote a true short story once about how a group of role-players used an unhinged door to defeat every trap inside a temple. The gnomish lift was designed with one limited task in mind. Of course, a group of cunning adventurers are going to find a way to misuse it in their own way. In every book of the trilogy, it finds a purpose that its creators had never envisioned.

TRIALS OF A YOUNG AUTHOR

If you want to get published, it is a hard road that involves a lot of work. After pouring my heart and imagination into nearly a quarter million words for <u>Inheritance of a Sword and a Path</u>, the task of finding a publisher was next. There is a lot of research available on getting published or looking for help writing. Check the self-help books at a bookstore or look online. These resources helped me narrow down who I should apply to and how. Sometimes there are local writers in your area who have a web forum and meet to critique their work. Remember, criticism may be hard to hear, but it is a good thing!

I put a lot of effort into polishing off my stories as best I can. After the writing is finished, you have to call upon more effort to see it through. A story doesn't sell itself. The author has to get out and meet people to promote his sales. For all the fun of the creative effort, one must also be willing to travel and beg.

Expect rejections. Publishers have many manuscripts sent to them, so one can expect long turnaround times. Months after I submitted to my first choice, the rejection letter was in my mailbox. I continued to write the rest of the trilogy as I awaited my eventual second rejection. That is one key right there. Don't put your creativity on hold expecting to hit it big with your first submission. More disappointing letters followed: some constructive, some simply dismissive. I turned to self-publishing instead...then changed self-publishing companies when the first proved a little shady. It is my hope that I will still be picked up by a major publisher. I have too many ideas in my head waiting to be shared with fans. Maybe my early work will gain some recognition and help get my foot in a door.

How did my first real attempt at a novel sell?

Friends and family applauded my story. My wife got to sample the first book before others, and while I was typing in the next room, I would hear her outbursts of emotion as she got involved with whatever passage I had shared. It feels good to hear a reader talk to your book! The first reviews popped up on Amazon.com, all giving me five stars for my work. I watched as copies were sold in Australia, Canada, England and Kyrgyzstan. It wasn't until I revised "Inheritance of a Sword and a Path" that a thousand copies flew out the door in short order, most of them digitally through Kindle.

The encouraging words from readers helps bolster my drive to write. The acclaim given to me by friends and critics makes the effort worthwhile. I still have a lot of tales to share. This trilogy may be a step that will help my work get noticed. Even if it doesn't, I will still write. The quiet boy that once daydreamed of heroes and magical worlds still yearns to share his imagination. As long as there are people that enjoy my visions, I will provide more scenes to entertain them.

Appendix A - Pronunciation Guide

(**Bold** indicates primary stressed syllable, <u>Underline</u> represents a secondary stressed syllable.)

Abriana – <u>ah</u>-bree-**ahnah**

Aburis – **a**-boo-ris

Agora'Seelie – **ey**-gohrah **see**-lee

Aijak – **ey**-jak

Alunetar – ah-**loon**-tar

Barkan's Crossing – **bahr**-kans **kross**-ing

Bortun – **bohr**-tuhn

Cassyli Wessail – **kas**-ilee **wes**-eyl

Chiaso – **kee**-ahsoh

Daerkfyre – **deyrk**-fīr

Dalios – **dal**-yohs

DeLaris – <u>dee</u>-**law**-ris

Deylirra re fa Thenguinal – <u>dey</u>-**lee**-rah rey fah theng-**gwin**-ahl

Dhea Loral – **dey**-ah **lohr**-ahl

Domid – **doh**-mid

Doranil Star – **doh**-<u>rah</u>-neel **stahr**

Eyldiian – **el**-dee-an

Faer'Seelie – **feyr see**-lee

Faunlessa – **fawn**-lesah

Muster of Heroes
    Firbholg – **fir**-bohlg

    Floranue Balshav – **floh**-rah-noo **bal**-shav

    Foyren Wessail – **foi**-ren **wes**-eyl

    Ganden – **gan**-den

    Gerlach – **ger**-lok

    Gheras – **ger**-ahs

    Gitouro – gi-**toh**-yuh-<u>roh</u>

    Gliel – **gleel**

    Hebden Karok – **heb**-den **ka**-rok

    Humut – **huh**-muht

    Ibleu Taraz – i-**blee**-yoo **ta**-raz

    Illwinu Wessail – il-**winoo wes**-eyl

    Inedra – i-**ne**-drah

    Jentan Mollamos – **jen**-tahn **maw**-<u>lah</u>-mohs

    Karet-Atriul – **kar**-et a-**treeool**

    Kashmer – **kash**-mer

    Katressa Bilil – kah-**tres**-ah bi-**līl**

    Kelor – **ke**-lohr

    Kemora Quickfeet – ke-**moh**-rah **kwik**-feet

    Kor – **kohr**

    Korrelothar Balshav – <u>kohr</u>-re-**loh**-thahr **bal**-shav

    Laedelious – <u>ley</u>-de-**lee**-uhs

    Leander – lee-**an**-der

Liijay – **lee**-jey

Lindon – **lin**-don

Loung Chao – **luhng chou**

Mel Bellringer – **mel bel**-ring-er

Mikhael – **mik**-eyl

Montanya su Troyeal bara Westonhout – mon-**tan**-yah soo troi-**yeel bah**-rah **wes**-tawn-<u>hout</u>

Mothrok – **moth**-rok

Naef'ad – **neyf**-ad

Nirahha – nee-**rah**-hah

Norzal – **nohr**-zahl

Orlaun – **ohr**-lawn

Orthymbar – ohr-**thim**-bahr

Pejena – pey-**jen**-ah

Petrow – **pe**-troh

Quoros – **kwoh**-rohs

Raulgan – **rahl**-gahn

Rayka – **rey**-kah

Revwar – **rev**-wahr

Rhijin – ree-**jen**

Sahbin – saw-**been**

Salgor Bandago – **sahl**-gohr ban-**dah**-goh

Savannah – suh-**van**-uh

Muster of Heroes

Serud'Thanil – se-**rood**-<u>than</u>-il

Shauntay Tessald – shawn-**tey tes**-awld

Sondra Oskires – **sawn**-drah **oh**-skīrs

Taef' Adorina – **teyf**-a-doo-<u>rey</u>-nah

Talo'Seelie – **ta**-loh **see**-lee

Trestan Karok – **tres**-tuhn **ka**-rok

Tuampor – too-**uhm**-pohr

Verantir Tessald – ve-**rahn**-teer **tes**-awld

Wendall – **wen**-dahl

Wilhelm Jareth – **wil**-helm **jahr**-eth

Woshan – **woh**-shawn

Yestreal – **yes**-tree-ahl

Appendix B – Deities Commonly Worshipped in Dhea Loral

This is not a complete list of all the beings that hold governance over the world of Dhea Loral. It is a glance at some of the major powers that exert their influence over the land, people and natural events. The gods make possible all the little things that keep the world from falling into disharmony. They each have agendas that are carried out by worshippers in the world, for the gods themselves are forbidden to tread the realms as they once did.

Abriana – Goddess of Love and Healing. She is the most loving goddess and a supporter of all that is good and wholesome in the world. She helps instill feelings in mortals of brotherly love, marital commitment, and care of the land. Many of her followers are pacifists and healers. There are others who do take up the call of arms, but only to fight for what they love and protect. Even those that become paladins are restricted from using weapons or incurring fighting on the first day of each month, as these days are sacred to Abriana.

Boyal – God of Justice. It is said when the Goddess of Death collects the souls of agnostics, unbelievers, and those who turned traitor to their god she must bring them before Boyal for sentencing. Once that is done, she is only too happy to carry out the sentence or deliver the wayward soul to its fate. The clerics of this faith often find themselves on city councils, in courtrooms, or even libraries of official records. The concept of law, and how it applies to different people, is carefully studied. Many clerics go on pilgrimages to explore how the cultures of other lands express their laws.

The Codex – Book on the Philosophy of Good. Not a god by itself, it nevertheless has inspired a large following. This way of life is based on a literary work that champions a strong belief in the morals and principles that are known as "good". The original Codex was brought into existence with the help of several deities devoted to good causes, and it took a life of its own. People who devote themselves to this following are able to tap into clerical miracles just as if they were praying to a genuine god. There are many that serve to fulfill the moral requirements set forth in the book.

Daerkfyre – Dwarven god of Strength, Valor and Courage. Worshipped as one of the dwarven "battle gods", this deity favors strong warriors. Daerkfyre is often referred to with the extension "the Valorous". Often worshippers of this god are as strong and stubborn in the mind as they are with their muscles. Physical strength is a domain honored by dwarven miners and certain craftsmen. Warriors often pray to this god before battle. Weapons blessed by his clerics are exceptionally strong and durable.

Dalios – God of War, as well as the humans' God of Strength and Courage. This deity can be wildly unpredictable. At times he sets forth destruction and strife, though sometimes for the benefit of oppressed people. Regardless, this god is a major influence on events that shape the course of the world. His clerics are often eager to go into battle on either side of the lines, and sometimes they do meet across opposite sides of a battlefield. To these clerics, life is met by facing trouble in a straightforward type of manner. The clergy spends their often short lives seeking out glory amidst fighting for a cause. Dalios is believed to look over the world from a huge feasting hall, toasting those who struggle and fight for their beliefs.

Dawn – Goddess of Life and Rebirth. Closely related to Abriana, this goddess shares some of the same ideals. However, this deity views life as chaotic, with a bit of mystery. She creates and shapes new life, from babies to new species. Sometimes the new species can be deadly, but that is only to balance out and strengthen other forms of life. This goddess has a special abhorrence of the undead, and her clerics fight to rid the world of their existence. Due to her zeal for all kinds of life, many of her worshippers include people who feel more at home in nature than in civilized areas built upon stone.

DeLaris – Goddess of Death. Death can never be anything but frightening. She resides in one of the many Lower Worlds, but travels between them often and freely to carry out her tasks. Her most ardent followers in life may pass into the afterworld to become *Karet-Atriul,* otherwise known as Death Angels. These souls become harbingers and servants of her will, assisting the goddess with the many aspects of her position. She ferries the dead across the other worlds and homes of the gods. Those souls who were unfaithful, traitorous to a god, and untrue in their worship may find an eternity of torture or simply a boring, never-ending imprisonment. Some of her most powerful clerics can raise the dead back to life, but only to prove her power over death. Her clerics are not very strong with social ties, for they serve as a constant reminder to others of the dark fates that might befall them in the next world.

Foyul – God of Balance. Foyul works on the principal that too much influence by one side or force tends to imbalance the world. He walks a middle line between anarchy and order, good and evil. His followers come from all walks of life, all serving to sway the balance in their own way when needed. Foyul has few friends among the gods or men, as he tends to fight for all sides in order to not let any one force hold too much sway. His clerics may be evil or good, and may act for any number of good or bad intentions, striving to maintain the balance of the world.

Ganden – God of Honor, Duty, Service. This god has followers in many races. Those that feel fulfilled by a calling of decency to their fellow man and sacrifice for the sake of others fit into his followers. Those who break promises, or serve only themselves, fall out of favor to this deity. Ganden serves the other gods in the same way, carrying out honorable edicts and being of service to those that require aid. Often symbols of this god can be found with militias, honor guards, healers, and others who perform even menial services to others.

Juliustan – God of Storms and Cataclysms. Many races fear the name of this god, without a full understanding of his focus in the worlds. The god has two sides that are apparent to people. On one hand, he strives to balance the natural forces of the world. This can only be done by allowing some of the pressure of the forces of nature to vent their wrath on occasion. He may hold back one storm, while allowing another to rage unchecked. On his other side, he also seeks to ease the suffering of the world's people through such terrible events. This aspect is apparent in his clerics. His followers bring relief to those who have been displaced by storms or cataclysms, and assist in rebuilding. People do not fully understand and tend to fear his name. Many blame him for catastrophes in the first place, and fear that it is somehow anger or wrath. His clerics believe that the world would suffer worse destruction than the Godswars if Juliustan relaxed his control.

Kelor – God of Luck. Although the other gods maintain that followers must have faith, this god prefers blind chance more openly. He champions games of chance, gambling, and random fate. This god tilts the tables in the direction he prefers, so one never knows how chance will turn up. This god rivals Dalios in unexpectedly bringing down great warriors. Many adventurers worship him, or at least pray for his blessing. Clerics of this god often throw themselves at adventure, or raise funds for the church in gambling houses. This god excels in finding small ways to thwart big plans.

Krakus – God of the Sea. The water is home to many creatures, and the oceans and seas have their own unique atmosphere. This god provides a home for some, and can bring down wrath on others with the power of water currents. Sailors pay homage to this god in return for passage over his domain. In time, Krakus can reshape the land with his currents, or smash cities in great waves, (and would do so more often, if not for the interventions of Juliustan). The influence of his domain resulted in several of his churches being built to float out on the water. His clerics have much influence over the element of water and some can walk over its surface.

Laedelious – Elven Goddess of Forests and Wildlands. Commonly referred to as the "Treemother", or "Lady of the Green", this goddess has worked through the elves to further the protection of nature. Due to her guidance, many elves build their cities within the trees and current topography, rather than cut down the woods. Many elves enjoy a certain harmony with the woodland creatures through their history with Laedelious. Though the race of man shapes the land around his needs, elves have learned to shape their civilizations and homes around the needs of nature. Although this goddess has many cleric followers, there are also a number of mystics that work in her name.

Mothrok – Goddess of Earth and Stone. Born of the element of earth, this goddess has a strong connection to earth and stone. She believes in the superiority of everlasting stone, and the plant life that flourishes from the ground. She sees animal life as a type of vermin that infests the planet on which Dhea Loral can be found. Given her perspective, one would think that she would have few followers. In actuality, Mothrok has many worshippers among the underground-dwelling races, and others that work with the land. Even goodly farmers spare prayers to her out of fear for their crops. As part of her control over the land, she has been known to bring forth the corpses buried within the ground and use them as undead abominations.

Nandorrin – God of Fire. Worshipped mostly by dwarven smiths, this god is also often seen as a smith. Whenever tales are heard of volcanoes running with lava, it is believed to be Nandorrin reforming part of the world. Many candle makers use his image or symbol on their work. Many wizards praise him for their destructive fire-based arcana. His clerics perform a lot of ceremonies around fire, and to an extent they can shape fire as well.

Noyugon – God of Knowledge and Learning. Often know as the "Lorekeeper", this god strives to preserve histories and knowledge, and is said to be a recorder of deeds for the gods themselves. He promotes academies and centers of learning. Needless to say, he does not have many followers outside of educated cultures.

Scriptum Verash – A Book on the Philosophies of Evil. Made by several dark gods, and by Foyul for the sake of balance, this tome is the exact opposite of The Codex. It details greed and lust, power and glory, and encourages the strong and cunning to take what they will. It is in every way a document of "evil", yet at the same time it also has a life of its own. These clerics practice in secret, with no room for honor or compassion. In the past they have lead armies filled with hate against enemies for no more reason than the cleric's own selfish needs.

Taekbol – God of Underworld. This dwarvish and gnomish god favors those who dwell under the ground, away from the light of the sun. This god also spreads gems and metals under the surface of the world, sometimes in competition with Mothrok's stone empire. Some human miners even claim worship to him.

Westrealei – Elven Goddess of Wind and Air. This goddess communicates with her followers by means of various flying creatures. Her own image is painted in the shape of a pegasus, whose head and neck is replaced by the upper half of a beautiful elven female. This elven deity is of the sky, and a force of nature. Elven arrows need to ride her winds to strike true to their targets. In this respect, a windy day is said to be a bad omen for going into battle, as the archers will have a harder time hitting their targets.

Yestreal – God of the Sun and Weather. This nature deity, worshipped by many who till the soil, exerts his influence on harvests and crops. Many times this puts him in direct competition with Mothrok for the success of farmers, but the two gods were once allied during the Godswars. The sunflower is often used as his symbol. His followers often come from agricultural regions, and are generally good at farming. Clerics of this god never condone weddings on rainy days, as they feel their god shuns the marriage. Elves also have numerous followers to this nature god.

Yurtash – God of Spirits. It is hard to define what spirits are to the common man, due to superstitions and drunken fireside chats. In short, spirits are creatures neither living nor dead that perform specific tasks in the world. They are the after images of once-living creatures. While the soul may depart to another world, a part of the spirit may remain in the world, trapped, only to be harnessed by magical means. Yurtash seems to store and nurture these lost energies of forgotten souls until they have a use in the world again. Mystics, greenmen and some arcane casters call upon the spirits in spells. Many of this god's clerics share the powers of mystics over these spirits.

304

Appendix C – The Calendar of Dhea Loral

The calendar of Dhea Loral is four hundred days long. That reflects the time it takes for one year to pass for the planet of Epos Goth. The calendar is divided into five seasons, with two months in each season, as follows...

Planting season: Primus, then Florum
Summer season: Jherad, then Doyal
Harvest season: Othgar, then Novak
Waning season: Tiquierum, then Norgrad
Winter season: Vientula, then Icethule

Each month is forty days long. Each week is ten days. The civilized societies of the land do tend to observe two-day weekends, however much work is still done on these days. The value of a weekend in Dhea Loral is seen more as a time for socializing and public events, but even on these days many merchants are still doing business. There is also a midweek day by which many government offices in the civilized lands take half of the day off. The evening on these days is usually reserved for balls, feasts, religious observations, or other relaxing endeavors. Note that many people do not observe such luxuries, as the struggle to work and survive has bred a strong work ethic into a number of cultures.

The New Season Day, which commemorates the start of the New Year, is held at the traditional end of winter. Usually, it begins to snow in most of the lands by mid to late Norgrad, and by the first of Primus the snow is melting away.

The calendar is measured by an important date in Dhea Loral history. In a time when war was sweeping the lands, several immortals and demigods were taking sides. Several were trying to attain more power, while some defended the common man. Several gods lent their powers to affect the outcome as well. It was a dark time in the world when great civilizations fell and new governments arose. During the waning season of 1 BC, (Before Covenant), the fury of the demigods and the use and destruction of several artifacts led to the destruction of the last great empires. The winter season that followed was a struggle for survival for many races. Even those living in the vast cave and underground systems of the world, while not affected by the surface winter, were weak and foraging for meager foods. The major powers, those gods who exerted the most influence in the world, stepped in and forced an end to the conflict. On the first of Primus, in the year now called 1 AC, (After Covenant), the gods and demigods signed a pact regarding the involvement of the deities in the future of the world. Although the gods were capable of capable of controlling the world much more directly, restrictions were placed and honored by all. In this way they voluntarily gave up several privileges, and bound their oaths. Even the most chaotic of gods can never break the covenant.

This was more or less the start of the churches and clerics, at least in their modern-day incarnation. Clerics are the necessary vessels through which the gods move the races, although the gods retain the necessary powers over nature and magic to make the world run smoothly and stay in balance.

About the Author...

Douglas was born on Nov 28th, 1971. He got the chance to live in many different places while growing up, courtesy of the assignments the US Army offered to his father. Too quiet and too shy for too long, there were always dreams of other worlds and places…and the desire to write about them. He got into fantasy role-playing games in his mid-teens. To this day he has friends whom he meets in tabletop role-playing games, as well as online adventures. Many of his characters evolved in games, and each developed their own personality.

Having to rely on self-publishing for his first novel, Douglas was surprised at the amount of good reviews and publicity it has received. Since going back to revise the trilogy, and re-release his titles under a new publisher, he has been surprised again at the amount they have sold. *Muster of Heroes* concludes the story set into motion in *Inheritance of a Sword and a Path*. The work continues on several other stories set in the world of Dhea Loral.

Douglas lives with his wife and two sons in Minnesota. He works in health care, serving people's needs in medical imaging. When most people see him, he is wearing scrubs.

Learn more about the author and the Realm of Dhea Loral at…

**Website – DheaLoral.com
Facebook – Dhea Loral
Twitter - @ThaminDheaLoral**

Want to experience more of the world of Dhea Loral? Explore the dwarf homelands through the eyes of revolutionary Duli! *The Widow Brigade* opened on Amazon with seven critiques praising the story, and each giving it a perfect 5 stars! This story features strong women, in a fantasy setting, rebelling against the traditions of a male-dominated society.

"I felt the plot was well developed, well paced, and the motivations of the characters really drew me in, caring about what happened as the plot progressed. I felt the main character was not your typical shiny hero, or dastardly anti-hero. She just felt real. I highly recommend this book..." - Tom H

"This book is very well written and as always with his stories, the battle scenes are intense, with details that pull you in and fully immerse yourself in the story. The characters are well developed and allow you to enjoy loving and hating them." - Lockhart

Muster of Heroes

Strangers thrown together, forced into service on a common quest, form a bond of camaraderie. Each seeks to find their focus in the world, amidst their private mysteries.

The half-orc savage, who takes pride in a company he no longer serves. The dusk-skinned archer, carrying a bow from her forgotten homeland. The dwarf who studies the past so he can create a future. The knight who pays fealty to no lord. The elf sorceress seeking knowledge, but what specific question is she trying to answer?

They will band together, seeking separate goals. How far will pilgrims travel to discover who they are?

-Pilgrims with Blades: Pressed into Service- (released Oct 2017)

Facing a crisis and looking for any excuse to strike in force against the orcs occupying the hills to their south, the city-state Kashmer conscripts privateers and adventurers into war. A band of strangers must learn to support and adapt to each other as a daring plan separates them from the main force in hostile territory. Each possess their own mystery, but without cooperation and trust, they will be doomed to failure.

Pressed into Service is the introduction to the bold Pilgrims with Blades series.

308

Douglas Van Dyke Jr.

The Boxer series features non-chronological adventures in an alternate Earth history. It's a Steampunk Wild-West flavor mixed with the old 1930s adventure serials that inspired Indiana Jones. This short novella, (19,000 words), will take you into a new reality.

Brian "Boxer" DuWold is feeling outdated in a booming industrial age of electricity, magnetism, and stiff competition between steam and fossil fuel engines. The tough conman makes a living off gamblers, using prize-fighting rings or shooting matches. Few realize his livelihood supports his blind sister; unfortunately, the suits of the United Republic Agency use this leverage to their advantage.

The United Republic has seen a lot of technological advances since defeating the southern rebels in its Civil War years ago. Now, the territory of Texico has won its independence from Meztica, and is considering joining the UR. One hitch: the mad scientist who helped win the revolution for Texico is pursuing his own agenda, which includes a train full of chemical explosives steaming straight for the capital! The doctor is rumored to have zombie soldiers, steam war machines, and high-tech weapons at his disposal.

Boxer barely has time to grab his brass knuckles and six-shooter before URA men send him on a mission that one team has already failed. He's loaded into the most advanced biplane of his time and tasked to stop the train. It's time to buckle in for a wild ride of an adventure.

Apprentice Storm Mage begins a new series of YA fantasy in the world of Dhea Loral. Thomena wishes to cast fire spells, but the guild must test her responsibility first. Events in this book precede the Earthrin Stones trilogy.

Thirteen-year-old Thomena is proving to be a talented storm-mage, though she doesn't like the title. Her mastery of wind and water elements allow her to pursue hobbies like foot-tall snowflakes and snowball fights in the oppressive summer heat. Yet, she yearns to study the element of fire at an age younger than guild rules allow.

Her master decides to test her responsibility alongside the tough, vigile fire-fighters of Orlaun. Thomena is tasked to protect these heroes from a safe distance, though they are an intimidating crowd for a young girl to impress.

But no one planned for her to get as close to the fire as events force. No one expected her to be a nearby witness as tragedy strikes. No one thought she would discover evidence that another mage is starting the fires.

Can a coming-of-age girl find the resolve and magical talent to seek justice when facing pressure from every direction to quit?

Book 1 of the Storm-Mage Chronicles opens up a new chapter in the fantasy world of Dhea Loral.

Douglas Van Dyke Jr.

www.ingramcontent.com/pod-product-compliance
Lightning Source LLC
Chambersburg PA
CBHW080918190726
48293CB00011B/2679